MW01045215

Roadside Ron

By

Ron Cox

Cox Publishing
San Diego, Ca

Published by Cox Publishing Co.
P.O. Box 99065
San Diego, Ca 92169
Fax/Voice: 619-274-2409

Printed in the U.S.A.

All characters in this book were generated by the
imagination of the author and have no relation whatsoever
to anyone bearing the same name or names, living or dead.
They were not inspired in any way, shape or form by any
individuals known or unknown to the author.
All incidents are pure invention.

Edited by Sandy Campbell, San Diego, Ca.
Cover art by Charles Held, San Diego, Ca.
Cover photo by Sandy Campbell

Library of Congress Catalog Card Number: 97-95324

Cox, Ronald J. Sr. (Ron Cox), 1949-
    Roadside Ron / by Ron Cox.
    ISBN: 0-9662586-0-6

10 9 8 7 6 5 4 3 2 1

Acknowledgements

I like to thank the following people who helped put this
Novel together and make this venture possible:
Sandy Campbell, Vicki Cox, Jennifer Valley, Cheryl Boyd,
Tom Elliott, Brenda Robinson, Frank Ciriza.

Dedication

To Richard E. Cox and Patricia M. Cox,
My parents who came before me,
May they rest in peace.

To Ronald J. Cox Jr. and Vicki L. Cox,
My children who came after me,
May they live in peace.

To Ginger L. Cox,
The mother of my children.

~ If you're willing to be still,
Pay attention and listen,
The answers will come ~

Chapter One

"Damn it's hot!" This climate has a way of sapping a person's energy, but not mine, not today.

Sweat dripped off my forehead into my eyes, stinging them and momentarily blurring my vision. I placed my forearm against my brow and wiped the perspiration onto my coveralls as I straightened up to lean against the fender of the car.

"Whew, it's more humid than normal." I peered out the garage doorway where the sun beat mercilessly onto the parched driveway. My hand searched for the rag stuck somewhere under the hood. Finding it, I held it up, looking for a clean spot to wipe my eyes. I stared outside, wanting to rip off my coveralls and get the hell out of here, now. As much as I wanted to bolt out the door, I couldn't. I had work to do.

It was only nine-thirty in the morning and already in the mid-nineties, common for late spring in the desert. It would probably reach one hundred fifteen degrees by early afternoon. Chicago was never like this. I'd lived in Borrego Springs for about two years now and was slowly getting accustomed to the temperature.

Shrugging off the heat, I focused my attention on the car in front of me. The customer would be here to pick it up soon. As I groped around under the hood for the wrench, I thought, *I've got to finish this carburetor job by lunch so I can take care of business.* The five hundred dollars was burning a hole in my pocket and I had trouble concentrating. *Only two more payments to make.*

Old John's voice snapped me back to reality. "Hey, Roadside, how ya doin' there? You almost finished?"

"All I have to do is bolt it back on and fire up the engine. It should work just fine. It'll be about thirty minutes."

"Okay, I'll leave you alone so's you can finish up," he said, limping out of the garage back to his office.

I set the carb on the manifold and at the same time thought, *I have to hurry so I can get to Oceanside and back, then to Jay's Pool Hall tonight.* I got into my hurry-up frame of mind as I tightened down the carb. The wrench slipped off the nut, slamming my hand into the steel manifold. I let go of the wrench and it fell to the floor with a loud, metallic clank. "Son of a bitch!" I yelled. I didn't have to look; I could feel it bleeding. The warm, bright-red blood oozed down my fingers in a slow, steady stream from gashes on my first two knuckles. *It's been a long time since I busted skin on a car.*

Gotta slow down. Gotta take it easy, I thought to myself as I stood up, walked over to the bench and sat down. *I've got a long way to ride today and there's no sense in killing myself before I get there.*

As I sat staring at my hand, my mind drifted back to when I first met John a little over two years ago. I was newly divorced after a long-term marriage and raising two children. My father passed away when I was young and my mother had just passed away from cancer at age sixty-five. The rest of my family was spread out all across the country. I couldn't stand the thought of going through the healing process of my divorce in Chicago and I didn't care much for the big fast city. My two children could take care of themselves now, so I did something I always wanted to do, move to the West Coast. I loaded up the old van with my tools and tied the 650 Yamaha motorcycle to the back and headed west. My mind played back my first day here as I waited for my knuckles to stop bleeding . . .

I'd been on the road three days when I pulled into Borrego Springs, a little town at the foot of the mountains in the Anza-Borrego Desert about an hour and a half from the California coast. I had to stop to gas up before heading through the mountains.

I spotted John's Gas Station just up the road and turned in. It was a station right out of the past. It looked like it came from of a fifties movie and the pumps were as old as I was. John limped slowly over to my van, shuffling in his oil-stained, threadbare coveralls. His short gray hair looked like it hadn't been combed in a week. He peered over his horn-rimmed glasses into my window and said, in a heavy western drawl, "Fill 'er up, sir?"

"Yes, I want to make sure I have enough gas to make it through

the mountains. I've never been this way before."

"Good idea," John replied, rubbing his gray, stubby whiskers. As he pumped the gas, he glanced at my Illinois license plate. "Long way from home, aren't ya?"

I looked at him with a tired grin, "Yep."

After he finished filling my tank, I decided to go inside the station and get a cold soda. I'd been driving all day and had a mouth full of desert dust, so I pulled over to the side and went in.

I noticed a stool off in one corner and asked, "Is it okay if I sit down?"

"Sure. Take a load off your feet and set a spell."

I sat down, trying to quiet my racing mind. I'd just done a lot of long, hard driving and was in a state of numbness from leaving everything I knew and loved, while at the same time driving headlong into the unknown.

The apprehension of not knowing where I was going or what I was going to do when I got there was beginning to overwhelm me. I took a sip of soda, hoping to settle my nerves, and watched John as he sat staring out the window. He had a rugged, windblown, wrinkled face from the scorching desert air. His hands were typical mechanics' hands with thick fingers and grease imbedded in each crack and under every nail. He moved slowly, as if he really didn't care whether whatever he was doing ever got finished or not.

"Nice town you got here."

"Yeah," he replied, "not much happening. But that's the way I like it. No big hurry, nothin' that important to rush about."

My eyes roamed around the garage. "I used to have a carburetor shop in Chicago. I had a pretty good business and was making some good money when I left."

"So why'd you leave if you was doin' so good?"

I stared out the window. "I just went through a divorce after eighteen years of marriage and lost the desire to keep the business going. I also needed to get away from that city." He looked at me and could see the pain in my face. I broke eye contact and looked back out the window, "I always wanted to live in California, so I packed up my belongings and pointed my van west. And now, here

I am three days later, only ninety miles from the coast."

John looked at me. "If ya don't mind my asking, what made you get a divorce after all those years?"

"We just grew apart. I figure people fall in love not of their own choice or making. It just happens. And I think people fall out of love whether they want to or not. We don't have any control over it either way. I guess that's what happened to us."

John remained quiet, staring into space. Then, looking at the floor, half-mumbling, said, "I was married for twenty-seven years. My wife died of cancer five years ago and I still ain't got over it."

"Sorry to hear that," I said, "It must be hard to lose someone that's been a part of your life for so long." He nodded. I took a couple of large gulps of soda, and asked, "So how's business, anyway?"

"Kind of slow, but it should start picking up pretty soon. We get a lot of tourists from the coast and from Arizona passing through. In this heat a lot of things can go wrong with a car, and they usually do." He looked at the motorcycle on the back of my van. "What kind of bike is that?"

"A 1979 Yamaha 650. It's just an old beater to get around on."

"Looks pretty good. You must take care of it."

"When I bought it, it wouldn't even start. Since I've had it, I've practically rebuilt the whole thing."

"So you know a lot about motorcycles, huh?"

"I do now," I replied.

"And you know how to rebuild carbs?"

"Well, I've been doing them for about twenty years."

"Do they work when you're finished with them?" John asked.

"Over the years, I've learned how to do them and do them right. I hate doing something twice, so I do it right the first time. It's the great American way, right? Quality is what's important, right?"

"That's the way it's supposed to be, but a lot of people just don't give a damn," John said.

"Yeah, I know."

"So, you're headed for the coast? Any particular place? Do you know someone there?"

"Nope. I have no idea where I'm going when I get there. This is a new experience for me and it's kind of scary but I feel like it's something I've got to do. Anything to get away from Chicago."

John gazed outside, tapping his fingers on his desk, then looked down the driveway at a car parked alongside the building. *"So, you had your own carburetor business?"*

"Yes, and I'm sorry I had to close up."

"I can do anything on a car except carbs," John said, looking down. *"I try, but my hands are just too big and clumsy. Too many tiny parts in them."*

John held up his hands for me to see. He was right. Then I looked at my own hands. *"I guess I'm lucky to have long thin fingers. I can reach all those tiny parts."*

"It's funny you should happen along now. See that Chevy parked over on the side?"

I looked out onto the driveway. *"Yes."*

"It needs a rebuilt carb. I have to drive ninety miles to get one and that takes up the better part of the day. If it doesn't work, I have to take it all the way back. It's a big pain in the ass. I could get all the rebuild parts from Jake's Auto about fifteen minutes down the road. If I could rebuild it myself or have someone do it for me, it would sure make life a lot easier."

"Is that a fact?" I asked, hesitantly.

"Yeah. I've been sitting here watching you. I'm a pretty good judge of character. I can tell an honest person when I see one. I got this feeling' you're honest."

"Yep, everything I've said is true." I was starting to wonder about John. I thought he had something on his mind.

"I'll tell you what. I don't know what your financial situation is, but if you can help me out maybe I can help you. It's already late and Jake's is closed. If you're not in any hurry to get to the coast, you can stay here tonight and rebuild that carb tomorrow. I'll pay you half the profit if it works right. I've got a shower and a bathroom in the back. It's nothing fancy, but it'll do the job. You can sleep in your van tonight."

I'd been on the road three days and could sure use a shower. Besides, it was really late, I was tired, and in no real hurry. After *all, this was the beginning of a new life, why not stick around a day or two. I had no pressing issues to take care of.* I looked at John, "Yeah, why not? I could use a few bucks."

"Okay! By the way, my name's John. John Phillips."

"Mine's Ron Healy. My friends call me Roadside Ron."

"Roadside, huh? Welcome to Borrego Springs, Roadside."

My mind drifted back to the present. *It's funny how a couple of days had turned into a couple of years.* I glanced down and saw my knuckles had stopped bleeding.

I looked at the clock, ten-thirty in the morning and I still had one tune-up left to do. All I could think about was driving to Oceanside and getting rid of the five hundred dollars in my pocket.

I finished the job and went into the bathroom to clean up. As I washed, I stared into the mirror. My hair had grown to shoulder length and was pulled back into a ponytail. It was bleached blonde from the intense sun. I'd had my left ear pierced and was wearing a small pearl earring that my daughter gave me. My skin was tanned to a dark brown, almost bronze, which made my blue eyes stand out even more than they usually did. My muscles were well defined, but not overdeveloped. I worked out every day to keep fit since I rode my motorcycle almost everywhere.

I stared at my image and thought, *Man, what a long way from that conservative, midwestern, homeowner, businessman I was two years ago.* I felt good about the way I looked. No one was able to guess my age. At most, they would say early thirties.

Looking over my shoulder, I walked away from the mirror and whispered, "Not bad for forty-two." I changed into riding clothes, felt my pocket to make sure the money was still there and walked over to my motorcycle. I got excited every time I made this monthly trip to deliver the payment.

John was standing in the driveway and as I backed my bike out he warned, "Take it easy and be careful out there. Remember, it's Friday and there're a lot of maniacs on the road."

"Don't worry, I will. I've made this trip many times."

"Don't matter. You I trust, it's the other idiots on the road I don't."

I couldn't help but feel that John had become emotionally attached to me and he really cared. I guess I'd become attached to him also.

"If I don't see you when you get back, remember to make sure everything's locked up. I'll see you tomorrow," he reminded me as he always did.

"Okay, I will. See ya," I replied as I rolled my bike out onto the street and pointed it towards the mountains.

I could feel the heat rising from the ground as the sun beat down unmercifully. The temperature was now close to one hundred fifteen. The base of the mountains was only about ten minutes away and I knew that once I got there and started climbing up, the temperature would drop to the mid-eighties.

Once on the plateau, the warm wind blew across my face as I followed the gentle curves and hills. I never surfed the ocean but knew how it felt to surf the asphalt highways, gliding through the hills and valleys of the beautiful countryside. Even though I'd made this trip many times, I still couldn't get over the diversity of this state. There were cattle ranches, horse ranches, farms and little towns. This stretch of ninety miles had everything a person could think of, from the hot, flat desert to lush green mountains, to the warm breezy coast with swaying palm trees. In winter, a person could snow ski in the morning and lie out in the sun at the beach in the afternoon. Amazing.

After a few minutes, I kicked back and let the sun caress my face and arms. The smell of pine trees and fresh-cut grass filled my lungs. The highway dipped and rose as I rode around the lazy curves. It was almost as though the road was holding me in its arms and gently rocking me back and forth. The wind felt like a soft, warm hand running through my hair. I let the road take over as it always did and I became one with everything around me. Before I slipped into the trance that the road always put me in, I decided to stop in Ramona, the halfway mark to Oceanside, for a cup of coffee.

I came back to reality as I reached the city limits of Ramona and pulled into a small coffee shop on the main drag. I could think better in the open spaces. Everything was slow-paced. It was as though life itself was clearer here for some reason. Maybe it was because of the simplicity of the town and its people. I always made it a point to stop here for coffee whenever I rode to the coast.

Most times, I would sit and watch the people walk by. I could see the bikers and their ladies glide by on their gleaming machines, usually on their way to the mountains or the coast. Sometimes, they would wave and I would wave back. Couldn't hang out today, though. Had to get moving.

I gulped down the last of my coffee, then pulled back onto the road fully refreshed. I was beginning to get excited the closer I got to Oceanside. I kept thinking, *just one more month, and just one more payment after this one.* My second dream was about to come true. The first one was moving to California. Although it still seemed like a dream, here I was.

The traffic started getting heavier the closer I got to the coast, so I had to concentrate on the road. As I focused on the traffic, I pictured Jim waiting for me as he did every month. I'm sure he wanted the five hundred dollars as bad as I wanted to give it to him. Just a couple more miles to go.

I turned right on Main Street in Oceanside, drove a few blocks, then stopped in front of the store. I looked up and read the sign as I had been doing for the past year: "Jim's House of American Motorcycles."

I peered through the window and could see Jim sitting behind his desk as usual. Then I looked over to the showroom floor to make sure it was still there. Something was strange. The bike had been moved closer to the door. Maybe he got some new cycles in and had to rearrange everything. It didn't matter, the bike was here and that's all that counted.

I cut the engine and slowly walked towards the door. Jim looked up as I entered the showroom. "How you doing?" I asked, waving as I walked over to the bike.

"Just fine, Roadside, and yourself?"

"Okay, nothing much to complain about."

Jim didn't look up. He just sat there shuffling papers. I made my way to where Jim was sitting, handed him the money and said,

"Just one more to go and I get to take the bike."

He didn't look up. He just kept shuffling papers. *That's strange*, I thought, *he's being awfully quiet.*

I walked over to the scarlet red, black and chrome Harley-Davidson that I'd been waiting for all this time. It looked so good. I slowly walked around it as I did every time I came here.

Jim said without looking up, "Don't worry, it's exactly the same as it was the last time you saw it. No dings or dents."

I thought about the first time I came to Jim's about a year ago. *I had saved some money and decided to start looking around for a Harley-Davidson. I'd wanted one for as long as I could remember. Almost every weekend I would stop at Jim's and check out the bikes. They were either too expensive or didn't appeal to me. Then one Friday, a Marine came in to sell his motorcycle. It was almost brand new. He'd owned it for only a few months and it had less than two thousand miles on the odometer. He was being shipped out and couldn't take it with him. I arrived a couple of hours after Jim had purchased the bike. As soon as I saw it, I knew I had to have it. Jim and I worked out a deal where I would make payments.*

I couldn't understand why Jim and Charlie, the counterman, were avoiding me. By this time we would usually be in an all-out discussion about mechanical things. Normally, as soon as I walked in the door the chatter would start. I looked over at Charlie behind the counter and he avoided my eyes. I was beginning to get annoyed. Something was up and I wasn't part of it.

I swung my leg over the seat of the bike and grabbed the handlebar grips. It was almost mine. I sat there looking at Jim, then at Charlie, but neither would return my glance. I gazed out onto the street, imagining myself on the road with my shiny new machine. I sat for a few minutes and was about to get off the bike when Jim walked over to me, holding something. He held out his hand and said, "Here's the keys. You mind getting off the bike?"

"What's going on?"

"Get off the bike so I can roll it outside for you."

"But it's not paid for yet. I still have one more payment to make before it's mine."

"Yeah, I know. But I'll make you a deal. This motorcycle has been sitting here for seven months and not a day goes by without someone coming in here trying to buy it. I tell them it's sold. Some try to talk me into giving them your phone number so they can talk you into selling it to them. I'm getting tired of other people trying to get this machine. Besides, I know how bad you want it."

I sat there with my mouth open.

"You owe just one more payment. I'll keep your Yamaha until you make the payment. With the shape that it's in, I know I can get at least five hundred dollars for it, maybe even a thousand. That's if you don't make the final installment."

I was unable to utter a sound as I looked over at Charlie. Charlie looked back and said, "I knew what was going on and I couldn't look you in the eye and keep a straight face. I had to avoid looking at you so I wouldn't ruin the surprise."

Jim stood there holding out the keys. "Take these keys and get off so I can roll it outside for you."

I still couldn't believe what was happening. I let go of the handlebars and took the keys from Jim's outstretched hand. I slowly stood up and swung my leg off the bike. I was not prepared for this. I knew that if I tried to speak right now it would be gibberish.

"Park your bike in back and I'll roll this out front for you."

I put my Yamaha in the rear lot. I stood there looking at the keys in my hand. I had to walk to the front and keep cool. My knees felt a little rubbery. I'd waited a long time for this moment and it was finally here. It was going to be hard to stay composed.

He had the bike out front by the time I got back. I had never seen it outside the showroom before and it looked even better in the sunlight.

Jim said, "I've got to run through these safety rules. I know you're an experienced rider but it's the law." After he was finished he said, "Did you get all that?"

"Yeah, Jim. I understand."

"You didn't hear a word I said, did you?"

"Yep, I heard every word." I just kept staring at the bike.

"Well then, that's it. Just ride safely and remember if you need any custom parts, come see me."

"Okay," I replied.

I put the key in the ignition and threw my leg over the seat. I hit the throttle a couple of times and turned the key to the "on" position. I hit the start button and the engine started, sputtered and died.

"It hasn't been started in a while," Jim said, "so it might take a couple of tries."

I twisted the throttle a few more times and hit the starter button again. The engine roared to life. I gunned the throttle to keep it running. I'd never ridden an American motorcycle, let alone felt one run. It was awesome to experience the throbbing power and to hear the deep, throaty rumble of the pipes. There was no other feel or sound like it in the world. I sat there for a few minutes to let it warm up. Jim and Charlie were standing outside the door watching.

I'd been riding for many years, but I was afraid to pull away. I felt like every eye in Oceanside was on me. If I made one tiny mistake, everyone in the world would know it. I knew that soon I would have to roll out of the driveway. I slowly let the clutch out and gave the throttle a twist. The bike lurched forward and I guided it down the driveway and onto the street. I figured it was best to turn right, less chance for an accident that way.

Once on the street, I waved to Jim and Charlie, rolled the power on and headed for the freeway. I could see heads turn as I cruised by. There was no describing how the bike felt. I took it easy the first couple of miles on the freeway to get used to my new machine. People passing me were giving the thumbs-up sign as I cruised. This was going to be fun.

Still shaking from the excitement, I twisted the throttle a bit more and the bike sped up. Giving it more throttle, it went faster and faster. I moved over to the left lane and looked down at the speedometer. The needle kept climbing, eighty-five now. Soon I had to move in and out of lanes. At one point, I had to cross from the left lane all the way over to the right lane to pass slower cars which looked like they were standing still. My heart was pounding and it felt like it was going to explode any second. The wind was pushing me back so hard I had trouble holding onto the handlebars.

I dodged in and out of lanes to avoid hitting cars in front of me. My eyes were beginning to tear from the fierce wind and it was getting hard to see. Before I knew it, I was going one hundred ten miles an hour. I didn't need a traffic ticket or an accident on this first day, so I let up on the throttle and the bike began to slow down. One hundred, then eighty, then seventy. Soon I was traveling sixty, a nice safe old man's speed. I didn't know which was vibrating more, the bike or me. The adrenaline was flowing.

I was headed toward San Diego, about twenty miles away. Coffee sounded good. I also thought that dinner in Yuma, Arizona, was a nice idea. It was one hundred eighty miles away. The temperature was in the mid-seventies along the coast and I didn't have a care in the world.

I turned off the freeway and onto the Coast Highway, the last major road before the Pacific Ocean. It was Friday and I had nothing to do. I kicked my black engineer boots up on the highway pegs, settled back in the seat and let the road take me. All I could feel was the sun, wind and the throbbing of the American machine beneath me.

After a stop in San Diego, I pointed my machine east and headed toward the mountains, then the desert, on my way to Arizona.

There were a lot of definitions of freedom, and this had to be one of them. . .

It must have been about two in the morning and I'd ridden almost five hundred miles. My body was sore and I was dead tired. But, man, did I feel good. I couldn't believe I went all the way to Yuma and wandered back through every side road I could find. I'd been in the seat almost twelve hours.

I was just outside of Borrego Springs and decided to stop at my special place in the desert. It was a large, flat, oval rock in the middle of nowhere where I would go to meditate and be alone to collect my thoughts and clear out the cobwebs. I had found this place while cruising one night right after I arrived in Borrego.

Coming out here helped me get through a lot of the pain of the divorce.

I pulled alongside the rock and slowly reached down to shut the bike off. My whole body was buzzing and most of it was numb from being in the seat so long. I grimaced as I lifted my leg over the seat and limped to the rock. I placed my hands on it and slowly crawled onto its flat surface, lying face up with my arms outstretched and my legs spread-eagle. I lay my head back and relaxed.

Even though I was in pain, I wouldn't have traded away one moment of today. I looked up, the sky was crystal clear and there were a billion stars out. The rock was still warm from the daytime sun and the heat began soaking into my body, easing the pain of my sore muscles. It was dead quiet and the only sounds I could hear were from the little desert creatures scurrying around the sand every now and then.

I started thinking about life in general, then looked straight up and said, "Hey, big guy in the sky, what's the deal? What's it all about? What's the point?"

I remembered some of the traumatic events that happened in my life. John F. Kennedy shot, the Vietnam War, Martin Luther King, Jr. and Bobby Kennedy assassinated, my parents gone. Many scenes kept racing through my mind. Why do men and women come together in relationships, then fall apart? Why did my marriage end when I thought it would last forever? There were too many questions and not enough answers. At times, I felt small and helpless and, other times, I felt on top of the world and there was nothing I couldn't do. I had trouble dealing with questions without answers.

I was on the verge of middle age and most of the people I knew or grew up with were dead. Some from drugs or alcohol, some from accidents, some from natural causes. It seemed that every time a person I knew died, a piece of me died also. There were beginning to be too many pieces missing. I was starting to feel incomplete and felt like I needed to build an emotional wall to protect myself.

I stared at the stars. "Hey, you up there! All I really want to do is live my life in such a way that I won't be afraid to go when the time comes."

Suddenly, I saw a bright flash streak across the heavens. It was an unusually brilliant meteor shooting through the atmosphere. It was probably billions of years old and had traveled billions of miles. In one instant it no longer existed and was now vapor. It had become part of the earth's atmosphere. Right then I realized that nothing stays the same. Not even very old, cold rocks.

I sat up straight. *Oh shit*, I thought, *I completely forgot about meeting Billy Jo, Paul and Diane. I knew Billy Jo would be pissed.* I'd also forgotten about Gloria. I hadn't heard from her in a couple of days and I forgot to check to see if she had written yesterday.

It was time to head home so I climbed off the rock and onto the bike. I fired up the engine and the roar of the pipes shattered the stillness. I think I scattered every creature around me.

I rolled slowly down the main street trying to keep the noise down, but that was not easy on this machine. There wasn't a car or a person on the street. I turned onto the station driveway, shut the bike off, pushed it into the garage and stood there admiring it. I still couldn't believe that I had it. Then I remembered the tradition that went with these motorcycles. When a person bought one, they had to spend the first night with it. I didn't know how that started or why, but I figured it would be best to keep with tradition.

I went outside to the van and got my sleeping bag and placed it alongside my bike. Then I went into the back room to check my computer for e-mail. I looked for the little white envelope to appear at the bottom of the screen to signal that I had mail.

No envelope. I wondered why Gloria hadn't written. *I'll write tomorrow, too tired to do it now.* I returned to my bike, lay down and fell asleep.

Chapter Two

It was six-thirty Saturday morning. John slowly rolled onto the station driveway, his eyes searching for my Yamaha, which I usually parked outside the garage door.

"Shit," he said, "doesn't look like Ron's here."

He drove his truck alongside the building and shut the engine off. Grabbing the door handle, he swung it open and slid out of the truck with a worried look on his face. Fishing the key out of his pocket, he fumbled for the door keys and, with a shaky hand, guided it into the lock. Pushing the door open, he mumbled, "I pray to the Almighty he's all right."

Stepping into the garage area, John saw me sleeping on the floor and momentarily smiled. The short-lived smile drained from his face as he exclaimed, "Well, gosh damn, you're alive! Everyone thought maybe you got killed on the road. Why the hell didn't ya call? You were supposed to meet Paul and Billy Jo last night. Did you forget?"

I opened my eyes and slowly sat up. "Sorry, John. I went to Jim's yesterday to make the payment. I didn't expect to pick up the bike until next month, but he let me take it."

John looked over at the bike next to me. "Yeah, so what happened to you?"

"I took a ride to Yuma."

"Yuma! What the hell's in Yuma?"

I'd never seen him upset before. "Take it easy, John. I just got lost for a while. I completely forgot about meeting Paul and Billy Jo."

"Well, after ya didn't show up at the pool hall by ten last night they called. I told them you should've been back by six or seven. It was too late to call Jim's, so all we could do was wait. We figured ya got in an accident. Billy Jo's really worried. Ya better give her a call."

"I'll call her in a few minutes. Give me a second to wake up," I replied, stretching my sore muscles.

John walked back to his office and I got up and splashed some water on my face. I stumbled to the phone, called Billy Jo and explained what happened. After some ranting and raving, she cooled down and then remarked, "Figures you'd do something like that. Just get lost without telling anyone. I should expect things like that from you."

"You want me to stop by later?" I asked hesitantly.

She shot a few more stinging comments at me, which I deserved, then said, "Yes, stop by later, I got some choice words for you. But right now, I'm going back to sleep for a few hours. I was up half the night worrying about you."

"Okay, I'll be by later this afternoon," I said, then hung up the phone.

I'd been dating Billy Jo for close to a year. Her father owned a horse ranch in the mountains not far from Borrego Springs. She would come to town on weekends and hang out at Jay's Pool Hall. It was the hot spot on Friday and Saturday nights. I noticed her right after I started going to Jay's.

The first time I saw her, she was wearing a cowboy vest with tassels, cut-off jean shorts with fringes and western boots that gave her legs real definition. She had long, flowing blonde hair. Her clear, blue eyes were wide and innocent and her face had soft, yet well defined features. She was a striking woman. When she spoke, her voice was soft, clear and direct. Her walk had purpose and she kept in good physical shape. The first time I spoke to her was when she drove her Jeep into John's for gas one afternoon. I walked back to my bench, sat down staring at my bike and reflected back to that first time we spoke . . .

"I've seen you at Jay's, haven't I?" she remarked as I filled up her tank.

"Yes, I've been there a few times."

"You're the new guy who just moved into town."

"That's me," I said trying not to stammer.

"All the girls have been talking about you."

"Is that so? Why would they want to talk about me?"

"Well, we're trying to figure why a good-looking, eligible guy like you would want to move here. Most guys who fit that

description are trying to get out of this tiny, dust blown town."

"It's a long story. Maybe I'll explain it to you some time."

I stood back as she started up her Jeep and drove to the end of the driveway. She stopped, turned her head and said, "I'll be at Jay's tonight. Maybe I'll see you there?"

"Okay, I'll be there," I said with a smile.

She shifted into gear and cruised down the street, her long blonde hair flowing in the wind. I leaned against the pump watching as she turned a corner out of sight.

Just talking to her made me nervous. She seemed sure of herself without being arrogant. I was looking forward to seeing her at Jay's . . .

I sat there blankly staring at my new Harley remembering that first time we got together. My mind drifted back to that night . . .

After finishing work at John's, I got ready to meet Billy Jo. I wasn't sure how to handle myself, as I hadn't been in the company of a woman since I left Chicago. I didn't know what to say or do and thought, to hell with it, just go and shoot pool. Whatever happens, happens.

It was close to five o'clock and John would be leaving soon. I wanted to shower and get ready to go, but I wanted to wait till he left.

After puttering around for a while, he came to the rear to let me know he was locking the front door. "I'll see you, Ron. Have fun and ride safe."

"I will, John, take it easy. See you tomorrow."

I grabbed a towel and soap, then jumped in the shower. While I was soaping up I started to think about Billy Jo. She was sitting in her Jeep with the door open. I thought about her long, tanned legs and her flowing blonde hair. She'd been wearing a brief, tight halter-top that hugged her breasts enough to show her large nipples. The more I thought about her, the more I began to grow. I rubbed my soapy hands across my stomach and down between my legs. I worked the soap into a foamy white lather. It was real slippery on my body. I pictured her firm thighs as I ran my hand up and down my lower stomach. I was fully-grown now and having trouble washing the rest of my body. I took hold of myself and started to fantasize about her. I squeezed myself and the soapsuds squirted out from between my fingers. I pictured her tight shorts and started to stroke. It felt real good. I thought about those nipples and moved my hand faster. I remembered her long, thin, fingers as she handed me the money to pay her bill. I positioned myself under the water so I could stay wet and slick. All I cared about now was taking myself to the end. I pictured her full, red lips and her slim, velvety stomach and was on my way to finishing when I stopped. What if I got lucky tonight? It'd been a long time since I'd had sex with anyone. Maybe I should save it in case it happens. It was very hard not to finish what I started, but I held off.

I rinsed and got out of the shower. As I towel-dried, I looked into the mirror. I stood there staring for a few moments. My stomach was still flat from working out. I looked down wondering if I was big enough. I guess I was bigger than some but not as big as others. Average would probably be the word. They say it's not how much you have, it's how you use it. I hope that's true or I might be in trouble. I took myself in my hand and tried to twirl it but it wasn't cooperating since it was still a little stiff. I'd better quit fooling around, I thought, and get ready to go.

I wrapped the towel around myself and went to the van to get some clothes. I looked through my tiny pile of stuff and took out my favorite jeans, the worn ones with the holes in the knees. It wasn't a hard decision to make since I only had three pair and two were dirty. I looked through my T-shirts for one that had no holes in it. I ran my hands to the bottom of the pile to the last two shirts. They were Harley T-shirts I bought from Jim's a couple of months back. I pulled them out and held them up. I wanted to wear one of them tonight but I couldn't. I made a vow to myself that I would not wear them until I got my Harley. I folded them back up and put them on the bottom of the pile. I grabbed a not-so-faded plain, black shirt and got dressed.

I locked up the station and put on my leather jacket, then got on my Yamaha and rode over to Jay's Pool Hall. I was getting anxious as I parked and made my way toward the door.

I walked in and saw her sitting with a couple of friends. She saw me and waved. I waved back. She was wearing a short, tight, black satin skirt and a low-cut, red silk, loose blouse and her long blonde hair was brushed to a silky luster. Her legs were crossed and I briefly glanced at her exposed thigh looking all the way down her leg to her black high heels. I walked over and asked nervously, "Care to shoot some pool?"

"All right. You want to get the table?"

"Okay, I'll meet you over there."

I racked up the pool balls and she walked toward the table gently rotating her hips, her heels making sharp contact with the marble floor. I let her break and as she leaned over the table her loose blouse exposed her firm breasts. I was having trouble watching the balls roll. I couldn't recall her ever being dressed this way the few times I'd seen her before.

As she was bent over ready to make a shot she asked, "You ride a motorcycle?"

I had trouble keeping eye contact while I answered, "Yes, it's outside. It's just an old beater to get me around. I've got a little money saved and I plan to get a Harley-Davidson soon. I've been waiting for the right bike to come into Jim's motorcycle shop in Oceanside. Hopefully, I'll be able to find one. In the meantime, my 650 will have to do."

"I've seen your bike. It's not a bad ride."

It was my turn. I was too nervous to make even a simple shot. I missed. "Must not be my night," I said, embarrassed.

She looked at me and didn't say anything. She walked slowly around the pool table, then stood with her back to me and leaned over it. Her skirt rose up and I thought I was going to die. It was almost as though she planned this.

I lost the first game. I looked at her sheepishly. "I had a long, day at the station. I didn't sleep well last night either." I don't know if she believed me. I was all thumbs and couldn't do anything right. She was making me sweat. She smiled at me again and we played more pool.

After a couple of games, she asked, "Would you like to sit down?"

"Yeah, my game is really off. I don't think I could make a shot even if my life depended on it."

"Don't worry about it, I have days like that," she said as we walked to the table with me following, breathing in her sweet perfume lightly floating through the air, while at the same time watching her body sway gracefully in front of me.

I sat there staring at her wondering why I hadn't noticed her like this before. She looked exceptionally good tonight. We sat for a while listening to music, then she spoke. "So you want to get a Harley?"

"Uh-huh. It's been a long-time dream."

"I like riding on motorcycles," she said. "I ride horses quite a bit. That's almost like riding a bike."

"Yep, the same, only different."

She looked at me and smiled.

"I'd offer to take you for a ride but you're not quite dressed for it. Too bad, it's a warm and beautiful night."

"Well, I've got a pair of jeans in my Jeep and I brought my leather jacket. It'll just take me a minute to change."

I wasn't sure if I could handle this lady sitting close behind me on my bike. She was stirring something inside me. Before I could catch the words from leaving my mouth I said, "Okay, let's go."

"All right. Let me change and I'll be ready in a minute."

I sat there wondering what to do. Where was I going to take her? What was I going to do when we got there? With a word she could easily turn me into a babbling idiot. It was too soon after my divorce. I wasn't looking for a relationship or even a one-night stand. I wasn't ready for any of this, or was I? The wounds were just beginning to heal. How did I get myself into this? Oh well, it didn't matter, too late to turn back now.

She came out of the ladies' room in tight jeans with her jacket flung over her shoulder and her skirt tucked under her arm, "Ready?" she asked.

"Yes, if you are."

I got up and we headed toward the door. She waved goodbye to her friends and they waved back with big grins on their faces. We walked outside into the warm, dry desert air. I was having trouble trying not to trip over my feet. I made it to my bike without falling over myself. I watched as she walked to her Jeep and put her skirt away, my eyes roaming up and down her womanly figure. Damn, she's good-looking.

I turned away as she walked back. "Well, this is it," I blurted out. "It's not much, but it's all I have till I get my Harley."

"Are you ready to go?" she asked with a look of anticipation on her face.

I nodded and got on the bike. She gracefully lifted her leg over the seat and carefully slid her body in behind me. My pulse jumped and my breathing quickened as she gently made contact with me. I fired the bike up, concentrated on the road and headed into the desert trying to maintain my composure.

I was a little tense at first, but settled back and relaxed after a few minutes. It was in the low eighties. Perfect weather for riding. I could feel her body pressing against mine. The stars were out and everything felt good. It was almost too comfortable. We rode for half an hour when I asked, "Would you like to pull over and rest?"

"Yes," she replied, in a small voice.

I turned off the road at my favorite spot by the large, oval rock. I felt at ease here. I rolled to a stop and let her get off. I shut the bike down and we walked over to the rock and sat down. I sat cross-legged on the ground sifting through the sand while she sat across from me with her legs tucked under her chin and her arms folded around them. The moon was half full and it made her eyes sparkle and gave her skin a soft glow.

As we sat there talking, the conversation turned to personal things.

"So, you were going to tell me what brought you to Borrego Springs?" she inquired.

I sat silent for a moment, then replied, "I lived in Chicago all of my life and I wasn't happy there. I always had a desire to move, but I had a house, a business and a family. I had too much responsibility to pack up and leave. Then my marriage started to fall apart and since my wife was self-supporting and my children were young adults, I decided to head west. What made it easy was

I asked myself a question: If I was from another planet and was dropped in the center of the United States, would I pick Chicago to live in? The answer was no. Leaving and starting over again was the hardest thing to do. But somehow I found the strength and courage to do it."

Billy Jo sat there rocking back and forth listening to me.

"I was on my way to the coast and had no plans. I stopped here to gas up before I went through the mountains. I started to work for John and I've been here ever since. Now, enough about me, tell me a little about yourself."

She looked at me for a minute, as though she was collecting her thoughts or I caught her off guard.

"Oh, okay. I've lived outside of Borrego Springs all of my life. My father owns a horse ranch in the mountains. I live with him and help maintain the ranch. I have an older sister, but she got married a couple years ago and moved to San Francisco. I was going to college in Los Angeles when my mother was killed in an auto accident. I was close to graduating when the accident happened, but I quit to be with my dad. He was devastated for a long time. He still hasn't fully accepted the fact that she's gone."

"Ever been married?" I asked.

"No. I've had a few long-term relationships, but nothing to get married over."

I grinned, "I think I understand that."

"When you live in a small town, there's not a lot of eligible bachelors available. I'm only thirty-two and I'm not in any hurry. Plus I haven't found the right man yet. Some women get desperate as they get older, but I don't think that's the case with me."

I paused for a second, then said, "Seems we're coming from two different aspects of life."

"Yes. Well, that could make life interesting," she said, softly.

I stared up at the stars. "I don't know much about relationships since I've had only one major one. It seems that there's a part of me closed off. It's hard to explain. I'm not sure if I can involve myself with another person. At least not right now."

"That will change in time. It always does. Everyone's different. It's been ten years since my mother's death and my father still

hasn't dated anyone. Hope it doesn't take you that long."

"Me too," I said, staring blanking into space.

We both sat looking at the stars without speaking. It was getting late and it starting to cool off. I don't know what it was, but I felt drawn to her now. I passed it off to her being a very sexy lady and me being a little lonely. What else could it be? I thought.

She looked at me, "Have you ever ridden a horse?"

"No. I'm a city boy, remember? The only thing I know about horses is what I've seen on TV, or in the movies. I don't think I've ever had the desire to learn how."

"Well, maybe I can teach you how to ride if you're not busy and I'm not doing anything."

"I don't know about that. Those animals look pretty big and they have a mind of their own. Seems to me they can do what they feel like."

"It's not as hard as it looks. You just have to have a little confidence in yourself. Anyway, you think about it and let me know."

"I'll do that. But for now, I'll stick with my cycle."

I looked at the moon now low in the sky, "It's getting late and I'm tired. We'd better head home."

She threw her head back and shook out her hair, "Yes, we'd better get going."

We stood up and walked over to the bike. I got on and started it, then she climbed on and said, "I had a good time. We must do this again."

"It was an enjoyable evening, we will have to do it again," I said as I looked toward the road and smiled wide.

She put her arms around me and the warmth of her body felt good in the cool of the night. I turned the bike onto the road and slowly drove home. Jay's was closed now, so I dropped her off at her Jeep.

"I guess I'll see you here again?" I asked.

"Yes, I'm here a lot. I had a good time. We have to go for a ride again soon."

She lingered for a moment, then turned toward her Jeep. I watched as she walked away, got into her Jeep and drove down the road. I felt good. Better than I'd felt in a long time, longer than I could remember.

I rode the short distance home to the station, parked the bike in the garage, then climbed into my van and went to sleep that night with a smile on my face . . .

I could hear John moving around in the front office and it brought me back to reality. I sat looking out the garage window remembering how I felt that first night with Billy Jo.

I was tired because I'd only had a few hours of sleep, but there was no way I was going back to bed. I was too excited about my new Harley to think about sleep.

Cruising through the desert all night got my new bike dusty and I figured I should wash it before riding through Borrego Springs. I also had to e-mail Gloria. I was beginning to worry since I didn't know much about her and she lived three thousand miles away in New York City. I met her on the Internet about the same time I met Billy Jo. The only way I could communicate with her was through the e-mail.

I knew nothing about computers before I came to Borrego Springs. A guy driving through town broke down as he was passing through. He didn't have much money and wanted to trade labor to fix his car for his computer. It was okay with John so I fixed his car and John let me hook up the computer in the back room of the garage. I'd heard about the Internet and they had a free offer going at the time, so I went on-line and met Gloria there.

We started writing each other on a nightly basis. She chatted freely about her feelings and about things in general, but she was very secretive about specific things in her life. I was up front about my life and myself since I didn't have anything to hide.

I was hoping she would open up and I felt like I had to know more about her. I had strong feelings for Billy Jo. But I also had feelings for Gloria, even though I'd never met her. It was as though I had to find out for myself by meeting Gloria in person. I was torn between the two. Seeing Gloria was part of my plan, but she didn't know it. I'd been keeping it a secret from her. Now that I had my new bike I could leave sooner. The only other person who knew of my plan was Paul and I was sure he would stop by. He always did on Saturdays.

I could hear John slowly approach from his office. He appeared at the doorway and made his way to the center of the garage. He stood in the middle of the room for a second, then walked over to his bench and puttered around. I knew he wanted to say something but was having trouble talking. I looked at him, "Gonna be hot again today, huh?"

"Probably," he said, without looking my way. He kept fidgeting at the bench. Finally, he looked over at me and said, "Ron, I'm sorry about hollerin'. I was just worried 'bout you. I never had a son and I kinda feel like if I had one I'd like him to be like you."

"That's okay, John. There's no need to apologize. I should have at least called Billy Jo."

"You know, Ron, the offer still goes 'bout taking the spare room in the house instead of living in your van."

"I appreciate that, but I don't mind living out of the van. Matter of fact, it's the best thing that could've happened to me. I needed time to be alone, to sort things out and this has been perfect. I couldn't have planned it better if I tried."

"Well, the offer is open anytime ya want."

"I'll keep it in mind. But for now it's just great the way it is."

"All right, whad'ya have planned for today?"

"I gotta wash my bike before I take it out. I think there's some kinda law about dirty Harleys. You can't ride one in public."

John looked at me funny. Then he looked over at the bike, "That sure is a mighty pretty motorcycle ya got there. Now I understand why ya been chompin' at the bit. I'd be in a hurry to get it myself."

"Yes, it sure did turn a lotta heads yesterday. I never owned anything that got this much attention. I had fun every minute of the ride."

"Lookin' at the bike I can understand how easy it would be to just keep ridin'."

A car pulled up to the pumps and John shuffled outside to take care of business. I rolled my bike to the back and started to wash the dirt off when I heard Paul drive up. He had an older Harley, which was spotless, and in perfect mechanical condition, probably the result of his being a former Marine. He still had that attitude. He kept his black hair short and combed straight back. He had a chiseled face and a tight square jaw. His frame was lean and muscular. We worked out at the same gym and started riding together soon after I arrived in Borrego Springs.

I could hear John tell Paul that I was in the back. Paul's boots made loud thuds as he walked towards me. He was dressed in his usual Saturday black leather vest, Harley T-shirt, and blue jeans. He broke out in a wide grin as he came into view.

"You dirty dog. How'd you get the bike? Thought you weren't supposed to get it till next month."

I explained what happened and told him about my trip to Yuma, while he walked around looking at every minute detail, poking at the chrome gadgets.

"Outstanding," he said. "Looks different than it did on the showroom floor."

"Sure does," I responded.

Paul stooped down balancing himself on one knee. He was looking at the engine and said, "Sure must be nice to have one of these new Evo motors."

"Man, this thing really flies when I hit the throttle."

"Come on, let's go out to Willow Road and see just what your machine can do."

"Paul, I don't feel like running a race with you right now. Let me get used to the bike a little more."

"Well, hell, you rode all the way to Arizona and back already! Besides, you said you'd race me when you got it."

"Listen, I know what this bike can do. I've been riding with you and I know what your bike can do. I can probably beat you with no problem."

"Then, come on, let's go out to Willow Road and check it out. Put your money where your mouth is."

I knew there was no talking him out of it. He'd been waiting for this ever since I put the bike on layaway. I'd been ribbing him for a long time about how I could beat him. I guess I had to go through with it now. "Are you sure you want to do this? We both have the same size motors, but my bike's lighter than yours is. I have a five-speed transmission and you only have a four-speed. I can take you off the line and when I hit top speed I can shift into fifth gear and leave you in the dust," I warned.

"Hey, my bike's not stock anymore. I've done some major work on it!"

I knew Paul was right. It would be close. But I knew I could beat him. Besides, he was gettin' me all fired up.

Paul looked squarely at me with his steely gray eyes. His brow narrowed and his nostrils started to flare. "Come on, bad boy. Let's get out on the road and see who's really bad!"

"Are you sure you want to do this?" I repeated.

"You bet I do. I've been waiting to shut you up once and for all," he said jokingly.

I knew Paul was having fun, but whenever he did anything, he took it seriously. "Let me finish wiping off my bike, then we'll ride out and settle this."

Before we left I went into my van and got one of my Harley T-shirts. I'd been waiting a long time to wear one. I walked outside and Paul started laughing, "Well, you finally get to wear a real shirt."

"Yeah, let's go. We'll see who laughs last."

We pulled out of the station and waved to John as we hit the end of the driveway. We slowly rolled down the main street, riding side by side. Paul's bike was about as loud as a Harley could be and my bike wasn't that quiet either. We turned every head we passed. People looked or gave us the thumbs-up as we rode by. The temperature was already in the low hundreds. We both fell into a trance and became stone-faced and expressionless as we cruised. It was hot out but we were cool.

When we got to the open road, we started toying with each other. Paul would crack his throttle and speed up. Then I would whack mine, catch up and pass him. We'd been riding together for a while and we knew what the other was going to do intuitively. It was as though we were connected by an invisible force.

Willow Road was about twenty minutes out in the desert. It

was where everyone went to race. It was a long, straight, four-mile stretch of road. You could see any traffic coming or going. We usually started at the top of the grade and raced to the bottom where the creek bed started. You couldn't race any farther because there was a sharp bend a half-mile past the creek bed that veered off to the right. On the left side of the road was a thirty-foot drop into a gully. On the right was a ten-foot-tall cliff wall. You couldn't see past the curve and it was too dangerous to take it over twenty-five miles an hour. There was no place to turn off the road at the bend. Many people tried to race around it and wound up in the gully or slammed into the cliff wall, never to return.

I watched Paul out of the corner of my eye as we headed to Willow Road. It felt good to be his friend. He was the kind of man who would do anything to help a person in need. I looked around at the desert. It was a place to be respected. It had a harsh beauty that most people couldn't see. It was delicately balanced yet very subtle. If you weren't careful it could kill. I turned my attention back to the road, the wind hot on my face. I wouldn't have traded this moment for any other.

We were getting close to the spot where we would begin. I pulled over at the top of the grade and Paul stopped alongside me. From here we could see all the way to the curve. I sat with my bike idling, looking at Paul. He looked back with a devilish grin.

"Now, remember," I said, "we have to stop when we get to the bottom, at the creek bed."

"Yeah, right, I know all about it," Paul snapped.

"Listen, I just don't want either of us to get hurt. We're just having fun. It really ain't important who wins."

"Man, I ain't going to do anything stupid. Besides, I'm going to win anyway."

I just looked at Paul, not sure if I should be doing this. Paul was too serious sometimes and I think this was one of those times. "Okay, it's all clear. There's no traffic in either direction. Let's pull out onto the road and at the count of three we'll go. The first one to the creek bed wins, right?" I asked.

"Yep, to the creek bed," he responded staring down the long stretch of pavement.

We pulled out onto the middle of the road. Paul had a crazy look in his eyes. I was beginning to worry about him. We both revved up our motors, then slowly counted to three. At three, we simultaneously popped our clutches.

It was about three and a half miles to the bottom where the creek bed started. When I popped my clutch, my front wheel leaped off the ground. I opened my throttle all the way and shifted into second gear. My front wheel lifted off the ground again. All I could hear was the roar of our pipes. I shifted into third and the front tire strained to come up off the asphalt one more time.

I could see Paul behind me in my rearview mirror. He was close but I was widening the distance between us. I shifted into fourth and Paul slowly drifted back. I knew when I shifted into fifth I would lose him. I looked at my speedometer, ninety miles an hour. I kicked it into fifth gear, one hundred ten miles an hour. The desert wind was getting hotter. I had to hold onto my handlebars with all my might. Paul was somewhere behind me but I couldn't see him anymore because my mirrors were vibrating too much. I knew he would never catch me now though.

I was almost at the bottom of the grade where the creek bed started. As I passed the bed, I was going faster than one hundred twenty miles an hour. I don't really know how fast because my speedometer only went to one hundred twenty.

The curve was coming up fast now and I started to slow down. I looked in my mirror to see where Paul was. He flew past me, going at top speed. My first thought was that he wasn't going to make it.

I screamed for him to slow down but I knew he couldn't hear me. I saw him hit his brakes but he was too close to the bend. His back end started to fishtail, then he drifted onto the wrong side of the road and I lost sight of him. If there was a car coming from the other direction, he was going to hit it. He disappeared, skidding around the cliff and I could only think that he wound up in the gully or slammed into the wall and splattered all over the road.

I dreaded riding around to the other side for fear of what I would find. I could see skid marks as I rounded it but, surprisingly, the marks stayed on the road. As I came to the straightaway, I could see Paul sitting upright on the shoulder. I was amazed. He hadn't crashed as I thought he would. I pulled alongside him and said loudly, "You stupid fuck! What's the matter with you?"

He didn't look at me. He just stared straight ahead. His skin was pale white, the deep tan drained from his face. I could see he almost crapped his pants. He was holding on to his handlebars so tight I thought his knuckles were going to pop out of his skin. He sat there stiff as a board. I let go of my handlebars and crossed my arms. I sat there for a few seconds, then sarcastically remarked, "You look like you just saw God."

Paul slowly turned his head toward me, his eyes bugged out, and weakly replied, "Yes, I think I did," his fists still tight on the bars.

"I don't care how fast you went around the bend, I still won," I snapped.

The color started to return to his face. His eyes were still real wide. I think he had some kind of spiritual experience. Then he started to smile and said in a weak voice, "Man, was that a rush! My heart is about to jump right out of my chest. I have no idea how I kept this bike up."

"Neither do I. You went around it at least fifty miles an hour. I don't think anyone has gone around it that fast and stayed in one piece. You're lucky. That was a real stupid move."

"My life flashed in front of my eyes."

"I'll bet it did, but I beat you fair and square. Well, are you satisfied now?"

"I want a rematch!"

"Paul, you're nuts, you know that. Are you going to be okay?"

"Yeah, I'm alright. Just give me a minute to catch my breath and let my heart slow down a bit."

Paul looked at me and I looked back at him, then we started to grin. We began laughing out loud and poking each other. I really thought he was a goner. He looked down at my bike, "Damn, that thing is fast. I'd really have to do some speed work on mine to beat that machine. And don't think I won't."

"You're the kind of guy that would do just that to prove a point." We sat there for a few minutes letting our bikes idle. "I want to stop by and see Billy Jo. I didn't get a chance to see her last night."

"I know. We waited for you till almost two before we left. She's really pissed. I wouldn't want to be in your shoes when you see her."

"She can't be that mad, can she?"

"Ron, that girl is really stuck on you. I guess I should say she was more hurt then mad. Either way, you gotta face her.

"Listen, Paul, I'm not sure how I feel. I didn't expect this to happen. I know I have feelings for her. I think about her all the time. But there's Gloria. I've got this strong urge to meet her."

Paul looked at me, then looked away. I stared him down. "You are the only one who knows about my plan, right?" He started shifting nervously on his bike. "Paul? You are the only one," I asked again.

"Well, I think I might've mentioned it to Diane."

"What? If you told her then you can be sure she's told Billy Jo."

"If Billy Jo knows, what's the difference? You were going to tell her anyway."

"Oh man, I wanted to be the one to tell her. If she knows, she hasn't let on. Now she probably thinks I want to dump her for some girl I haven't met."

"Isn't that what you're going to do?"

"No. I told you what I want to do. I just have to meet her to satisfy my mind. I was married for eighteen years and I'm not going to make a commitment unless I'm absolutely sure. If I don't do this, I'll never know. I can't go through life not knowing."

"Billy Jo is probably the best thing that could happen in your life. If you go, you might be sorry," Paul warned.

"I know you'd like to see Billy Jo and me together. But try to understand why I have to take this trip. Try to be objective, if you can."

"You're a smart man, Roadside Ron, but you're also one stupid S.O.B."

"Yeah. Well, I'm going to ride over to Billy Jo's ranch. Wanna come along?"

"You bet. I wouldn't miss this for the world."

The ranch was a half-hour away in the mountains. We pulled onto the road and kept to the speed limit. One close call today was enough.

The scenery changed to lush green and the temperature dropped to a cool eighty-five at the higher elevation of the mountains. We rode side by side and waved to fellow riders we passed on the way. The road felt good and so did the bike. I was looking forward to fulfilling my third dream. I had only imagined what it would be like to own a Harley. Now, I could feel the thrill. It was an experience I couldn't put into words.

The ranch entrance was fast coming up so we slowed down to turn onto the gravel roadway. It was a very big spread, one of the largest and most successful ranches in the area.

Paul backed off so I could pull into the driveway first, then followed me onto the dirt road that led through the center of the ranch to a house at the other end. I could see Billy Jo's father working with some horses at the far end of the field. He glanced up for a moment, then went back to his work.

Her father never said very much. For that matter, he didn't speak to anyone, much less me. In business matters, he was direct and to the point, never using any unnecessary words. I think he was still hurting about his wife's untimely death. We just said hello to each other whenever we met. He was the spitting image of Clint Eastwood and his attitude fit his appearance. If he hadn't become a horse rancher, I'm sure he would have made a good movie cowboy, the strong silent type.

I stopped in front of the house and couldn't see Billy Jo anywhere. If she was around, she should've heard us drive up. I looked back at Paul and he shrugged his shoulders. I revved my engine a couple of times hoping to get her attention, then looked around and saw her walking toward me from the back of the house. She was wearing jeans and boots and had on a flannel shirt with the tails tied around her waist showing her slim stomach. Her hair was pulled back in a ponytail and her bright blue eyes peered at me from under the brim of her white Stetson hat. She looked good no matter what she wore, but she didn't look too happy to see me.

"Looking for someone?" she asked sharply.

"Uh, yeah, Jo. I was lookin' for you."

"Are you sure? Maybe the person you're looking for is in Yuma. Or maybe in New York?"

I looked back at Paul. He avoided my glance. I turned back to Jo. "Uh, what do ya mean by that?

"You know what I mean. What about your computer girlfriend? Didn't think I knew about her, huh? You know, the one in New York."

"I told you about her and the Internet."

"You told me about the Internet and about some girl you occasionally talked to, but not about seeing her."

"Well, I didn't know about that myself until recently. I was going to tell you about it but someone else seems to have done it for me."

I looked back at Paul and glared at him. He looked like a kid caught with his hand in the cookie jar. I lowered my kickstand and set my bike down on it, then reached down and switched off the ignition. I swung my leg over the bike and stood facing Jo. She had her arms folded across her breasts with her body cocked sideways. This was not the time to explain anything.

Paul hollered over the noise of his engine, "Hey, Ron, maybe I should head out and meet you back in town?"

"No. You stay right here. We're going back to town together."

He shut off his bike and walked down the road a bit to look at some horses. I walked to where she was standing, slid my arms around her and gazed into her eyes. I moved forward to kiss her and she turned away and said, "Oh, no, you don't, you Bozo. You stood me up last night. You plan to go visit some babe in New York. Then you come up to me as though nothing's going on! I don't think so, buster."

"Aw, come on Jo. I didn't mean to stand you up last night. It just happened. I got on that bike and it took me for a ride. I've been waitin' all my life to get a Harley and I guess I lost it."

"Yep, you lost it all right!"

"And about Gloria, I was really going to explain that to you. I was waiting for the right time."

"When? After you left?"

"No. I didn't quite know how to put it into words. And I wasn't going to try until I knew how to say it. If I try to say anything now, it will come out all wrong. If you want to tell me something I have to wait till you're ready to say it, right?"

"Well . . . yeah."

"Okay, the same with me. If I have to wait till you're ready then you'll just have to wait till I'm ready."

"I guess it's the way it'll have to be," she replied meekly.

"I'll explain it to you, just give me some time to sort it out."

She looked into my eyes and I could tell she was trying hard not to smile. "You bastard, all I have to do is look at you and I can't stay mad." She swung her fist, lightly hit me on the arm and at the same time broke out in a big grin. She put her arms around my neck and softly put her lips against mine. I could feel her body press against me. My pulse began to quicken and I started to breathe hard. This happened every time we kissed.

"We better take it easy. Your father's right over there."

"I missed being with you last night. We've spent every weekend together for the last couple of months, and your damn Harley got between us and you've only had it one day. I knew that bike was going to be a problem."

"Come on, Jo, my bike's not going to be a problem unless you make it one."

"Yeah, we'll see."

"Your dad's looking over this way. We better stop kissing or he'll see us."

"So? What's the big deal if he sees? He knows I'm going out with you."

"I don't think he cares too much for me. I get the feeling that he'd rather see you with someone else."

"Oh, yeah, who?"

"Anyone but me."

She pulled away from me. "Ron, he's that way with everyone. Don't take it personally."

"If you say so. Check out the bike. Jim let me take it early. Didn't expect that."

She walked around the Harley and nodded her head in approval. She'd seen it many times before when I made the monthly payments.

"Come on, Jo, let's go for a short ride."

"I can't leave now. I'm supposed to be working."

"Your boss is your father. He's not going to say anything. You come and go as you please any other time. 'Sides, what's he going to do, fire you?"

"All right. Half an hour, no longer. I'll see you tonight anyway."

I motioned to Paul to come back. I got on my bike and put the passenger pegs down for Jo. She took off her Stetson and set it on the porch. Then she walked to the bike, swung her leg over the seat and put her arms around me. She squeezed me tight and laid her head on my back. Whenever she got close to me, something inside tingled. Paul got on his bike and kick-started it.

"Me and Jo are going for a short ride. Wanna tag along?"

"No. I should stop by and see Diane. I'll see ya back in town."

I nodded to him, then we turned around and slowly rode down the driveway. Jo's father looked in our direction and stood up when he saw that Jo was with me. She looked at him and waved. He just stared at us.

"I really think he's not happy with me."

"That's just the way he is. How many times do I have to tell you?"

"Whatever you say."

When we got to the road, Paul turned left and I made a right. We waved to each other as we headed in opposite directions. I rolled the power on and Jo clung tight. The sun was out. It was a beautiful day and the road was all mine.

Jo ran her hands gently up and down my sides as we rode along the highway. She started to kiss the back of my neck and put her hands on my stomach. "Ooohhh, I love the way your body feels," she said as she let her hands fall to my lap. She began caressing the inside of my thighs, then put her lips next to my ear and said, "You feel so . . . good."

She pressed her body tighter against me. Her hand slid between my legs, which started to arouse me. "This bike feels good and rides nice," she said. "It's making me real horny. Every time I get close to you I get horny. I was looking forward to being with you last night. We can make up for it today though."

I was having trouble concentrating on the road. Her hands were in all the right places. She put her lips close to my ear again, "Let's stop somewhere soon."

"That sounds like a good idea. You want coffee or lunch?"

"No, stupid. I want you. Pull over and stop where there aren't any people."

I knew of a secluded out of the way place up the road by a small creek. We'd stopped there a couple of times before. It was mid-afternoon and we'd never made love outside in the middle of the day before. I was excited about this prospect and was having trouble concentrating on driving.

I slowed down and rode onto the dirt road, then pulled into a small clearing alongside the creek. There was no one in sight and people rarely came this way. Jo looked around. "Stop here."

I did and shut off the engine. She got off, walked to a grassy spot and sat down. She looked at me with half-closed eyes as I set the bike on the kickstand. I walked over to where she was, took off my T-shirt and placed it behind her on the ground so she could lie on it. I sat down beside her and she softly ran her fingertips across my shoulders and down my arms. She grabbed me and pulled me down to the ground with her. I unbuttoned her shirt and lifted it over her shoulders. She nibbled on my ear and unbuttoned my pants, then pulled my zipper down and took hold of me.

"Oh yeah," I stammered, as I unhooked her bra and exposed her soft, well-formed breasts. Her hair was lightly scented and smelled fresh as the country around us. I reached down, unbuttoned her jeans, and slid them down her legs. Then I pulled her boots and jeans off. She wasn't wearing any underwear. I sat up and looked at her naked body and touched her soft breast. I put my lips on her stiff nipple and sucked while licking it with my tongue. I ran my hand over her stomach, then down between her legs and caressed her. She was already real wet. Her hips rhythmically moved against my hand. She still had hold of me and started to stroke faster. She shivered as I fingered her. I took my pants off and she pulled me down on top of her body. She guided me to her, then sighed and moaned softly as I slowly slid into her.

"Oh, Ron, don't stop," she whispered into my ear, "you feel so good." She wrapped her legs around my waist and took my hips in her hands as she slowly pushed and pulled. I watched her breasts rise and fall. "Oh, God, you're doing it," she said as she lifted her hips to feel all of me.

I kissed her lips and felt her hot breath on my face. I was almost there. She started to move faster and I could feel her nails grabbing at my back. I thrust harder and she moaned loudly. She reached up and wiped the tiny beads of sweat off my forehead, then grabbed my hips again and pushed and pulled harder. I could feel she was on the verge of cuming, so I put my lips on hers and searched for her tongue. I felt her body stiffen as she groaned, her inner muscles starting to pulse around me. She threw her head back and I could tell she had just orgasmed. Her body slowly relaxed and I stopped thrusting so she could feel all of me. After a minute or so, she grabbed my hips and started to push and pull again.

I was trying to take my time and move slowly but she pushed and pulled me faster. I couldn't hold back any longer. She took me all the way to the end. I exploded with a big groan and could feel her shudder as I lost control. She vibrated, arched her back, and sighed loudly, "Oh, Ron!"

We both relaxed at the same time. I put my lips on hers and I could feel them quiver, then let my body go limp on top of hers. She put her arms around me, pulling me tighter against her. We stayed in that position for a few minutes, then she whispered, "We better get our clothes on in case anyone happens along this way."

I agreed and rolled off. "Oh, man, you feel so good," I said as I watched her firm breasts slowly rise and fall with each deep breath she took.

She looked at me and smiled softly, "I'm glad you liked it." She closed her eyes and reached out and ran her hand over my chest. "You do something no one has ever done to me before."

"What's that?" I asked.

"You make me feel out of control."

I looked into her eyes and I knew what she was talking about. She looked back at me. "There's something I want to say to you but I can't bring myself to say it just yet. Maybe in time."

I stared at her and didn't say anything. I thought to myself, *I know what's she's talking about but I'm not sure how I feel. I'm going through too many emotional changes to know how I feel about anything right now.*

"My dad's probably wondering what happened to me. We'd better start heading back."

"Okay. I wouldn't want him to feel any worse about me than he already does."

"Ron . . . quit it."

"Sorry, forget I said that." I sat up and handed her jeans to her. I looked at her body again and couldn't help getting excited. I turned away and picked up my clothes. I knew she had to get back and didn't want to keep her any longer.

We got dressed and walked over to the bike. I got on and fired up the engine. She leaned over and kissed me. It was a long, wet kiss and I started to get excited again. "Better stop or we'll have to stay here a little longer," I snickered.

She kiddingly slapped me on the back, "Don't worry, I'll see you tonight. Whatever we start, we can finish later."

I turned the bike around and Jo got on. We rode toward the highway and headed back to the ranch. When we got there I looked around for her father, but he was nowhere in sight. I stopped in front of her house and she hugged me tight for a moment.

"Where's your dad?" I asked.

"Don't know. I'm sure he's around somewhere." She got off the bike and turned to face me. "I'll see you tonight at Jay's?"

"Of course."

"You blew me off last night. Wasn't sure if you might do it again."

"Come on, Jo, I didn't blow you off. It's not every day I get a Harley. I had to get the first day out of my system. 'Sides, had to make sure she ran right."

"Uh-huh. That's a good one. Just don't let it happen again or you'll feel my full wrath."

"Oooohhhhh, I'm scared."

As we hugged each other, I glanced over her shoulder and noticed her father looking at us through the living room window. I kept it to myself. "Time for me to get out of here and let you get back to work."

"Yes, get out of here! I've got work to do," she hollered playfully as she kissed me goodbye. I revved my engine a few times as I eased the bike into a big circle and headed towards the highway.

On the way back, I thought about what she had said and I knew what she wanted to tell me. She wanted to say she loved me. I wasn't sure if I was ready for that. I was confused about the whole situation. I felt like it was too fast, too soon. Not that I didn't like the idea, I just couldn't commit to anyone unless I was absolutely sure. I had to find some things out first. *Why did life have to be so damn complicated?* I screamed inside my head. I hit the throttle hard and sped through winding roads back to Borrego Springs.

Chapter Three

It was late afternoon by the time I got back to the station. I parked and made my way towards the front door. John was inside the office as I walked in. He glanced up at me, squinting, while adjusting his glasses. He looked tired sitting there in his threadbare coveralls and his scuffed, wingtip shoes without laces. Not from working, but from life in general. I walked over to the three-legged stool he kept for customers and sat down. It was a challenge to get the stool to sit level on the uneven floor. Sometimes I would get it right, but not today.

"Hi, Ron. Did ya get to see Billy Jo?"

"Yeah, we went for a short ride."

I got up, walked over to the soda machine and felt for change in my pocket. After shoving some coins into the slot, I punched the button. The can dropped with a flat clunk. I grabbed it, then sat back down. John ran his hand through his unkempt hair trying to make it behave, but it fell back to the same position. He cleared his throat, looked at me and said in his scratchy voice, "Looks like you got something eatin' at you?"

"Well, you know how I've been talking about riding cross country ever since I've been here."

"Yep. You mentioned it more than a couple of times."

I leaned one elbow on the counter trying to steady myself on the stool. "As long as I can remember I've wanted to ride a Harley from one end of this great country to the other, long before I moved here. I have the Harley now and I've saved a few bucks. I didn't plan on getting the bike this soon, but it doesn't matter. I've got to make a couple of changes to it so I won't have any problems on the road. One reason I went to Yuma was to feel it out to see what I would have to do to make the trip smoother. Billy Jo's upset because I'm going to ride to New York and I have mixed feelings about this myself. When I first moved here, everything was simple and clear. Now, it's fuzzy and complicated."

John shifted in his old, wooden rocking chair on wheels. Every time he moved, even slightly, the chair would squeak or creak loudly. I could swear it was used as sound effects for those "grade B" haunted house movies. His eyes peered at me over the rims of his glasses as he took in every word.

"I met this girl, Gloria, on the Internet awhile back and I plan on seeing her when I go to New York. I don't know what the attraction is but I've got to do it."

With a straight poker face he looked at me for a few long seconds. I could never figure out how he was feeling by looking at him. He would be great at bluffing in a card game. I said nervously, "I feel like I'm the bad guy. I don't want to screw anything up, but I've got to follow my gut."

John cleared his throat again. "I'm not any expert on people or situations so I don't know if I should say anything. Seems people have to do what they have to do, right or wrong. What's right for one person might not be right for another. If you got an achin' in your heart to do something, I think you should do it. If it isn't right, then you can always change it. If you take that chance and you lose what you had, then it wasn't meant to be."

"I wanted to let you know I was going, but I didn't know I was going to be leaving early. I should be gone about three weeks. Hope that's okay with you?"

John looked at me with that poker face again. "Ron, you're young and you have a lot of livin' to do. I understand your desire and I can only hope the best for you. If I were in your situation, I would probably do the same thing. I'm set in life. If I never work another day, I would have enough to last me the rest of my life. The only reason I keep this station going is so's I can keep busy. Otherwise, I would shrivel up and die. So, if you want to take off three weeks, or more, go ahead. If you need anything just ask and I'll be more than glad to help."

"Thanks, John, you've done a lot for me already and I really appreciate it. You let me work here and I was able to save some money. You let me live in my van on your lot and I was able to buy the Harley."

"You livin' on the lot didn't cost me anything. 'Sides, you helped my business." John got up, walked to the water cooler and took a couple long gulps of cold water. He then walked to where I was sitting. "When you're ready to go, let me know. Take your time and enjoy yourself, ya hear?"

"I will. And I'll let you know ahead of time just when I'm leaving."

John put away his records, took the cash for the day and locked it up in the safe. "If I don't see you tomorrow, have a good Sunday. I'll see you Monday mornin'."

"I will, and you have a good weekend, too."

I watched him leave and sat staring out the window. It was getting late and I had to get ready to go to the pool hall and meet Jo, Paul and Diane. But first I had to check if Gloria had written. I locked the front door, went to the back room and turned on the computer. I sat watching the screen flick its opening text, too fast for any human to read. I went into the on-line program and stared at the lower right hand corner of the screen for the little white envelope to appear. There it was. She finally wrote. I recognized her e-mail address. I opened up the mail and started to read:

Ron, I'm sorry I took so long to write back. I'm going through some personal problems and it's taking up a lot of my time. I can't talk about it right now. Maybe in the future when I get things sorted out I'll be able to let you know what's going on. Anyway, how are things in Borrego? Not too hot I hope. You must be looking forward to getting your Harley soon. I hope you have a lot of fun with it. I envy you living out in the desert where there's a lot more room and freedom than here in New York. I might be making some major changes in my life in the not too far future. Maybe I'll move to a place like where you are. Wide open spaces and room to breathe. But before I do that, there are a lot of things I have to do here. Let me know how things are going with your motorcycle and what your plans are when you get it. I'm going to have to sign off now. Write back soon and have fun in the sun.

Gloria

I stared at the words on the monitor. I had to write back and tell her I was going to be off-line for at least two weeks, but I couldn't tell her why. I wanted to ride to New York and surprise her. I had to make something up, like maybe I was going to ride up the coast for a week or two and I wouldn't have access to a computer. Yeah, that would work. I wasn't big on lying but sometimes you gotta do what you gotta do. She might wonder why I was taking this ride a couple weeks before I get my bike and not after. If she asked, I'm sure I would think of something to tell her. I fingered the keys on the keyboard, trying to decide how I was going to start this lie:

Hi Gloria, got your message. I was beginning to worry 'cause I hadn't heard from you in a while. I hope things work out for you. I don't know what the problem is, but that's okay. We all have our own little problems to deal with. Well, some not so little. As long as we have our health and our sanity, things usually take care of themselves. So, you plan on getting out of the big city some day. I can certainly understand that. Most people have the desire to break away, do something different. But they can't seem to fully let go of what they have in order to make a clean break. It was hard for me to make that move, but I did. If you really want it to happen I hope you find the courage to do it. I'm going to be traveling up the coast for a few weeks, kind of a mini-vacation. I won't have access to a computer so I won't be writing to you for a while, at least a couple of weeks. I'll make sure I write the day before I leave. In the meantime, let me know how things are going. Looking forward to hearing from you. Have a good day.

Ron

I sent the e-mail and turned the computer off. I leaned back in the chair staring at the blank screen, tapping on the keys. "What was going on with me?" I whispered out loud.

All I knew about her were the bits and pieces she would give me every once and a while. She said she was attractive, had short, light-brown hair and green eyes. She was five-feet-six inches tall, weighed one-hundred-twenty pounds and was thirty-four years old. She belonged to a gym and jogged ten miles four times a week.

All the while we were communicating on-line, I got the feeling something was going on in her life. At times, I wanted to ask her but I figured if she wanted me to know she would tell me. I didn't know if she was married or had a boyfriend. If I even hinted at anything personal she would change the subject or just avoid the question. I still felt connected to her, somehow.

I pushed my chair away from the computer table and got ready to take a shower. I stepped under the stream of water with a very uneasy feeling in my stomach. My mind started racing. I had a good thing going with Billy Jo and I might ruin it by meeting Gloria when I ride to New York. Funny, when I left Chicago I swore I would never get involved with another woman again. Yet, here I was going back and forth. This was really getting crazy and I was starting to feel guilty.

I got out of the shower and dried off. I had to hurry up and get to Jay's. I dressed and headed toward my bike. I was looking forward to taking it to Jay's for the first time.

I locked up the station for the night and turned the bike towards Jay's. It was Saturday night and everybody would be there. I was starting to get excited again. One reason was because of the bike, the other was I thought it was time to explain to Billy Jo about my trip to New York. I didn't know why I was going myself, so I didn't have any idea what I was going to say. I'd just have to play it by ear.

There was a small crowd in front of Jay's as I pulled up. A couple of people looked and pointed. A few walked over and said, "Nice bike." I just nodded. I looked around for Jo's Jeep but didn't see it anywhere. I parked next to Paul's bike and went inside. The place was packed and Paul was sitting alone at our usual table. He looked up as I walked in and half-smiled. I nodded and went over to the table, "Jo's not here yet?"

"No, not yet. She's probably with Diane shopping or something."

I pulled up a chair, turned the back of it toward the table, then sat backwards on it facing Paul. I hung my arms over it and rested my chin on the back of the chair. I stared at Paul for a few seconds and watched him fidget in his chair, "So, tell me how Jo found out about Gloria."

He looked around at the crowd for a moment, and said, "I guess I must have accidentally mentioned it to Diane in the heat of passion or something."

"The heat of passion, huh? That's a good one. Do you happen to remember which particular passion it was?"

"Not really. I didn't mean to tell her. We just got to talking and it slipped out. Does it matter?"

"No, I guess not. She was going to find out anyway, but I wanted to be the one to tell her."

"Sorry, Ron. Hope you're not too pissed?"

"No. I've let some things slip that I was supposed to keep to myself. No big deal. I'm sure I'll probably make that mistake again. I just gotta figure how I'm going to explain this." I stood up. "I'm going to get a beer, you want another one?"

"No, thanks, I'm set. You're not much of a drinker. Why the beer?"

"I'm kinda stressed out and tired. If I drink when I'm riding, one's my limit. Besides, I have a lot of mental stuff going on and I've got a feeling things might get a little warm tonight, if you know what I mean?"

"I think I do."

I stepped up to the bar and, while waiting for the bartender, I realized someone was glaring at me at the other end. It was Jerry Harden, the town bully. He came to town on the weekends, usually to start some kind of trouble. He worked on a dairy farm about fifty miles outside of town. He never came to Jay's alone. He would always bring a couple of farmhand friends with him. By himself, he was nothing.

We almost got into it a few times. I didn't know what his problem was and I wasn't looking for trouble, so I just avoided him as best I as I could. He reminded me of an overgrown kid who never lost his baby fat. His face was round and chubby and he had tiny beady eyes. His hair was short, and he was almost bald. He looked like Curly of the Three Stooges, only six feet tall. He always wore farm coveralls. I don't think he has much going on in his life, so he came to town to harass people. No one here really likes him. A few times, the sheriff had to escort him out of town.

I got my beer and walked back to my table, avoiding Jerry's gaze. Paul looked at me. "Seems you got farm boy's attention."

"Well, he's not my problem right now. I've got other things on my mind and he's not one of 'em."

"He's been on your back ever since you moved here. You know you might have to take him on someday. I watched you work out at the gym. You're fast and you've got a real nasty punch. I wouldn't want to be on the receiving end of your right hand." Paul paused, then added, "I know you can kick his ass. Why don't you go over there and punch his lights out once and for all and get it over with? No one in this town would blame you. He's not going to let up."

"He probably won't. But not right now."

The jukebox was turned up real loud and my head was pounding. I sat there watching people playing pool and dancing off to the side. There was a lot of motion and energy in the room. It seemed like it was swallowing me up.

I caught Paul staring at me. "What's buggin' you, Ron?"

"This is starting to drive me nuts. What am I going to do?"

"You mean about New York and that girl on the Internet?"

"Yeah. I'm getting older and if I don't make this trip now I might not get another chance to do it. I didn't plan on a girl being on the other end. But that's the way it is. I can't change that. There's just something I gotta find out and I don't quite know what that is."

"Hey, why don't you ask Jo if she wants to go with you?"

"I thought about that, but I don't think it would work out very well. I have to do this solo. I think I've got some things to work out in my mind, and besides, I don't think Jo would be too interested in meeting Gloria. I need time by myself."

I took a swig of beer and let my eyes wander around the room. The bully was still trying to stare me down. He was starting to irritate me but I wasn't going to provoke him, so I looked in the other direction. I figured that if I ignored him he might go away.

Billy Jo and Diane walked in and came over to where we were sitting. Jo was wearing jeans and a red, well-pressed, tight flannel shirt. She looked hot as usual. Diane walked up to Paul and kissed him. "How you doing, honey?"

"Fine," Paul responded, "how was your day?"

"Pretty good," Diane said, "we did a little shopping and took a ride out to Jo's ranch for a while."

Diane looked at me and winked. "There's a hot new motorcycle parked outside."

I returned her glance and smiled weakly. Jo remained silent and gazed around the room, uninterested.

Diane then remarked, "So, you guys were already out playing today, huh? Heard you and Ron took a ride up to Willow Road. You didn't do anything stupid, did you?"

Paul's eyes darted over to me and I kind of peeked back at him. He looked back at Diane. "No, we wouldn't do anything stupid, would we, Ron?"

"Nope, not us. We're just two straight and narrow guys."

"Yeah, right. I can really believe that."

Jo pulled up a chair and sat down next to me, leaned over and gave me a small kiss on the cheek. "And how was your day, Ron?" she asked, winking at me.

"Well, this afternoon was kind of exciting. I sorta got lost in the bushes."

"You did, huh?"

"Yep. Got an opportunity to really get into nature."

She grinned back at me. "Glad you could appreciate the fine qualities of our great state."

I smiled and winked back at her, "You want a drink? How 'bout you, Diane?"

They both wanted a beer. I got up and walked to the bar. The bully was watching me even more hawk-eyed and his two friends were stuck close to him. I picked up the beers and made my way back to the table.

Diane looked at Jo, then at me. "I hear you plan on riding cross country. Heard you always wanted to do that on a Harley."

"Yes, it's been one of my dreams. I just want to experience how it would feel to wander from coast to coast without any plans. To experience the freedom."

"I envy you, Ron," Paul said. "I'd like to go with you, but I know I'd get fired for sure."

"That would be great if you could go," I replied, trying not to rub it in. Jo was unusually quiet. I didn't think she was too happy with this particular conversation. I figured I'd better change it. "So Jo, how's things going on the ranch?"

"Same old stuff. Not much that can get different on a horse ranch." She shifted around in her chair. I could tell she wanted to talk about my plans to ride cross-country. But she didn't want to pry. We all sat there for a few seconds without speaking.

Then Paul asked, "How'd you get the name Roadside, anyway?"

"It started out as a joke. When I was getting ready to leave Chicago, I was talking to a couple of friends about what I was going to do and how I was going to support myself. I didn't have any real plans and I didn't know anyone. I decided that if worse came to worst, I would park alongside the road, fix cars or rebuild carbs to feed myself. I would live in my van and roam the countryside, working only when I needed to. I wanted to be totally irresponsible for the first time in my life. Hence, the name 'Roadside Ron.'"

"That's interesting," said Jo, "a bum living in a van. Seems like you're not too far from that right now."

I looked at her surprised, "That's a cheap shot, Jo."

"Sorry, you're right. I'm just a little on edge right now. Don't pay any attention to me."

Paul jumped in. "So, you just wanted to roam the country and be irresponsible?"

"That was the idea. I had no plans to stop at any particular place. I could have never guessed I'd be sitting here with a Harley outside."

"Are you sorry it happened the way it did?" Jo asked.

"I have no regrets. I'm glad about the way my life is unfolding. There are some things I wasn't expecting."

"Like what?"

"Jo, could we talk about this later?"

"Sorry, let's drop it."

"How about shooting a game of doubles pool?" Diane asked.

"Sounds good to me," I said. Everyone agreed and Paul went to get the pool table.

The first couple of games I played partner with Jo. Then we switched and I played partner with Diane. Jo was sitting on a stool next to the pool table. I walked over to her and put my arm around her. She leaned her head on my chest and softly sighed. The longer I knew her the better she felt.

Paul ribbed me. "Come on, lover boy, it's your shot.

I made my ball, looked over at Jo and could see the stress on her face. I missed the next shot and by now I really didn't care who won or lost. The cook waved to us that our pizza was ready, so we picked it up and sat down at our table.

I looked at Paul. "So, what's on for tomorrow?"

"How 'bout going for a ride?"

"Sounds like a plan to me. What about it, Jo?"

"It's Sunday and I don't have any plans."

I looked at Diane. "That okay with you?"

She looked at Paul. "Well, Paul, aren't you going to ask me?"

"Of course, you're going, right?"

"Now that you asked, yes, I'd like that very much."

We were eating our pizza and I noticed that Curly of the Three Stooges fame and his two friends had moved to the middle of the bar, a lot closer to where we were sitting. He was glaring in my direction again.

"What is that guy's problem?" I asked.

Jo looked over at the bar. "You mean Jerry the dork?"

"Yeah, he's been staring at me all night!" Jo glanced at Diane. They both looked at me like they knew something was up. "Alright. What's going on?" I asked.

Jo looked away and took a bite of her pizza. "I think you should tell him, Jo," Diane said.

"Tell me what?"

I looked back at Jo and she said to Diane. "Thanks a lot, now I have to tell him."

She set her pizza back down on her plate, "Not many people know this and I'm not too crazy about more people finding out. Jerry's had a major crush on me for as long as I can remember. I can't stand to even look at him and I wish there were some way I could get him to snap out of it. God knows I've tried. But anything I do seems to make him like me more, so I just ignore him. I don't think he can stand the thought of me being with you."

"Great, now it all makes sense. Why would it have to be him, the town nut? I don't think he's working with a full deck and that makes him dangerous."

"Sorry, I should've told you sooner. But just saying it gives me an upset stomach."

I peeked over at the bar and sure enough he was staring, and now I knew why it was directed at me. "Any other skeletons I should know about?"

"It's not my fault. I've tried to shake him."

"You're right. If I were him I'd want to be in my place, too."

Jo looked at me sort of funny. "That's supposed to be a compliment, right?"

I smiled, "You bet. A lot of guys would love to be in my shoes." Jo smiled back, reached out and softly put her hand on my forearm.

We finished our pizza and sat listening to music for awhile. Jo and Diane got into a conversation about girl stuff and Paul and I shot a couple more games of pool. We went back to the table and I asked the girls, "Are you ready to go?" They nodded yes as they stood up.

On Saturday nights, we sometimes rode into the desert and slept overnight in sleeping bags. Paul and Diane had their special spot and Jo and I had ours, a little ways from them.

"We have to use the ladies' room," Jo said as she and Diane headed in that direction.

"Yeah, we better go too, before we leave," I said.

We finished and Paul walked out the restroom door ahead of me. Jo and Diane hadn't come out yet. I was following Paul towards the front door and had to walk past Jerry. Paul passed him and as I walked by he stuck his foot out. I stumbled and caught myself a few steps up. I stopped and turned around and he had already stood up. He took a couple of steps toward me and I could tell he was about to swing. I was prepared for it as his fist came around and I backed out of the way. His big, fat arm missed me by quite a bit. Paul turned around and saw what was going on. Jerry seemed kind of stunned that he didn't connect. I put my arms halfway up anticipating another swing. His two friends were standing behind him not doing much of anything. Paul placed himself in position in case Jerry's buddies decided to jump in. The place got deadly quiet and all eyes were upon us. I stood my ground waiting for his next move.

"What's the matter, biker boy, having trouble walking?" Jerry asked.

I just stood there with my eyes locked onto his beady little eyeballs.

"Nail him, Ron," Paul snapped. "I'll back you. Don't worry about those other two guys. There's enough people in here that won't let those two jump you."

I stared into his face and part of me wanted to rip into him and part of me felt sorry for him. "What the hell's your problem?" I yelled, all the while knowing what it was.

"All you biker punks think you're bad asses. Just cause you ride bikes you think no one can touch you. Well, you ain't so bad," Jerry taunted.

"Whatever you say, big guy." I was tempted to nail him right in the nose. I don't think he would even know what hit him.

"Smack him, Ron," Paul said again.

"Yeah, come on biker punk, smack me."

Just then Jo and Diane came out of the restroom. Jo saw Jerry and me facing off and she hurried over. "What's going on?"

I kept my eyes riveted on this bald-headed jerk in front of me. "Seems this guy's foot got in my way."

"He doesn't know how to walk, my foot was not in his way."

"Come on, Ron, it's not worth fighting over," Jo said.

"You go with Billy Jo like a good little boy," Jerry said, making a face.

"Don't listen to him, Ron. Let's just leave," she said quickly.

I had to make a decision, swing or leave. The whole place was waiting to see what I was going to do. I don't think he was too crazy about fighting after I easily ducked away from the punch he threw. But he was too stupid to back out now. "I'm not looking for any trouble tonight," I said, choking on every word.

"That figures, all you biker punks are the same, cowards."

"Ron, don't listen to him, he's had too much to drink. And besides, we're supposed to go for a ride, remember?"

I didn't want to ruin the evening any more than it was, so against my better judgment I let my hands fall to my side. "Some other time big boy. I gotta go."

"You bet, there'll be another time." He turned around and sat back down.

"You should've whacked him good, Ron," Paul said as he mockingly swung his fist in the air.

"Paul, be quiet. Just let it die," Jo snapped.

"Yes, Paul. Don't push it any more," Diane said, as she grabbed Paul's arm and guided him towards the front door.

I felt like a fool not punching his face in. I knew what I did was right, but it was still hard to swallow. Everyone in the place probably thought I was a coward.

As we reached the door Jerry yelled out, "Next time, biker bum."

I stopped at the door for an instant, but Jo grabbed my arm and led me the rest of the way out. "Don't pay any attention to him. He doesn't know what he's saying."

"He does know what he's saying. And I'm probably going to have to take care of this 'cause he's not going to quit."

"Well, don't worry about it right now."

We walked to where the bikes were parked. "Do you have the blankets and sleeping bag, Jo?" I asked.

"They're in my Jeep, I'll get them."

"I'll get ours out of my car, Paul," Diane said.

While the girls were away, Paul looked at me. "Why didn't you whack him, Ron? He swung at you first. You had every right to take him out. He couldn't hit you if you stood still and closed your eyes for him."

"I know. I just didn't have the stomach to punch him. Besides, I sort of felt sorry for him."

"Ron, he's a big jerk. He's done a lot of bad things to people. He deserves everything he gets."

"Maybe so, but I'm not the one to deal out justice."

"It's not like you were doing it out of the blue. He started it, remember?"

"It doesn't matter, I don't feel like fighting tonight. I've got other things on my mind."

"Okay, but if he gets in your way again, punch his lights out."

"We'll see."

The girls came back with the blankets and sleeping bags. Paul and I rolled up our bags and tied them onto the back of our sissy bars and started up the bikes. We sat there for a few minutes letting them warm up.

Paul leaned over towards me. "Any particular direction?"

"Just head into the desert and let's ride for awhile before we stop for the night."

"That's all right by me," he smiled.

The girls got on and we slowly rolled out of town into the warm desert night air. Paul took the lead and I fell in behind him. The moon was three-quarters full and lit up the sky in an eerie grayish light. The moonlight also made the desert ground look like the lunar surface. It was as though we had crossed some time line and were in a different world, a world all our own. Paul and I both settled back and let the gentle, curving roads guide our bikes. The rumble of the pipes seemed to be tuned to each other and it put me into a trance. I could feel Jo cuddle close to me and I could tell she enjoyed being out here. We were riding in the direction of the Salton Sea, the biggest inland body of water in California. Bob Segers' "Against the Wind" played loud and clear in my head.

It was a thirty-minute ride to the Salton Sea. When we arrived, Paul pulled over towards the shore and I followed. We got off the bikes and found a place to sit by the shoreline. The moon was high over the water, and after we sat in a circle I said, "I feel like a real wimp. I should've hit him."

"You did the right thing, Ron," Jo said as she put her head on my shoulder.

"Naw, I think you should've kicked the shit out of him," Paul snapped.

Diane elbowed Paul. "No, he shouldn't have. If he did fight him, we would still be there and so would the sheriff. He would have ruined our whole night, and that's just what he wanted to do. So, Ron, you did do the right thing."

"Maybe so, but I still think I would've got some satisfaction from decking him," I replied.

Jo looked at all three of us. "I can't believe we're sitting around still talking about that Bozo. If we keep this up, this talk will ruin our night."

"Jo's right, forget about him," Diane said, "He ain't worth it."

Jo put her hand on my thigh. "Yes, we got better things to do with our time."

I looked into her eyes. "Yep, I can think of a few."

"Beautiful night, isn't it?" Diane said. We all agreed. I leaned back on the sand and Jo laid her head on my stomach. Paul and Diane got up and went for a walk on the beach. "When do you think you'll be leaving on your trip?" Jo asked.

"I'm not sure, a couple of weeks, maybe."

"Are you coming back?"

"What kind of a question is that? Of course, I'll come back, everything I own is here."

She fell silent and we watched the reflection of the moon on the water. It was smooth as glass and a perfect picture of the heavens. I knew we would have to talk about my leaving and I didn't know what to say. I was mixed up about my feelings and my future. Was now the time or should I wait? My mind started racing again. If only people didn't get connected like they do, life would be a lot simpler. But that was a simple solution to a complicated problem. I didn't want to cause anyone any pain, especially Jo.

"Ron? How do you feel about me?"

I looked at her amazed she would ask that. "You're a wonderful person, Jo and I think a lot of you. You should know that."

"Just thought I'd ask."

"We've been together almost a year. You should know that by now."

"Never mind, it was a stupid question."

She started to rub the inside of my thigh and I felt my pulse quicken. She ran her fingers up to my stomach and across my chest. I had my arm around her shoulder and reached down and touched her breast. I felt her respond. She looked up and put her lips on mine, moist and warm. I was getting aroused and I whispered, "Paul and Diane are right there. We better not start anything now."

"Ron, you're such a midwestern prude," she whispered back into my ear.

"We really should wait till we get to the spot where we usually sleep. It's more private there."

She sat up and faced me. "Oh, loosen up. You're not in Kansas any more, Toto."

"Very funny. You know I'm kind of shy. Give me some time."

She got that pouty look on her face, "Okay, we'll work on it."

Paul and Diane came walking back and sat down next to us. "You guys ready to head out?" Paul asked.

"Yes, Ron's kind of edgy. We wouldn't want to embarrass him."

"Come on, Jo, they don't have to know our personal stuff, do they?"

They both laughed and walked to where the bikes were. "Sounds like it's time to go," Paul said over his shoulder.

"This is not my night," I said, as I got up and brushed off the sand.

Jo pinched my ass as she got up behind me. She grabbed my hips with both her hands and guided me towards my bike. I turned around and she raised her hands over my head and let them fall on my shoulders. "Take a joke, big bad biker dude, take a joke." She kissed me, then we got on the bikes and started them up. They sounded especially loud by the quiet shore. We rolled back onto the road and headed to where we would spend the night.

The place we slept was just outside of Borrego Springs. It was off the road and secluded. From the road, we couldn't be seen.

It took about twenty minutes to get to our special place. I pulled off the road and Paul rode a couple hundred more feet away and pulled off. We stayed far enough away from each other for privacy, but not so far that we couldn't hear each other holler. Being out here could be dangerous. The only protection we had was what we could provide ourselves. I usually brought my .357 magnum with me, but I forgot it in all the excitement of the day. Sometimes, drug runners came through the desert or illegal aliens trying to get jobs. Most of the time, they weren't out to hurt anybody, but occasionally, a criminal would come through. A couple of times, a group of people had come by and looked us over. We just stared them down and they moved on. I didn't know if Paul brought his gun, but it didn't matter now.

This spot was good because it wasn't far from a nature trail and the trail had an outhouse on it. All the conveniences of home except a shower. In the spring, a creek flowed along the trail, especially when it rained in the mountains.

Jo got off the bike, "I'm going to the outhouse, I'll be right back." She hollered to Diane, "Hey, Diane, come with me."

Diane yelled back, "I'll meet you there."

I took the sleeping gear and blankets off the bike and spread them out on the ground. Paul hollered, "Sleep tight and try to keep the noise down."

"Right, Paul, you're the one who makes all the noise. Try not to wake up too many animals."

I had everything out by the time Jo got back.

"Do you have to use the bathroom, Ron?"

"No, maybe later."

I was lying on my back looking up at the stars as Jo lay next to me. I was awestruck every time I came here at night and gazed up to the heavens. "Look at all those stars. There must be billions and billions of them," I said. "There must be life out there somewhere. It's stupid to think that out of all that space we're the only ones here."

Jo looked up. "I think there must be something out there, too. It's just too big to think otherwise." She propped up on one elbow and started to unbutton my shirt. "Are you sure it's all right to do this now?"

"You're making fun of me, Jo."

"You deserve it. You're too conservative."

"Well, I'm sure you'll help me get over it."

"Maybe I will," she whispered. "I want you to just lie there and relax. Don't think about anything. Just surrender to me, Ron."

Jo leaned over and put her lips on mine. Her tongue darted into my mouth and I slid mine into hers. Her mouth was wet and she was breathing heavily. She sat up, unbuttoned my pants, then unzipped them. She took off my boots and socks. She slid my pants down my legs exposing my half-hard penis. She ran her fingertips across my stomach, down my thighs, then back up the inside of my legs, stopping just short of my hardness. Her hand felt cool against my warm skin. She took hold of me again and slowly stroked. I started to rub her back and she took my hands and placed them over my head.

"I don't want you to do anything, just completely relax."

I kept my hands over my head. She sat up and positioned herself over me. Her hair fell onto my chest and she slowly drew it up and down the length of my body. It was silky soft.

"Do you like that?"

"Yes, very much."

"Good, I want to do the things you like."

She knelt down between my legs and took me in her hand, letting her hair fall onto my stomach. She started to stroke again, at the same time rotating her head in a circle so her hair would caress me. I was losing any control I had. She touched me with the tip of her tongue while she stroked me. Then she put her lips on me and started to move up and down its length. I moaned and had trouble keeping my hands over my head.

"Does that feel good?" she asked.

"Yes, very."

"What would you like me to do? Would you like me to continue to suck you?"

"Yeah . . ."

"Mmmm, you smell like sex," she said, as she slid her tongue around the tip of my penis.

Breathing hard now, I looked up at the dark sky and the bright stars seemed brighter, then I closed my eyes. She had me in her hands and put her lips back on me, her mouth wet and warm. She started to move her head faster. I stiffened up and she moved even faster. It was only a matter of seconds now. I opened my eyes again and stared at the sky. I think Jo knew I was about to let go. I threw my head back and stiffened up even more. I was right there, then closed my eyes and let go. My stomach muscles tightened and I came in several erratic spurts. I forced myself to open my eyes again and looked up at the sky as I finished. It was awesome.

"Mmmm," she cooed. Jo slowed down and softly stroked me as I relaxed. The desert air blew across my wet body and gave me a chill. "Did that feel good?" she asked.

"Oh, God, it was better than good. There's no words to describe it," I said with deep breaths. She stretched out beside me and laid her head on my chest, gently caressing me.

I lay there with my eyes closed and ran my hand through her hair not wanting to move a muscle. I started to say something and she put her fingertips across my lips and said, "Shhhh . . . don't speak, just lie still."

We didn't move for at least fifteen minutes and I almost dozed off. I opened my eyes and ran my hand along her arm. I started to roll over and she tried to keep me in that position. But I rolled on my side and gently pushed her onto her back. I unbuttoned her shirt and took it off. Then I took her boots off and licked the bottom of her bare feet.

She jerked her foot away. "Oh, don't, that tickles."

I felt for the button at the top of her pants and lightly brushed my finger across her bare stomach as I unbuttoned it. I undid the rest of the buttons on her fly and when I finished with the last one, I pushed my hand against her pelvis and she parted her legs slightly. I then pulled her jeans down her legs and over her feet. I unhooked her bra and put my lips on her stiff nipple. At the same time, I put my hand inside her thighs and moved it up and down. I sat up and looked at her body in the moonlight, then slid her panties off and looked at her naked body again. She had tan lines that made her look like she was still wearing a bikini, only I could see all of her womanhood. The narrow white band around her hips seemed to point between her legs. I bent down and placed my tongue on her belly button. I moved it past her groin and down her long, tanned leg. I felt her shiver as I moved it back between her legs. I brought my tongue up above her opening and stopped.

"Would you like me to lick you?" I said, holding my mouth right next to her while breathing on it.

"Okay," she said, in a faint, squeaky voice.

I put my tongue back on her and moved it around in circles. She was smooth and silky. I spread the lips of her vagina with my fingers, found her hard spot and took it between my lips. She was dripping wet. I breathed in her womanly scent as she groaned and arched her hips. I put the tip of my tongue on her clit and slowly moved it up and down at the same time sucking on it. She started to move her hips against my lips. I slipped my hands under her, cupped the cheeks of her butt and pushed a little harder with my tongue.

I stopped and looked up. "The moment it happens, I want you to force yourself to open your eyes and look up at the sky."

"Don't stop!" she stammered.

I put my lips back on her and moved my tongue back and forth. She opened her legs as far as she could and moved her hips faster against my lips. She started to moan louder. I could feel her start to shiver uncontrollably. It was about to happen so I sucked a little harder and moved my tongue faster. I reached up and grabbed her breasts. She put her hands on top of mine and squeezed hard. She was moving her hips faster against my lips and I could feel her jerk as she screamed softly and pushed her pelvis against me. I put my finger in her and moved it in and out. She stiffened up and clutched the back of my head with her hands. She held still at that position for a moment and I could feel it happening. She stopped moving her hips and began to pulse. She jerked a few times, then slowly relaxed. I sat up and put my lips on her nipple.

She shivered. "Oh, I'm super sensitive right now. If you even touch me, it'll drive me nuts."

"Good. How nuts do you want to be driven?"

"Just let me lie here for a moment. That was so intense. I can't believe how good it felt." She reached over and ran her fingers through my hair. I lay next to her, put my hand on her breast and we both stared up at the sky.

"Did you open your eyes when it happened?"

"I don't remember. How do you expect me to remember? I lost all control."

We laid next to each other, spread-eagle naked under the huge night sky. "Do you realize how small and insignificant we are compared to the big picture?" I asked.

She didn't say anything for a minute, then looked at me. "You're not sure when you're leaving on this trip?"

"No. I've got some stuff to do to my bike before I go. I have to change the shocks and handlebars and I have to put bigger tanks on it. I have to get the tanks painted before I put them on too. It'll be at least a couple of weeks."

She stared into my eyes not speaking. Hers sparkled in the moonlight. "A couple weeks, huh?"

"I want to make sure I'm as comfortable as can be and not have any mechanical problems on the road. It's a long ride."

"It certainly is," she said, a little moody.

Jo sat up on her knees facing me and started rubbing my shoulders. She lifted her leg over my body and sat on my lap. I could feel the warmth and moisture of her womanhood on me. She leaned down and put her lips on mine. I ran my tongue around hers and she responded.

"You're making me hot," she said as she slid her hands down the side of my body.

"I don't know if I can. We already did it twice today and I didn't get much sleep last night."

"Oh, Ron, you can do it. Just lie here and let me take you there one more time."

"I think I'm gonna die of pleasure. But what a way to go."

She moved her hips against me and I started to rise. I reached up and took her head in my hands and pulled her to me. I guided her lips to mine and searched for her tongue. She lifted her hips slightly and took me in her hand. I was almost fully erect and she guided me into her. She was thoroughly wet. I took her hips in my hands and moved them slowly up and down and at the same time she moved back and forth.

"You feel so good," she whispered into my ear.

Her hips began to make longer up and down motions. I was completely hard now.

"I love to feel you deep inside me."

She sat all the way down on me and moved her hips in a circular motion. I put my hands on her waist and even though we were in the dry desert air, she had a light coat of perspiration on her body. I could smell the freshness of her perfumed hair. It blended well with the desert smell of eucalyptus. Her breath was hot and heavy on my face and her hip movement got more erratic as she came closer to orgasm, forcing herself down hard on me.

"Oh, God," she said, as she threw her head back and grabbed my shoulders. She sat straight up and dug her fingernails into my chest and pushed down even harder with her hips. Her whole body stiffened up and she shuddered as she let out a low moan. Then she bent over and put her lips on mine and I felt her inner muscles vibrate, then rapidly contract. Her body relaxed and she sat on top of me, not moving.

I started to push up and down again. Jo sat upright and started to rotate against me. She was extremely hot and slippery. She reached back between my legs, took my balls in her hand and caressed them. I grabbed her hips and pushed harder against her. I could feel tiny beads of sweat begin to form on my forehead. I looked at her in the soft moonlight, her breasts dancing up and down with every push.

She looked at me with half-closed eyes. "I want you to finish. I want to feel you cum inside me. I want all of you."

We were both moving fast against each other. My penis was hard and throbbing. I was getting close and I knew she could tell. She still had her hand between my legs and touched me just right. I grabbed her breasts, made one final push and lost control. My body jerked back and forth and she pushed down hard on my groin. I felt the blood throb in my temples. I flexed several times, then ejaculated into her. My whole body went limp and I was completely drained. I couldn't move if my life depended on it. I was utterly useless.

"I knew you could do it. I love when you cum inside me."

"Yes, but I think I died somewhere along the way," I said, not able to speak another word.

"Not bad action for a dead man." She bent down and put her lips against mine. They were warm, soft and gentle. I took a deep breath and inhaled her scent. For that moment I felt completely at ease and at peace. It scared me.

She straightened out her legs, laid on top of me and buried her head in my chest. I slowly ran my fingertips up and down her body. I could feel her heart beat and her slow, deep breathing. She was relaxed but there was an uneasiness about it.

"Ron?"

"Huh?"

"I think I'm falling in love with you." She lifted her head and looked into my eyes, waiting for a response. I stared back into her deep blue eyes and honestly didn't know what I was feeling. I was so mixed up in my head. She kept staring.

"Jo, I'm not sure how I feel. I don't want to speak words unless I'm sure. It wouldn't be fair to you. I'm still going through a lot of changes, emotional changes."

"Doesn't all the time we've been together mean anything to you?"

"Of course it does. I wouldn't be with you if it didn't mean anything to me."

"You're going on this cross-country trip. You're going to meet some girl in New York. A girl you know nothing about. I don't get it."

"Jo, I don't know either. I'm only going to meet her. It's not like I'm going to run off with her. I don't even know her. Is that what you're worried about?"

"How would you feel if I said I was going off to meet some guy?"

"You meet a lot of people on any given day. It doesn't mean you're going to run off with them. You also have friends that you've known for a long time. So what? You have old boyfriends who live around here that you see all the time. Does that mean I should worry about you running off with them?"

"That's not the same."

"Oh yes, it is. I've had this dream as long as I can remember. If I don't do this, I'll always feel cheated. I've been talking with Gloria for awhile now and I'd like to meet her. New York City is as good a destination as any and I feel like I've got a friend there."

"And in the meantime, I just sit here and wait?"

"You're not a possession and neither am I. I don't expect you to do anything you don't want to do, and I'm not going to ask you to. I've still got some questions to answer and some unresolved issues to deal with." I searched deep into her eyes, looking for some sign of understanding as I continued. "This trip will give me the time and the opportunity to do that. Maybe I'm not emotionally free yet like I'd like to be."

"What do you mean, 'not emotionally free'?"

"I've been gone from Chicago two years. I've heard that it takes two to five years to completely get over a relationship. I don't know if that's true, but I feel like I've got some things to work out in my head and my heart. That's not your fault or your problem, it's mine and I'll have to deal with it."

"Can't I help you somehow?"

"I wish you could, but I'm on my own with this one."

"Oh, Ron, I feel so confused and worried."

"I didn't want to say this, but I guess I have to. I don't think you realize it but you're not emotionally free yourself."

"What do you mean?"

"Let's say I'm not going to meet Gloria, I'm just going to ride cross-country and I want you to go with me. I'm asking if you want to go with me."

She sat there looking at me, not answering.

"Well, I'm asking you to go with me. Will you?"

"I can't leave the ranch. I've got too much work to do to just leave for a few weeks."

"I knew you'd say that. That's why I didn't ask you to go. In the past ten years, how many vacations have you taken?"

"Hmm. Now that I think about it, none."

"Why is that?"

"Because my dad needs my help on the ranch."

"Your dad has plenty of hired hands to help him. If you left for a month, he would do just fine without you being there. You're emotionally tied up with your dad and his ranch. I'm not saying that's bad, it's just the way it is."

She looked away from me and stared off into space. I wasn't sure if I should continue, but I did. "Your dad needed your help and your emotional support after your mother was gone. You needed each other in that time of distress. That's understandable. Don't get me wrong, I'm not asking you to change it, just be aware of it. We both have some things to work out."

She looked at me like I just dropped a lead weight on her. The last thing I wanted to do was hurt her. She rolled over and stared up at the stars. "My dad's been my whole life for the past ten years. I don't know what I'd do without him."

"Maybe I shouldn't have said that. Maybe it's none of my business."

"No. That's all right, Ron. I just never thought about it. I guess I didn't have any reason to think about it until now."

"Before I can make any kind of commitment to anyone I have to straighten some things out. I have to make this ride. I don't know how it will come out or how I will feel, I just know I have to do it. I hope you understand that?"

"I understand. I don't like it, but I understand."

"You have to do what you have to do. If you don't feel you have to do anything, that's not a problem. Only you know what's best for you. I didn't expect to meet anyone this quick. Everything's happening so fast that it's making me dizzy. It's as though I'm being swept up and I can't stop it."

"Ron, you make too much damn sense. Why can't you just be like everyone else and stop thinking about things so much?"

"I can't help it. It's the way I was born."

We heard a coyote howl in the distance, probably up in the mountains. We both fell silent and held hands. She cuddled next to me and put her head on my chest. I put my arm around her and held her close. I could feel her pulse against my side. I buried my face in her hair and lost myself in her scent.

Paul and Diane had probably fallen asleep by now. I looked up at the stars, and the moon was setting. It would be dawn soon. This was the second night in a row I wouldn't get much sleep. Even if I hadn't ridden to Yuma or not made the trip out here with Jo, I probably wouldn't have gotten much sleep anyway. Getting the Harley was just too much excitement. I looked over at my bike and the moonlight made the chrome look like it had a blackish tint to it. The red and black paint glistened in the pale light. Everything seemed perfect at this moment. I figured that I should get a couple of hours of sleep because I knew that Paul, Diane and Jo would want to go riding again tomorrow. We always did on Sunday.

I pulled the sleeping bag over us. She turned over and I snuggled up next to her, like spoons. She pulled my arm around her drawing me close to her naked body, then she placed my hand against her breast and sighed softly. Her breathing became slow and regular and I could tell she had fallen asleep. It wasn't long after that I closed my eyes and drifted off.

Chapter Four

I heard Diane's voice, "Hey guys, wake up, wake up."

I thought I was dreaming. I opened my eyes, it was morning and Diane was standing over us. I squinted trying to blot out the intense rays of the new sun. I groaned as I rolled over and covered my head with the sleeping bag, "What time is it?"

"It's seven-thirty. Time to hit the road and have breakfast at Connie's. Come on sleepyheads, get up."

Jo stirred under the bag, "Go back to bed. It's too early."

She sat down next to us, "It's gonna get hot real soon and you guys are gonna fry under there. Paul and me have been up almost a half-hour now. What'sa matter, didn't get enough sleep last night? Too much nooky?"

Jo peeked out over the edge of the sleeping bag. "You're going to bug us until we get up, aren't you?"

"It's a beautiful morning. Look at that gorgeous motorcycle over there. It's just begging to be ridden. Come on, if we ain't crusin', we're losin'."

I looked over at my bike. I couldn't argue with her there.

Jo poked her head out, "Take a walk so we can get dressed."

"Aw, come on, let me watch you two naked people dress."

"Diane . . .!"

"Okay, okay, I'll leave. Killjoy." She got up and walked toward the nature trail.

Jo scooted up next to me, "I could stay here forever," she cooed into my ear. Her skin felt cool and smooth against my body.

"Sounds good to me but I don't think Diane and Paul would let us."

She turned over, faced me and wrapped her arms around my shoulders, "Good morning, sweetie."

"Morning, honey," I said placing my lips on hers.

"We better get up or we'll have the biker friends from hell on our backs again," Jo snorted.

We started to put our clothes on under the sleeping bag. This wasn't easy especially since we kept playing with each other. After we finally got dressed Jo went to the outhouse and Paul rode his bike over to where I was. His bag and blankets were packed up and ready to go.

"It's about time you guys woke up. We let you sleep an extra half-hour."

"That was mighty nice of you, Paul."

"I know. We figured you love birds were busy late into the night."

I rolled up our stuff and tied it to the back of the bike as Jo and Diane came walking back from the trail. "You have to go, Ron?" Jo asked, as she walked up to me.

"Yeah, I better before we leave."

I walked along the trail to the outhouse. It was close to eight o'clock and it was getting warm already. I finished and went by the creek to see if any water was flowing. It was completely dry. It hadn't rained in the mountains for awhile. I stood on a small mound and looked around at the scenery, quite different from the concrete and asphalt of a big city. The warm, dry air blew across my face and there wasn't a cloud in the sky. A person couldn't really get the full flavor of this country till he'd been out west awhile. I tried to imagine what it would have been like to be an American Indian here a couple of centuries ago. It probably looked and felt exactly the same. I gazed out over the landscape for a few moments, then walked back to where the others were waiting.

"You ready for breakfast? I'm starved," Jo said, as she rubbed her stomach.

"I'm ready," I nodded, "let's go."

Paul kicked his bike over a few times, then turned on the ignition and kicked it one more time. It sputtered and died. He turned off the ignition and kicked it a few more times. Then turned it back on and kicked it again. It came to life with a roar. I turned my key on, twisted my throttle a couple of times and hit the start button. The electric starter cranked the engine over and it sprang to life. Paul looked over at me, "Must be nice to have a kick start button."

I smiled, "You bet it is."

Diane got on Paul's bike and Jo got on with me. I looked at

Paul and he nodded. I nodded back and rolled onto the road first. Paul followed and we both kicked up a big, gray cloud of desert dust as we roared down the road.

Connie's Cafe was about ten minutes away. It was early Sunday morning and we were the only ones out. I opened my throttle and Paul stuck close right behind.

Jo leaned back on the sissy bar, held her arms straight out in the wind, "Ain't this great? Don't you just love it?"

I nodded, reached back and patted her on the thigh.

We were almost at Barrett Junction. Connie's cafe was right on the corner. It was in the middle of nowhere but was situated where two major state roads crossed. Her customers were travelers and locals from small towns nearby. Every time we slept in the desert, we came here for breakfast. It was beginning to be a regular thing and Connie knew us on a first-name basis.

Paul and I drove onto the dirt driveway in front of the cafe. I stopped and set my bike on the kickstand, as did Paul. The aroma of fried potatoes, bacon and eggs cooked in butter filled the air. It was so thick I could taste it.

The cafe was in an old building, probably built around the turn of the century. The dry desert air preserved it well. It served as a grocery store with a four-table restaurant in one corner.

I got off the bike and took our toothbrushes out of my saddlebags. We used the restroom to wash up and brush our teeth. Connie wasn't busy this time of the morning and she didn't mind the company.

We all walked in and Connie was in the kitchen preparing food. She came out front, "Good morning, guys and gals," she said, with a big smile.

We said hi and sat down in the back. The old wooden tables and chairs were covered with plastic coated tablecloths and had large, red and white checker patterns on them. The wooden floor creaked when you walked across it. The walls were barren except for a couple of old pictures of sailboats. I thought that was odd considering we were in the desert. The radio was tuned to a country western station and was playing a heartbreaking song. The grocery section was not overly stocked. It had the basic necessities and the fast food snacks tourists and travelers would likely buy. The menu was short and handwritten, but the food was homemade and very good. She cooked everything herself.

Connie came over to our table, "You ready to order or do you want some time to freshen up?" she asked in her soft-spoken voice.

"Give us a few minutes," I said.

"Just holler when you're ready."

I watched as she walked back to the kitchen. She was about sixty, I would guess, and a little overweight. She always wore a plaid dress and an apron and her hair was gray and short. I don't know if she had any children but she would make a perfect mother. Everytime we came here she always made sure we had enough to eat. Most people I've met since I've been here have made me feel welcome. It must be the nature of the west. I looked at everyone, "Well, who's going to the bathroom first?"

"I will," Jo said. She took the toothpaste and toothbrush and headed towards the bathroom. One by one we made our trek to freshen up.

I was the last one to wash up. I stood looking in the mirror after brushing my teeth. My eyes were a little bloodshot and I had a couple of bags under them. I thought, *a little cold water on my face and a couple gallons of coffee and I'll be set.* I walked back out to the table and sat down.

"I can't wait one more minute to order," Diane said as she looked as though she was about to eat the paper menu.

I knew how she felt. No normal human being could sit here for any length of time taking in the smells of the kitchen and not be overwhelmed.

Connie soon came and took our orders. As we waited, Diane looked at Jo and me, "What time did you two finally get to sleep?"

"Oh, I don't know. I didn't really look at my watch. How 'bout you, Ron, did you happen to look at your watch?" Jo said with a gleam in her eye.

"I wasn't wearing one. Besides, I was too busy to notice the time," I replied, staring blankly at Diane, then I looked at Jo and winked. She winked back.

"Ohhhhh, you were making whoopy."

"Diane," Paul said, "that's really none of our business."

"Well, Paul, if you had more energy maybe I wouldn't have to pry into other people's affairs."

"Sheesh, how many times a week are we supposed to do it? I only have so much energy you know."

"You're getting complacent. We have to perk up our relationship. That's the way you keep it alive," Diane said as she looked for Connie with our food.

Jo and I just looked at each other and shrugged. I searched under the table for her leg and rubbed her calf with the instep of my foot. She reached under the table and touched my knee.

I grabbed my coffee and gulped it down, then fingered the empty cup craving more. Diane was impatiently waiting for the food and I needed more coffee. Jo and Paul were sitting back relaxed, taking everything in stride.

Connie finally arrived with our order. She placed the plates in front of us. I had ordered eggs and potatoes with bacon. The potatoes had steam rising from them with melted cheese clinging to the crevices. They were fried light brown, crisp on the outside, white, moist and meaty on the inside with a touch of garlic. The eggs were fried over-easy in butter and looked as though they were staring at me begging to be eaten. The bacon was perfectly cooked, not too crisp or limp. Jo had pancakes, large and fluffy with a huge pat of melting butter right in the middle of the top one. Her bacon was perfectly cooked also. Paul and Diane both ordered eggs and potatoes. Everything was right off the farm. This was a heart attack waiting to happen but it was well worth the risk. Besides, we only did this once a week.

Diane looked as though she was about to start drooling. She grabbed her fork and almost got Connie's hand as she harpooned her potatoes. "This is the best food," she mumbled as she took in a big forkful.

"Do you guys need anything else?" Connie asked.

"I need more coffee, much more coffee," I replied.

"I'll bring the pot. You know, Ron, if you need anything, feel free to get it. You don't have to wait for me."

I was hungry but I didn't feel like eating. I sat there looking at

Jo. Her words, "I think I'm falling in love with you," kept running through my head.

She looked back at me puzzled, "Is everything all right?"

I sat straight, "Yeah, I'm just thinking."

"You shouldn't do that," Paul interjected, "it could be dangerous."

I ate my breakfast while staring out the window, hoping the view of the desert would carry my mind to some faraway place. A place free from worry, pain and stress. I thought about the love between a man and a woman. It was such a strange concept. At times, it could be stronger than the strongest steel, even stronger than death itself. Other times, it could be forever shattered by the slightest wrongdoing. It always eluded definition, reason or rationale.

After a few minutes of staring, Jo's words broke my mental escape, "Do you want some pancakes?" she said, guiding her fork to my lips.

She shoved them into my mouth as I opened it to say no, but I never got the chance to get the word out. The pancakes were dripping with syrup and a small stream ran down my chin. She scraped it up with her finger and put it in my mouth and said, "Yummy, isn't it?"

"Real good. Would you like a bite of potatoes?" I asked, lifting a large fork full to her mouth.

She opened wide and said, "Hmm, good."

Jo went back to finishing her breakfast and I stared out the window again. I started thinking how people seem to be on an eternal search for something never quite knowing what that thing is. They keep looking though. There was a time I thought getting that right car would make me happy. Getting married and having children, that would do it. Or, once I bought the house I would be set. Then it was setting up the business. That would put my life on an even keel. When I moved to California I won't have anything to worry about. Maybe if I could get a Harley that would smooth out my problems. Everytime I got the thing or got to that certain place, it was time to move on to the next thing or place. It seems that people either had love or lacked happiness or had happiness and lacked love. I guess the trick was to get both of them at the same time. Not an easy task. The more I sat here thinking about it, the more I realized there probably is no final destination. Not in mortal life anyway.

"Ron, Paul asked you a question. Aren't you going to answer him?" Jo asked, nudging me.

"Huh? Sorry, Paul, I didn't hear you. What did you say?"

"Sometimes I think you leave the room without moving. Do we have a plan for today?"

"I don't know. Where would you like to go? We could go north or south. We could go to Arizona or to the coast."

"You're a big help. I could've done that by flipping a coin," Paul said, flipping an imaginary coin in the air.

"Well? Does anyone have any suggestions?" I asked. No one spoke.

"Okay, let's ride to Tecate, Mexico. It's straight south right across the border. Paul do you have your gun with you?" I asked.

"No, I didn't bring it. How 'bout you?"

"I forgot mine. I guess we're legal then. So, how 'bout it?"

We agreed to ride to Mexico. Tecate is considered a small, quiet, family town. A place to go and not be badgered like the tourists in Tijuana. We didn't go there often because the Mexican police have a reputation for being a little dishonest. A person could lose what they had without any legal recourse whatsoever.

"Let me finish this one last cup of coffee and then we'll head out of here," I said between gulps.

"You drank that whole pot of coffee, Ron," Jo said as I downed the last drop. "We're going to be making a lot of pit stops."

We all finished eating and Paul picked up the check. As always, we took turns paying and it was Paul's today. The menu prices were out of the sixties so we made sure we always left a tip at least fifty-percent of the bill.

Connie came out from the kitchen and yelled out to us as we were leaving, "Have a fun day and be careful on those motorcycles, ya hear?"

"And miss your fantastic cooking? Never," I said as I reached the door.

"Oh, go on now, you're just saying that."

Diane stopped at the door, "He means it, you have the best food."

Connie blushed a little and waved bye to us as we walked outside to the bikes. It was ten o'clock and the wind began to pick up. You'd think the blowing wind would make it a little cooler, but it was like trying to cool off in a dry steam room with a hair dryer turned all the way up. I took the sunblock, my long sleeve shirt and Jo's shirt out of my saddlebag. I put the block on my face and handed it to Jo. She in turn handed it to Diane and Paul. They put on their shirts and sunblock also. We tied our bandanas on our heads. I slipped on my riding gloves and Paul did the same. Almost all of our skin was covered except our faces. You couldn't ride a motorcycle in the desert with unprotected exposed skin any length of time. If you did, you would pay the price at the end of the day.

I mounted my shiny steel steed and Jo got on behind me. I waited for Paul to kick-start his bike before starting mine. The older Harleys were temperamental. Sometimes they would fire right up, other times they could be stubborn and start when they felt like it. So far today, Paul's bike was behaving. After kicking it several times, it sprang to life and they hopped on it. I pushed my start button, then looked at Paul and we rolled onto the road heading south. I hollered over the loud, roaring pipes, "Onward to Tecate, Mexico!"

We went smoothly through our gears and soon were up to highway speed. Both our bikes purred as we rode side by side along the gently sloping, curving roads. I glanced over at Paul and Diane, the tails of their headbands flowing in the breeze. The wind took hold of the loose folds in their shirts and beat them back and forth. The air was hot and dry and the sun was high in the sky. We looked like a small band of homeless nomads aimlessly wandering the desert wasteland in search of a place to rest our weary bones.

I pulled closer to Paul's bike on a long straightaway. I got to within a couple of feet of him when Diane and Jo reached out and held hands. We rode that way for the full length of the straightaway as though we were held together by an invisible thread. We broke away at the next curve and Paul took the lead.

I watched the scenery roll by. I was always impressed by the desert's clarity. Everything had such clear and sharp definition, maybe because of the dry air and intense sunlight. Nothing was distorted. It was as though God had turned up the contrast and brightness knob on the TV of life out here. I could almost see the graininess of the sand on the side of the road as I rushed along. When I looked at the sparse vegetation I could see the skinny, bent, contorted twig branches reaching in all directions as if pleading for moisture, however slight. The desert colors were very subtle, not like the brilliant greens and lush browns of a more rainy area. But they were present none-the-less. The ground would shift from a soft reddish to a brownish hue then back to red again. The light green, flat, round and prickly cacti scattered throughout the sandy hills seemed to be daring anything to try and steal their precious water hidden underneath their sharp, spiny needles. Then there was the dead, round sagebrushes blowing across the face of the landscape. A reminder not to take anything for granted out here.

Every once in a while a little creature would scurry across the road in front of us. The lizards would sun themselves along the edge of the pavement, trying to capture all the heat they could, then scatter as we roared by. It wasn't uncommon to see a rattlesnake making its way across the sand looking for a moving morsel to make its day. The desert was teeming with life, all you had to do was look for it.

As we made our way to Tecate, the road carried us in and out of the Cleveland National Forest, which ran along the edge of the Anza-Borrego Desert. The forest was in stark contrast to the desert; its wild grass and green trees lining the roadway. The animal population was different also. The most notable was the presence of mountain lions. These big cats had been getting more aggressive in the past couple of years. There had even been a few attacks on humans. The largest animal I had ever encountered as a city boy was an overgrown dog. From what I hear, these lions would have dogs for lunch. I wasn't sure which was worse, getting stranded in the desert and dying from exposure or getting stuck in the forest and being some big cat's toy mouse. Neither prospect was very appealing.

Occasionally, we stopped in some out of the way place and took a walk into the desert or the forest. Most of the times we did, I felt comfortable even when I didn't have my gun with me. This was truly a wild and still untamed part of the country. Paul and I were the type never to ride the beaten path and so far nothing serious had happened to us.

Paul slowed down and motioned with his hand. He held it up to his mouth holding an imaginary glass to his lips. It was a strange sensation to become dehydrated without even realizing it. My body moisture would evaporate as soon as it appeared on my skin. It was as though I wasn't even sweating but in reality I was. That was the danger of the desert, it would suck you dry without you even knowing it. I nodded to Paul that I understood.

We drove off to the side of the road in the first town we came to. It was on Old State Route 94, the original east-west road from San Diego to Yuma, Arizona. There was a small grocery store right in front of where we stopped. I had water in my saddlebags but I needed to get something cold to drink. I shut my bike down and Jo got off. I put my kickstand down and slowly lifted my leg over the seat.

"What's the matter, Ron, a little stiff?" Jo asked, as I strained to straighten up, "A little too much riding the last couple of days?"

"Not really, just tired is all," as I tried to hide the aching in my bones.

"Why don't you go sit over in the shade and I'll get us a nice cold soda."

"That sounds good to me," I said, walking over to the shady side of the building and sitting down on the ground. I closed my eyes, leaned my head back and let it rest against the building.

Diane came over and sat down next to me, "Well, how's your new bike doing?"

"Couldn't be better. It's what I expected and a lot more."

She picked up a twig and started fidgeting with it, "Think it'll make to it New York and back?"

I didn't like where this conversation was going and I looked over for Paul and Jo hoping, they would hurry up. I had a feeling Diane was about to mention Jo and how she felt about my leaving.

Even though her intentions were good, I still didn't feel like trying to explain something I had no explanation for.

"I don't foresee any problems. I've got a couple of weeks to make sure before I leave," I replied.

"Do you have any plans when you get to New York?" she inquired.

"Like what?" I knew exactly what she was talking about. But I figured that if I play dumb she might get the hint.

Before she could ask another question, Jo and Paul came out of the store with the sodas. Jo sat on the ground next to me and Paul sat next to Diane. Jo handed the bottle to me and it was ice cold. I held it to my forehead for a moment then took a long gulp. It felt so good sliding down my parched throat. I paused with the bottle at my lips then took another long drink. I handed it to her and she took a big swallow.

"Damn, it's hot," I complained, as I watched the cars whiz by on the road, kicking up desert dust.

Even in the shade, it was still very hot. I closed my eyes and leaned my head back again.

"You must be tired, honey," Jo said as she slid her arm through mine and laid her head on my shoulder. "You put on a lot of miles and your nights have been kinda busy too."

"Yeah," I whispered with a faint smile.

"We can head back home. We don't have to go to Tecate."

"It's only ten minutes away. Let's rest a few minutes here. I'll be all right.

"Just like a man. You say you're going to do something and you can't back out," Jo said under her breath.

"Huh? What'd ya say?"

"Oh, nothing. Just talking to myself."

We rested about twenty minutes when Paul's voice snapped me out of my semi-trance. "Is everyone ready to hit the road?"

I opened my eyes and Jo sat up. The places where our bodies touched had sweat on them. But it evaporated in a couple of seconds. We all stood up, got on our bikes, then fired 'em up and rolled back onto the road. I felt refreshed and I'd learned a long time ago that when you ride a motorcycle, you had to make frequent stops to rest. To ride any other way would be stupid.

We made our way to the border and there weren't many places to cross into Mexico. Tecate had only one road in and one road out and was in a remote area along Route 94.

We turned onto the short road towards the Mexican border. After a couple of miles we reached the guard station. I slowed down expecting to be waved on, but he looked us up and down, then motioned for us to stop at the gate. He stepped halfway out of his booth holding his arm out, blocking our path. He stood there in his light blue police uniform with his gun belt loosely hanging low on his hip.

"What is the nature of your business in Mexico, sir?" he asked with a thick accent.

"Just going for a Sunday ride in Tecate," I answered.

"How long do you plan on staying?"

I could barely see his lips move under his thick mustache. "A couple of hours at most." I glanced over at Paul with a puzzled look. We never had a problem getting into Mexico before.

"Do you have any firearms or contraband to declare?"

"No."

He peered at us from under the bill of his baseball-type police cap, then locked his eyes on mine and said, "You may pass. Enjoy your stay in Mexico," he said, in a monotone voice.

"Thanks, we will," I said and I rolled away from the guard. I looked at Paul and he shrugged his shoulders.

We drove slowly toward the center of town, making sure we kept well under the posted speed limit. I got an eerie feeling whenever I came here. It was immediately clear that you were in a different country. The whole town seemed to have been put together by engineers with a different set of plans under a different set of rules. As fast and hi-tech as Los Angeles and New York were in the extreme, Tecate was just the opposite. I didn't speak or read Spanish and all the signs were written in Spanish. I had to guess at what they were saying and so far I'd been guessing right.

We rode past the little park in the center of town. It was Sunday afternoon and everybody was out lying out on the grass under the shade trees. It was so peaceful and serene. People watched us as we drove around the park. Some nodded and some waved. We nodded back. There was a small cantina a couple of blocks away where we usually stopped when we were here. I turned my bike in that direction and Paul followed.

We pulled up in front of the cantina and parked. The owner saw us and waved. We waved back.

"I think it's time we got some fluids," I said as I licked my dry, cracked lips, which didn't help any.

"I gotta get something to drink before I shrivel up and blow away, too," Diane said as we all walked into the cantina.

We all got a cold soda and went back outside to sit under the canopy on the sidewalk where we watched the families stroll by. I looked around, "If I spoke Spanish, I don't think I would have any trouble living here. This is about the pace I can handle."

Most of the people who walked by nodded and smiled as they passed. Every now and then, one or two people would stop and look at the bikes. Sometimes, they would walk around them pointing at things and speaking. I couldn't understand what they were saying, but I'm sure it was in approval. The language might be different but the feelings were the same.

We were there a couple of minutes when a young couple walked by with a small child. He must have been no more than five years old. He stopped in front of my bike and pointed to it. He didn't say anything, he just stood there and pointed.

"Looks like you got a young admirer," Jo said.

"Well, at least he picked the right bike," I said, snickering at Paul.

"Okay, Ron, don't start," Paul barked in a defensive voice.

"Oh, come on, I'm just kidding. You have a real pretty bike, too."

He just growled a little. I got up and walked over to the couple and motioned to lift the child onto the seat. At first they didn't understand. Then they put his hand in mine. I lifted him onto the seat and put his tiny hands on the handlebar grips. He sat there with an awestruck look on his face. Then he started to smile. I reached down and turned the key on and pressed the start button. The bike cranked a couple of times then sprang to life. The boy's eyes got real big and his jaw dropped wide-open on his little round face. I placed my hand over his and turned the throttle a few times and the bike revved up. Each time I did that, his eyes got wider. He started to laugh nervously and jump up and down in the seat. I took my hand off his, he looked at me then turned the throttle all by himself.

"Better watch out, Ron, he looks like he learns things pretty fast. He might just kick it into gear and take it for a spin around the block," Jo said laughingly.

"You never know, he might. Just as long as he brings it back with a full tank of gas," I snickered. I turned the key off and the little boy looked disappointed. His parents said something in Spanish and reached out to take the child. They smiled and said, "Gracias." As they walked away, the little boy kept looking back pointing to the bike.

Diane said, "Looks like you just made a friend, Ron."

"Yep, at least he's got good taste." I sat back down and we finished our drinks.

"It's about time we started back home," Diane said, "I have to get things ready for work tomorrow."

"Yes, it's been a kind of a long weekend for me and I could use a good night's rest before I start the work week," I remarked in a tired voice.

Both Jo and Paul agreed. The sun was getting low in the sky and it was starting to cool off a little and should make for a pleasant ride back. We said "Adios" to the cantina owner and walked to our bikes.

As we rode through town, I looked around and felt very fortunate to live in the USA. I took a lot of things for granted and being here made me aware of the things I had.

When we approached the border, there was a line of about ten cars waiting to cross. Usually there were no more than two or three cars. *No big deal,* I thought, *we were in no hurry and the temperature was getting bearable.*

We fell in line behind the last car and shut our bikes off so they wouldn't overheat. "Did you have a good time so far?" I asked, looking back at Jo.

"I always have a good time when I'm with you," she said, rubbing her hands up and down my sides.

I didn't respond. I sat there with my head turned toward her. I couldn't see into her eyes because she was directly behind me but I knew exactly how they looked. I pictured the look in her eyes when she told me she thought she was falling in love with me last night. A strong, familiar feeling stirred inside me.

The line moved slowly and when there were only five cars in front of us, we got off our bikes and sat in the shade. Paul glanced at me. "You look real tired."

"Seems I've forgotten what sleep is. Anyway what'd ya expect? This is my first experience on my new Harley. I'm gonna ride it as much as I can. That's what new Harley riders do, don't they?"

"I guess I did the same thing when I got mine," Paul said.

"You sure did, Paul," Diane said. "You guys and your bikes, I'll never understand it. You almost treat them as though they were living things."

Paul and I looked at each other and grinned.

Jo looked blankly at my motorcycle, "There's no worse feeling than having to compete with a piece of steel." Then she turned her head away and said under her breath, "Among other things."

"Aw, come on, Jo, it ain't like that. I'm not gonna let the bike run my life."

"Well, we'll see 'bout that," she snorted.

"Right," Diane said, sharply. "It happens to everyone who gets a Harley."

"Not everyone, Diane," I replied defensively.

While looking at Diane, Paul said, "Don't worry 'bout it, Ron, It's just a woman thing. They get over it after a while."

Diane looked at Paul with raised eyebrows and wide eyes, her lips poised to respond to Paul's comment, but before she could speak I said, "There's only a couple of cars in front of us now, we better get back on our bikes," hoping that would end the conversation.

We rolled forward pushing our bikes as the cars passed through the crossing. When there was just one car in front of us, we started our bikes, waiting for the border agent to wave the car on. After it passed through, Paul rode his bike up to the agent and he punched up Paul's license plate number on his computer, then asked, "Where do you live?"

"Borrego Springs," Paul answered.

"I'll have to ask you to move to secondary."

I watched as Paul pulled over to the side, wondering what was going on. I said to Jo, "I bet he's going to pull us over, too."

I rolled up next and he punched up my license number on his computer. I watched him as he gazed into his screen. He appeared to take his job seriously. From his short haircut and the way he had his hat pulled down tight over his eyes, he had to be a former military man. The muscles in his arms were very well defined under his skintight, forest green shirt. He was all business.

"Who is the registered owner of this motorcycle?" he asked.

"I am."

"What's your name and where do you live?"

"Ron Healy and I live in Borrego Springs."

He grabbed my handlebars and said, "Shut off the ignition and hand me the keys."

I looked at him, "What's the problem, officer?"

"Do as I say. Turn off the bike and hand me the keys!"

I shut off the engine and handed over the keys.

"What the hell's going on?" Jo snapped.

"Push the bike over by the station and wait for me there," the officer barked. He motioned for another officer to escort me to the secondary area.

Paul was waiting at the side of the building and when I pulled next to him, he asked, "What's up with this shit?"

"I don't know. He took my keys and told me to wait here. He ran the plate number and it's still registered to Jim's dealership. I think that's why he pulled me over. I got the registration in my pocket, so there shouldn't be any problem, I hope. Why'd he pull you over?"

"I don't know but I'm sure we'll find out."

Another agent took his place at the crossing gate and he came over to me, "Can I see both your licenses and registrations, please?"

Paul got out his paperwork and handed it to a second agent standing next to him. I got off the bike and so did Jo. I reached back in my pocket for my wallet, "What's the problem?"

"This motorcycle's registered to a dealership in Oceanside and I have to check it out."

"I just bought it Friday and I'm sure it's not in your computer yet. But I have all the paperwork right here." I handed it to him and he shuffled through it. He checked the serial number on the registration with the numbers on the frame.

"I'm going to have to ask all of you to step inside and submit to a personal search. We also want to look through your saddlebags."

"What!" I screamed. "You got the paperwork and it's all legal. Now you want to look through my bags and search us, why?"

Jo grabbed my shoulder, "Take it easy, Ron. There's nothing you can do. We don't have anything to hide so let him look in your bags and search us. That way, we can get out of here sooner."

"Yeah," Paul said, "let him do what he's gotta do so we can get on our way."

"I don't like it, okay! I've got a bill of sale from Jim's in my name. I've got a transfer of title again from Jim's in my name. What's the point of carrying this paperwork if it doesn't mean anything? These papers are supposed to satisfy any questions of ownership."

He didn't pay any attention to me. I watched him go through my saddlebags. I was starting to loose it. I think he was thoroughly enjoying this. The other officer said, "Would you mind stepping inside."

"Let's go. It's hot out here and I could use a drink of water," Jo said in a smooth, calm voice.

I looked at the agent and sarcastically said, "Is it okay if we get a drink of water?"

"Yes, there's a fountain inside."

We all went into the station house and sat on the hard wooden benches. I slapped my hand on the bench, "This really sucks. Does that idiot think it's a stolen bike or something? If it were stolen, I sure wouldn't be trying to bring it into the country. I'd be going the other way. Maybe he thinks we're drug runners. Do we look like drug runners?"

Paul looked hard at me, "Well, you haven't taken a shower or shaved today. Neither have I. You look like you're all strung-out from lack of sleep. Yes, you look like you could be running drugs."

"Come on, give me a break. You know better than that. Where would I be hiding them? In my shoes?"

"Doesn't matter, they're going to strip search us no matter what we look like."

"Maybe you're right. I guess he's just doing his job. I still don't have to like it though."

Jo put her hand on mine, "We should be out of here in a little bit."

"I hope so. I just want to get home and get some sleep. I can't remember the last time I covered so much ground in three days."

Two agents came in, one male and one female. The male agent came up to me and said, "Please follow me," and led me to a small room. He closed the door behind me and said, "Empty your pockets on the table." I did as he asked. "Take off all of your clothes and set them on the bench."

"Why is this necessary? Do I have to do this? Is this legal?"

"Yes, it is. And yes, you do or we will hold you here and put a hold on your motorcycles."

I stared at him for a second, then thought, *I better do as he asked or we will never get home.* I took off all my clothes, then set them on the bench and stood there feeling totally stupid. This was really embarrassing, not to mention that I was all dirty and grubby from being in the desert all night and day. He looked through my pile of clothes and looked me over, then said, "You can get dressed now and wait outside."

I stepped outside and they called Paul into the room. Diane was sitting on the bench. I looked at her and asked, "Where's Jo?"

"The lady agent took her in the other room while you were gone. Did they make you take off all of your clothes?"

"Yep. It wasn't fun."

Diane didn't look too happy. Just then, Jo came out of one of the rooms. The lady agent said to Diane, "Come with me."

Diane got up and followed her and Jo sat next to me, "Well, that was interesting. I've never been strip-searched before," she said, blankly.

"Neither have I. I wonder why they're going to all this trouble?" Jo shrugged her shoulders. Paul and Diane came out of the rooms at the same time and sat on the bench.

The agent said, "You can wait here, someone will be with you in a little while."

We stayed silent for a moment, not really believing what just happened. Then Paul asked, "Hey, what's the worst thing that's ever happened to you on a motorcycle?" Trying to break the tension.

I thought a minute, then hesitated before I said, "I guess the worst thing really didn't happen so much to me as it did my old riding buddy. We were out cruising late one Saturday afternoon. His name was Kevin."

"Was?" Diane asked.

"Yes, was. He had a habit of trying to adjust things on his bike as he was riding down the road. Well, this one day he was reaching around trying to fix things and wasn't paying attention. We came to a curve, I was on the inside next to the center line and he was on the outside next to the shoulder. Suddenly, he veered off the road and went head first into a light pole."

I could feel my eyes starting to get wet. I looked away for a minute. It was always hard to talk about the accident. Jo put her hand on my leg and softly caressed it. Anytime she touched me it felt soothing. I continued on, "I stopped and by the time I ran back there, he was already gone. His head hit the pole and he died instantly."

"Sorry to hear that. Maybe I shouldn't have brought it up," Paul said.

"No, that's all right. It's something I can't hide or run from. Things like that happen. Now you tell me the worst thing that happened to you on a bike."

"Tell him about the time you ran off the road with me on the back," Diane said.

Paul shifted on the bench, "Oh, yeah, the ditch. That was really wild. We were riding on Old 94 not too far from here, up where it gets real curvy. I was going around a left hand curve and I heard a loud clunk."

"I heard it too," Diane said.

"I was going about forty miles an hour and I looked down at my front wheel in the direction of the noise. I shouldn't have taken my eyes off the road. By the time I looked up, I was heading straight for the shoulder. I was going too fast to swerve and before I could react I drove into the three-foot ditch alongside the road. I don't really remember being in the ditch, it all happened so fast. I guess I bounced around the bottom of the ditch and all I could think about was to try to keep the bike upright."

"I almost jumped off," Diane said, "but I stayed on. I'm glad I did."

"We rode along the ditch, must'a been about twenty feet. I guess while bouncing around I accidentally hit the throttle and it powered the bike right back up the side of the ditch. The next thing I knew, I was back on the road rolling along. I slowly came to a stop and sat there not believing what had just happened. I felt behind me and Diane was still there."

"I couldn't believe it either. I thought for sure we were going to get hurt real bad. That's when I realized it was a good thing I didn't jump off."

"There was an older guy riding behind us and saw the whole thing. He pulled up behind us and asked if we were all right. We said yes and he said that was the best piece of driving he'd ever seen. I explained to him that I had no idea how I got out of the ditch. All I remember was seeing the edge of the road coming up and the next thing I remember was being back on the road. He said I must have some pretty good reflexes, but I think it was my guardian angel."

Diane nodded her head in agreement, "Someone was watching out for us, for sure."

"I remember when that happened," Jo said, "you guys were real lucky."

"I guess I picked up a rock in the treads of my front tire and it hit the fender. I never did find out what made the noise," Paul said as he stared blankly across the room as though he was reliving the incident.

I looked out the window. "I wonder how much longer this guy is going to keep us here. I bet he's just trying to harass us."

"Naw," Jo said trying to keep me from going off the deep end again, "it probably takes time to check the registration 'cause it's Sunday and a lot of people are crossing the border going home after the weekend."

"Maybe," I replied, not really believing it. I went to the water fountain and took a long drink of water, then splashed some on my face. The coldness against my skin shocked me wide-awake. I walked over to the benches, then began pacing back and forth. I stopped in front of Jo and stared at her. Everytime I looked at her and tried to figure what was going on between us, I got all confused.

"What's wrong?" she asked.

"Oh, nothing. Just thinking."

"Thinking? 'Bout what?"

"People. Life in general. You."

"Are they good thoughts?"

"Yes," I nodded.

"You want to tell me about them?" she asked meekly.

"No, not right now. Maybe sometime when I get it all sorted out. 'Sides, anything I say right now will come out all distorted."

"Okay, whenever you're ready. There's no hurry."

I nodded and continued to pace. Paul looked at me, "Sit down and relax. We should be outta here soon."

"I'm antsy. I have to move around."

Just then the border agent came through the door and said almost nonchalantly, "Everything checked out. Sorry we had to detain you. You're free to leave."

As I walked up to him he handed me my keys and paperwork. I stood squarely facing him, "I'll bet you're sorry you had to detain us! So, we didn't commit any crimes or do anything illegal! Let me ask you a question. How many people on European motorcycles have you stopped and detained today?" His eyebrows started to quiver under the bill of his cap. He didn't respond.

"How many people riding Japanese motorcycles have you stopped and detained so far today? Huh, Mr. Border Agent Man?" His pencil-thin upper lip started to twitch but he stood steadfast and remained silent staring over my head. Jo, Paul and Diane got up and quickly walked over to where I was standing.

"Don't pay any attention to him," Jo said, "he's not normally like this. He's just hot and tired."

"Yeah," Paul said, "he doesn't know what he's saying. He'll be back to normal after a good night's sleep."

I looked the border agent in the eye, "Well Mr. Agent Man, how many? Huh?"

Paul was standing on my left side and Jo on my right. Paul looked at Jo, "Take his other arm and let's get him out of here before he gets us all thrown in jail." Jo and Paul started to push and pull me toward the door. They damn near lifted me up off the ground.

"Well," I screamed over my shoulder as we went through the door, "How many? Huh?"

Once outside Paul let go of my arm, "Forget about it, it ain't that important. Let's just get out of here."

"All right," I stammered, "let's go." I had to rearrange everything in my saddlebags in order to close them, then I buckled them shut and said, "For some reason, I feel like that guy rubbed his hands all over my body. I still think he was harassing us."

"So, you think you've just been harassed by the police, huh?" Paul exclaimed, raising an eyebrow.

"Yes, I do!"

"Maybe you're right. Maybe he was harassing us. You better get used to it," Paul replied, and smirked.

He stood on his kick-starter and jumped down on it. His bike roared to life and Diane got on the back. He looked at me and started to grin. He reached over and slapped me on the back, "You are now fully initiated, man."

"What'd ya mean?"

He kicked his bike in gear and started to laugh. He hit the throttle and as he sped away he hollered, "Welcome to the world of

Harley-Davidson."

I grinned real wide and screamed, "You S.O.B." I stood there for a second, then got on my bike and started it up. Jo jumped on and I chased after Paul, laughing all the way.

I caught up with him and he still had a grin on his face. I gave him the thumbs-up and he responded with his thumb-up. I adjusted myself in my seat. Jo put her arms around me, pressed tight against my body and laid her head on my shoulder. We drew a bead on the road and headed toward Borrego.

It took about forty-five minutes to get home. We drove straight through without stopping. It was almost dusk when we pulled up to the first stop sign in town. As we came to the stop, Jo said, "You want to get something to eat?"

I looked at Paul and Diane. They nodded. "Let's go to the hamburger stand and grab a quick burger. I don't feel like making a long drawn out thing out of it," I said.

Everyone agreed and we rolled slowly through town to the fast food place. When we arrived at the hamburger joint, we parked and I walked over to one of the outside tables and sat down. Everyone followed. "Boy, do we look like a bunch of banditos or what?" I asked, as I looked at everyone.

"Yep, we sure do look like a skuzzy bunch," Diane replied.

Jo rubbed the back of her neck, "I feel like a dusty, dirty bandito that could use a long hot shower. And then a good night's sleep," She put her hand on the back of my neck and started to rub, "You should be just about dead by now. What do you want? You sit here and I'll get it for you."

"Just a burger and a Coke. That's all I can handle right now."

Diane and Jo went inside to get the food. Paul and I sat quiet for a few minutes. I stretched my legs as far as they would go, raised my hands over my head and yawned loudly, "What a ride. I think I'm really going to enjoy this cross-country trip. It's gonna be a real challenge."

Paul leaned forward, rested his elbows on his knees, tilted his head down a little and squinted, staring at me. "Come on, don't do that to me," I said, waving my hand at him.

"What? I didn't say anything."

"Oh yes you did. Loud and clear with that look you just gave me."

"Well, I can't help it. I hate to see anything bad happen between you and Jo. I care a lot about both of you," Paul said.

"I know you do. If you had to do something to satisfy your mind, I would give you all my support."

"I know you would. Maybe I'm not as open minded as you are," he said, sitting back in his chair.

"Sure you are. I can sit here and say I wouldn't get involved. But if the time came for me to put it into practice, it would be hard for me not to say anything, to sit back and let you do what you were going to do," I replied.

"I just hope you come back and don't blow what you have here."

I looked around at the town and its people. "I can't say what's going to happen 'cause I don't know myself. I have to do what I have to. That's the kind of guy I am. That might sound cold but believe me, I'm going through one hell of a head trip over this."

Paul leaned forward, cupped his hands together and let out a big sigh. He stared at his hands, "What happens when you meet this babe and she puts some kind of spell on you?"

"Do I look like the kind of guy that can be led around by the nose?"

"You never know. New York, the lights, the glitter, it can get the best of some people."

I sat straight up, "This is my home, out west here. The fresh air and the wide-open spaces. Remember, I came from a big city and it didn't work for me."

"Okay, I hope the best for you and I hope it all works out."

"I'm sure it will . . . and thanks."

Jo and Diane came out with the food and sat down. Jo looked at Paul and me. "You guys are real serious. What were you talking about while we were gone?"

I grabbed a hamburger off the tray she had put on the table and fidgeted with the wrapper, "Oh nothing, just guy stuff."

Paul looked away and took a Coke off the tray avoiding Jo's eyes. "Come on, Paul," Jo said, "what's up?"

"It's like he said, just guy stuff. Nothing important."

"Right," Diane said, "you guys are up to something."

I grabbed a Coke, "Hey, it's been a long day and we're all a little edgy and tired. We shouldn't take anything serious right now. Let's eat and relax."

Jo looked at me, "You're right. How's your burger?"

"Good. Well, as good as a burger can get." I took a big bite of my sandwich. "I can't wait to get in the shower," I mumbled in between chewing.

Jo looked at me with a devilish grin, "Would you like company?"

"No way. I wouldn't survive. Please, no."

"No problem. Take a shower by yourself. I know you need your space. I'll go home and take one. Anyway, I don't have any clean clothes with me."

"If you come over, you know I won't get to sleep till late and I have to get up early tomorrow," I said.

"Don't worry, I understand. It's no big deal. We should take a breather. I need to get to bed early, too. Just thought it would be a nice way to end the day."

"It would be but I'm really too tired. Another day."

She nodded and smiled. We finished eating and everyone sat staring blankly into space. It must have been five minutes before Paul broke the silence, "Well, this was one hell of a nice weekend. Ron got his shiny new motorcycle."

I grinned ear to ear, "I guess it'll do."

Diane chuckled, "Yeah, right, it'll do, huh? Look at that smile on your face."

They all started laughing. "Okay, okay, so I'm stoked. Ain't nothing wrong with that."

Jo smiled and tapped me on my shoulder, "There's nothing wrong with being excited, and it's all right to show it."

I tried to wipe the grin off my face and act like just another Harley-riding tough guy but it wasn't working. We looked at my bike and Paul said, "Yep, that's one nice ride ya got there, bud."

Diane stood up and stretched, "I think it's time we get going. You ready to take me home, Paul?"

Paul looked at Jo and me, "Yeah, we better be on our way. It's getting late and I also gotta get some rest. See you guys."

"You guys ride safe and I'll probably see you tomorrow, Diane," Jo said. Paul fired up his bike and they both got on. I watched them roll onto the street and slowly disappear down the road. Jo looked at me, "Well, finally, you and me alone. What a concept."

I picked up a cold French fry and fiddled with it, "There are plenty of times when we're alone."

"Well, maybe. It just seems that we don't spend a lot of time together. I guess it's just me." She reached over and took the French fry out of my hand, "Ron, you really frustrate me sometimes. You are so evasive. Talking to you about anything specific is like trying to nail Jell-O to the wall. It can't be done."

"I'm not doing it on purpose. I don't mean to be that way. Right now I'm confused. Everything is vague in my mind. I think I'm going through some kind of transition. I feel a little numb inside. Like I can't make a real life choice right now if I tried. I really don't know how to explain it. I spent a lot of time caring about and caring for people. It's like I need a break now, as though my emotional side has shut down. I really don't know what's happening. Believe me, I wish I did. It would make my life so much easier."

"Are you sure you're not sorry you moved away from Chicago?"

"No. I have no regrets. I know I did the right thing. That's not the reason I feel the way I do. At least that much I know."

"I wish I could help you deal with whatever it is that's troubling you."

"I wish you could, too. I think I just need a little time."

Jo sat back in her chair and sighed loudly. "You need time. I can do this. I'm going to be adult about this," she said in a strained voice.

"Please try and be patient with me."

"Patience. I got plenty of patience. The operative word here is patience."

"Jo!"

"Sorry, sometimes I get carried away. Don't pay any attention to me. I better get home. Can you give me a ride to my Jeep?"

"Of course I can. You don't have to ask."

She shrugged her shoulders, "Sorry again."

"Stop apologizing."

"Okay."

As we walked toward my bike I put my arm around her shoulder. "Have faith, Jo, let's not try to force anything."

She looked deep into my eyes, "All right, I won't."

I drove slowly to her Jeep and we stayed silent. Partly because we were exhausted and because of the stress between us. I pulled up behind her Jeep, she wrapped her arms around me and laid her head on my back. We stayed that way, motionless for a few minutes.

We got off the bike, stood facing each other and I looked into her ocean-blue eyes. She took both my hands in hers, "See you again this week?"

"Of course. Either I'll stop by the ranch or I'll see you at John's."

She nodded as she put her arms around me and hugged me tightly. Then she put her lips to my ear and whispered, "I really meant what I said last night."

I whispered back, "I know you did." I hugged her close and could feel every curve on her body against me. It was awkward not knowing how to respond. I wanted deep inside to make her happy by saying what she wanted to hear, but I couldn't, not right now.

She brought her lips to mine and gave me a soft, long kiss. "I better get going," she said, as she pulled away from me.

"Me too." I watched her walk away and climb into her Jeep. I stared as she drove down the road out of sight. I sat on my motorcycle and kept staring down the empty road. *Damn, I thought, what the hell's wrong with me?* I smacked my handlebar really hard. *I better get a shower and get to bed.* I started the bike and headed for the garage.

The sun was low in the sky. I didn't have a watch and I guessed it to be about seven p.m. I rolled onto the driveway of John's station and shut off the bike. I sat facing the door just staring at it, too tired to move.

After a few minutes, I gathered enough strength to get off, stretch out and open up the garage door and push my bike inside. Taking a shower would be a real chore, but I had to do it. I walked past the computer and stopped. *I wonder if Gloria had written since Friday night. I was tempted to look, but after I get out of shower, I thought. Otherwise, I might fall asleep before I got on-line.*

I got undressed as I walked toward the bathroom, leaving a trail of clothes behind on the floor. I stood under the showerhead and turned on the water. It was cold at first and shocked me as it flowed over my body. I turned on the hot more and more until I could barely stand it. I let it run over my body for a few minutes not wanting to move. After the heat of the water reached down to my bones, I soaped up. I rinsed off and stood under the scalding water for another ten minutes before I got out.

Man, that felt good, I thought as I towel dried. *It kinda woke me up.*

After putting on some clean clothes, I sat down at the computer. Part of me wanted to check the e-mail and part of me didn't. If only I hadn't gotten a computer or met Gloria on-line. Wait a minute, that's stupid to try and wish things had happened differently. It's a waste of time to do that. Things happen exactly the way they're supposed to.

I flipped on the switch and waited for the text opening to roll by. I went into the on-line software and waited to get connected. I saw the little white envelope appear to signal that I had mail. I clicked on the envelope and the mail appeared on the screen:

Hi Ron,

I got your letter about your trip up the coast. I envy you. I wish I could go with you. I would love to ride along the California coast on a motorcycle. It must be nice to be able to live the way you live. Free to travel whenever you want. Is your steady girl, Billy Jo, going with you? I bet she's one happy lady. How are things between you and her? Good, I hope. Do you think you'll be getting serious about your relationship with her? Oh, never mind, that's none of my business. I have to learn to mind my own affairs and keep my nose out of other people's lives. If you want to tell me, I'll listen though. I've always enjoyed writing to you and I enjoy it when you write back to me. I'm going to miss your e-mails while you're on your trip. Is it okay if I keep writing anyway? You'll have a lot of mail when you get back. I hope we continue our correspondence. I would hate to lose you as a pen pal and a friend. I better get going. I have a lot to do. Take care and I hope to hear from you soon.

Gloria

I wanted to write back but I was too tired. I'll wait till tomorrow when I can think straight. I turned off the computer and sat in the chair looking at the darkened screen. I strained my eyes to see the clock on the wall. It was almost nine p.m. I picked up my clothes off the floor and took them outside to my van. I sat on my bedroll and thought, *I should lie down right now and go to sleep.* But I knew I wouldn't be able to do that.

I went back into the garage and got my bike out. I started it and locked up the station. I headed out to the desert to my big oval rock. It was the only place where I could get things straight in my head. It only took a few minutes to get there. I pulled alongside the rock and got off. The sun had set an hour ago. The stars were beginning to get brighter and more numerous in the sky. I slowly climbed onto the boulder and laid on my back looking up. The sun had heated the rock nice and toasty. After a few minutes the heat began to penetrate my aching muscles. The soreness in my back began to vanish and I started to relax. I gazed into the vast, cloudless night sky. It was almost as though I could connect with the energy of the universe by staring out into space.

The thoughts started to race through my mind as they always did when I came here. They were more in the form of questions than anything else. Why was my life unfolding the way it was? Why were the people in my life the way they were? How come I couldn't make a definite decision about my relationship with Jo? What was holding me back? Maybe I'm just stupid. Maybe I have some sort of brain damage that's keeping me from making a rational decision. Why does everyone seem to have the answers to how and with whom I should be with? How long will it take to free my heart again? What will it take to free my heart again? Will it ever be free to love another?

"Hey, big guy in the sky, what's up with this stuff, huh? Come on, I need answers. I got all the questions and I need some answers." I stared deep into space waiting for some kind of sign to appear. I closed my eyes and let the heat of the rock caress my sore body. Everything was absolutely still. I think I dozed off for a few minutes, then I opened my eyes and sat up, "Well, I guess you're not going to give me the answer tonight, huh? At least I feel a little better even if I still don't know what's going on." I rolled off the rock, fired up my bike and headed back to the garage.

I put my bike away, crawled into my van, got undressed and laid down. I think it must have been ten seconds after my head hit the pillow that I fell into a deep sleep.

Chapter Five

I clenched my teeth, put the wrench down and walked to the front of the garage. I sat on the three-legged stool and looked at the clock, ten a.m. I didn't feel like finishing the car. It'd been two days since I talked to Jo and I hadn't written back to Gloria since I got her e-mail Sunday night. John was at the VA Hospital in La Jolla for his doctor's appointment. Every other Wednesday he had to go for a checkup on his diabetes. I stared out the window, not wanting to do anything.

Maybe I should pack my stuff and head straight north, to Alaska. Yeah, that way I wouldn't have to worry about anything. I started over once. I could do it again.

I got up and walked over to the soda machine. I slowly and deliberately dropped the coins, one by one, into the slot. The can fell down to the opening. I took it and sat back down.

Naw, going to Alaska is not going to solve anything. Just what the hell am I afraid of anyway? It's been two years since I left Chicago. Do I still need more time to get over my marriage? That's what must be bothering me. What else could it be?

I looked out the window just as the sheriff pulled up to the gas pumps. I walked outside as he was putting the nozzle into his tank.

"How's the Harley man doing today?" he quipped.

"Okay Pete, how 'bout yourself?"

"I'm fine. Is John around?"

"No. He went to La Jolla for his doctor's visit."

He thought a second. "Oh, that's right, it's Wednesday. I forgot it's his day to go to the VA. He's lucky to have you here to watch things for him."

"I'm the one who's lucky. John's done a lot for me."

"I guess it's a two-way street," he said, as he finished pumping the gas. He put the nozzle back and followed me into the station. I made out a receipt and handed it to him to sign. "It's gonna be another hot one today. Hope we get a Santa Ana soon to give us a break from this heat," he said as he walked toward the door.

I hadn't even noticed the heat. Probably 'cause of all the stuff on my mind. "I hope we do, too."

I watched as he got into his patrol car. He waved and hollered as he rolled away, "Have a good day, Ron."

"You too, Pete. And stay safe." Pete was an all right guy, I thought as I walked back to the stool and sat down again. It wobbled back and forth and I really didn't care to try and level it. "Story of my life, not even the chair will co-operate," I said under my breath.

It was slow for Wednesday and I had just one car to finish but I couldn't bring myself to get up and go back to the garage and do it. I stared out the window again.

"Just what does Jo mean to me?" I asked myself. I wasn't sure. *Just what did Gloria mean to me?* I've never met her. All I had was a vague description of her. But by the things she wrote, I could really relate to her. It wasn't what she said, but how she said it that made me feel close to her. "Damn this anyway," I said as I plunked the soda can on the counter.

Just then the phone rang. I slowly got up and answered it, "Morning, John's Service Station."

"Hi, Ron," it was Jo's voice, "how you doing? Haven't heard from you in a couple of days so I thought I'd give you a call."

"Hi. I'm all right. And you?"

"I'm fine. Working a little. Hey listen, I hope I didn't scare you off by what I said the other night."

"Uh. No, why?"

Jo hesitated on the other end, "I've been thinking the past couple of days and I have no idea what it feels like to be married eighteen years, let alone how it feels to split up after that. It must be a real hard thing to do. I can't even imagine it. So I want you to know that you can do whatever you have to do or go wherever you have to go to get to the end of this. I just gotta have faith that it'll work out the way it's supposed to."

"Thanks, Jo, you're really an understanding person."

"Not really, I just don't want to spook you or scare you off. I want you to tell me if I start putting any pressure on so I can back off."

"That's being kind of harsh, isn't it?"

"No. I still don't know a lot about you or what your boundaries are. And I want to make sure I don't cross them and push you away."

"That sounds reasonable. And the same goes for me. Let me know if I cross some lines I'm not supposed to."

"I will. So, what are you doing today? Are you busy?" she asked.

"I'm here alone right now. John should be back in a little while. Why?"

"Do you have any cars to work on?"

"Just one and I think I'll be finished for the day."

"Why don't you stop by then? My dad's going to Temecula on business. He'll be gone the whole afternoon."

I couldn't resist her. "I'll have to wait for John to get back. If it's all right with him, I'll stop by. If not, I'll call you."

"Okay, hope to see you. Take care and I'll talk to you later, hon."

"Bye," I hung up the phone with an excited feeling in my gut. I was looking forward to seeing her.

I got up. *Better finish this car so I can get outta here.* I gulped down the last of the soda and tossed the can into the trash across the room. It made a loud clang as it hit the trash container dead center.

"Not bad for an old man," I said, as I hurried into the garage.

It was half-an-hour later after I finished the car when John arrived. He walked through the door as I was washing up. "Hey Ron, where are you?"

"I'm in here," I hollered back from the bathroom.

I came to the front and John was sitting in his chair. "How'd your visit go?" I asked.

"According to the doc, I'm doing all right."

"That's good." I had a sneaky suspicion that he wouldn't tell me if he wasn't doing well. He was the kind of person that kept his problems to himself.

"Were you busy while I was gone?" he asked.

I sat down on the stool, "No, Pete was in for gas and I finished the last car."

John looked at me with that eagle eye of his as I fidgeted on the stool, "So there's nothing doin', huh?" he asked.

"Nope, everything that I had to do today is finished."

John looked around the room, "Well, Ron, you put in some long hours the past couple a days. We've been real busy and you worked your butt off."

"It wasn't that bad. I made some money."

"You haven't even left the station for two days," he reminded me.

"I had a lot on my mind and working is good therapy for me."

"Since there ain't nothing happening here, why don't you take the rest of the day off. Enjoy yourself. Take a ride on that new cycle of yours. Maybe go visit your girlfriend."

I looked at him with a raised eyebrow, "I swear you have ESP sometimes."

"After you been around as long as I have, and if you're willing to keep an open mind and pay attention to nature, people ain't that hard to figure."

I sat antsy tapping my foot on the floor, "I hope to reach that state of mind someday."

"It's one of those things you can't get by trying. It's a funny kind of thing, it just happens. If it ever happens at all."

I slowly stood up stretching, "Well then, if it's all right with you I'll take the rest of the day off."

"Have fun and be careful out there."

I walked back to the garage and pushed my motorcycle outside. I could hardly keep from breaking out in a wide grin thinking about getting out into the country and seeing Jo.

In the past two days I'd just been back and forth to the diner on my bike. But I needed the rest. I'd put over eight hundred miles on it between Friday and Sunday night, and I loved every minute of it.

I went into the back of my van and found my black Harley T-shirt and put it on along with my black leather boots. I got on the cycle and pushed the start button, then twisted the throttle and the engine revved up. I sat there for a minute listening to the mellow roar of the pipes and feeling the powerful throbbing of the motor. I don't think a person could ever get used to that sound and feel enough to take it for granted.

I pulled out onto the street and headed for the mountains. Once I got several miles outside of town, I settled back, took a deep breath and smelled the fresh air. There was something soothing about the wind blowing through my hair and across my face. Each and every time my tires hit the open road, something inside my soul stirred.

It seemed like only a few minutes had passed and I was already approaching the entrance to the ranch. *Man, that was quick,* I thought.

I slowed down and turned onto the dirt driveway. I looked around for Jo and all I saw was a few ranch hands over in one of the fields. As I got closer to the house I saw Jo talking with her father. I pulled up and shut off my engine, keeping my distance. I didn't want to get too close 'cause they looked like they were into a serious discussion and I didn't want to irritate her father anymore than I already did.

Jo looked my way, "Hi, I'll be there in a minute."

"No problem," I said, "Hi, Mr. Thompson." He looked in my direction more or less and grunted what sounded like a weak hi, but it was debatable. I remained sitting on my bike while they talked. After a few minutes he went into the house and Jo walked over to me.

"Hey, Ronnie baby, I'm glad you could stop by."

"Jo, don't call me Ronnie."

She stepped in front of me and took my hips in her hands, "The big bad Harley man doesn't want to be called Ronnie," she said, shaking my hips back and forth.

"I don't like to be called that. It's what everyone called me when I was a little kid."

"Oh, you're so damn serious sometimes. Lighten up a little. Do you have to be back soon?" she asked.

"No. I'm pretty much done for the day. Whatever work that comes in, John will take care of, or save for me to do tomorrow. Do you want to go for a ride?"

"No, maybe later. If you don't have to be back, then you can help me around here," she said, as she put her lips to mine and gave me a soft, lingering kiss.

She pulled back and I hesitantly said, "As long as you don't make me shovel horse pooh."

"Come into the barn," she said as she pulled me off my bike. "Leave it here, it'll be all right."

She put her arm around my shoulder and held on to it. Then she slid her other arm around my waist as we went through the stable door. I'd been in here a few times and only for a few moments at most. The stable had about twenty stalls for horses which was big, I guess, not really knowing much about these things. Most of the stalls had horses in them. There were also a lot of outdoor stalls, but most of the pampered horses were kept in here.

Jo guided me to one of them and we stopped in front of the gate. I looked at the nameplate. "Bad Boy" it said. I peered inside. There was a large, caramel-colored horse with a big white patch on his nose and chest. He didn't look bad. But then, all horses looked the same to me.

"Is this a mean horse?" I asked.

"No, he's just the opposite. He's a real gentle horse. That name's just a joke. Sometime I'll explain to you how he got it."

"I'll bet."

She pulled open the gate and went inside, then grabbed a brush and started to stroke across the horse's back, "Come on in, he's not going to bite you."

"No thanks, I'll wait out here."

"Ron . . . come on. Just come in and pet him." The horse looked at me, "See, he wants you to pet him," she said, as she rubbed his nose. "You're a good boy, aren't you."

I looked at her, then at the horse. I took a step forward into the stall and the horse took a step in my direction. I stopped and started to back up.

"He just wants to get close to you to get to know you. I promise he's not going to hurt you."

"Are you sure?"

"Yes, I'm sure. This horse has been with us for about seven years."

I took another step forward and Jo grabbed my hand and placed it on the horse's nose. She moved it up and down and the horse shook his head. I jerked my hand away. "He wants to bite me."

"He's not going to bite you, but I might if you don't stop acting like a little kid, Ronnie."

I straightened up and stuck my chest out, "I'm not afraid to pet him," I said as I stuck my hand out and placed it on his nose again. I gritted my teeth and kept petting as he nodded his head up and down.

"See, he likes you. Here, take the brush and stroke it across his back like this," she said as she moved the brush in long, slow motions along the horse's back.

I took the brush and ran it along his back. He made funny breathing noises as I brushed him. She reached up and stroked his nose, "Yes, Big Boy likes Ron, huh? See I told you there's nothing to be afraid of."

"I wasn't afraid. Just that I've never been this close to a horse before. And this guy's awfully big, too." Jo walked out of the stall and I said, "Hey, where you going? Don't leave me here alone."

"I'll be right back. Relax, just keep brushing."

She came back a minute later with two carrots in her hand. She broke one in half and handed a piece to me. "Hold your hand wide open and flat. Put the carrot in your palm and hold it under the horse's mouth like this," she said as the horse took the carrot out of her hand.

I looked down at the orange thing in my hand, "Okay, I can do this," I mumbled. As I reached out, the horse took the morsel from my palm.

She handed me another carrot, "Here, give him another piece."

I let the horse have it and he made horse noises, in approval, I think. Just then her father appeared, his tall thin frame filling the doorway. He looked at me hard with his dark blue, steely eyes, then turned to Jo.

"Are you leaving now, Dad?"

"Yes. I'll be back later." He shot a darting glance at me, then turned and quickly walked away. He certainly was a man of few words. I wondered if it was because of me, or if he was that way all the time.

"Let's get this horse ready for the trail," Jo said.

"Is someone taking him for a ride?"

"Yep, and you can help me get him ready."

Jo walked over to the bench, picked up the blanket and threw it over Bad Boy's back. I walked around to the other side of the horse where Jo was, "Has your father dated since your mother died?" She walked back to the bench, picked up the saddle and threw it over his back, "No, he hasn't."

I had the feeling she didn't want to discuss it. She stood leaning against the horse staring at me. After a minute she said, "God knows I've tried to get him to break out of his shell. I've tried to get him to go out. I've tried to set him up with women who were interested in him. I've even gone so far as to take him out myself so that he could meet people. He wouldn't have anything to do with it."

I felt funny now as I said, "You don't have to talk about it if you don't want to."

"No. I've been holding this inside for a long time. I wish I could get him to open up, just a little. It's been ten years and he is still the same, as though my mother had just passed away."

"Well, it's like you told me, it takes whatever it takes."

"Ten years, Ron?"

"I don't know what to say. I'm certainly not an expert here."

"It's not your problem and I don't expect you to have any answers, just support."

"I can do that."

She changed the subject, "You have to make sure the saddle is strapped tight or the rider will get an unpleasant surprise." She then got the bridle and placed it over the horse's head and strapped it on. "Let's walk Bad Boy outside," she said as she took the reins and led him through the door.

Once outside, she let go of the reins. "Come on," she took my hand and walked back into the stable, "I've got one more horse to saddle up."

We walked to the back of the stable and stopped in front of another stall. Jo opened the gate and stepped inside. I recognized the horse, "Isn't this your horse, Jo?"

"Yes," she said as she threw the blanket and saddle over his back.

"Are you letting someone else ride him?"

"No. I'm riding him," she said with a funny smirk on her face.

"Uh . . .Who's riding Bad Boy?"

"You are."

"Jo, that's sneaky. Why didn't you tell me?"

"Because I didn't want you to chicken out," she said as she led her horse out of the stable. She dropped the reins of her horse, took my hand and walked me over to Bad Boy. "We're going for a ride and the first thing you have to know is that horses can sense fear. You have to take charge of him or he won't respond to you."

"Well, that's good to know. If he thinks I'm afraid, he'll do whatever he wants. I'm not sure I like that."

"It's easy. Just get some confidence in yourself. Come on, you do it everytime you ride your motorcycle. You expect me to get on the back and have confidence that you won't kill me. If I can ride a horse, you can too."

"I guess I can't back down now."

"Good. Now take the reins and walk him out to the corral and we'll practice mounting and walking him around."

I did as she said and she took her horse's reins and followed me into the corral. I walked him around a bit and it felt pretty good. He followed me with no problem. "I'll be right back, I've got to get my hat."

She went into the stable and came back out wearing her white hat and holding another one in her hand. She walked up to me and handed me the hat, "Here, try this on. I wasn't sure of your hat size so I had to guess."

I reached out and took it, "You got this for me?"

"Try it on and see if it fits."

I lowered it onto my head and it fit perfectly. Jo looked at me and smiled, "Oh boy, you look hot, Ron. That looks real good on you. How does it fit?"

"Perfect."

"I don't think I can let you out by yourself wearing that hat.

The women will be all over you."

"Come on Jo, cut it out," I said as I turned away. I turned back, reached out and put my arms around her waist, "Thanks. That was really nice of you."

"Well, if you're gonna ride a horse, you've got to have a hat. Now stand on his left side and I'll show you how to mount him." I stood along his left side and she said, "Put your left foot in the stirrup and grab the saddle horn right here."

I did as she said.

"Now lift your body up and swing your right leg over the saddle."

I hesitated, "What if the horse doesn't like the idea?"

"Confidence, and show no fear, remember."

"Yeah, no fear." I pulled myself up onto the saddle, the horse swayed a little and sidestepped, "Whoa," I said nervously.

"There you go, you did it. Now hold on while I walk you around the corral a little." She took the bridle in her hand and slowly walked me and the horse around in a big circle. It started to feel comfortable.

"How you doing up there?"

"Okay, I guess. He seems to be doing what he's supposed to, so far."

"Now we'll go through the ways to control a horse. When you want him to go forward you press on his sides with both your legs. When you want him to stop, you pull up on the reins with both hands. When you want to turn, you pull the reins in the direction you want to go while applying light pressure with your knee. You got all that?"

"I think so. It doesn't seem to be that hard."

"It's not," she said as she let go of the bridle.

"Hey, don't let go! I don't know how to do this yet!"

"Just do as I said and you'll be all right."

I gritted my teeth and said under my breath, "Look horsey, better pay attention or we're going to have it out." I applied a light pressure with my knees at the same time saying, "Giddy-up." The horse moved forward. I pulled left on the reins and he turned left, then I pulled right on the reins and he turned right, "Hey, this is all right." I made a full circle around the corral and the horse responded to me.

I walked him up to Jo and stopped in front of her. She walked to her horse, got on and said, "Follow me." She guided her horse out of the corral and I followed. There was a trail a few yards away and she headed for it.

"Are we going on the trail already?" I asked nervously.

"Yes, you're doing just fine. Keep right behind me and you'll be all right. Bad Boy is a good trail horse."

I pulled down on the brim of my hat and said against my better judgment, "Okay." He did seem to be behaving, though. We rode about a mile when we came to an open field and I rode up alongside Jo.

"How's he feel?" she asked.

"He hasn't thrown me off yet and he hasn't run away with me."

"I guess I can tell you now why his name is Bad Boy. When we first got him, he threw everyone who tried to ride him."

My eyes grew real wide, "What?"

"It took awhile but we broke him of that. He hasn't thrown anybody in years. He's the best horse we've got now."

I sat straight up in the saddle, "Jo!"

"Calm down, just keep doing what you're doing and you won't have any problems."

"You could've told me."

"If I did you wouldn't have got on that horse." I didn't answer. I knew she was right and I was beginning to relax.

She trotted in front of me. I fell in behind her and a little to the side. I watched her as she rode through the trail, the wind softly blowing her long blonde hair back and forth under her hat. She sat straight in the saddle and rose and fell each time the horse took a step. My eyes wandered down past her slim waist to her buttocks. They were nice and firm and fit the saddle well. Her solid thighs hugged the horse with just the right amount of pressure. My eyes lingered on her for a while, then I turned my attention to the scenery.

We rode through the dense forest and into open meadows and the scent of sweet grass filled the air. The horse rocked me back and forth as I closed my eyes and took deep breaths in through my nose and slowly let the air out. I could hear the birds chatting to each other what was probably important to them. It reminded me of being in the forest preserves back home, only it was a little different on horseback. I remembered how there was nothing like the intense summer smells of fresh flowers and new grass after a harsh Chicago winter. I kept my eyes closed, taking in the sounds and smells as the horse continued to rock me back and forth.

Several minutes passed when I heard Jo's voice. "You're awful quiet back there, Ron. Are you all right?"

I opened my eyes. "I'm enjoying this. It's not as bad as I thought it would be."

"I knew that once you got past your stubbornness you'd probably enjoy it."

"I'm not stubborn, just careful."

"Uh-huh," she said, with a hint of sarcasm.

We went a little further and came to a small stream. Jo led her horse to it and I did the same. We sat on the horses while they drank. Jo's eyes scanned the horizon. "This has been my whole life. The only time I've been away from home for any length of time is when I went away to college in L.A. I can't imagine ever moving away from here. I know people do move to new places. My sister did. She had no problem relocating. This life wasn't for her. You left your home and it must have been hard."

I stared into the stream. "You gotta do what you gotta do. Mine was leaving Chicago. That's the only way I could handle it."

We sat silent and watched the horses drink, then Jo asked, "Want to sit down for a while?"

I nodded, we got off and Jo dropped her reins. "Hey, aren't we supposed to tie them to a tree or something?" I asked.

"No, they won't go anywhere. They'll just stand here and graze."

"But in the movies the cowboys always tie up their horses. How come?"

"I don't know. I'm not an expert on cowboy movie stuff. I just know they won't go anywhere." She walked over to a shade tree and sat under it. I stood by the stream for a minute then walked over and sat next to her. She looked down and picked at the grass, "You know how you get on your bike and get lost in the mountains and desert to escape from life and its problems?"

"Yes."

"This is how I get away and escape. When I was a young girl, my father and I would ride this trail a lot. We haven't done that in a long time."

She stared out into space, probably reliving memories.

"If I was brought up on a ranch, I would do exactly the same thing," I remarked. "I guess everyone has to have a place to get away. The only problem is that in a big city there are not many places to go. A lot of times I had to retreat into my own mind. I'd much rather do it this way, though." She stayed quiet while picking at the grass. I didn't know what to say, so I waited for her to speak.

A few minutes passed and she looked at me with those eyes, the kind with a twinkle in them. "God, you look good in that hat," she sighed.

"Hey, you're a knockout yourself, with or without the hat." She blushed a little and smiled. It made me feel good to see her smile. "How far is it back to the ranch?"

"Not far. We've been riding in a large circle. Every time we came to a fork I took the right one," she said waving her arm in a wide circle.

"I didn't even notice."

She looked at me with a smile, "I think you're hooked."

I didn't want to say it, but I did, "I think maybe you're right. This horse stuff isn't so bad."

She laughed out loud and reached over to tickle me. I tickled her back and we rolled around in the grass. After a few minutes of tickling each other to the point of tears, we lay on the ground and paused for a moment to catch our breath.

"We better start back," she said.

I got up and put my hand out to help her up. She took hold and I pulled her to her feet. She continued her forward motion, pressing her body against mine, wrapping her arms around me and hugging tight. "You're so much fun to be with," she said.

"We do have a lot of fun, don't we?" She put her head back,

closed her eyes and parted her lips slightly. I gently put my lips on hers. I could feel a sensation all the way down my body. We pulled away from each other a little. She gazed into my eyes and I felt that feeling stirring deep inside. "We better get back," I blurted out.

She pushed me away almost knocking my hat off, "You can really ruin a moment."

"Well, it's getting late. Aren't you supposed to be working today?"

"All right, let's head back," she said in a huff as she walked back to get her horse.

I'd upset her and I didn't mean to. Lately, if I didn't respond the way she wanted me to it would affect her. I stood there for a second, feeling real stupid. Then I ran after her, "Jo, wait a minute." I caught up to her just as she got to her horse. "Come on Jo, remember what we talked about?"

"Men. They don't have an ounce of romance in their bodies."

"That's not true." I turned her toward me. "Just because I'm not acting the way you think I should, that's no reason to be mad at me."

"Oh, I'm not mad at you. Forget it, you wouldn't understand."

I slipped my arms around her waist and pulled her close to me. She laid her head against my chest. "I don't know what's happening to me. I've never felt this way before. It's scary. It's like I can't control my emotions and I don't like feeling that way," she said in a soft, almost child-like manner.

I laid my chin on her head, "I know that feeling and I know what you mean. The last thing I want is to be out of control."

"One thing you're certainly not is out of control of yourself." I wasn't so sure that was a compliment, but I kept my mouth shut. Now was not the time to kick up any dust. She sighed and looked at me, "We're having a good time and I don't want to ruin it. So let's just enjoy the rest of the day." She reached up and adjusted my hat. "Looking good," she smirked.

I pulled down on the brim of her hat. "Women," I said.

"Uh-huh, you love it," she replied, as she spun around toward her horse in a sexy manner.

I watched her as she put her foot in the stirrup, lifted herself up and swung her leg over the saddle. Anytime she moved, she did it gracefully and with a sexual overtone. I was always amazed at how she could take an old pair of tight jeans, a beat-up flannel shirt with the sleeves rolled up to the elbows and tied around the waist, and look so good. She always had a tiny bit of cleavage showing. I bet it drove the ranch hands wild. It sure made my pulse beat faster.

"Well, are you going to just stand there?"

I caught myself gawking at her and quickly turned toward my horse, "Uh, no. Let's see if I remember how to do this." I walked around the left side of the horse, went through the motions of mounting and quickly found myself sitting on top of him. "Nothing to it," I said with a wide smile.

"Oh boy, now you're an expert. Sheesh." Jo tugged on her reins and her horse made a tight right turn. I followed her back onto the trail.

I focused on her as we rode along. She was quite a woman. She had everything a man could want. As I watched her jog back and forth in her saddle, my mind drifted back to my thoughts at Connie's place last Sunday. I thought about the happiness and love thing. It's as though I was stuck between them. There were times, like right now, I was happy being with Jo. I wanted to experience all of her. The more I watched her, the more I wanted her. I wanted to feel her smooth, naked body against mine. Then there were other times I had to be alone, away from everybody. Why was that? Was it wrong? I knew that if I told her this she might take it the wrong way. She might think I didn't want to be with her or something. This thing I had to satisfy was not just in my mind, it was deep in my soul. I thought about meeting Gloria. Why did I have to do that? I didn't know. At times like this, I wish I had a switch to shut my mind off. I would definitely flip it.

Jo's voice broke my train of thought, "You're being quiet again, Ron."

"Just enjoying the ride and the scenery," I said, afraid she might sense I had something on my mind.

"Are we getting close to the ranch yet?" I asked, hoping that would distract her from asking further about my silence.

"It's right up the trail. Are you in a hurry to get back?"

"Not really. Just like to know where I am," I said in my manly voice.

"Don't worry, I won't get you lost."

"Getting lost out here might be fun."

"Now you tell me when we're almost back. I would have taken you for a real ride but I didn't want to overwhelm you on your first time out." I wasn't sure if she meant horse ride or a ride with her. Either way, I was beginning to get aroused watching her. I hope this horse doesn't feel the bulge starting to grow in my pants and take it personal. Once the urge for Jo started, it was almost impossible to stop.

I looked away from her and could see the ranch fence through the brush about three hundred yards ahead. I guessed we'd been gone about an hour and a half. The more I tried to ignore this urge, the more intense it got. I rode up alongside her and with a devilish grin asked, "Wanna stop for a while before we get back to the ranch?"

"Ahhh, a little while ago you didn't want anything to do with me. Now you want to stop?"

"Well?" I stammered, like a stupid little kid.

She had an *I'll show you* look on her face and tilted her nose slightly up in the air and said, "Nope. We're almost back and we're not going to stop until we get back."

Now I felt even more stupid. But the desire was still there, strong as ever. I think she was punishing me and I'm not sure if I deserved it or not. I figured now was not the time to go into it.

She took the lead and trotted through the ranch gate. I followed her as she stopped in front of a ranch hand. She dismounted and handed the reins to him. Then she looked at me and said, "Let Dave take your horse." I dismounted and handed my reins to him.

"Take care of these mounts for me," she said, as she walked toward the stable. He nodded and walked the horses toward the corral. I stood there as Jo kept walking. I didn't want to be left behind, so I hurried after her.

As I caught up with her, I said, "I had a great time. We gotta do that again soon."

"Huh," she huffed.

God, I wanted her so bad and I think she knew it. I continued to follow her into the stable. Once inside, she stopped suddenly and whirled around. I ran into her, my chest just touching the tips of her breasts making me catch my breath. "Ops," I said as we made contact.

I backed up a step. She looked at me and blurted out, "He, city slicker, have you ever seen a hayloft?"

"Uh . . . no, I haven't."

She took a deep breath and her shirt opened up a little to expose her breasts. I looked at them and could see her watching me. This was getting unbearable. "I should have known you've probably never seen a hayloft being the city boy that you are. Follow me," she said as she walked to a ladder near the back.

I was right behind her as she started to climb the ladder. She was about four rungs up, her butt was face high when I reached out and brushed my hand against it. She stopped, caught her breath and leaned back against my hand for a moment. I felt a surge of desire rush through my body and I knew she felt it, too. We continued up the ladder with me close behind. We reached the loft and Jo walked a little ways and stopped.

She turned around and said, "This is hay." Jo grabbed a handful and threw it down into one of the stalls then turned to me. Her eyes had that faraway look in them. I unbuttoned the top button of her shirt exposing more of her breasts as I ran my finger along her cleavage. She closed her eyes for a second and tilted her head back slightly.

"This is how we feed the horses," she said as she fumbled with the button on my pants.

"Is that a fact," I replied with heavy breath as I undid the rest of her shirt showing both of her breasts. I cradled them in my hands and bent over placing my lips on one of her nipples. It was already hard. She moaned a little as I sucked on it.

She finished undoing my pants and pulled them down to my ankles, at the same time dropping to her knees, "Let me make you hard."

I was already hard as a rock but I kept silent as she took hold of me and started to suck. My knees almost buckled under me and I began to sway. The rush of pleasure was almost too much to handle. I felt myself starting to cum but I held off. After a few moments she stood up and said, "Let's lie down over here," as she led me to a pile of hay.

She took my hand and I hobbled after her. I sat down and took my boots off, then finished taking my pants and underwear off. She sat watching me as I took off my shirt. I was now completely undressed, "Hey, this isn't right. I'm naked and you're not."

"Then take off my clothes," she said, smiling.

She laid back and I scooted down to her feet. I took off her boots and rubbed her feet. Then I slowly undid her jeans, she raised up her buttocks as I tugged them down past her thighs. She held her legs high in the air as I pulled them over her feet. All she had on was her unbuttoned shirt. One of her breasts was covered and the other one was exposed. She lifted up to take off her shirt and I said, "No, leave it on. It's sexy."

"Okay," she panted.

I positioned myself between her feet and gently pushed her legs apart. I ran my hands along the inside of her calves, then up her thighs, past her groin to her stomach. I purposely avoided touching her. I looked at her face and she had her eyes closed. I moved her shirt aside and took her breasts in my hands. I manipulated her nipples and she wiggled under me. I slowly drew my hands back down her body and when I got to her lower stomach, she arched her hips up into the air. I put my hand between her legs and moved it back and forth. She was very moist. Keeping my hand in place, I moved up and put my lips on hers. Jo parted them and put her tongue in my mouth searching for mine. She rotated her hips against my hand as our tongues darted into each other's mouths. I moved my lips away from hers and ran my tongue down the middle of her body. As I got closer to her abdomen, I looked up and said, "Let me make you wet," well knowing she already was.

"Uh-huh," she said barely audible.

I placed myself between her legs and spread her lips open with my fingers. I touched her with my tongue and she shivered uncontrollably for a second. I started to suck and move my lips up and down. She let out a loud groan and her hips began to move faster.

She reached for me and pulled me on top of her. I raised my hips, and she took hold of me and stroked me, then guided me to her wet groin. I just barely entered her and held there for a moment. She grabbed my hips and pulled me the rest of the way into her. I immediately became dizzy with passion, the feelings racing from my head to my toes. My mind could not hold thoughts any longer. I became totally consumed with Jo and her very being. It was so intense all I could do was to press myself even further into her. I started to move my hips slowly up and down and Jo moved with me. I wanted to make this feeling last as long as I could. I put my lips against hers and kept the slow rhythm going. Suddenly I heard someone walk through the barn door.

"You up there, Jo?"

Jo whispered, "It's one of the hands."

She sat up slightly, "Yeah, Frank, I'm up here. I'll be down in a minute. What do you need?"

"Should we walk the Bartons' horse?"

"Yes, take care of it for me, please."

I heard him leave, "Whew, that was close."

"Don't worry," Jo said with half-closed eyes.

She lay back down, then began to pull and push on my hips faster to get the rhythm back. I took hold of her buttocks and rolled her over on top of me. She sat up and her shirt hung loosely over her breasts, just barely exposing them. I reached up and cupped them in my hands as she moved up and down. I was on the verge of cuming and she moved even faster. I tried to slow her down to make it last longer but she kept moving on me. My body stiffened up and I couldn't hold back any longer.

"Oh, you're so hard," she said as I let go and jerked with every spasm. She moved faster and harder against my groin and I could feel her begin to cum. She threw her head back and pressed herself hard against my erection and let out a loud moan. She stayed stiff for a moment on top of me, then we both relaxed at the same time. She bent down and laid her head alongside mine, letting her hair fall across my face.

"God, that was the best yet," she whispered, breathing heavy.

"I know. We both did it at the same time."

"Yes," she breathed. We kept that position for a while, then she said, "We better get dressed before anyone else wanders in here."

I agreed and we both sat up. I picked up our clothes and handed Jo's to her. I stood up and as I put my pants on Jo grabbed me and wiggled it. "That's not a good idea if you want to get out of here," I said with a smile.

"Okay, okay, we better not fool around anymore," she playfully growled.

As we finished dressing I said, "So this is how you feed horses, huh?"

She laughed and said, "Well, not exactly."

"Anytime you want to feed horses you give me a call and I'll be right over, ya hear?"

"You promise?" she asked.

"You bet."

Our clothes were full of hay, "Wait, we better brush off before we go outside," I said. We did and got dressed.

I had a light, easy feeling as we climbed down the ladder. We walked outside and I squinted against the bright sunlight.

"Come over to the corral with me," Jo said, as we headed in that direction.

I followed her with weak knees. I was hoping none of the ranch hands could guess what we had been doing in the loft. I wouldn't want word of that to get to her father. Somehow I felt like it was written all over my face.

When we got to the corral, Jo sat on the fence and motioned for me to sit alongside her. She pointed to a horse in the corral, "That one belongs to a wealthy family in Temecula. That's where my father went to see about boarding some more horses. He should be back in a couple of hours."

"He does a lot of business here, huh?"

"We keep pretty busy."

We sat on the fence for a few minutes watching the hands working the horses in the corral. It felt great to relax and feel the warm, gentle breeze from the mountain slopes blow across my body. "Would you like to go in the house for a while and get something cold to drink?" Jo asked.

"That sounds good."

I jumped off the fence and almost lost my Stetson. I readjusted it and reached up to help Jo down. She pushed away my hand and said, "I think I can get down myself. Thanks anyway, that was a gallant gesture."

I was a little embarrassed as we walked toward the house. Jo was a woman in every sense of the word, but could definitely take care of herself.

We reached the house and I stood close behind her, taking in her scent as she opened the door. We stepped inside and I was always amazed at the furnishings. Over against one wall was a gun cabinet with at least a hundred assorted pistols and rifles, from very old collectors' guns to new, modern ones. Under the cabinet on the floor was a bear rug. There were also two deer heads and a cougar head mounted on the wall. I wasn't sure what western furniture looked like but this had to be western. This was the first time I'd ever been inside the house when Jo's father wasn't somewhere on the ranch.

"Have a seat and I'll get us a couple of sodas," she said as she went to the refrigerator.

I walked to the sofa and sat down looking around. She came back with two sodas, handed one to me, then sat down next to me. "Let's take this off," she said as she reached up, took my hat and expertly threw it on a chair across from us.

"Did your father shoot all these animals?"

"Yes, but he hasn't hunted in a long time. He said the taste of sport hunting has grown bitter for him."

"Has he hunted since your mom passed away?"

She looked at the animal heads, then at the guns, and remained silent. By doing so she answered the question.

"You have a nice house. This is the first time I've really had a chance to sit and relax."

"Thanks," she said as she set her drink down, got up and sat on my lap. Her warm body felt good. "Ron, I want you to promise me something."

"What?"

"When you go to New York and you find you want to be with this girl, you let me know right away."

"Jo, I'm just going to meet her, that's all."

"Or if you sleep with her you have to tell me."

"Just 'cause I'm going to meet someone doesn't mean I'm going to sleep with them. Do you jump into bed with every man you meet?"

"No. But men don't know what they're doing."

"Ah, and women do? Come on, gimme a break. You act like I have no control over my emotions. Did I jump into bed with you right away?"

"Uh . . . no."

"I went out with you about four months before we slept together, right?" I asked.

She sighed, almost in disgust, "Believe me, I know. I didn't think we were ever going to do it. I was starting to think there was something wrong with you, or me. Just the same, sometimes men don't have control over their emotions."

"I thought you had more faith in me than that."

"Just be careful. Women can be real sneaky."

I fidgeted in my seat. "I like sex. I'm a normal, healthy male but that doesn't mean I don't have any control. I've planned to take this ride as long as I can remember. It just happened that I met a girl on the Internet who lives where I wanted to ride to and I would like to meet her, that's all."

"Just tell me if you find out otherwise. Don't make me sit here waiting, not knowing."

"Whatever you say. I'll let you know. Are you happy now?"

"Not really. Just be careful."

"I will."

Jo put her lips on mine and gave me a soft, warm kiss, "I feel like taking a shower," she said, "would you like to join me?"

"What about your dad?"

"We have enough time before he gets back. He should be gone at least another hour. Besides, I'm a grown woman and it's my business what I do."

"Uh-huh, right," I said.

She ignored that comment, took my hand and we went upstairs to her bedroom. I'd never seen her room before. I expected to see non-feminine things but I was surprised by the overall pink decor. Her bed was neatly made with a pink comforter that had white-laced edges. The drapes matched her bedcover and had white lace around them, too. She had stuffed animals on her bed and dresser and there were pictures of horses hanging on the walls. There was also a poster of a cowgirl whom I didn't recognize. She looked like she might be someone famous but I didn't ask.

I sat on the bed and she took a towel and a washcloth out of the closet and handed them to me. She had her own bathroom adjacent to the bedroom. "Do you want to go first?" she asked.

"Okay."

I walked into the bathroom and she followed, "Everything you need is here. There's shampoo and soap."

It'd been over two years since I'd been in a regular shower. The one at John's station was a survival setup. Jo's smelled like perfume, like a woman. And it was nice and clean.

She walked out and left the door open. I undressed, stepped into the shower and slid the door closed. I turned on the water and let it run over me. It felt soothing and refreshing.

"Everything all right in there?" she asked over the noise of the water.

"Yes, just fine." Then the shower door slid open and Jo was standing there nude. I couldn't keep my eyes from looking at her breasts then trailing down to the light blonde patch of hair between her legs. That "feeling" started to stir in me again and my breathing quickened.

"Well, there's a naked man in my shower. Move over, we have to conserve water here," she said with a grin.

I stepped aside so she could stand under the water flow. She put her head under the nozzle and as her hair got wet, it clung to her breasts and her back. She slowly turned around full circle letting the water run down the front of her body, then the back. Her wet skin glistened in the dim light. She stepped aside and motioned for me to get under the water, "Now you get wet."

I did as she asked and she took the bar of soap in her hands. I looked down at myself and could see I was throbbing. She lathered up her hands, then rubbed them across my shoulders and chest. I closed my eyes and put my head back. She slowly rubbed my chest and stomach with her soapy hands. She picked up the soap again and lathered her hands some more, then went to my lower stomach, "Oh, looky. What do we have here?" she said as she grabbed my hard-on.

Whenever she touched me like that, it felt like every nerve in my body was going to scream. I reached out and took hold of one of her breasts as she teasingly stroked me with both hands.

"You like that?" she asked. I couldn't speak, I just nodded my head. "Hmm . . . I bet that feels real good." All I could do was moan with sheer pleasure. She picked up the soap and holding it out to me, said, "Now you wash me."

It took a second for me to regain my composure. I took the soap and lathered my hands. She closed her eyes and waited for me to touch her. I gazed at her nude body, wet and tanned. I placed my hands on her shoulders and started to soap her up. She sighed softly. I guided my hands to her firm, well-developed breasts. I traced her nipples with my fingers, then firmly grabbed hold of them and she giggled for a second. I took her nipples between my fingertips and manipulated them. She chuckled some more. I soaped up my hands again and moved out of the way so the clear, sparkling water would hit her. The soapsuds ran down the front of her body in well-developed lines, over the top of her breasts, then dripped from her nipples in a steady stream. A large line of water also funneled between her breasts and down the center of her body to the hair between her legs, then finally running down the inside of her thighs. Watching the water dance over her body excited me tremendously.

I took my soapy hands and put them on her waist, then lightly caressed her lower stomach. I then moved my hands back to her hips. She drew her hands across her body to soap them up and grabbed me. I was acutely sensitive now and when she touched me I jerked back a couple of times. I slid my hands toward the center of her body, between her legs. She squeezed me a little harder and gasped as I rubbed my hand back and forth on her.

"I don't think I can stand any more of this," I said, panting heavily.

"We can take care of that," she said as she turned around, bent over and grabbed the faucet offering her vagina to me.

She arched her hips in the air. I took hold of myself and rubbed the head of it up and down on her clit. I paused a second at her opening, then guided it in. I started to pump fast holding onto her hips. The water ran between our bodies as my groin slapped against her buttocks with each hard thrust I made, making us even more slippery than usual, if that was possible. The feeling was almost there. I grabbed onto the top of the shower door and pumped as hard as I could. I watched the water splash on Jo's back and along the sides of her breasts as I released myself in erratic spasms. I had trouble keeping my balance on the wet shower floor as every muscle in my body tightened. I threw my head back, then slowly relaxed.

We held that position for a moment, then Jo started pushing against me. I knew she wanted to finish, so I moved with her. I reached down around her hips between her legs. As I pumped I stroked her clit with my finger and she responded by arching her hips a little higher.

"Oohh . . . that's just right," she moaned.

She moved against me, her back muscles tightening as she grabbed the faucet. I knew she was cuming so I thrusted harder and she groaned louder. She held firm on my hard-on for a moment, contracted a few times, then moaned loudly as she came. Her head fell limp for a second, then she stood up, faced me and put her arms around my neck. I put my arms around her waist and we stood there letting the water run over our bodies.

"This feels real good, but if we stay in here any longer, our skin's going to shrivel up like prunes," I said.

Jo agreed, so we rinsed off and got out. I picked up a towel and handed it to her, "Your father's going to be home soon. Don't you think we should hurry?"

"Ron, stop worrying about my father. I'm a grown woman, I can do what I want."

"Whatever you say. I still think we should hurry up." I didn't think being caught in the shower with Jo would go over too well with him.

"You worry too much. Just relax and take it easy. We have plenty of time."

I finished drying off and picked up my clothes, "I wish I had clean clothes to put on. Oh well, you can't have it all, I guess."

"No, you can't," Jo said as she wrapped the towel around her hair and came into the bedroom naked.

I watched her as she walked to the dresser and rummaged through her drawer for undergarments. I walked over to the window just as her dad drove up to the front of the house, "Jo, your father's home."

"Oh, really," she said with a surprised look.

"Yep. He just pulled up." She got a funny look on her face and started to move faster, hopping around the room trying not to fall as she tugged on her jeans. *I could say something smart right now,* I thought, *but I'll keep my mouth shut.* I knew she was nervous and I didn't want to make her more uncomfortable than she already was.

Just as she finished dressing we heard the downstairs door open.

"Jo! Are you here?"

Her eyes widened, "Yes, Dad, I'm in my room."

I heard his footsteps walking slowly up the stairs. He had to know I was here 'cause my motorcycle was parked out front. He probably figured we were in bed and picked up a gun with each hand as he walked past the gun cabinet to shoot me full of holes. *It's been a nice life so far,* I thought, *too bad it has to end right now. Wait! Maybe if I jump out the window. Too late, he was standing in the doorway.* I cautiously looked at his right hand, no gun. Then his left, no gun. *Whew,* I thought, *I'm safe for the moment.*

He looked at me, then my wet hair. He looked at Jo with the towel around her head. The room was full of shower steam from being in there so long. He had to know we just got out.

Jo quickly said, "Ron helped me around here so I let him take a shower, then I took one." I'm glad she worded it the way she did. She was quick on her feet and probably saved my life.

He stood there like a rock, not saying anything. "How did things go in Temecula?" she asked quickly.

He stood silent for what seemed an eternity, then answered, "It went okay. I have to talk to you about it." He turned and walked down the stairs.

I looked at Jo and she looked at me. We didn't speak for a moment, then I said, "He wants to talk to you and I think I better get going."

"Good idea. I've got to see what happened in Temecula and I should get back to work."

I wasn't sure if he was waiting downstairs or if he went outside. In my mind I pictured him sitting on the sofa with a rifle in one hand, a pistol in the other and a large knife between his teeth, waiting for me. I thought about exiting through the window again but just my luck I'd break my leg in the fall.

I had to be a man about this so I beat Jo to the bedroom door making sure I was the first one down the stairs so that if anyone got shot it would just be me. I didn't want her to get caught between her dad and me in case he decided to get nuts.

I gritted my teeth and slowly took the steps one by one. As I got further down the staircase, the living room came into view. Why did it have to be so damn big? When I got to the bottom I quickly glanced around, no dad. I walked to the middle and looked around again and couldn't see him anywhere. *Wow, another reprieve. Must be my lucky day.*

I walked past my hat still sitting on the chair where Jo had thrown it. "I better leave this here," I said as I walked by it. "I won't be able to wear it on my motorcycle."

"It'll be safe here. I'll put it away for you so you can wear it next time you come by."

"Sounds good. By the way, where'd your dad go?" I asked nonchalantly.

"He must be outside. I'll walk you to your bike."

We went outside and I saw him by the corral talking to some ranch hands. Jo walked me to my bike. "Did you have fun today?"

she asked as I turned to face her.

"It was great. I wouldn't mind riding that horse again. That was soothing on the trail. Almost like riding my cycle out on the open road. The whole afternoon was great."

She blushed a little. "We'll go out again soon, but right now I have to get going." She kissed me and turned to walk away. "Will I see you Friday?" she said over her shoulder.

"Of course you will. Don't we always get together on Fridays?"

"Oh, just don't get lost on that machine again," she said over her shoulder.

I got on my bike and sat there a minute. I ran my hands across my chest and stomach feeling for any gunshot holes or knife wounds. There were none. I couldn't believe I got out alive. I fired up my machine, trying to be quiet so as not to draw any attention to myself. I just wanted to be inconspicuous. I hit the main road and it was already late afternoon. I got up to highway speed and the wind felt cool on my damp hair. As I rode, my thoughts turned back to the horse ride, the hayloft and the shower. I smiled, hit the throttle a little harder and roared along the winding mountain road.

I rolled onto the driveway and could see the station was locked up and John was gone for the night. I opened the garage door and walked my bike inside. It was almost dusk so I turned on the light to the back room where the shower and computer were. I sat down at my makeshift desk and looked at the darkened screen. I hadn't turned it on in three days now. I'm sure Gloria had written since Sunday. Should I turn on the computer or not? I dragged my fingers over the keys. I wanted to know, yet I didn't. I would be leaving on my road trip in about two weeks and I knew I would meet her when I got to New York. I still wanted to surprise her so I had to keep it a secret. I was getting nervous about the whole thing. What started out as a simple dream has turned into a lot of mental turmoil. I was on my way to becoming a basket case.

I fingered the switch on the computer then pushed it to the on position. *To hell with it, I might as well look and see.* The little white envelope appeared in the lower right hand screen as I thought it would. I opened the mail segment and there were two letters and a photograph waiting.

"She sent me a picture," I said out loud. Everyone was sending e-mail photos over the Internet lately. It was the big craze. I thought about getting a photo of myself scanned but I hadn't gotten around to it yet.

Now I was getting excited. Should I read the mail first or should I open up the photo? The suspense was killing me. I dragged the arrow down to the photo and clicked. It started to appear from the top down. It took a few seconds as her picture filled the screen. First her hair came into view, then her face. I couldn't believe what I was seeing. She was absolutely beautiful. The photo stopped at her waist. She was definitely in good shape. She had short, light brown hair and green, innocent, captivating eyes. She could easily be a cover girl or model. Her features were perfect. I sat there staring at the image on the screen.

"This is not what I need to be seeing right now. This is the last thing I need," I said.

I couldn't get over her natural beauty. I was awe-struck, to say the least. Her eyes were so intense they seemed to be staring a hole right through me. I sat there at least five minutes just looking at the picture, then I heard Paul's bike pull up in front. He must have seen the light on. I shut the monitor off and went to open the door.

"Hi, Paul, what's up?"

"Was driving by and saw someone was here, so I figured I'd stop by. Were you busy?"

"No. Just playing with my computer." I wasn't sure if I should tell him about the picture, let alone show him. I surely didn't want Jo to find out about this. Paul let one thing slip already and I wasn't sure if he could keep a secret. But if I try to keep this to myself I was sure I'd explode. "Come in, I want to show you something. But you have to promise not to say anything about it."

"I won't," he said, following close behind me.

"You already told Diane about my going to New York and she told Jo. You weren't supposed to say anything about that."

"That was a mistake. I won't tell her anything more."

I walked to the back room with Paul hot on my heels. I placed my finger over the monitor button. "You've got to promise that what I'm about to show you will not leave this room."

"I promise. So show me already." I flicked the button and the monitor came on. Paul stared at it, "That's not that girl in New York, is it?"

"That's Gloria."

"Oh, shit. You better not go visit her. That girl will steal your heart for sure."

"Let's not start that stuff again. Just 'cause she's beautiful still doesn't mean anything."

"You better open your eyes, pal, that girl's a knockout. And that's just what she might do to you." I had to admit he was right. She was a real looker. Paul slowly let out a deep breath, "Remember, you're going to be a long way from here. And by the time you get there, you're going to be tired and beat. She will look awfully good when you're in that frame of mind."

"I'll be okay, you gotta have a little faith in me. You've known me long enough to know I'm not flighty. It took a long time before Jo and I got together. That's the way I am. I don't just jump into things."

He gazed at the picture, "Man, you're in trouble. I wouldn't want to be in your shoes."

"You better not tell anyone about this. I don't want to cause any trouble that doesn't need to be caused."

"I won't say a word."

I turned off the screen and changed the subject, "I pick up my gas tanks Friday and I have to drop them off to get painted. I get my new high-rise handle bars next week and I should have it all together by next weekend."

"Your bike's gonna look real good with the new tanks and the handlebars. You'll be leaving soon after that, right?"

"Uh-huh, in about a week. I should be gone two, maybe three weeks. A little longer depending on the route I take. I want to follow old Route 66 as much as possible. It has a lot of detours so it's hard to be accurate about the amount of time. This is a once-in-a-life-time thing so I'm not concerned about how long it will take."

"All I can say is be careful and make sure you come back in one piece. I've sort of grown attached to you. Even though I think you're stupid about some things." I'd grown fond of Paul too, and I understood how he felt. I would feel real bad if something happened to him. "Well, I better get home and get to bed," he said, as he got up and walked to the door.

I followed him out to his bike, "Not a word to anyone, especially not Diane, you hear?"

"Don't worry, my lips are sealed."

I watched as he started his cycle and rode away. I walked back into the garage and turned on the monitor again. I opened up the other mail. The first one was just the usual thing about not hearing from me. The second one was about the picture:

Hi, Ron, I had this picture scanned and I thought I would send it to you. I hope you like it. I've never done anything like this before but since everyone else is doing it, I thought it would be okay. I hope you're all right. I haven't heard from you in three days and I worry that maybe you got into an accident or something. Maybe I shouldn't do that but I've really grown accustomed to writing to you over the past few months. You're the only one I write to so I would miss it if you stopped. I don't have many friends here and it's hard for me to make new ones, so I really treasure the friendship we have. I better go now. I hope to hear from you soon.

Bye, Gloria

I didn't know what to write so I thought I would wait until later to respond. I shut down the computer, walked outside and sat by my van. The sun had already set and the stars were coming out bright and numerous. My mind was racing a thousand miles a minute. Now I was beginning to worry about meeting Gloria. Why couldn't I just make a decision about Jo and stick with it? It seemed a simple thing to do. I guess it's not like ordering dinner. This had emotional feelings involved with it. I didn't know if a person could make an intelligent decision about love.

I stared into the night sky. It was hard to imagine the stars were so very far away. I wondered if there was another planet racing around one of those suns with a person on it just like me. A person going through the same stuff I was. Of all the countless trillions of stars in the heavens there had to be others with intelligent life. They were probably so far advanced that they didn't have these problems. Or did they? I guess you can be technologically advanced and still have emotional problems.

"So, is there any hope for us?" I said as I got up and went back inside.

I better write back to Gloria and let her know I'm all right. I flipped on the computer and, tapping onto the keyboard, started my message:

Hi, Gloria, I'm all right. Thanks for your concern. I've been busy and I haven't been able to write back sooner. It's summer and we get a lot of seasonal repair work from tourists and travelers going to and from the coast. I got your picture and you are a very beautiful lady, if you don't mind my saying. I was thinking about getting my picture scanned and if I do, I'll send it to you. I hope everything is going good. I know you were having some problems and I hope they're better now. If you want to talk about them, please don't hesitate, I'm a good listener. I'll be leaving for my trip up the coast soon and I won't be on-line for a while. Well, it's late and I better get to bed. Thanks for the picture and I'll be talking to you soon.

Bye, Ron

I sent the e-mail and sat back in the chair looking at the screen. I started thinking about all the major changes I'd made in the past couple of years. It's funny how you can never foresee where you'll wind up. I had some loose plans and they seemed to be working out except for a couple of things. Would I want it any different if I had the choice to change it? I really couldn't answer that. If it were different that wouldn't automatically mean it would be better.

I should get to bed. It's been a long day. I thought about looking at the picture of Gloria one more time but I shut down the computer and locked up the garage. I stood by my van and looked to the heavens again. I think I'm going to have trouble sleeping tonight.

I climbed into my van and laid down staring through the window at the stars. I tossed and turned for a couple of hours before I fell into an uneasy sleep.

Chapter Six

Damn, it's already Friday again, I thought, *the weeks seem to be zipping by. They say the older a person gets the faster time flies. I'm not sure if that's true, 'cause I remember when I was a little boy in school, summer vacation seemed to be over as fast as it started. And the weekends always came and went in the wink of an eye. I think people just forget the way things used to be.*

The hot sun beat down and the scorching wind blew across my face as I pumped gas for a customer. I glanced at the station clock on the wall. Eleven a.m. I had to pick up my gas tanks from the painter so I could install them and my new handlebars this weekend. Everything was coming together for the trip. I bought a bigger set of saddlebags to hold all my stuff for this long ride. As far as I could tell, I was doing everything right to make this a comfortable and safe trip. I felt good about the bike but I had to see how it handled with the new parts. I knew one thing for sure, it was going to look real cool.

I went inside, made change for the customer and he drove off. John didn't have any of the new self-serve gas station gadgets. We pumped gas the old-fashioned way and I got to meet a lot of people because of it.

I sat down on the three-legged stool and as usual it was not level. I was excited about getting the things for the bike and about getting close to the time to leave. I hadn't been sleeping too well lately. I had a lot of other feelings running through my soul but I was having trouble nailing them down. It was like they were all mashed together and I couldn't sort them out. I thought that if I could just separate them somehow, then I could get a handle on them. But every time I tried to, it almost made me feel dizzy. How do people deal with this kind of thing? I hated feeling this way but there was nothing I could do about it. If I didn't go on this trip, I wouldn't be truc to myself and if I do go, I feel like I'm doing something wrong. Damned if I do and damned if I don't.

John came out of his office, "Hot enough for you, Ron?"

I looked out the window, "Not as hot as it's going to get." He looked at me and didn't say anything. I think he knew what I meant. He paced back and forth a couple of times. "Is there something bothering you, John?"

He stopped for a minute, then turned and looked at me, "Uh, no. There's nothin' wrong." He had something on his mind and he wasn't telling me. I'd known him a couple of years now and I could tell he wanted to say something but I knew better than to push it. Another car drove up to the pumps and I got up to go outside. John stepped in front of me and said, "I'll take care of him. You sit and rest a bit."

I sat back down and watched him as he limped out to the car. It looked like he was moving a bit slower than usual. I wondered if something was wrong. I'd grown real attached to him since I'd been here. I would hate to see anything happen to him. It would break my heart.

He came back in and leaned against the counter, "I've been thinking, Ron, if something should happen to me . . .well, I wanted to ask you if you'd be willing to take care of the station for me?"

My eyes widened, "If what should happen to you? What's going to happen?"

He gave me a long, hard stare. "I'm gettin' on in years. I'm going to be sixty-six soon and I'm starting to feel it. I don't have any relatives or anyone close to me," he paused, "except you."

I knew what this station meant to him. This was his whole life. I didn't believe in getting something for nothing but if anything did happen to him there would be no one but me to run things.

John shuffled his weight, "I been working this station for forty years. I came to work here when Bill and Nona owned it back in the fifties. I was a young man then. It was just before I got married. They sold it to me in the sixties and moved back east 'cause they couldn't handle the heat here." He paused for a moment reminiscing about the old days, "And 'sides, the cars are gettin' too complicated to work on and I can't lean over the fenders like I used to." He walked over, pulled up his squeaky rocking chair and sat down. I watched his face as he gazed out the window. I hadn't noticed but he did appear to be a little thinner and was a bit more tired looking.

I glanced around the room. I wasn't sure if I was ready to take on a job like running the station. Up till now, the only things I had to worry about were my van, my bike and me, and that gave me a real sense of freedom. But was that freedom real or imagined? I wasn't sure. Did the abundance of things take away a person's freedom or was freedom in the mind? When I left Chicago, I thought the lighter I traveled the more freedom I would have. But I wasn't so sure about that now.

John's voice broke my train of thought, "So, Ron, you haven't answered my question."

"To take care of the station? Uh, yeah, I can do that." I didn't know for sure if I wanted to settle down in Borrego Springs but I could stay a little longer till I made up my mind. I looked at John's face again and he had a look of relief about him. I think it was real hard for him to ask for help. He was the kind of man who was extremely self-sufficient.

"Thanks. It's good to know I have someone to depend on."

"No problem. I'll probably be here for a while. I have no plans to move on right now."

I had no idea how things would turn out between Billy Jo and me. I'm sure John knew I was having a hard time with that situation. And I had mixed feelings about taking on responsibility again. Not that I didn't know how, since I'd already had a successful business of my own. I think I was scared to be tied down again. Whatever the reason, it made me uncomfortable in some ways, and good in others.

He turned in his chair, a bit perkier, "You go on and have a good time on your trip. When you get back, we'll talk about it."

Funny how John was sure I'd be back, "Sounds good to me."

John got up and walked toward the garage, "I'll finish up this brake job and then you can go pick up your tanks. I know you're itching to see 'em."

As I waited for John to finish so I could leave, I thought about my future. *If I did move on, where would I go and what would I do? Good question and I had no answer.*

I took care of a few more customers and John finished up. I told him I'd be back in a little while and fired up my van, which I hardly drove any more, and went to the painter's to get my tanks.

I was back at John's in about an hour and drove into the driveway and parked in my usual spot. As I was unloading the tanks, John came out and said, "Billy Jo called and said she'd be at Jay's at about seven-thirty tonight and that she'd see you there." He took one of the tanks from me and looked it over. "He did a mighty fine job."

"They came out real good," I replied. "They'll look just right on the bike."

"I'm sure they will," John said. "I'll be leaving in a little while so don't forget to lock up tight." He turned to walk away and stopped, "Oh yeah, I almost forgot, Paul called and said he'd stop by in a little bit."

"I'll be here. I'm not leaving any time soon."

He went into the station, set the tank down, then continued into his office to lock things up for the day. I brought my tanks into the back and set them on the bench. I took a couple of steps back, eyeing them. The painter did an excellent job. I wanted to take my old one off and begin installing the new ones right now, but if I did, it would take the better part of the evening and I didn't want to keep Jo waiting. I didn't think she would understand so I'd wait till tomorrow like I planned even though it took everything I had to keep from starting on them. I covered 'em up with towels so they wouldn't get scratched and went to the front of the garage.

I stood in the doorway and leaned against the doorjamb looking at the mountain range off in the distance. The sun was starting to get low in the sky and would be setting behind the mountains in a couple of hours. In the morning, it would hit them in such a way as to expose all the hidden crevices and make everything bright and clear. In the late afternoon, the sun was at such an angle so that there were shadows and dark spots, giving them an eerie look. When the sun was just above the mountain range, you had to look directly into the rays and all you could see was a gray outline of the mountains, all detail was gone. There were days in my life that would pass that way; they started out clear in the morning and were gray and muddled by nightfall.

John came out of the office and I stepped aside to let him through the doorway, "I'll see you tomorrow. Have a good night and stay safe on your motorcycle."

"Okay, John, see ya."

I watched as he walked to his old Chevy pick-up truck. That truck was almost as old as I was. The intense sun had long ago burned the paint off the body. He got in and pumped the gas pedal a couple of times and turned the ignition key. The motor sprang to life with a smooth, low rumble. It was old and ugly but ran better than brand new. It was a perfect example of the type of guy he was; it had quality about it. He slowly rolled out of the station and waved as he hit the road. I waved back and watched as his truck disappeared around a curve.

I stood there a few minutes staring at the empty road. Everything got real quiet for a moment and I was acutely aware of the peacefulness of my surroundings. For an instant, I felt completely at ease, as though no matter what happened, it would be all right. I went into the station and repositioned the stool and sat down. One of the few times I got it level, "This must be my day," I said under my breath.

I took care of a couple of gas customers and was about to close when Paul drove up. He parked in front of the door, revved up his engine a couple of times and shut it off. I got up from the stool and walked to the door, "Hey Paul, what's up?"

"Not a lot. How ya doing?"

"Pretty good. I got my tanks today. You got to see 'em." We went to the back room and I took the towels off them.

"Yeah, they're awesome. When you going to put them on?"

"I want to do it right now but Jo's going to be at Jay's at seven-thirty and I don't want to make her wait. I'll probably do it tomorrow."

"Good idea. It's not the smartest thing to keep her waiting again. If I'm even a little late, Diane has a fit."

I sat down and Paul walked over to my bike, "You sure got one nice machine here." He grabbed the handle bar and swung his leg over the seat and sat down. He took the other grip in his other hand and assumed a position like he was riding, then said, "Man, I'm real jealous. I want to go with you, but I need my job and I can't afford to get fired. It's the only one I've had since I got out of the corps and jobs are hard to find. I envy you, I wish I had the guts to chuck the job and ride. But I know I'd kick myself in the ass if I did."

Paul worked for a private road resurfacing company and I knew his job was important to him. He looked at me with a serious face and said, "I waited a whole year after I got out of the military to get this job. I lived off my separation pay and applied every couple of weeks to let them know I was serious. Right now we've contracted a road job with the state. We're short-handed and we have a deadline to meet. I have full benefits and they take care of me."

I didn't say anything. I just watched him sit on my bike. I felt bad that he couldn't go, almost guilty.

"You're a free spirit," he said, in a faraway voice. "I wish I could just pack up and leave like you did in Chicago."

"Whoa, I had reason to leave. It's not like it was on a whim. You have no reason to just split."

He thought a second, then replied, "I guess you're right, but I still envy you. It must take a lot of guts to do what you did and what you're about to do."

"I wouldn't call it guts. I'm paying a big emotional price for this. Maybe I hide it well but it's still there. I don't know if I'm searching for something, or just trying to satisfy some inner desire. I guess I'll find out when I get to that place in life. If I ever do."

"When I think about it, I did the same thing," he reminisced, "I joined the Marine Corps 'cause I needed a change. I considered making a career out of it but after twelve years I knew that it wasn't right for me. So I came back to Borrego Springs. I'm happy with Diane but the rest of it's gettin' old again. Why the hell do people have to go through this unsettled state of mind anyway?"

"Good question, if you ever get the answer to that, you're gonna make a lot of bucks."

He sat on the bike and stared straight at the wall, "I still would like to go cross-country."

"I'd like you to ride along, but the price would be too high for you right now, your job, and you would really get a lot of friction from Diane."

"Yeah, now's not the time for me. Damn, you better have a good time and keep me in mind when you're sailing in the wind, you bum."

We sat silent for a few minutes listening to the desert wind blow hard and steady across the sand. I got up and covered my tanks again and Paul stood up, "One day, I'm gonna get a new bike and maybe all four of us can go for a long trip. Maybe north to Oregon or further."

"That sounds like a plan to me. The last thing I would do is turn down a good ride," I replied. I faced Paul. "I want to tell you something but keep it to yourself."

He nodded, "Sure, what's up?"

"John's gettin' old and today he asked me if I would take care of his station if anything should happen to him."

"Is he all right?"

"As far as I know he is. I think he's starting to feel the years and he just wants to make sure his station doesn't fall into the hands of the state and wind up wasting away. I hope that's all it is."

"Hey, that means you'll have to stay," he said with a wide grin.

"Yeah, it looks that way. Just keep it to yourself. I'm still not sure exactly what he plans to do."

"Sure, no words outta my mouth." We both walked to the front door and Paul sat on his bike, "So, you're gonna be a permanent resident of Borrego Springs?"

"I'm not sure how permanent just yet. There's still some things up in the air and one of 'em is my mind."

He flipped on his ignition switch and placed his foot on the kick-starter, "I'll see you later at Jay's."

"Yep. I'm gonna lock up here and take a shower. I'll meet you there 'bout seven-thirty."

He stepped down on the kick-starter and pushed. It sputtered once. He hiked up his leg again and pushed. It sputtered and roared to life. "See you later," he said, as he rolled away.

I turned and stepped back inside. I could hear Paul go through his gears as he faded away in the distance till I couldn't hear him any longer. I locked the front door and went toward the back to take a shower. I walked past John's toolbox and stopped. I looked at it for a minute then went over to it. It was an old box but was still in almost brand new condition. I slid open one of the drawers and gazed at his wrenches. They were all lined up in order and clean as a whistle. I picked one up and held it in my hand. It didn't feel like an ordinary wrench. It was almost as though it had John's energy attached to it. I ran my fingers across it, wondering how many cars it had repaired. John was a major fixture in this town and it wouldn't be the same without him. He was just as much a part of this town as his energy was a part of this wrench in my hand.

I carefully put it back in exactly the same spot and slowly closed the drawer. I stood in the middle of the garage and turned a complete circle. Everything was old but in excellent shape, probably a combination of John's touch and the dry desert air. I felt strange at the thought of taking over something another person had built up through the years. It was a mighty big pair of shoes to fill and I didn't think I could even come close. I wanted to think that John was the kind of person who would be around forever. But, too many times I'd seen people leave this earth to be that naive.

I better get in the shower and get to Jay's. I passed the computer and stopped. I hadn't checked yet today to see if Goria had written. Should I look? I wouldn't get another chance till tomorrow 'cause we'd probably sleep in the desert tonight. I had this overwhelming urge to check. No, I thought, I'll wait till later. I turned, took a couple of steps toward the shower and stopped.

"Damn it," I said as I turned, went back to it and sat down. "I'll just check for any new mail I have. I won't send any back now," I vowed.

I flipped on the switch and waited for the on-line program to start. I tapped my fingers randomly on the keys while the screen flicked rapidly by. "Why do I have to do this?" I asked myself.

Before I could think of an answer, the on-line program appeared. I went into the mail section looking for the envelope to signal I had mail. There it was. I opened up the mail program and there was a letter waiting. I opened it and started to read:

Hi, Ron, I've decided to make some major changes in my living arrangements. I can't go into detail just yet but they're going to be big. I know you're going up the coast and will be off-line a while. I will be off-line for a while, too, when I make this change. It won't be for another month or so. But when I get resettled, I should have the same e-mail address. I wish I could tell you more but not just yet. Please have patience with me. I know I haven't said much about myself personally but in time I will. Right now things are emotionally hard for me so please bear with me. I have to go now, have a nice day and I'll talk to you soon.

Bye, Gloria

I wondered what kind of living situation she had. This was getting more mysterious by the day. I shut down the computer. *I'll write back later; it was seven o'clock and I'd better get moving.* I walked to my tanks and couldn't resist taking another look at them. I pulled off the towels and reached out to touch 'em. It was hard to believe that the time was getting near for me to leave. It still felt like a dream, like I was going to wake up in Chicago in the middle of a fierce winter snowstorm, not able to go anywhere. I couldn't deal with the winters. When they came, I felt like a prisoner in my own home. I used to sit and wait for spring to arrive, then dread the first cold snow. I guess I was just born in the wrong place. Well, that was no one's fault, it's just the way things happened.

I looked at the tanks, the garage light danced off the newly painted, bright red, glossy finish. Nope. This was not a dream. It was really happening and I better get outta here or I'll be late too.

I threw the towels back over them and made it all the way to the shower this time. I hurried up and washed, then wrapped the towel around me. I went outside to my van and dug through my T-shirts for a Harley one. I found my Friday go-to-town jeans and got dressed. I rushed through the station, turning out all the lights and pulled my bike outside. I locked the garage door and fired up the bike. I hopped on and cranked the throttle and sped off to Jay's. I made it there in record time.

It was a little past seven-thirty when I pulled up to the door. Paul's bike was out front and Jo's Jeep was parked down the street. I parked next to Paul's bike and got off. I adjusted my clothes and started toward the entrance. I could hear the music blaring and the place was jumping. I walked through the door and people were shooting pool and dancing. It was as though someone had given the place a jolt of electricity.

I took a few steps inside and saw Paul, Jo and Diane sitting at our favorite table. Paul and Diane had on their weekend Harley attire and Jo was dressed in faded, tight jeans and a loose plaid shirt tied at the waist. She wasn't caught up in the *"Harley"* look yet. I wasn't sure if she ever would. It didn't matter, whatever she wore she looked good in.

I glanced around the room and I caught Jerry, the goon, staring a hole right through me. He had his two goonies with him as usual and he looked like he was half drunk already. I broke eye contact with him hoping he would focus on someone else. But that was probably too good to be true. "It's going to be one of those nights," I told myself as I weaved my way through the crowd to their table.

Jo stood up as I pulled a chair out to sit down, "Well, you're on time," she said, then put her arms around me and kissed me. I hugged her back and we sat down. She looked at me, "How was your day?"

"The usual. I picked up my new gas tanks."

Paul interrupted, "They're awesome. It's gonna look like a different bike when he gets 'em on."

I nodded and looked back at Jo, "And how was your day?"

"It was busy. We got a new customer today. We're almost getting to the point where we might have to hire more help."

"Well, that's good."

She nodded her head. Diane was be-bopping to the music in her seat and Paul was looking around the room, "Man, it's moving tonight."

I quickly looked around, "Yep, I noticed that when I walked through the door."

I tried not to meet Jerry's glare as I could see through the corner of my eye I was still the object of his attention. I really wished I would have nailed him last week and got this damn thing over with once and for all. "I need something cold to drink. Anybody want anything while I'm up?" I asked. Diane wanted another beer and Paul and Jo were set.

"Are you going to want to order something to eat, Ron?" Jo asked, as I stood up.

"In a little bit. I just want to get a drink first and relax."

I walked over to the bar and the only open spot was a couple of stools away from where Jerry was sitting. As I stood waiting for the bartender, I overheard him say, "Biker punks think they're bad shit 'cause they ride motorcycles. They ain't nothin'."

He spoke loud enough to make sure I heard him. I just looked the other way, got the drinks and walked back to the table. "Jerry's in a good mood tonight," I said, as I sat down.

Jo touched my arm, "Why? What happened?"

"Just his everyday sarcastic self, is all."

"Don't pay any attention to him. Don't let him get you down or it will ruin your night," Jo said as she rubbed my arm, "He ain't worth it."

"Okay, I'll ignore him," I said, swallowing a big gulp of my drink.

Diane tapped the table, "So, guys, what are we gonna order? We better do it quick 'cause I'm starving."

"How 'bout pizza?" I suggested.

Everyone agreed, "Why don't we get two medium pizzas', half and half," Paul said, "and we'll each have a few pieces of all four different toppings."

"Sounds good to me," Jo said.

"I don't care how we do it, I just want to get some food. I worked all day and I gotta eat before I shrivel up and blow away," Diane quipped. I had to admit that girl had one healthy appetite. She was still slim and trim but as she gets older, she's gonna lose that girlish figure if she keeps eating the way she does. But it wasn't my job to bring it up. I learned the hard way, you don't talk weight with women.

Paul looked up, "Oh-oh. I think Jerry's headed this way."

I looked over in the direction of the bar and sure enough, he was making a beeline right for us. He looked like he was weaving slightly. I would prefer him to be stone, cold sober or sloppy drunk rather than in between. I think he was more dangerous that way.

He walked around the table, "Hey, Jo, you want to shoot a game of pool?"

"No, Jerry, I don't think so."

"Are you sure? I might even let you win."

"No. Not today."

"Aw, come on, just one game." He wasn't taking no for an answer and I was starting to get pissed. If he didn't leave soon, I wasn't sure what I was going to do.

Diane spoke up, "Look, Jerry, she doesn't want to play pool right now!"

"Well, all right. But if you wanna play later, let me know."

"I'll do that," Jo snapped.

He took a step back and almost lost his balance. He turned and walked back to the bar.

"Boy, that guy needs to be set straight," Paul snarled.

Diane picked up a napkin, "Let's order already. It's gonna take at least a half hour."

"She's right, so we better order now," Jo added.

Jo and Diane walked to the counter. As they walked away, I looked over at Jerry. His eyes were glued to Jo. He watched her all the way to the counter.

Paul looked at me, then at Jerry, "He's sure got it bad for Jo."

"Yes, he does, but it's not normal. The attraction he's got is the sick kind. 'Course what do you expect from a natural born sick'o." I looked at Paul. "I got a funny feeling it's not going to be a good night. The energy's high and everyone's moving too fast. It's not the easy, fun energy. It's a tense, nervous, edgy kind here tonight."

"Is there a full moon or something?" Paul asked.

"I don't know. But it sure feels like one," I answered.

Jo and Diane came back and sat down.

Paul looked over at the pool tables, "Hey! There's an empty table. Why don't I go get it and we'll shoot a game while we wait for the pizzas?"

"Maybe it'll make the time go a little faster," Diane said in a monotone voice.

Paul got up to get the table. We all picked up our drinks, went over and waited for Paul to bring the balls. I flipped a coin and Diane called heads. Heads it was.

"We get to break," Diane told Paul as he set the balls on the table.

Jo was in a kind of funk and I felt bad whenever she was not in a good mood. I hoped she wasn't worried about my trip, but I was sure that was the problem. I racked up the pool balls and Paul broke. I walked over to Jo and put my arm around her, "How you doing?"

"I'm just in a down mood. Doing a lot of thinking lately."

"About what?"

"My life and where I stand in it. You said some things a while ago that made me start thinking about my relationship with people."

I knew what she was talking about but I wasn't going to mention it. I would wait for her to bring it up, if she wanted to. "That's a hard thing to deal with, relationships. I've been wrestling with them since I left Chicago."

"People say there's pain in growing emotionally. Maybe that's what I'm feeling," Jo said as she twisted her pool stick in her hands.

"I know what you mean. I felt the pain for the past couple of years."

Paul missed his shot and Jo was up next. I glanced at the bar and saw Jerry walking our way, "Aw shit, here comes trouble again," I said as I set my pool stick down.

He walked up to the opposite end of the table and turned to Jo, "Hey, I thought you didn't feel like shooting pool, huh?"

"Listen, I'll do whatever I please. Right now, I feel like playing and I'll play pool with whomever I want. Do you understand that?"

"I think that sucks. I asked you first."

I started to walk toward him and Jo stepped in my way, "He's not worth it, Ron, just stay calm," she whispered to me.

"Why don't you mind your own business and take a walk before I lose my cool," I growled.

"Why don't you make me, big, bad biker punk."

I started to walk around Jo and she said, "Go sit down and mind your own business, Jerry! NOW!"

"Well, since you asked, I will."

I wanted to hit him right between the eyes but Jo kept a stance between us. He went back to the bar and Jo turned to me, "Don't you see he's just trying to provoke you? If you fight him, that's what he wants. He's got to prove something. God knows what, but he's got to prove it."

Diane interjected, "It must be that male thing. They always have to prove something."

I looked at Jo, "Well, whatever he's doing, it's starting to work 'cause I'm about ready to oblige him."

Paul waved his pool stick around the room, "Don't worry, if you have to fight him, this whole bar will back you."

"Well, that doesn't make fighting him any easier," I said.

Diane pointed to the pool table with her stick, "Let's play pool and forget about that overgrown moron."

It was Jo's turn to shoot. She missed an easy shot, "Oh well, I'll get it my next turn. It's your shot, Diane."

Diane took her shot and missed too, "Well Ron, go for it," she said.

I walked to the table. The anger was starting to build up in me to the point of rage. I bent over the table and lined up my stick with the cue ball. I brought my stick back and hit the cue ball with all my might. It hit the cushion on the other side of the table and shot across the room. My stick almost ripped a hole in the table felt.

"Damn," Paul said as he ran after it.

It narrowly missed hitting a guy in the head sitting on the other side of the room. He looked in my direction, "Hey, Roadside, this ain't no pistol range. Stop shooting them pool balls at us."

"Sorry 'bout that. I'll try to keep 'em on the table."

He smiled and waved. He was a regular customer at John's. I'd hate to lose a customer that way. Paul walked back tossing the white cue ball in the air, "I think you set some kinda distance record with that shot."

It took a while but we finally finished the game just in time for the pizzas. Paul and I went to get them and the girls sat down.

Diane grabbed a slice off of the one Paul was holding before he could set in on the table, "Sorry, Paul," she said, "I gotta have it. I can't wait any longer."

Jay knew how to make a good pizza. I think he learned back east somewhere. We had ordered a half-and-half sausage and mushroom. The other one was green pepper and onions.

"After I finish eating, I want to dance," Diane said between mouthfuls, "I got to work off all this energy."

Paul just looked at her and kept eating. The music was loud and people were moving about everywhere. You couldn't help getting caught up in the mood of the place. We ate most of the pizza and were sitting back relaxing when Jerry decided to pay us another visit.

"I'm gonna wind up smacking that guy," I said, as he got closer.

He walked up to Jo and asked, "You wanna dance?"

Jo didn't even look up, "No, Jerry."

"It's a good song playing. Doesn't it make you want to dance?"

"Not with you, Jerry."

I started to shift back and forth in my chair. Jo reached over and grabbed my forearm and shook her head. I gritted my teeth and sat still.

Diane looked at Jerry. "We're going to be leaving in a few minutes so stop bothering us!"

Jerry didn't hear a word she said, "Just one dance?"

"Are you hard of hearing, I said NO!"

"Maybe later, huh?"

I felt like a spring wound as tight as it could be, straining to let go. I didn't feel very good about fighting but sometimes it just can't be avoided. I sat there and tried to keep my cool as best as I could. He started to turn and walk away, then stopped, reached out and grabbed a piece of pizza. He laughed as he quickly turned and zig-zagged back to his stool. "That stupid asshole," I said as I started to get up and chase him.

"Don't do it, Ron," Jo exclaimed, "it's exactly what he wants."

"He's not going to quit. It's going to happen sooner or later," I said through gritted teeth.

Paul agreed, "He's too stupid to quit, Jo."

"Just the same, I don't want you starting it," Jo said as she rubbed my shoulder.

Diane wiped her mouth, "Men! The only way they know how to solve anything is to beat each other up." Diane bounced up and down in her chair, "Come on Paul, let's dance."

"Not right now. I just ate and I can't move."

She looked at Jo, "Jo. Come on dance with me."

"Oh, Diane, not right now."

"I just have to get one dance in before we leave."

"All right. Just one," Jo said reluctantly.

"I need some fresh air. I'll be out front," I said, getting up.

"I'll go with you," Paul said.

Paul lifted himself out of his chair like a man who just over-stuffed himself. We walked outside and the cool, night desert wind blew across my face. It felt good. "Temperature sure did drop," he said as we stopped outside the door.

I nodded, "It's a little cooler than usual. I'm gonna put my jacket on." I walked over to my bike and Paul followed. I had my leather coat wrapped up and strapped across my handlebars. I took it off the bike and put it on. "I don't know what I'm going to do about that jerk, Jerry. He's really bugging me and Jo lately."

"There's only one way out, you're going to have to kick his ass."

"I don't like that idea. I wish there were another way. I know I can't reason with him 'cause he's unreasonable. So that's out."

I sat down on Paul's bike and he sat on mine, "I know you don't like fighting but if you do this and get it over with, I think he'll stop," Paul said sternly.

"I'm not too sure about that. He doesn't have a lot of common sense. I don't think that'll be the end of it."

Just then Diane came storming out the door and stomped up to me, "You better get in there. Jerry just grabbed Jo's ass and she's trying to smack the shit out of him."

"WHAT!" I yelled.

Paul hollered, "Wee doggie, there's gonna be a fight tonight."

I jumped off the bike and threw my jacket to the ground. I almost pulled the door off the hinges as I swung it open. There was a crowd gathered around the dance floor and I couldn't see anything. All I could hear was Jo swearing at Jerry. I shoved people out of the way to get to the center of the floor. I saw Jo pick up a chair and throw it at Jerry. He ducked out of the way. I ran up to her, picked her up and set her aside. I turned to face him, and he said, "Well, if it ain't the big, bad biker pu . . ."

He never got the last word out. I took a step toward him, at the same time swinging my fist with every ounce of energy I had. I locked my eyes on his chin and felt my knuckles make contact. His chin gave way under my fist and his eyes rolled back in his head. A small spurt of blood squirted out from his face. I wasn't sure if it was from my hand or his mouth. At the same time, I heard a loud crack and knew something had broken. He wobbled back and forth for a second, then his legs gave out. He crumbled to the floor in a big bundle of limp flesh. He was out cold.

His two buddies were standing not very far from me and both took a step towards me. Someone in the crowd hollered out, "You guys jump on him and you'll never get out of here alive!"

They stopped in their tracks and I looked at them, "Come on. I'll take you on one at a time!" I screamed, as I held my hands up to fight, "Come on, you bastards, let's do it!"

They looked at each other and one of them said, "We don't want any trouble."

"Well, if you do I'm ready to lay you out just like I did your punk friend here."

They walked around me and tried to revive Jerry. Paul came over to me, "Damn, that was some punch."

I turned away from the crowd and shook my hand, "Ouch, that hurt! I think I broke his jaw." My hand was pounding and my knuckles started to swell. Jo came over and hugged me. I put my arms around her and could feel her shaking, "It's okay," I said, "he ain't going to bother anyone for a while."

"Oh, Ron, I wanted to kill him. If I had a gun I would have shot him," she said as she shivered, tears forming in her eyes.

"Well, if I had the gun I would have shot him too. He's going to be hurting for a while," I whispered in her ear. I looked at Paul, "I think we'd better get out of here. I'm sure the sheriff's gonna show up. And this jerk's gonna need an ambulance." I looked at Jo. "I don't want to be here when the sheriff gets here."

"Okay," she stammered.

Jo and Diane went outside and I looked at Jerry on the floor. He started to come to and I wanted to smack him again but I didn't. I turned to leave and saw Jay standing by, "Hey, Jay, I'm real sorry about this."

I took out two twenties to pay the tab. I tried to hand them to Jay, but he put up his hands, "You don't owe me a thing. It's on the house. I'd pay to see that jerk get knocked out any day. I haven't called the sheriff yet. I figured you might want time to get out of here. As soon as you get on the road, I'll call. That way you won't wind up in jail tonight. After I talk to him, I don't think you'll be going to jail."

"Thanks, I appreciate that and again I'm sorry for the disturbance."

"He caused it, not you. So don't worry about it."

"All right, I'm outta here. Come on, Paul, let's go."

He nodded and as we walked to the door I could hear people say, "Way to go, Ron," and "Nice punch, Ron," but I didn't feel good about it.

When we got outside, I shook my hand out again, "I'm sure glad those other two guys didn't want to fight. My hand's really killing me. When I hit him, I heard, and felt something snap and I wasn't sure if it was my hand or his jaw." There weren't any cuts on my hand so the blood must have been Jerry's. I stood outside the door and moved my fingers around one by one, "Ouch, that hurts, but I can move all of them. I guess I just sprained my knuckles. The crack must have been his jaw."

Paul looked at my hand. "It was 'cause it was out of line when I looked down at him on the floor."

"That's just great. I hope I don't have to pay for his hospital bill."

Jo and Diane were standing by the bikes. Diane looked at me and said, "You sure walloped him good, Ron. He deserved every bit of it."

I didn't respond and walked to Jo, "You all right?"

"I'll be okay. I just need to get away from here."

"Do you want to stay in the desert tonight?" I asked.

"Yes, it'll be peaceful and relaxing there."

Diane responded, "A night in the desert would probably be good for all of us."

"We better hurry," I said, "Jay has to call the sheriff and he's waiting for us to leave." Jo and Diane quickly got the sleeping bags out of their cars and we strapped them to our bikes. I waited for Paul to start his bike, then I started mine. "Let's get the hell on down the road," I said, as I let out the clutch and poured the power on. I could see the flashing emergency lights in the distance coming from the opposite direction as we headed out of town. It was either the sheriff or the ambulance. It didn't matter 'cause we were history.

It didn't take long to get to where we usually slept in the desert. I pulled off to the side of the road and stopped. "Hey, Paul, why don't we look for some firewood and build a campfire?" I suggested.

"Sounds like a good idea."

We got back on the road and went to the foot of the mountains about fifteen minutes away and scrounged around for old pieces of wood. We each got a small armful, tied it to our bikes and headed back to the campsite.

We parked the bikes and left the bedrolls on them for the time being. I set my wood down in a pile and Jo set hers on top of mine. Diane and Paul set theirs on the side for later. We got some dead brush and stuffed it around the edges of the woodpile. "Who's got a light?" I asked. Diane reached in her pocket and pulled out a lighter. "Why do you have a lighter?" I asked, "You don't smoke."

"Because people are always asking me for a light so I carry one."

We soon got the fire going and Jo and I sat together on one side and Paul and Diane sat on the other. "I wonder what's going to happen when I get back to town tomorrow?" I said, leaning on Jo as I stared into the flames.

"Don't worry about it," Diane said, "If we have to, we'll say he started it and you were only defending yourself."

Jo sat straight. "And if he tries to press charges, I'm sure I can get him on some kind of sexual assault rap."

"Just the same, I ain't lookin' forward to going back to town tomorrow and seeing the sheriff."

"Well, you have to go back. It's your home, isn't it?" Jo asked.

I thought for a second, "I guess I could consider it home. It's the only one I got right now."

"And you can't run," Paul said.

I looked into the flames again and listened to the wood crackle as it burned. Jo took my arm and slid under it while pulling it around her shoulders. "No, I'm not going to run. I've got no reason to," I said, calmly.

I buried my face in Jo's hair and breathed in her sweet scent. She cuddled up close to me and we all sat silent as the crackle of the fire filled the air. The yellow flames jumped off the wood and lit up the desert floor several feet out in a wide circle. The smoke drifted upwards and disappeared into the darkness of the night sky.

It was amazing how just forty-five minutes ago we were in a hectic, violent place and now we were sitting here in peaceful, serene surroundings. Just as the mood of Jay's place had taken me to its height, the mood of the desert night was taking me to its peaceful depth. I started to relax, allowing myself to enjoy the moment and forget about Jerry.

Diane looked into the night sky. "I wonder how many of those stars have life on them? They're probably staring back at us wondering if there's life here."

Paul said, "And we can't reach any of them. Not even the closest ones."

"Uh-huh, we're prisoners on our own planet," I added, "except now we can travel to the moon and maybe Mars. But that isn't far compared to the big picture."

The fire started to burn low and Paul got up to get some more firewood. He carefully laid it on the burning wood and in a few moments the fire flared back to its original height.

It was strange how a flame from a campfire could be so soothing and mesmerizing, I thought. But it had its destructive side, too. It was like a lot of things in life.

We sat around the fire not saying much and used up the rest of the wood. The flame was getting low and there was more red ember than fire. Every time a light breeze blew across the pile of burnt wood it would go from a deep, dark red to a bright, almost orange glow, then quickly die down to deep red again.

Jo sat up. "We better get some sleep. I have to get back to the ranch tomorrow morning. I have things to take care of."

Diane stirred, "Me too. I have things to do also."

I had to get to the station so I could start work on my new tanks. "Paul, do you want to take the spot down the way or do you want us to?" I asked.

"We'll take it. You guys can stay here and enjoy what's left of the fire."

"Thanks," Jo said.

Paul started his bike and he and Diane rode a little ways down the trail. I heard him stop and shut off his bike. I got up and took the sleeping bag off my bike and brought it over by the fire. Jo took it from me and laid it out on the ground. I started to get undressed. "Oh shit," I said.

Jo looked at me, "What's wrong?"

"I didn't bring my gun. I'd feel much better having it with me after what happened with Jerry tonight."

"I don't think he's in any shape to cause any more trouble tonight," she assured me.

"I hope you're right."

We both got undressed and slid into the sleeping bag together. We faced each other and Jo slid her arms around my neck, her cool, soft, smooth skin felt good against my body. "I talked to John this morning," I whispered.

"About what?"

"He asked if I would take care of his station if anything were to happen to him."

"Is he all right?"

"As far as I know. I think he's just tired. And he's getting to that age where he realizes he's not going to live forever so he's worried about the business."

"Hmm, if you stick around you'd have a permanent job with John," she said under a hidden grin.

I think she liked that idea and the more I thought about it the more it grew on me. I pulled her close to me. "Before I make any major decisions, I have to think it out. Or maybe the right word would be to feel things out. I'm not sure thinking is going to get it."

"I can relate to what you're talking about, "Jo said, "I have to make some decisions about my future, too." She took my right arm and pulled it around in front of her, "How's your hand?"

"A little sore, but what the hell, I'm a real he-man, right? I ride a Harley," I said jokingly, "Besides I heal fast. I gotta admit though, I'm glad it wasn't my clutch hand. I'm not sure if I could drive the bike if it was."

"You're my hero, Ron, but not because you ride a Harley. It has nothing to do with the bike." She looked at my hand. "It is a little swollen." She lifted it to her lips and slowly, softly kissed each knuckle, it felt so good. "You punched him for me and I'm grateful to you for that."

"Hell, I'd punch him again for you if I had to."

"I really hope you won't have to do that. I hope he leaves both of us alone from now on." I didn't say anything. I wanted to tell her that he wouldn't bother us anymore. But unless I knew that for sure, I couldn't. Jo kissed me softly on the lips, "Is it okay if we don't tonight?" she asked, "I really don't feel like it."

"Sure, it's fine with me. It's been a hectic night and I understand." This would be the first time since sleeping together that we didn't make love. Actually it was sort of nice to just lie here and relax.

Jo turned over and snuggled up next to me. I put my arm around her and slowly rubbed her breast, then guided my hand to her stomach and stopped there. I didn't want to go any further so I brought my hand back up to her breast and gently cupped it in my hand.

She softly sighed, "Good night, my he-man."

I snickered and replied, "Good night, my she-lady."

I could feel her body start to relax and it didn't take long after that before I could tell she was in a deep sleep. I watched the fire as it died to a few red embers hidden under the ashes. Whenever a breeze blew across it, the embers would flare up slightly trying to ignite again. But there was no more wood left to burn.

I turned my gaze to the stars with half-closed eyes. The temperature was cool enough that it was comfortable to lie next to each other. The wind made a subtle howling sound as it blew across the desert floor and put me into a sleepy trance. The last thing I remember before falling asleep was the howl of a coyote somewhere off in the distance.

Chapter Seven

I felt Jo stir beside me. I could see the brightness of the day through my closed eyelids, making me duck my head into the sleeping bag.

"Are you awake?" Jo whispered.

"Yes, but I don't want to be."

"That's a nice idea, but you can't sleep forever," she said, rolling over to face me, "Besides, you have to take me back to my Jeep. I have to get to work."

"Oh, all right, you killjoy," I said jokingly, "I need to get to the garage and do some things myself. That's if I don't wind up in jail."

I had to go back to town and face the music. I'd rather just stay out here in the desert and become a hermit, I thought to myself. I opened and closed my hand several times. It was sore and stiff, but I thought if I kept moving it, it would be all right.

She wrapped her arms around me. "You're not going to jail. The sheriff wouldn't put you there even if everyone said you started it, which you didn't. If you did go, I wouldn't let them keep you."

"Well, that's good to know."

She gave me a long, soft, wet kiss, "How's your hand?"

"It'll be fine. It's just a little sore."

"Come on, let's get dressed and see if Diane and Paul are awake yet," Jo said as she got up.

"Good idea," I chuckled, "let's go bother them for a change." I shook out the sleeping bag and tied it to my bike while Jo walked to the outhouse.

She came back down the trail, "Do you have to go?" she asked.

"Yeah, then we'll go pester Paul and Diane."

I walked to the outhouse and when I came back we got on the bike. I started it up and revved it so Paul and Diane could hear it. I didn't want to surprise them or embarrass them in case they were doing adult stuff. 'Course, it might be fun if we did.

As we got close to where they were, I hollered over my pipes,

"Hey, you guys, we're coming over so you better not be doing anything naughty."

When I got to within sight of them, they were still in the sleeping bag. I rolled up next to them and revved my engine a couple of times. Paul stuck his head out, peeled one eye open then said, "Ron, turn that thing off."

"What's the matter, too much nooky last night?" I asked.

Diane stuck her head out, "Ron, you're gonna get it."

Jo replied, "Can we watch you naked people get dressed?"

"Real funny, Jo," Diane said with squinted eyes, trying to block out the sun.

I looked at Jo. "Don't you just love it?"

"Yep," she said, "it's great."

Diane stuck her arm out of the sleeping back and made a circular motion, "You guys turn around so we can get dressed."

"Well, Jo, what'd ya think? Should we turn around so they can get dressed or should we sit here and stare at them?"

"Hmm . . . I don't know. What do you think?"

I looked back at Jo, "Not an easy question to answer."

Paul looked at us with a grin, "Don't make no difference to me. You want to watch me get dressed, then enjoy."

Diane said through gritted teeth, "You guys better turn around!"

"Oh, all right," I said. We got off the bike, faced the other direction and folded our arms across our chest. I looked at Jo. "Kill-joys, aren't they?"

"Yeah, they sure are."

They got dressed and we turned back around. Paul rolled up his sleeping bag and tied it to his bike, then they both went to the outhouse. By the time they walked back, they were pretty much awake and in a better mood. "It's about time you guys woke up," I said.

Diane just grumbled and Paul said, "Touché."

"Let's get back to town so I can find out the rest of what happened at Jay's last night. And what's going to happen to me," I said as we all got on the bikes.

"Nothing's going to happen to you," they all answered back in unison.

Paul drove onto the highway and I followed. We headed toward town in silence. As I got closer I began to get a knot in my gut. Even though everyone was sure nothing would happen, I couldn't relax until I heard it from the sheriff's mouth.

It was early Saturday morning and Jay's was closed when we pulled up to the front. It looked so calm and peaceful, quite a contrast from the night before. Paul dropped Diane off so she could get her car. They both looked at me and Paul asked, "Are you gonna be here tonight?"

I hesitated, "I'm not sure."

"Well," Diane said, "I think you should."

Paul revved up his engine. "I gotta git. I'll stop by the station later." I nodded and he rolled away while Diane walked to her car.

Jo got off the bike. "I have to get going, too." She faced me as I sat there, "Call me and let me know what happens."

"As soon as I find out I will. But if your father answers, you never seem to get my messages."

"Just call and let me know. I think Diane's right, you should be here tonight. You have a lot of friends here and you can't let one jerk interfere with your life."

I nodded, "You're right, I'll be here. I'm not going to let some stupid fool keep me away."

She put her arms around my neck, "Good. I'll see you around seven-thirty?" She gave me a lingering kiss then turned and walked toward her Jeep. I watched as she climbed into it and started it up. She stuck her hand in the air and waved as she pulled away from the curb. I waved back and sat there for a few minutes. I looked at the locked front door of Jay's. *Funny how you never know where life's gonna take you.* I started my bike, made a U-turn and then headed back to the station.

John was already open when I pulled into the driveway. I rode up to the garage door and shut my bike off. John came out of his office and said, "The sheriff was here a few minutes ago lookin' for you."

"He didn't waste any time, did he?"

"Said he wants you to call him or stop by his office." I walked into the station and John followed, "He told me what happened. He said he just needed your side of the story."

"Did he say what happened to Jerry after I left?"

"Yeah, he's got a broken jaw. They took him to the hospital last night."

"A part of me feels good about that and a part of me doesn't."

"You got one hell of a punch. I figure he deserved it from what the sheriff said."

"I don't know, John, it was real strange. I was outside Jay's when Diane came out and told me Jerry grabbed Jo's ass. Suddenly, all rationale and reason left me. I saw red and all I could think about was smashing him in the face. It was like I had absolutely no control."

"I ain't much on fighting but seems to me you did the only thing a person could do in that situation."

"It was as though I crossed some line and there was no turning back. Like I had to go to the bitter end. It's scary to be in that frame of mind."

John kept silent, walked over to his chair and sat down. He stared out the window in his usual pose. I looked at his face and he seemed to have a few more wrinkles than he had before. It also looked like the ones he had were deeper. He looked at me, "Something wrong, Ron?"

"Naw, I was just thinking. I guess I better get over to the sheriff's office and explain my side of the story. You gonna be okay here for a while?"

"Sure. You take care of business and I'll see you in a little bit."

I had a major knot in my stomach by now and it wasn't getting any smaller. I'd never done anything like this before: broke someone's jaw. I stopped at my bike and thought, *should I take my van in case he locks me up? I wouldn't want to leave my bike in the parking lot all by itself. To hell with it. I'm riding my bike, whatever happens, happens.*

The sheriff's office was a few minutes away from the station. As I rode, thoughts went racing through my head, *what if I can't make my trip now? What if that jackass Jerry sues me and takes everything I own? Which wasn't much, 'cept my Harley and he'd have to pry that out of my cold, dead hands.* I wanted to shut my mind off but I didn't know how. I turned right and drove into the small parking lot then, shut my bike off. "Well, let's get this over with," I said to myself.

I walked toward the office and could see the door was open. I stopped at the doorway and looked in. Pete was at his desk and looking up at me said, "Oh, hi Ron. Come on in and have a seat." Well, this was a good start. He didn't say put your hands on the wall and spread your feet. "Heard you had some trouble at Jay's last night with Jerry and his boys."

"A little," I responded.

"Let's see now, I got everyone's story and I have to get your statement. But before you say anything, let me tell you what everyone else said. If what you say matches what they said, then it's pretty clear cut and you have nothing to worry about." I sat down on the plain, gray plastic chair next to his desk. He shuffled through a small pile of papers, "Ah, here it is," he said, as he pulled out a sheet. I didn't know much about police work but it seemed to me that he should ask me first so that he could get my side without leading me on, then read what everyone else said. But I'm sure he knew what he was doing. "Okay Ron, I got a statement from Jay and a couple of witnesses and here's what they said happened. You were outside and Jo and Diane were dancing together."

"That's right."

"Then Jerry came up behind Jo and grabbed her buttocks."

"I didn't see that part but that's what Jo said."

"Then Jo started to slap and punch Jerry and Diane went outside to get you."

"Uh-huh," I nodded.

"Now, this is the part where Jerry and his friends differ from everyone else. He said you walked up to him and without any warning or provocation punched him. Everybody else said you were just defending yourself. They said it looked like he tried to swing at you first and you just swung in self-defense. If that's the case, I have no reason to charge you with anything. Matter of fact, if you had stayed around last night I would have arrested him after they got through with him at the hospital."

I don't remember Jerry trying to hit me first. I think Pete was telling me this so I would know what to say. I could go with that. It wasn't entirely true, but what the hell, it beats going to jail. "As far as I remember that's what happened. It all was over so fast, it's hard to recall everything."

"No matter, I have enough people to back it up. I also need Jo to give me a statement and if she wants to press charges against him, I'll issue a warrant for sexual harassment. If you still want to press charges for assault, I can arrest him for that, too."

"I can't speak for Jo, but I'll let her know. As for me, I think a broken jaw is enough. Maybe he'll back off now. He's been harassing Jo and me for a long time."

"I'll give you a copy of this report so that if he ever tries to file any kind of civil suit or criminal action against you, you'll have the official record that he caused everything."

I nodded and asked, "Is that all you need from me?"

"That's it. Jerry's been a pain to me for years. He's caused nothing but trouble here ever since I can remember and if he gives you any more trouble, don't hesitate to call me. Try not to take it into your own hands if you can possibly avoid it."

"I don't want any more to do with him and I'll try to go the other way." I stood up and he handed me a copy of the police report. I folded it up and put it in my pocket.

Pete reached out his hand and I shook it, "Take care, Ron, and don't hesitate to call."

I said goodbye and walked to the door. I stopped for a second, *maybe I should tell him I didn't really see him try to swing at me. No, let it be. That would be real stupid on my part,* and continued to walk outside. I looked up at the sky and let out a deep breath, "That was easy," I told myself.

I stood in the parking lot and looked at the mountains and the open sky. I don't think I could ever take losing my freedom from being locked up. Just the thought sent shivers up my spine. I looked at my bike, the sun glistening off the shiny chrome. It was a pretty machine and I couldn't imagine the thought of not riding it.

I got on, started it up and sat there feeling the engine rumble. I had a funny feeling as I pulled away that no one really wanted to know if Jerry swung first and no one really cared. I drove back to the station with a sense of uneasy relief. The legal part of this was over but I still had a crazy man to deal with.

John was filling up a car at the pump when I got back. I parked the bike and went inside. I walked over to the bench and took the towels off my new tanks. I wanted to get them on the bike before I went to Jay's tonight. I went outside and rolled my bike to the bench. Before I started, I had to see if John had anything for me to do.

I was about to walk to the front when he appeared, "How'd it go with Pete?"

"Everything went pretty good. He said Jo can file charges against him if she wants to."

"She should. Teach that donkey's ass a lesson."

"Sheriff said as long as I hit him in self-defense there's nothing Jerry can do. 'Cept I really don't remember him trying to swing first."

"It don't matter, sometimes justice don't follow the letter of the law. As long as it feels right, just let it be."

"Yeah, why should I get all worked up since he started the whole thing anyway?"

"That's right. Are you gonna put your new tanks on now?"

"I was. That's if you don't have anything for me to do?"

"Go ahead, all I got is gas customers so far."

"If you need me just give a holler."

"I will," he said as he walked to the front.

I started to take the bike apart. I wonder if Jo should press charges. That goof might try to do something to her and I wouldn't be around for a few weeks. It wasn't fair to let him go free, but then again, he might hurt her if she did press charges. I guess I couldn't decide that, it was Jo's decision to make.

I was about finished taking my old tank off when I heard Paul pull up out front. He asked John if I was here and I heard him say I was in the back.

"Hey, Ron, you're getting to it, huh?" he said, as he came into view.

I nodded as he walked to the bench, "I better get this done if I'm gonna do this trip."

"Have you talked to the sheriff yet?" I explained what happened and Paul said, "I think you both should have him arrested." I didn't say anything. I picked up one of the tanks and Paul picked up the other and as we walked over to the bike, he said, "I didn't want to say this when the girls were around and I'm not sure if Jo knows. There's a rumor that Jerry got into a scrape with a guy some time ago and Jerry pulled a gun on him. There were never any charges filed and I don't know who the other guy was. I'm not even sure if it's true."

"I'd rather be safe and believe he did than not believe it. This is gettin' worse by the minute," I said, concerned now.

"Just be careful and watch your back."

Paul took a seat at the bench. I picked up the brackets, fitted one tank on the bike and stepped back, "Doesn't look half-bad," I said.

"Hell, that looks great," Paul added.

I put the other tank on and connected all the hoses. I drained the gas out of the old tank and put it in the new ones, then started the bike up. "Now let's see if I got any leaks," I said, letting it run for a few minutes. I didn't see any so I shut if off, "Well, I guess I did that right. Now for my new handlebars."

The handlebars would take a little more time. They were the high-rise bars and I would have to change some things to make them fit right. For the most part Paul sat and watched me work. When I got the old ones off, I decided to take a break.

"Hey, Paul, you want a soda?"

"All right. You buying?" he asked.

"Sure. I'll buy you fly." I handed him some coins and he went up front to the soda machine. I pulled up a stool next to his and sat down. He came back with two sodas and handed me one. He sat next to me and we stared at the bike. I leaned on the bench with my elbows, "Gonna look bad when I get those bars on."

"Man, you got one of them new 'Evo' machines with a five-speed tranny and a belt drive. You're gonna cruise the highway cross-country. Ron, you got it dicked."

"You're looking at me thinking I got it made. I got a lot of things up in the air. Shit, I look at you and you're pretty well set. You know where you stand and your life is pretty clear cut."

"That might be but I'm awfully bored. I'd give anything to trade places with you."

"You might not like all the mental stuff that goes along with it. The idea was to go carefree and let the country swallow me up. Let the wind take me wherever it blows."

I got up and went back to working on the handlebars. Paul looked around the room. "Things couldn't have worked out better for you."

I nodded, "I can't complain. When I left Chicago, I figured I'd wind up on the coast roaming around working for scraps."

"And here you are getting your new machine ready to make this big ride."

I knew Paul was right but I couldn't get my mind off Jerry, though. I looked at him, "I thought I had enough to worry about before. Now I got that idiot, too." I felt like taking the wrench in my hand and flinging it across the room, "Man, this is beginning to get to me," I said as I walked away from the bike.

"Take it easy. Everything will be all right here. Don't worry about it. Just get your bike ready and have a good trip. We'll all be waiting right here when you get back."

I stopped for a moment and gazed out the back window at the open expanse of desert. I was starting to lose it and I had to get a grip. Looking out at the desert helped to calm me down a little.

I turned to Paul. "I don't know what to do. I'm really getting confused. I didn't want my life to ever get complicated again and now I feel like I'm in this big mental cipher being whirled around and around." I stood still for a second, then walked back to the bike. "I better finish this. It'll help take my mind off things."

Paul changed the subject, "You gotta show me how you do the computer thing."

"That might not be a good idea. You meet a lot of people on-line and I can just see Diane jumping all over you. And kicking my ass for showing you."

"Hey, she don't tell me what to do." I didn't say anything. I kept my head down and continued working on the bike. "What," he said, "you don't believe me?"

"Sure. I believe you. She has no say in your life."

"Listen, I only do what she says 'cause I want to. Not 'cause I have to."

"I believe you."

He sat at the bench with a puzzled look, trying to figure out if what he just said was true or not. I don't think anyone has complete control of his or her own life, but now was not the time to mention that to him. I was almost finished with the bars. All I had to do was attach the lines and I could take it for a test ride. "I almost got this baby together. I'll be able to try it out in a few minutes."

"Good," Paul said as he fidgeted on the stool, "I could use some fresh air about now."

I attached the last line, then got a rag to wipe off the smudge marks and fingerprints, "I'm gonna have to wash this when I get back."

"Right, it looks real dirty," Paul teased.

"It is," I said defensively.

"You keep that thing so clean I'd need a magnifying glass to find any dirt on it."

"Maybe so. Are you ready to go?"

"Let's hit it," he said as he jumped off the stool.

Paul walked out to his bike and I sat on mine to feel it, then walked it out front. When I got outside to where Paul was, I said, "This feels completely different. I'm going to have to take it easy the first couple of miles to get used to it."

"Good idea," he said, "it looks completely different, too."

John was standing by the door as I said, "I'll be back in a few minutes. I gotta try it out to see how it feels." John nodded and waved his hand.

"Hey, Paul, ride behind me in case I have any gas leaks. You'll know right away, 'cause you'll get sprayed."

"Well, thanks, what are friends for?" he said sarcastically.

"I'd do it for you."

"Okay, okay, let's go. I'll ride behind you."

I sat on my bike and started it. Paul did the same. The bars were a lot higher and made me lean forward in the seat. That changed my whole point of balance.

I looked at Paul and he nodded that he was ready. I slowly rolled out onto the street with Paul behind me. Steering was a lot different. I took it easy till we got to the open highway, then I took it up to highway speed. I rolled from side to side to get used to the different handling. Paul stayed close behind. I was riding along and I took one hand off the bars to feel the tanks to make sure they were tight. I momentarily looked down taking my eyes off the road. As I looked up, I was right at the shoulder about to drive onto it. It was soft gravel and dangerous to drive on at this speed. There was no way I could jerk the bike back to the center of the road so I held tight and rode onto the gravel. All I could do was hold onto the handlebar grips with all my might, trying to keep the bike from falling over. My heart felt like it shot right up to my throat. I bounced around on the gravel, fighting to stay upright. As I slowed down, it got easier to regain control. I sat stiff in the seat and rolled to a stop.

Paul pulled alongside me and stopped too. "Whoa, for a minute there I thought you were gonna loose it."

I took a big gulp trying to get my heart back to my chest, "You're not the only one," I said, peeling my fingers off the handlebars.

"You're going to have to drive a little better than that if you expect to make it cross-country and back," Paul said, half-jokingly.

"I can't believe I did that. I only took my eyes off the road for a second. Don't say anything about this to Jo."

He nodded, "No problem."

I put the kickstand down and got off the bike. I slowly walked around it to make sure everything was all right. It seemed to be. I looked at Paul, "Did you see anything out of whack when you were behind me?"

"Naw, just you trying to do some trick driving on the shoulder."

"Real funny. It feels good so far. I'll put a few more miles on it tonight. And if we go for a putt tomorrow, it'll give me a chance to check it out some more." I got back on, pulled onto the road in front of Paul and we headed back to the station. I could still feel the adrenaline running through my veins. It was kind of a numb, buzzing sensation.

As we drove into the station, Paul pulled alongside me. "I better get going. I'll see you later at Jay's. Try to keep that thing on the road."

"Just for you, I will." He grinned at that and drove off. When he got to the street he opened his throttle wide and roared away. I shut my bike off and sat for a minute.

John walked up to me. "Did everything go okay?"

"Everything's fine."

He looked at me, "You sure?"

"Yes, everything's just fine." I knew I couldn't fool him, "Well, not really. I almost ran the bike into a ditch a few minutes ago and I'm still a little shaky."

"You look a little spooked."

"I should have known better than to take my eyes off the road."

He looked down at the bike, "Looks like nothin' serious happened. We all make mistakes. All's we gotta do is pay attention to 'em. If we don't and keep doing the same ones over and over again, then they become problems." He turned and walked back toward the station. I looked at him and wondered where he got all that wisdom. Most things to him had simple, straightforward answers.

I slowly got off the bike and pushed it into the back of the garage. I sat down on the stool, looking at the machine in front of me. Then I blankly stared out into space. I played the scene of me running off the road in my head again. It made me shudder. My thoughts drifted back to my friend who got killed while riding his bike. It's funny how one minute you're here alive and healthy, the next minute you're gone.

I have to shake this feeling, I thought, as I got up. *I better get busy.* I checked the brackets and the bolts I'd just put on the bike to make sure they were tight. Then I went to the front of the station where John was sitting in his usual spot. I walked to the soda machine, got one, then sat down.

"Looks like everything's coming together for your trip," John said.

"I got a couple more things to do, then I should be ready to hit the road." I sat quiet for a few minutes. "God, I want to take this trip so bad, just once is all. If I never do it again, I'll be happy to have done it just once."

John nodded. "I imagine a lot of folks would love to be able to take a ride like that."

"I want to travel on the parts of old Route 66 that still exist to see all the small towns and the people who live there." I started to get excited as I looked out the window, "You know, stop at the restaurants and talk with the townsfolk. Travel down the side streets and look at the houses, check out their neighborhoods, see the countryside away from the interstates. Watch it slowly change as I head east over the mountains and prairies. Take my time and breathe in what America is all about." John rocked back and forth in his squeaky chair with his eyes closed, listening to me. "If I find a town I like, maybe stay the day. Get to know the people."

"Sounds like you're gonna have a good time," he said without opening his eyes.

"When I made the trip out here, I didn't get a chance to enjoy it. I had too much on my mind, going through the divorce and all. Only thing I cared about was getting to my destination and I couldn't see the things around me."

John cleared his throat, "A lotta people go through life that way, not seeing things around them."

"And I don't want to be that way. I want to take time and experience all that I can. The first part of my life I just ran through, so I want to slow down and enjoy the second part. That's one reason this trip's so important to me." Just then the phone rang. "I'll get it," I said as I got off the stool. I picked up the receiver, "Afternoon, John's Service Station."

Hi, Ron, how are you doing?"

It was Jo. "I'm okay, how about you?"

"I'm working. Did you find out what happened to Jerry and did you talk to the sheriff?"

"Yep, everything went smooth. I'm not going to jail. Matter of fact, it might be him that goes to jail. I'll explain it all to you later at Jay's."

"So you'll be there around seven-thirty?"

"I finished my tanks and handlebars so I should be there about then."

"See you later."

I hung up the receiver and sat back down on the stool, "That was Jo," I said.

He nodded and opened his eyes. "I guess I better get these old bones moving before I fall asleep."

He got up, stretched and went into his office to take care of the daily paperwork. I was a little worried about going to Jay's. Just my luck, Jerry would show up with a machine gun and mow me down along with everyone else. I knew I had to go, or everyone might think I was a wimp. I usually didn't care what other people thought, but I also had to prove something to myself.

I took care of a couple more gas customers and John was ready to close up for the afternoon. He came to the back as I was staring at the dark screen on the computer. He looked at me, "So, have you figured out that contraption yet?"

"A little too much. Sometimes I wish I never had it. I should have made that guy pay cash for the work I did on his car."

John didn't respond. He stood there in his usual quiet way, making me come up with my own answers. He looked at me, then at the computer. "Well, I guess I'm finished for the day. Do you have any plans for tonight?"

"Go to Jay's and hang out. Then maybe spend the night in the desert."

"Well, have a good time and drive that thing careful," he said as he swung his arm in the general direction of my motorcycle.

"I will. See you."

The sun was low in the sky and shining bright through the window as he walked toward the front. All I could see was the silhouette of his body against the glare. The light rays were darting through the clumps of his hair sticking up in the air. He looked more frail than usual as he limped away. He also looked like he was stooping a little more.

He walked out the door and shut it behind him. Then I heard his truck start up and pull away. I turned back to the computer and started to go back and forth in my mind about whether I should check my e-mail or not. Damn it. I'm going to look, so why do I play these mind games with myself? I turned it on and the e-mail program came to the screen. I pulled up a chair to the desk and sat down. There was a letter waiting, I knew it was from Gloria. I opened it and started to read:

Hi, Ron, how's everything in the sunny desert? It's raining here. It's been raining here off and on for the past couple of days. When the weather's like this, I feel like a prisoner in my own home and I want to break out. I feel this way even when it's not raining. God, I wish the sun would come out, even if just for a little while. I guess I'm in a depressed mood and I shouldn't bore you with it. How are you doing? Good, I hope. When you get that Harley, you've got to take me for a ride someday. From what you've told me, it's always sunny there. Must be a perfect place to own a motorcycle. You're going for a ride up the coast? Why don't you wait till you get your new bike, then go? Oh well, it's none of my business how you do things. How are you and Jo doing? Good, I hope. It's nice to see two people in a relationship who are getting along. Is Jo going with you on your ride? There I go again, that's none of my business either. Enough of the third degree from me. I better get going, I've got plenty to do around here. Talk to you later.

Gloria

This is crazy. I'm not even sure where she lives and I can't ask her or she might catch on to what I'm going to do. She described her neighborhood and the street she lives on. I could probably figure it out when I get to the east coast. From the way she's talking, she might even be living somewhere else by the time I get there. I've never been to New York City and finding her is going to be as much an adventure as going cross-country.

I brought her picture to the screen and looked at it. She certainly was beautiful. I wouldn't have any problem recognizing her in a crowd. Enough of this. I'd better take a shower and get ready to go.

I shut off the computer and headed toward the bathroom. I finished washing and got dressed. Jo hasn't seen my new tanks and handlebars yet. I hope she likes them. I don't see how she couldn't.

I took the bike outside and locked up the station, started it up and headed toward Jay's. I had a tense feeling. I had no idea how Jerry or his friends were going to react to my breaking his jaw. This uneasy feeling grew the closer I got to the bar, but I gritted my teeth and kept driving.

When I got there, I looked to see if Jerry's old, beat-up truck was around. I couldn't see it anywhere. Paul's bike and Jo's Jeep were parked outside. I pulled up next to Paul's, parked and walked to the door. I took in a deep breath, swung the door open and stepped inside.

I stopped and looked around the room. I didn't see him or his friends anywhere. He was the kind of guy that if he was here, I couldn't miss him. Jo waved at me from our usual table. I slowly walked over to her, looking from side to side. Paul and Diane were dancing. She stood up and turned to me. I reached out and slid my arms around her waist and she reached up and put her arms around my neck.

"Hey there," she said as she put her lips softy against mine. I ran my tongue around the inside of her lips and I felt her quiver. She took in a deep breath and let it out slowly, then laid her head on my chest. "You make something inside me burn," she said as she hugged me tightly.

I knew the fire she was talking about. I felt something inside me stir also. I just wish the hell I knew exactly what it was. Every time I thought about it, I got pissed at myself 'cause I couldn't come up with an answer. I looked around the room again as we sat down. "Not a lot of people here tonight," I said.

Jo glanced around, "I guess not. Probably too much excitement last night."

I settled in my chair, "I don't see Jerry here."

"Nope. He hasn't been here and I don't think he will."

"I hope you're right."

Just then, a couple of guys walked by our table on the way to the bar. One of them said, "Way to go, Roadside. You should've kept whacking on him, though."

I smiled weakly and nodded. Jo looked at me after they walked away. "I think you're the town celebrity."

"I really don't want to be."

"Well, you blew into town, got a sweet-looking Harley and took out the town bully. Guess that makes you the hero whether you like it or not."

"That reminds me. You gotta see the bike with the tanks and bars on it."

The music stopped and Paul and Diane came back to the table. As Paul sat down he said, "Glad you showed up."

Diane nodded in agreement. "People have been talking about you. They've been waiting a long time for someone to clean Jerry's clock."

Why'd it have to be me? I thought.

I told Jo what the sheriff said and Diane asked her, "Are you going to press charges?"

"I don't know," she replied. "I'll have to think about it."

"This isn't an easy decision to make considering the main character here," I said. "He might do something stupid to Jo or me."

Jo hesitated, "I don't think he would do anything to hurt me. I can't really be sure. But he might go after you, Ron."

"That's why we should wait a day or two and feel things out," I suggested. "We can always go ahead and file them later."

We ordered pizza and ate in silence. Once in a while, someone would come up and congratulate me for smacking Jerry. I would smile and politely nod. Every time the front door opened, my stomach would tighten, expecting to see Jerry and ten or twenty of his thugs walk in.

We finished eating and played a couple of games of pool. I really wanted to get out of Jay's so I could relax and not worry about whether Jerry was going to show up. We sat down and I said, "Is everybody ready to leave?"

Jo stretched in her seat. "I'm about ready to take a ride."

Paul and Diane agreed. "Want to ride up into the hills and get some firewood before we get to the desert?" Paul asked.

"Sounds like a good idea," I said. "What do you think, Jo?"

"It might be a little cool, so it wouldn't hurt to have it. A fire would be nice anyway."

We took care of the bill and walked outside. We went over to my bike and looked at the changes I made. Diane stood alongside it. "It's real bad with those high bars on it. And those tanks make it a lot bigger."

"I'm happy with the way it turned out. It should get me through the long stretches between gas stations. Considering I'll probably take a lot of out-of-the-way side trips."

Jo looked at me. "I hope you don't get lost on any of those side trips."

"I don't plan on it. I have a pretty good sense of direction."

"Just watch where you put your compass. You wouldn't want to break it."

I didn't respond to that remark. I just smiled and nodded. We packed up our gear on the bikes and got ready to leave. "I have to stop by the station and get my revolver before we head out to the desert. I want to make sure I have it with me. Just a feeling."

"Okay," Paul said. "I didn't bring mine and I think we should have some protection."

We mounted up and rode to John's station. I went inside and got my gun, unloaded it and carried it out to my bike. I always transported it according to the law. As long as I had the pistol in one saddlebag and the bullets in the other, it was legal to carry. I packed the gun and the bullets and we set out on the highway.

We rode to the foothills to get some wood, then headed out to our usual spot in the desert. It was a still, quiet night. The sky was crystal-clear and the temperature was somewhere in the seventies. Perfect for riding and sleeping.

Tonight would have been one of those exceptional nights to kick back and really enjoy. I had Jo riding behind me. The bike looked, felt and rode just right, and nature was providing the perfect backdrop. The air was crisp and the stars were so bright I could almost reach out and touch them. Except for one thing, this knot in my stomach over some immature jerk. Seems like whenever things start to get good, someone or something comes along and screws it up. People have an uncanny sense of timing. I decided I'd try to not mention anything more about Jerry tonight. I didn't want to ruin anyone else's night.

I made an effort to enjoy the evening as best as I could. I let myself get lost in the sound and feel of the bike and the vastness of the night sky. We rode into the desert and stopped by the ashes of last night's fire. Paul and I took the wood and got the fire going while Jo and Diane unloaded our sleeping stuff. We sat in a circle and watched the flames start to build.

Jo threaded her arm through mine. "This is perfect. The temperature is just right."

Diane laid her head on Paul's shoulder. "Yes, life is good," she replied.

We watched the flames jump up from the wood and listened to it crackle in silence. Just then, a truck drove by and slowed down. I looked over but couldn't make it out 'cause my eyes were not accustomed to the dark from staring into the fire.

Paul looked in the direction of the truck. "Look's like someone's checking us out."

The truck idled on the road about two hundred yards away. After a minute or two, it picked up speed and drove on. "Maybe the flames caught their eye," Diane remarked.

Paul and I looked at each other as we both said at the same time, "Maybe."

I knew what he was thinking and he knew what I was thinking. We both kept quiet so as not to worry the girls. *That might be Jerry,* I thought. *I hope it wasn't.*

Paul changed the subject, "Should be a comfortable night to sleep, huh?"

Everyone agreed. We went back to watching the fire again but the peacefulness was gone. I had a gut feeling that there was going to be trouble. My gun was still in the saddlebag and I wanted to get up and get it, but if I did, I was sure it would make everyone uneasy.

Jo picked up a twig and tossed it onto the burning wood. It landed on top of the pile and caught fire. It twisted and contorted as it burned. She started to hum a tune and we all fell into a trance as we stared at the flames. She had a mellow voice and could probably sing professionally if she practiced.

We used up all the wood and the fire started to get low. I figured we'd probably go to sleep soon. I was about to suggest that when I saw what looked like the same truck come down the road again. I could make it out a little better this time and it resembled Jerry's truck. The others peered in that direction. "That's Jerry," Diane cried out.

I got up to get my gun and said, "You're right, that's him." I took my pistol out, loaded it, and put it into my clip-on holster. I clipped it to my belt and went back to the fire. I sat down as the truck rolled by slowly again. This time in the opposite direction.

"This might get a little hairy," I said as we all kept our eyes on the truck. It rolled slowly past, then took off down the road again. "I think we all better sleep here together by the fire tonight," I suggested.

Everyone agreed and we sat by the fire watching the road. We waited for about forty-five minutes and when he didn't come back again, Paul said, "I don't think he's going to drive by anymore so maybe it's safe to hit the hay."

"I think he's just trying to spook us," Diane added.

"Could be," I said. "Let's all get to bed."

We rolled out our sleeping bags and climbed into them. The fire was just about out and we settled in for the night. I knew I was going to have to sleep with one eye open in case that stupid jerk came back and started something. We kept our clothes on mainly because it was cool and Paul and Diane were close to us. I hated to sleep with clothes on, especially when I was with Jo. I loved to feel her soft skin against my body, but I guess one night wouldn't kill me.

I laid my gun right outside my bag just above my head in case I needed to reach it quickly. Jo faced me and put her lips on mine.

She reached her arms around my waist and pulled me close to her. After giving me a long, wet kiss she said, "Good night, honey. Sleep tight."

"You too. And don't worry about anything."

"I won't. You're my hero, remember."

"Uh-huh. I remember."

She turned over and snuggled up next to me. I slid my hand around the front of her body, then reached under her shirt and put my hand on her soft breast. I cupped it gently in my hand and she placed her hand over mine. She squeezed, then sighed softly.

"Good night you two and no hanky-panky," Paul said, "and if you hear anything, Ron, take care of it."

"Thanks, Paul. You know you don't have to sleep so soundly either."

"Hey, you got the gun."

"I can give it to you, then you can keep an eye out."

"No thanks, it's your gun. You can do the shooting."

"Sheesh. What are friends for?" I replied flatly.

Diane barked, "Will you guys cut it out. Nothing's going to happen!"

"Yes," Jo added, "nothing's going to happen so shut up and go to sleep and stop trying to scare us."

"See you in the morning," Paul chuckled, then went silent.

Everyone got quiet and I lay there listening to the night sounds. They were always pleasant and would put me to sleep, but not tonight. Each desert noise made my stomach tighten up a little. I laid there for what must have been an hour. Paul was snoring and I could tell Jo had fallen asleep. I guessed Diane was sleeping also. I didn't think Jerry would be back since it was getting late. I figured it was safe to go to sleep, but I knew it would be an uneasy one. It took some time, but I finally drifted off.

Chapter Eight

A hand grabbed my shoulder.

I immediately reached for my gun, at the same time sitting up while opening my eyes. I squinted against the morning sun as Jo said, "Ron, Ron, take it easy. It's me, Jo."

I froze for a second, looking around. Paul and Diane were buried in their bedroll, still sleeping. Jo placed her hand on my arm, "I'm sorry I startled you, but you were in a deep sleep."

I let out a long, slow breath and set the gun back down. "That's interesting since I tossed and turned all night. It must have caught up with me."

I lay back down and gazed up at the blue sky, "Damn, I'm really edgy."

Thoughts were racing through my head. I would be leaving in a week and I wasn't sure if I should go right now. I couldn't leave not knowing what Jerry might do.

I felt like my brain was being whirled around in a large washing machine. The only time I could slow it down was when I was riding my bike. It put me in a pleasant, trance-like mood. It didn't take away my problems, but it sure did minimize 'em.

She curled up next to me, laid her head on my chest and put her arm around my waist. "Don't worry, everything's going to be all right."

"I sure hope so," I said reluctantly.

"Should we wake them up?" she asked.

"That's probably a good idea if we're going riding. I'm awake now." I stretched and yawned, "Okay, let's do it. Let's get on the road before it gets too hot."

Suddenly I was all perked up and full of energy. Maybe because I wanted to get on the open road. It didn't really matter, I just wanted to ride.

We climbed out of the sleeping bag and Jo said loudly, "Hey, you guys, wake up."

They both stirred and groaned. Then they stuck their heads out and grimaced at the bright sunlight. "What time is it?" Diane asked.

"About seven-thirty," I answered.

Paul asked, "Did Jerry come back again last night?"

"I don't think so," I replied.

They moaned a little more, then slowly crawled out of their sleeping bag. After stretching, they walked to the outhouse. When they got back, we packed up our gear and got ready to ride to Connie's. We checked our bikes, then hit the road.

When we got there, we cleaned up and ate, then went for a ride through the mountains. All I could think about was whether I should leave now or postpone my trip. I would feel real guilty if I left and something did happen to Jo.

We rode through the hills and valleys and I tried to shake this feeling, but it hung on like a bad cold. After being on the road for about an hour and a half, I pulled up to Paul and motioned with my hand to stop for a drink. He nodded and we rode down the main street in the first small town we came to. I took the lead and drove to a small outdoor coffee shop. "I need a strong cup of coffee. How 'bout you guys?" I asked.

"A cup of java sounds good," Jo said. "There's a little chill in the air, it'll warm my bones."

"I just want to wake up," I replied.

We each got a cup and sat down at an outdoor table. The sun was high in the sky and it warmed me. I wrapped my hands around my hot cup and let the heat soak into them. It felt real good. Jo, Diane and Paul had a discussion going on as I gazed at the hilly countryside. It was the middle of summer and everything was deep green.

After a few minutes, Diane looked at me. "You look like you got the weight of the world on your shoulders."

"Naw, just thinking."

"You do a lot of that," she shot back. "Too much of that might not be good for your health."

I didn't feel like defending myself so I kept quiet. I had a lot on my mind and sparring with Diane was not on my list of things to do. Jo looked at me with her big, blue eyes. She didn't say anything. She just gazed at me as though she was trying to understand me. I wanted to open up and tell her, but I didn't know where to start or how to put it into words. I felt like a little kid who didn't know how to express himself, with a bunch of bottled-up feelings waiting to burst.

"About time we got back on the road." Paul suggested. I was beginning to believe there were times when he knew just what I was thinking.

"I'm good to go," I said, glad that I wouldn't be grilled about my frame of mind any further. We rode around the rest of the day and it was late afternoon when we headed back towards Borrego Springs. Once there, I needed to get out to my favorite place tonight, the big rock, and have time to myself.

When we got to Jay's, Paul and Diane took off to Paul's place to watch a movie. I parked, expecting Jo to head home like she usually did, but instead she asked, "Are you in a hurry to leave?"

"Not really," I answered.

"Are you going back to the garage?"

"Yeah, I was planning to."

"Do you want some company for a while? I'm not ready to head home yet."

"Sure," I said, "it's still early."

It was almost dusk when we got back to the station. I parked in the driveway and Jo got off. I shut down the bike and unlocked the front door. I let her in ahead of me and turned on the lights.

"It's quiet here," she said as she started to walk toward the back.

"It's nice to have this peace and quiet after a hard day's work or a long ride."

She turned toward me and posed like a little girl. "So, where's your computer? You never did show me how it works," she said in a sheepish voice.

I knew she'd seen it before, but I never turned it on while she was here. I nervously shifted back and forth, "It's in the back room. You really don't want to see it right now, do you?"

"Yeah. I'd like to get an idea how they work. I'm trying to talk my dad into getting one for the ranch, but he's old-fashioned so it's going to take some doing." She tilted her head down and with a devilish look said, "That way, we can e-mail each other. I know how you like to get, and give, e-mail."

I was starting to get uncomfortable with this. If I turn on the computer, I'm sure she'll want to see how the e-mail works and I'm almost positive that there'll be a letter from Gloria. She walked over, took me by my arm and said, "Come on, show me how it works."

There was no way I was getting out of this. We walked to the desk where it was and she positioned me alongside it. She sat in the chair and ran her fingertips over the keys on the keyboard. "How do you turn it on?"

I flipped the switch for the monitor, then the switch for the computer. The screen flashed through its opening dialogue and the little white envelope appeared showing I had mail waiting. I didn't have anything to hide, yet I was still nervous. I knew Jo would read whatever Gloria wrote.

"So, what exactly can you do with this computer?"

"You can run programs, store data, play games and a lot of other things."

"What about this e-mail business? I want to see how that works."

"You see that little white envelope at the bottom of the screen?"

"Yeah," she nodded.

"That means I have mail waiting."

"Aren't you going to read it?"

"I will," I replied, fumbling with the keys.

I positioned myself behind Jo, reached around her and grabbed the mouse. As I leaned over her, I could smell the light scent of her hair. My arm brushed against hers as I guided the mouse to the envelope and it sent an electric rush of pleasure through me. Standing this close, I could feel her energy and began to get aroused. This was probably not the time to feel this way, but I couldn't help it. I clicked on the envelope and the mail program appeared. The only mail I had waiting for me was from Gloria.

"Is it from Gloria?" she asked innocently.

"Yes, it is," I answered.

"Well, aren't you going to read it?"

I gritted my teeth and said, "Yeah, why not." I opened the letter and Jo leaned forward, reading every word. All Gloria wrote was the usual things about the weather and wishing she were somewhere else.

"Is this the kind of stuff she writes?"

"Yeah, for the most part."

"Well," she said as she sat upright in the chair and grinned, "doesn't sound very important to me."

"It's not," I responded.

I still had her picture saved and wondered if I should show it to Jo. Maybe that wouldn't be a good idea, but I didn't have to ask. She beat me to it. "Do you know what she looks like?"

"Uh . . .yeah, she described herself."

"So tell me, what does she look like?"

"I have a picture of her. Do you want to see it?"

She shifted in the chair and looked around the room. "Yeah. Where is it?"

"It's in the computer. She sent it to me through the e-mail."

"You can send pictures through the e-mail?"

"Uh-huh."

I hesitated, then took the mouse, went into the file manager and clicked on her photo file. It took a second for her image to come up and I had a queasy feeling in my gut. When it came to the screen, Jo sat up and starred at it with wide eyes. I knew then that it was a bad idea.

Without taking her eyes off the screen and with a funny look on her face, she said, "So this is Gloria! She's a very pretty lady."

I didn't say anything. I just watched her stare at the screen. I didn't think Jo was too happy about Gloria's physical appearance.

"Well," she exclaimed after a few moments of deafening silence, "you're going to visit her?"

"It's like I said before, we've been communicating back and forth for about a year. I feel like she's a friend."

"A friend?"

"Yes, a friend. I'm heading to New York, which is where I would've gone anyway. And since I'm going to be there, I want to stop and meet her."

"Just stop and meet her?"

"Yes, that's all."

Jo stood up, faced me and laid her hands on my hips, "Remember what I said, if you find you like her once you get there, please let me know."

"Jo, that's not going to happen."

"You can't tell the future, Ron."

"Neither can you."

"Let's stop. I don't want to get into this right now," she said as she put her warm lips on mine. It sent a hot flash through my body and I felt my pulse quicken. It'd been a while since we'd made love and it was hard for me to hold back. I slid my hands around her waist and pulled her close to me. I was beginning to grow so I pushed my pelvis against hers and she responded by pushing back against me. I got hard immediately.

I let my hands fall to her buttocks and pulled her even tighter to me. I darted my tongue into her mouth. She backed away from me, then placed her hand between my legs, rubbing the length of my hardness. The passion raging inside me was almost uncontrollable. All I could think of was becoming one with her. Her breasts began to heave against my chest and everywhere her body touched me burned into my soul. I wasn't sure if making love was the right thing to do now, but it sure felt like the natural thing to do.

"Is there any place we can get comfortable here?"

"My van," I said, barely audible.

It was dark now and there wasn't any traffic passing John's this time of night. We walked to the front of the garage, my pulse was racing and I was light-headed. She took my hand and led me to the van. I opened the door and she crawled into the back onto my sleeping bag. "It's getting warm in here," she said, as she unbuttoned her shirt and pulled the shirttails out of her jeans. I crawled in and laid alongside her. She reached over and started to unbutton my shirt, "You must be warm, too. Let me undo this for you."

Her fingers brushed against my chest with each button she undid and sent ripples of excitement rushing through me. I opened her shirt, exposing her breasts. It was dark but her nipples stood out from her milky white patches of skin where the sun hadn't tanned.

She pushed my shirt over my shoulders and down my arms. "There, isn't that better?" she asked as she threw it aside. She took her fingernails and ran them around my chest muscles, then down across my stomach. I threw my head back, gasping from her touch. "You like that?" she asked, in a deep, scratchy voice. I blurted something inaudible.

"It's still warm in here. Let's take off these hot, stuffy boots," she said, pointing to my feet.

"You know we've been in the desert all night and all day and I could probably use a shower," I said defensively.

"You can take one later." She sat up and tugged at one of my boots till it came off. She pulled at the other one and I watched her breasts bounce as it popped off my foot. She pointed to my groin while straddling over me and sitting on my thighs just below my lap. "You must be hot there, too?"

"If only you knew," I said with heavy breath.

She pulled her shirt off her shoulders and tossed it over her head, "Oh, I think I do." She fumbled with my trouser button, "Let's get these hot, stuffy pants open so you can breathe better."

I reached up, took her breasts in my hands and played with her nipples. Her long, silky, soft hair brushed across my stomach as she bent her head down, undoing my pants. I was so hard I thought it would burst right through the fabric. She started to unzip me and I pulled in my stomach so she could get it past my penis. After she opened my pants, she ran her fingernails softly up and down its length through my underwear. I stiffened up my buttocks and lifted my hips in the air. She took hold of my pants and began tugging them. I picked up my midsection even higher so she could pull my pants down past my hips, exposing all my flesh to her.

"God, you're so big and hard," she exclaimed, as she took me in the palm of her hand and caressed me. Her fingertips were soft and smooth against my skin. Her touch made me dizzy with desire.

I was almost at the peak of ejaculation, but I held off trying to prolong the ecstasy. She wrapped her fingers around me just right and stroked the length of me slowly. "Do you like this?"

I couldn't speak any words. I just nodded my head and grunted, "Uh-huh."

"Good," she whispered, stroking from the tip to the base of my penis. I didn't think it was possible for the feeling to get more intense, but it kept building.

"Don't let it happen yet," she whispered, "hold on and make it last."

She blew her hot breath on me, but didn't touch me with her lips. I think she knew that if she did, I wouldn't be able to hold back. After a few moments of stroking me she sat up and pulled my pants and underwear all the way off. She positioned her head above me and let her hair fall between my legs. It was smooth, soft and cool on my loins as she rotated her head around in large circles.

She sat up, looked at my naked body and placed her palms on my flat stomach. "God, I want to just crawl inside you," she whispered.

I gently took her arms and sat up. I laid her on her back and undid her jeans. She closed her eyes and let out a deep breath as I scooted down and pulled off her boots and socks. I tugged her jeans past her hips and looked at her womanhood as I took them all the way off her legs. She bent her knees and raised them up in the air. I pushed them apart and sat between them in a kneeling position. I placed my hands on her inner thighs and slowly rubbed them while moving my hands in the direction of her lower stomach. Her hips started to move up and down and she moaned when I guided my hands past her vagina. I moved them up her stomach then to her heaving breasts. I took hold of them and squeezed. My body was positioned over her and the tip of my penis brushed against her vagina. She caught her breath and took hold of me. "I need to feel you," she gasped.

I felt myself throbbing in her hand as she placed it at her opening. I slid myself inside her as I lay on top of her, resting my weight on my elbows. My body made contact with hers from my waist up. I slowly started to move my hips up and down, never breaking that contact. I laid my head alongside hers and could feel her heavy breathing in my ear. I wanted to touch as much of her as I could. It was as though our flesh was melting together. She grabbed hold of my buttocks and rammed me harder into her. I responded by pumping even faster. It only took a few seconds and I was there. I tightened my muscles and so did Jo. We clenched one another closely. I came in erratic spurts and she pulsed with me. We held still for a few seconds, stiff against each other. Spasms of pure pleasure rushed over me like never before. I could feel her inner muscles throbbing wildly against my penis. I lifted my head and placed my lips on hers. They were quivering as though she was frightened.

I raised myself up, looking into her eyes, "Is something wrong?" I asked.

"No . . ." she whispered.

"Are you sure?"

"Yes, I'm sure. Just lie here with me and be quiet," she said, pulling me close to her. The sweat between our bodies seemed to merge us even further into one. I laid my head alongside hers again and let my body relax. Her breathing slowed to a steady, deep rhythm. I was so at peace I dozed off for a few minutes. I think Jo did, too.

I woke up with my face buried in her hair as I breathed in the sweet scent of her perfume. I lay motionless on top of her, feeling her heart beat and slow breathing, trying not to wake her. She stirred under me and said, "It's getting late and I better get back to the ranch."

I sat up between her legs. "I'll give you a ride back to your Jeep."

I slid my hands along her outer thighs all the way up the sides of her body. She shivered, "I love it when you touch me."

"And I love to touch you." I caught myself at the word I just used. It'd been many years since I used the word love when speaking to a woman.

I quickly spun around and grabbed my clothes. Jo got up with a surprised look, "What's the matter?"

As I put my clothes on, I blurted, "Nothing. It's getting late and we better get going." She grabbed her clothes and put them on, all the while looking at me.

I looked back at her, "It's not your fault, it's me. My head is still screwed up."

"Don't worry about it right now. You're going to take a long ride and you'll have time to yourself."

We finished dressing and walked out to the bike. I swung my leg over the seat and Jo got on behind me. She wrapped her arms tight around my waist and I reached back and pulled her close to me. She put her lips next to my ear, "I had a great time this weekend. I'm going to miss you while you're gone."

"I had a great time, too, and I'll miss being with you."

I started the engine and headed to her Jeep. *What's happening to me?* I thought to myself as we pulled up to Jay's. *It felt like my feelings were running wild.* I stopped and we both got off. We faced each other and Jo looked into my eyes, "You're leaving next week?"

"After next weekend, maybe Monday."

"So, we have one more weekend together before you leave?"

"Uh-huh."

"Good," she said, as we kissed each other. She stared deep into my eyes for a few long seconds, then said goodbye and hopped into her Jeep. I watched as she drove away.

I got back on my bike and as I reached for the key, I noticed Jerry's truck parked on the side, but he was nowhere in sight. It sure didn't take him long to get back into town. I cautiously started my bike and rode back to the station. I stopped before I drove onto the driveway, "I'm going to take a ride to the rock," I said to myself.

It took about five minutes to get there. I pulled off the road and stopped alongside it. I shut my bike down, walked over to the rock and laid my hands on it. It was warm from the sun as usual. I let the heat soak into my hands for a minute, and then I climbed onto it. I laid on my back and gazed up into the heavens. The air was still and the desert was quiet. I closed my eyes and let the heat caress my body from top to bottom. Each time I took a breath, I smelled Jo's scent on me. I opened my eyes, "What the hell's wrong with me, big guy? There's something good happening to me and I'm fighting it every step of the way."

The night sky remained still and quiet. The stars just continued to twinkle brightly. I closed my eyes again and thought about Jo and me in my van. I smiled as I went over the feelings I had and how intense they were. "God, she feels so good," I screamed into the open sky.

I didn't think I could open up my heart to anyone again, so when I left Chicago I vowed I would never get emotionally involved with another woman. But here it was happening all over again. I didn't know what to do, I didn't know what to say and I didn't know what to think.

I laid there with my eyes closed, trying to stop thinking and become one with my surroundings. A few minutes passed when I heard a vehicle ride by and stop. The road was in the direction over my head so I had to twist it and look up to see who it was. The headlights were shining into my eyes, temporarily blinding me. My gut tightened up when I realized it was Jerry.

After shining his lights on me for what seemed like an eternity, he turned back on the road and squealed his tires as he sped off. He went around a curve and I lost sight of him, but I could hear him slow down. I knew he stopped down the road and would be back. I still had my pistol in my saddlebag and I leaped up to get it. I quickly took it out of the holster and got the bullets out of the other bag. I loaded it and ran back over to the rock. I laid down again and shoved it under my hip with my hand resting on the butt. I didn't want any trouble and I didn't want to shoot anyone, but I would if I had to.

I lay still and waited for him to return. My adrenaline was pumping and my heart was beating a mile a minute. It felt like it was going to pop right out of my chest, but I kept my cool.

I saw his headlights approaching from the inner desert. He must have turned off the road, circled around and thought he would surprise me. I had my gun under my right hip and he was coming up on my left side so he couldn't see it. He came to a sliding stop, kicking up a big cloud of dust on the sand about ten yards from me with his lights shining in my eyes. I couldn't see past the lights but I knew he was sitting in his seat looking at me. I didn't know if he was alone, but I figured he never went anywhere by himself. I stayed motionless, watching the truck out of the corner of my eye. I could feel tiny beads of sweat forming on my forehead. I was holding the butt of the gun so tightly that my hand started to shake. I kept my finger off the trigger so I wouldn't accidentally shoot myself in the leg.

I heard the door swing open and I saw his huge form walk to the side of the lights. I still couldn't see him very well through the cloud of dust he had stirred up. I heard the passenger door open and gulped. "Shit, he's not alone," I whispered to myself.

He stepped in front of his lights and I could see he had a rifle or a shotgun swinging at his side. All I could make out was a dark figure against the haze of the bright lights. The other person stayed by the door and I couldn't see him at all. Jerry kept the gun at his side and I figured if I was going to make a move I'd better do it while he still had it pointed at the ground. I was counting on the fact that he was too big and sluggish to raise his gun before I got a bead on him, and the fact that he didn't know I had a gun.

I clenched my teeth and thought to myself, *well, big guy in the sky, if I have to die here and now, let it be fast and painless. I hope Jo forgives me.*

"Damn you, asshole," I said, as I sat up, at the same time swinging my arm around as fast as I could while pointing my magnum at his head. It took him completely by surprise.

"Don't move a fucking muscle!" I screamed as I stood up, keeping him between myself and his friend on the other side of the truck. That way, if he were armed, he wouldn't get a clean shot at me.

"If you breathe, I'll blow your fucking brains out all over this desert and I won't miss from this distance," I said as I cocked the hammer back.

Jerry froze in his tracks. I walked slowly around the side of him to get out of the path of the headlights so I could see him and get a better view of his friend. He mumbled something that sounded like, "Don't shoot." His jaw was wired up and he couldn't talk right. I pointed the gun past his head and in the direction of his friend and I yelled, "Get away from the truck and stand alongside this fuckhead!"

I saw the figure come toward me, at the same time saying, "Don't shoot. I didn't want anything to do with this. I didn't know he was going to pull a gun on you. I don't want no trouble."

"Well, you got it, mister. Now, get over by this bastard and shut up."

I pointed my gun back at Jerry's head, "This magnum's got a hair trigger and goes off by itself sometimes. Wanna see, you stupid prick?"

He mumbled something inaudible and I could see he was shaking. I took a couple of steps toward him holding my gun eye-level. "I'm only going to say this once, so listen very carefully. Don't move that rifle at all, just open up your hand and let it fall to the ground. If it moves any other way but down, I'll blow a hole in your head so big your mamma won't recognize you."

He was shaking violently by now and was too scared to move a muscle. He mumbled what I think was, "Please don't shoot."

"Do it now or I won't hesitate," I said again very deliberately. He slowly opened his hand and the rifle fell to the ground. "Now back up a couple of steps."

I moved forward, picked up his gun, then backed up a little, all the while keeping my gun on him. *Before I let him leave I'm going to have some fun*, I thought to myself. *I'm going to try to scare the shit out of him.* He looked like he was on the verge of pissing his pants.

"You've been messing with me ever since I got here. I guess there's only one way to get you off my back and that's to put an end to your life here and now."

He responded as though he had a mouthful of marbles. "Please, let us go. I won't fuck with you anymore."

"I don't think I can do that. I don't believe you."

His partner added, "I promise you won't see me again. This fool's gonna get someone killed and it's not going to be me."

"Let me explain the three possibilities we have here." I held his rifle in the air. "I've got your gun and I could shoot you both with it, dump it next to your body, cover up my tire tracks and footprints, then leave. You've got enough enemies so they'd probably never pin it on me."

His chin started to quiver and he squeaked out, "No."

"Or I could load both of you in your truck, shoot you with your gun, then drive your bodies out into the desert. I could bury both of you, then ditch the truck. They might never find you."

I wasn't sure but I thought I could see tears forming in his eyes.

"Then there's the third option, which I really don't care for myself. I could let you go, take this rifle to the sheriff tomorrow and make a full report. I'm sure he'd believe me. And you could pick it up from him," I said, shaking his rifle in his face. "That's if he'll give it back to you."

He nodded his head so fast and hard at that idea I thought he would break his neck, "Yeah, yeah, let us go, please."

"Naw, I can't do that. I wanna live my life in peace, not having to worry whether you're going to get into one of your stupid moods again."

"I won't. I promise. I'll never say another thing to you again," he mumbled.

"Get down on your knees, both of you." He started to cry and his partner looked like he was going to try to run. "I said get on your knees! I want to check your truck to see if you have any more guns before I let you go."

I could see a sigh of relief on both their faces. They got down on their knees. Then I said, "Now don't move or I'll blow holes in both of you."

I checked the truck and the only gun he had was his rifle. I stood in front of them. "You can pick this up at the sheriff's office," I said as I held up his gun.

"Thank you, thank you," he said, whimpering.

"Shut up and get the fuck out of here. Now!"

As they ran back to the truck, his partner reached over and punched Jerry on the shoulder, "You fucker. You almost got me killed. When your jaw heals, remind me to break it for you again."

They jumped in the truck and Jerry slammed it into reverse, throwing up a bunch of gravel trying to get back to the road. He laid down a large patch of rubber as his tires hit the blacktop. It only took a couple of seconds before he was out of sight.

I walked back to the rock, laid both guns down and climbed onto it. I sat cross-legged and closed my eyes. I let out a long, slow breath. "I can't believe what just happened. Well, big guy, I'm glad no one had to get shot. Especially me."

I wonder if anyone would really believe this. I thought about calling Jo and telling her, but why bother her tonight. I'll give her a call tomorrow after I see the sheriff.

I unloaded both guns, put mine back in my saddlebags and tied his rifle on my handlebars. I was tired and when I got back to the garage, all I wanted to do was sleep. It'd been a rough weekend. I walked past the computer and noticed I forgot to shut it off. I reached out and held my finger over the off button. *Should I write back to Gloria or should I wait?* I flipped it off, locked up the garage and crawled into my sleeping bag in the van.

Chapter Nine

I raised the shotgun off the table and held it in front of me, staring at it. *It could have been a lot worse than it was. I wonder if he'll really quit now or will we have to go to the bitter end with this?* I wrapped the gun in paper because I didn't want to alarm anyone on my way to the sheriff's office. I called John at home to let him know where I was going and that I'd be back later. After tying it onto my handlebars, I made my way to Sheriff Pete's. It was 6:30 Monday morning and I hoped he would be there.

I swung the door open and Sheriff Pete was sitting at his desk. He looked up at me, "Hi, Ron. You're out and about early. How you doing?"

"Fine. I've got a present for you."

He looked at the newspaper-wrapped thing in my hand, "What's that?"

"Jerry's rifle," I said.

"What are you doing with it?"

"I took it from him last night." I placed it on his desk. He leaned back in his chair and listened as I told him what happened the last few nights.

"So, let me get this straight. You had an altercation with him Friday night. Then Saturday night you're in the desert with your friends and he buzzes you."

"Yep."

"Then last night, you're in the desert by yourself and he drives by, then comes at you and stops."

"Uh-huh."

"Now, this is important. I have to know exactly what he did after he got out of his truck. Did he ever point the rifle at you?"

"No. I never gave him the chance."

"Did he ever say he was going to shoot you or threaten you in any way?"

"Nope. He just walked toward me holding the rifle."

"And you thought your life was in danger?"

"After what happened Friday night? You bet I did!"

"Given the circumstances and under those conditions, you had every right to defend yourself and do what you did. The only thing I can charge him with is brandishing a weapon. And I'm going to charge him. I can't let this go."

"That's fine with me. And I'll do whatever I have to on my end."

"I'm going to contact him and get him down here."

"Do you need me any more?"

"Nope. I'll take care of the rest," he answered. I shook his hand and said goodbye, then rode back to the station.

John was under the hood of a car as I parked next to the garage. He stood up and as I walked through the door, he asked, "Did everything go okay?"

"Yeah. Pete said he was going to charge Jerry with brandishing a weapon."

"Pulling a gun on someone is a serious thing. I think Pete was right to do that." I nodded in agreement. John walked to the front office and I followed him. He seemed to be favoring his bad leg more than usual, "Is your leg all right?" I asked.

"Sometimes it pains me more than others. When I have a bad day, it takes longer to get over than it used to. Guess that comes with age."

I didn't say anything as I watched him sit in his squeaky rocking chair. I walked over to the window, shoved my hands in my pocket and stared out at the dry, dusty street. I still thought something was going on with his doctor's visit. I turned and faced him, "Are you sure everything went all right at the doctor's?"

He looked at me long and hard, then said, "Now I have to take insulin shots. My diabetes is getting worse."

"How bad is it?"

"I have to watch my sugar level a lot closer. I guess things start happening when you get to my age."

I sat on the stool and thought about the roles people play in each other's lives. *I hope nothing happens to John. He's an important person in my life. I'm getting tired of people dying around me. Maybe the only way to avoid that was to move to a mountaintop where there were no people, but that wouldn't work for me.*

"I better get this car finished," he said as he pushed himself out of his chair.

"Want me to take care of it for you?"

"No. I still got a lot of life left in me. It'll be quite a while before I can't finish a job I start." He had the right attitude. There are places where stubbornness can be a benefit. I hope I have the same drive when I'm his age.

The rest of the day dragged on. It was slow for a Monday and that didn't help any. Plus, I was counting the days. Just one week and I'd be on the road. It was almost four p.m. when the sheriff came by. I was restocking oil on the shelves as he walked in. "Hi, Ron. Jerry came by a little earlier and I filed charges against him."

I stood up and turned towards him, "That's good. He's been messing with people and it's about time he got what's coming to him."

"He bailed himself out and I warned him that if anything should happen to Jo or you, he'd be the first one I'd go after."

"Well, I hope he gets the message."

He handed me the court information. "I hope so, too. I'll talk to you later."

I felt a little better knowing he'd been warned. But we'd all have to wait and see. Pete went into the garage, talked briefly to John, then left. I hadn't told Jo yet, I knew I'd better call her.

I dialed the number and the phone rang once, twice. I figured the machine would pick it up when her father answered, "Hello, Thompson Ranch."

"Hi. This is Ron. Can I speak to Jo?"

"She's not available at the moment. Can I take a message?"

"Could you tell her I called?"

"I'll see that she gets the message."

I heard a click and I hung up my receiver. For some reason I didn't think she'd get it, as usual. That man was starting to piss me off. I sat back down on the stool and tapped my fingers on the counter. It wobbled back and forth as I shifted my weight on it. I fumbled through my pockets, searching to see if I had the right amount of change for a soda. I walked to the machine, got a can and sat back down. I couldn't sit still.

John finished the car he was working on, "That's the last one for me today." I stared out the window. John looked at me and didn't say anything for a while. I drank the soda, fingering the can, and he said, "Thinking about your trip?"

"Yeah. I've been thinking about all the things that could go wrong. It's weighing on my mind."

"I'm sure you'll handle anything that happens. You're a good mechanic, and you got a good head on your shoulders."

"I'm not so sure about that anymore. Seems I just keep screwing things up lately."

"You'll be okay. Just drive safe and have a good time."

"Maybe once I get on the road, I'll be able to kick back and enjoy it. I'm getting antsy waiting for Monday."

"It'll be here soon enough. One thing about time, it don't slow down or speed up for no one." I watched him as he sat in his chair, relaxed. He had such a mellow mood. I wonder if it was because of the desert or it was his personality, probably a combination of both. A person had to have a certain personality to live out here. He got up out of his chair, "I better git," he said as he locked up the office and headed for the door, "I'll see you in the morning."

I nodded, "See you."

John got in his truck and drove home for the night. I walked past my computer, thinking about writing to Gloria. I wanted to try to get her address so it wouldn't be hard to find her once I got to New York. I knew the name of the street she lived on and she'd mentioned a couple of landmarks near her home. I figured I could find her, but an address would make it a lot easier. I sat down at the keyboard and turned it on:

Hi, Gloria. I'm leaving for my trip up the coast next Monday and I'd like to drop you a post card or two while I'm gone. I don't know your mailing address. If you could give it to me, I'd be able to send a couple of cards to you. So, could you e-mail me before I leave? Anyway, how are you doing? I hope things are

*working out for you. I'm sure they will, they always do
if we have a little faith. I'm about to go to bed. Things
have been hectic around here and I'm mentally
exhausted. I've been having a lot of trouble with the
town idiot, but I think it's over now. Anyway, I'll fill
you in later. Talk to you soon.*

Ron

I sent the e-mail, then turned off the computer and got ready
for bed. I felt like a little kid before Christmas. Thoughts were
running through my head about the last-minute details. I started to
go out to my van and I realized Jo hadn't called back. She probably
didn't get the message. I thought about calling one more time, but
it was late. I'd ride by the ranch tomorrow and give it to her in
person. That way, I could be sure she'd get it. I went to bed and
tossed and turned before finally falling asleep.

I held the carburetor in my hand, wondering if I'd put all the
parts back in it. It was Wednesday and Gloria hadn't written back
yet with her address. I was having trouble concentrating on my
work the closer I got to leaving. I'd never done anything like this
before, and it was totally occupying my mind.

I stopped at my bench, making sure I replaced everything back
into the carb. I'd hate to do this job over again, and I'm sure John
wouldn't be happy about it either.

All I could think about was checking the computer to see if
Gloria had sent her address. I'd hate to ride all the way to New
York and not get a chance to meet her.

I put the carb back on the car and started it. I drove it around
the block and it seemed to work fine. I was surprised that it did,
given all the stuff going on in my head.

The past couple of days had dragged on, but today seemed to
be zipping by. Probably because it had been busy. I still had some
minor things to take care of on the bike. I could finish them up
anytime.

"How's the car?" John asked.

"It purrs, and runs like a charm."

"Good. The customer's on his way here to get it."

I went inside and made out the bill. I wrote so fast, I almost couldn't read it. I set it, and the pen, aside. "Slow down," I whispered to myself.

I was working myself into a frenzy. I sat down and closed my eyes. I said the word relax over and over in my mind and took deep breaths. A lot of good things were happening to me and I had to pace myself. Take things a day at a time. Do what I can today and leave the rest for the other days.

I started to calm down when the customer came in. "Is my car ready yet?" he asked.

"Yeah. I just finished it and it runs great." The man smiled, paid the bill and drove off.

John came in and I handed him the money. He took it and said, "I'm sure he'll be happy with the way it runs. I haven't had any complaints about your work yet." I gave him a tired smile and nodded. It was a good feeling to know I did something right and someone else appreciated it.

The day was almost over when Paul stopped by. I was in the garage cleaning up the floor when he parked his Harley and came in. "Dude! What happened Sunday night between you and Jerry? I heard you drew down on him!"

I explained what happened.

"You should've shot him!" he exclaimed.

"I thought about it, and I hope he doesn't do anything to make me regret not shooting him. Once I pull the trigger though, I have to live with it the rest of my life, even if he is an asshole."

"If he came at you with a rifle, you had every right to drop him."

"I know, but it's just not that easy to kill someone. Maybe there are people who could do it and live with themselves, but I'd rather not try if I have the choice. Besides, it was more fun just to fuck with him."

"If that happened to me, I would have blown him away."

"I'm not so sure you would have, Paul. It's easy to sit here and say that."

"Naw, I would have done it."

I didn't respond 'cause I knew he wouldn't quit. I changed the subject, "How's your bike running?"

"Great. It needs a little fine tuning, but that's the nature of the beast."

"Yeah, I got a couple of things to do to mine."

"Then you're off into the wild blue," he said as he stared at my motorcycle.

"I'm busting at the seams waiting for next week to get here."

"I still say you're one lucky dog. I want to go with you so bad I can taste it. If I didn't have responsibilities here, you can bet your Harley I'd be on the road with you."

"Man, that'd be great to have you ride along. But you can't throw away what you have just to do that."

"I'm seriously considering it. To see the country on a Harley. To get in the wind for a few weeks, not caring how fast you go or which direction you're headed. Just the thought gives me chills."

"Well, if just thinking about it gives you chills, imagine how I feel. I'm actually going to do it."

I set the broom aside, walked over to the stool and sat down. I looked at the floor and kicked a piece of dirt with my foot, "You know, nothing's free. People pay for everything they do. Sometimes the payment's pleasant and other times it's painful. I don't know how this is going to turn out, but I hope it's pleasant for everyone involved."

Paul looked at me and didn't say anything for a moment. I think he could see the stress in my face. He took a deep breath, then said, "No matter what happens, I think Jo will be here for you when you get back, and I think you'll be back."

"Of course I will. Why does everybody think I'm going to ride off in the sunset and never come back?"

"Maybe 'cause you did it once already when you just packed up and left Chicago. You were married a long time and had a lot going on in your life and you left. You're not sure about what's going on in your life now and you're planning to take a long ride."

"I guess you're right. I never thought about it that way."

"You live in your van. You could be packed up and gone in

less than a couple of hours."

I looked at my van, then at my bike. "Uh-huh, I could be outta here in the wink of an eye, couldn't I?"

"I saw that picture of Gloria. If she looks half as good in person as she does in that picture . . ."

"That's not going to happen. I'm not flighty and I do have morals."

"You asked why everyone thinks you might just vanish. All I'm doing is telling you."

"Okay, okay, I get the picture."

Paul looked around with a smirk of a grin. "So, you got a few things to fix on your bike?"

"I'll probably get to them Saturday."

He walked over to it and sat on it. "You haven't let me ride this baby yet," he said jokingly as he grabbed the handlebars and gripped them tight.

I could see the muscles in his forearms bulge as he gripped tighter. I stood up, "When John leaves and after I lock up, we'll go for a putt. I'll ride yours and you ride mine."

"You mean it? I get to ride your bike?"

"Sure, why not. Long as I get to ride yours."

He nodded as he said, "Outstanding!" and turned the handlebars slightly as though he was on the road.

John took care of his business and said goodnight as he headed for his truck. I could see Paul was anxious waiting for me to lock up so he could check out my bike.

I finished cleaning up, then rolled my cycle next to his, locked the door and handed him my keys. His keys were already in his bike. "You want me to kick start that for you?" he asked.

"Hell no, I can do it myself."

I'd seen him do this many times, so I think I had the procedure down. I could see him out of the corner of my eye sitting on my bike watching and waiting. I'd never kick-started a Harley before. I cranked the throttle once, then stepped on the kick-start. I pushed down twice to prime it, then hit the throttle again and flipped on the ignition switch. I lifted all my weight onto the kick-starter and pushed down hard. The bike sputtered and died. I shut off the switch and went through the ritual again. I flipped the switch back on, then pushed down hard on the kick-starter one more time. It sputtered and I hit the throttle. It came to life and Paul smiled. "Not bad," he said, as he turned on my ignition and hit the start button.

"Man, this is wild," he said, as the engine came to life under him.

"Let's both take it easy for the first couple of miles till we get used to each other's bikes," I suggested. He nodded, as we headed toward the road.

We took a short ride to the foothills for about a half an hour. Paul's bike handled well for an older Harley and I could see he was having fun zipping around the curves on mine. I wanted him to keep the lead 'cause I wanted to check out my bike. It was at least three thousand miles to New York one way. And probably more depending on how many side trips I took. So, I was looking at maybe seven thousand miles total round-trip. That's a lot of riding no matter who you are. I couldn't see anything wrong as Paul whizzed around in front of me putting it through its paces.

We rode back to John's and as we pulled up to the door, Paul said, "Damn, this is one sweet machine. This Evo engine with the five-speed tranny and the belt drive sure is smooth. It really accelerates with muscle. Sometime down the road, I'm going to have to get me one of these."

"Since I tweaked the carb, it runs a lot better than when I first got it."

We got off and he asked, "Could you take a look at my carb when you get back? I'm sure it could run better if it were adjusted right, but I'm no expert."

"Sure, that's no problem." I wondered why he waited this long to ask me. Maybe riding my bike convinced him I knew what I was doing.

Paul got on his cycle. "I gotta git. I'll see you this weekend before you leave."

"Yeah, I'll be at Jay's Friday night."

He roared off and I went into the station. I walked to the computer to see if Gloria had written. I turned on the monitor and the envelope was there. I opened it and started to read:

> *Hi, Ron. Sorry it took so long to write back. I can't send you my address now because I'm not in a position to receive mail. When you get back from your trip maybe you could e-mail me about it. I'd love to hear the details. I have some unpleasant things going on and talking to you helps me get through them. So please write me all about the trip. I have to sign off now. Write me before you leave, okay?*

> *Bye, Gloria*

I looked at the screen. *Why wouldn't she want me to have her address?* I asked myself. *She didn't have to hide anything from me.* Now I was really curious. I guess I would have to find her on my own. I thought I had enough information to locate her house and surprise her. One thing was puzzling me, though. Her messages were getting shorter and shorter now. When we first started writing to each other, they were almost a page long. It seemed as though she was afraid to tell me anything personal.

I finished up in the garage, ate dinner and got ready for bed. I locked up and stood by my van. It was warm and there was a gentle breeze blowing. I walked to the road and looked both ways. The moon was three-quarters full and I could see quite a distance. I started to think about how some people couldn't be alone, while others liked being by themselves. I wasn't sure if I could handle being alone when I left Chicago. The time I spent by myself before I started seeing Jo was good for me. It's probably good for everyone to spend some time alone once in his or her life to get to know who they are.

I stared down the road leading out of town. Just a few more days and I'd be on that road fully packed. I got a chill down my spine. I wanted so bad to do this and I didn't think anything, short of an act of God, would stop me.

I stood there still having trouble believing this was really happening. It almost had to be a dream. Yeah, some entity was playing a cruel trick on me and I'd wake up any moment.

I looked up at the stars, felt the warm wind on my face. "Nope, this ain't no dream."

I walked back to my van and climbed in. I got undressed, laid on my back, and gazed out the window. The dark outline of the mountain range stood tall in the moonlight. Suddenly, I got a deep inner feeling that everything would be all right. That was one thing about the desert. If you took the time to stop and listen, it would do that to you. I laid there for hours peacefully watching the moon glide across the silent night sky, not caring if I went to sleep or not. Sometime during the night I drifted off.

Chapter Ten

It was barely dawn when my eyes snapped open. This was the big day, the day I'd been waiting for . . . early Monday morning and I thought, *I have to finish packing. I have to stop and see Jo before I leave. Would I forget anything? How's the weather going to be?* I've only been awake a few seconds and already I was driving myself nuts.

I looked out the van window and the sun was hardly over the desert plain as I leapt out of my sleeping bag to get dressed. I rolled up the bag to take it with me. I figured I'd be sleeping alongside the road as much as I could. It was only six a.m. and John wouldn't be here for at least another hour. It'll take me that long to get ready. I didn't want to leave this early anyway because I wanted to make sure Jo was up and dressed before I got there.

With most of my stuff packed, I unlocked the garage, tied my sleeping bag onto my back fender and washed up. I made myself a cup of coffee and had a sweet roll. The adrenaline was pumping through my veins. I wanted to leave right now but I figured I'd better get something into my stomach, even though I wasn't hungry, and I wanted to say goodbye to John. I hadn't seen him since late Saturday afternoon.

I took the roll and coffee and sat down at my bench, looking at the motorcycle all packed up and ready to go. As I sipped my coffee, my mind wandered. *This time I'd really get to see the country up close. Meet the people who make up this nation.* The excitement was building inside.

"Let's see, did I forget anything?" I asked myself.

I got up and checked my saddlebags. Then I looked at my computer. I'd written Gloria last night and still hadn't got her address. No problem. This way it will really be a surprise when I show up on her doorstep. I had said goodbye to Paul and Diane last night.

Jerry was last seen at Jay's Saturday night drinking beer through a straw. He kept to himself and minded his own business. He didn't even look at me once the whole night. I felt pretty good that he would leave everyone alone. Things seemed to be falling in place.

I sat back down and finished my coffee and sweet roll, waiting for John to arrive. I started daydreaming again when the phone rang. I wondered if I should answer it or not. We didn't open till seven and it was only six-thirty.

"Oh well, what the hell," I said, as I got up to answer it.

"Good morning. John's Service Station. Can I help you?"

"Hi, Ron. I thought you'd be up already," Jo said on the other end.

"Hi, you're up early yourself."

"Yeah, a little early. Are you going to stop by?"

"Yes, I'm just waiting for John to get here before I leave. I want to say goodbye to him."

"I'm sure he'd like that. He thinks a lot of you. I'll see you when you get here."

"Okay," I said as I hung up the phone.

I went back to my bike and walked around it in a big circle. This was maybe the hundredth time I'd checked it. I looked at the clock, six thirty-five.

"Damn, it was going to take forever for seven o'clock to get here," I blurted to myself.

I checked my bags and made sure my leather coat was tied tightly to the handlebars. I got a wrench and double-checked all the nuts and bolts. Harleys had a habit of shaking things loose. It's probably the only machine that takes itself apart on a regular basis if left alone.

It was going to be a hot day so I got out my long-sleeve shirt, sun block and a bandanna for my head. I sat back down on the stool and tried to be still. I closed my eyes for a moment, then opened them and looked around. Suddenly I noticed how quiet and peaceful it was. I leaned back on the bench, propped myself up on my elbows and looked around the room.

It would be a few weeks before I would see this place again. I was really going to miss it. When I looked at my toolbox, then over at John's, I choked up a little. The thought of leaving was starting to make me sad. My eyes were beginning to get a little damp when I heard John's truck pull up. I quickly jumped off the stool and fidgeted around with my bike trying to regain my composure. I didn't want anyone to see me in a frail mood.

I heard his key slide into the lock, then his footsteps walking to the garage, "Hey, Ron, morning."

"Hi, John. I was just finishing with my bike here," I said without looking up.

"Looks like you're all ready to go."

"Just about. I'm gonna ride by Jo's ranch on my way out." I was still trying to avoid his eyes 'cause I knew I couldn't hide anything from him. I finally looked up. "I'm going to miss this place while I'm gone. It's like home to me."

"You'll be back. 'Sides, it's good to have that feeling of belonging. It sure beats wandering aimlessly."

"Yeah, I guess you're right."

I rolled my bike outside and John followed. I turned and stuck my hand out. "I'm glad I stopped here for that soda and gas two years ago."

He grabbed my hand firm and solid. "I'm glad you did, too. And remember what I said. If you need anything on the road, you better give me a ring on the phone, ya hear?"

"I will." My eyes started to get moist again and I figured I better get out of here. I turned to get on my bike. "I'll see you when I get back."

He walked up and slapped me on the back, "Drive careful now and enjoy yourself."

"You bet I will."

I fired up the engine, rolled out of the driveway and headed towards Jo's place. I took my time so I could get hold of myself. *It's amazing,* I thought, *how I got here friendless and now I have a whole new world of friends. And one very, very special lady, Jo.*

It wasn't long before I pulled into the ranch driveway. I saw her father standing next to the stable and Jo was sitting on the porch, waiting. When she saw me, she got up and went into the house. I parked and got off. *I wonder where she went?*

After a few minutes, she stepped through the screen door holding the hat she bought me. She slowly walked down the porch stairs swinging it at her side. With her head cocked to one side and strutting her shoulders, she walked up to me, "Here, put this on," she said, as she handed the hat to me. I took it and set it on my head. She reached up, adjusted it and grinned, "Damn, you look handsome."

I shrugged, slightly embarrassed. "Gee, thanks, Jo," I said as I peered down and shuffled my feet. I looked up and down her body, then gazed into her ocean-blue eyes. "You're one lovely lady yourself."

She giggled and slid her arms around my neck, pressing her body tight against mine. I put my hands on her waist, then put my lips on hers. I felt the familiar spark as soon as we made contact. I breathed in her morning-fresh scent.

She pulled her lips from mine. "You don't have to leave right away, do you?"

"Uh . . . no. Why?"

"I saddled up two horses. Let's go for a short ride, half hour or so." I looked at her a little suspicious. She caught the look and quickly shot back. "No, not that. Just a ride together before you leave. If that's okay with you."

"Sure, I'm in no hurry. It's still early yet. Yeah, a ride would be nice."

"Wait here and I'll get the horses."

I leaned against my bike and watched her walk away. If I could put together a woman anyway I wanted to, I think it would be exactly like Jo. I wouldn't make any changes.

Her father started walking toward the house and as he passed I said, "Hi, Mr. Thompson." He looked in my direction and glared. I wasn't quite sure if the looks he gave me in the past were hateful, but there was no question about the one he just shot at me. He stared at me long and hard, then turned away without speaking. I wanted to run after him, grab him and ask him why he hated me so. But I thought, *now's not the time.*

He went into the house and slammed the door shut. A couple of seconds later, Jo appeared from the stable with two horses saddled and ready to ride. She handed the reins to me. "You remember how to do this?"

I quickly responded, "Yes, I do."

She smiled at my defensiveness and mounted her horse, "Well? Let's get to it."

I fumbled with the reins, put my foot in the stirrup and lifted myself over the saddle, "Easy horsey," I said as he adjusted himself to the weight of my body. I tugged on my hat, "See, nothing to it."

Jo didn't say anything. She looked at me with quiet confidence, then pulled the reins and her horse turned and walked in the direction of the bridle path. I did the same and my horse fell in behind.

It was a little after seven-thirty and the dew was still on the leaves and flowers. The morning dampness had a sweet smell to it. I followed Jo until the path became wide enough for me to ride alongside her. As I came up beside her, I asked, "Are we going anywhere in particular?"

"No, just down the path a ways. Ride in front of me for a while."

I nodded, snapped the horse's reins and his step quickened.

She didn't talk at all and I figured she was just watching me. I kept silent and took in the scenery. When we got to the stream where we stopped the last time, I asked, "Wanna rest here for a bit?"

"Sure, let's sit for a while."

We got off and let the horses walk to the stream's edge. I found a dry spot in the grass and we sat down. Jo laid her head on my shoulder. "It's a beautiful morning," she said.

"It sure is. It's a little different from the desert with all the trees and grass here."

"Let's just sit here for a while and not speak." she replied softly.

"All right."

She took my arm and pulled it close to her body and nestled her head into my shoulder. I could feel her heart beat slowly and steadily. I closed my eyes, smelled the flowers and listened to the birds singing to each other. The stream was making a steady rushing sound and began to hypnotize me. I let my mind slip into a state of semi-consciousness.

We sat in that position for ten or fifteen minutes before Jo stirred, "Will you keep in touch with me?"

"I'll send you post cards from as many places as I can. I'll call you every so often, too. But I doubt if you'll get the messages, though."

She playfully slapped my shoulder, "Oh, yes I will."

I ignored that last remark and looked into her eyes. "I sure wish you were going with me."

"I wish I was, too." She paused a moment, then looked down at the grass. "I have a lot to do here and my dad needs me."

I wanted to take her by the shoulders and shake some sense into her, but I knew that wouldn't work. We had already talked about this and Jo was not the kind of lady to be pressured or pushed into anything. She'd have to come to that realization on her own, in her own time.

She put her hand back on my shoulder. "I'm really going to miss you while you're gone."

"I'm going to miss you," I said, pulling her close to me.

She laid her hand on my knee. "I don't know how, or why, but I have a feeling that this time apart is going to be good for us."

Maybe she was right. I think I had to take this trip now. Not just for myself, but for both of us. A part of me wanted to stay right here in this spot and never leave, but I knew that wouldn't work. We both needed time to sort things out.

"We better get going," she said as she got up. "I'm sure you're itching to leave and I have to get back to the ranch."

I picked myself up off the grass and followed her to the horses. We mounted up and headed towards the ranch. I let her take the lead and stayed behind her the rest of the way back. It was getting close to eight-thirty and I was anxious to get on the road, but I enjoyed being with her. I'm glad we saw each other before I left.

We rode back to the stable and her father was nowhere in sight. I was happy I didn't have to face him again. I was sure now that he hated me. *Well,* I thought, *that's not my problem. Maybe in time he'll change, or maybe he wouldn't. Either way, I wasn't going to let it get to me. Or so I kept telling myself.*

I got off my horse and Jo did the same. She walked me to my bike. "You got everything you need?"

"I think so. I couldn't fit anything else on here if I tried. I got enough cash that if I need anything on the way, I can always stop and pick it up."

She stood right in front of me and I looked deeply into her eyes. I felt something tug at my heart. I could see the moisture start to build in her eyes as she took my hands in hers and said, "I want you to know before you leave, I love you. I can't hide it and I'm not ashamed to tell you."

Something inside wanted to say I loved her, but I couldn't bring myself to say it, not just yet. "I really care about you, Jo. I'm not sure just yet that it's love. Whatever it is, it's real strong. Please give me time to get my head straight." I could see her eyes begin to tear up. I slid my hands around her waist and pulled her close to me. Her body was shivering slightly and I put my lips next to her ear and whispered, "It's going to work out, just have faith. I know it's going to be all right."

I felt her nod her head. "I know it will." We stood there in each other's arms for a while. I didn't want to let her go until I was sure she was all right. She pulled away. "You better get going. I'll see you when you get back."

I kissed her a long, soft, tender kiss, then stepped back so I could see all of her. I wanted to burn her image into my mind. I took off my hat and handed it to her. "Here, take care of this for me till I get back."

She smiled and took it, "I sure will."

I turned and swung my leg over my bike. "I'll see you in a few weeks."

She stood there for a second looking at me, then ran to me and kissed me one more time. "Drive safely and don't do anything stupid."

"Me, do anything stupid?"

"Yes, you. I want you back here in one piece."

"Will do. I'll ride safe just for you. No, for us."

She smiled. "Good. Now get outta here."

She moved back a few steps and I started my bike. Her dad

came out of the house and stood on the porch watching me. I kept tabs on him out of the corner of my eye, made a U-turn and slowly headed down the drive. I waved to Jo and she waved back.

When I got to the road, I stopped and looked over my shoulder. Something deep inside me wanted to turn around, and something equally strong urged me to go on. "It's okay," I told myself, "I'd be back in about three weeks or so."

I rolled onto the highway and headed east. It had been two years since I made this trip, only from the other direction. *It's funny,* I thought, *coming out here I was going through the mental turmoil of a breakup. Now, going in the other direction, I'm going through the mental turmoil of getting together with someone.*

I looked down the road, the sun was high in the sky and the California wind in my face. The bike was purring at sixty miles an hour and felt just right under me. I slowly settled back and began to enjoy the scenery. It started to hit me that I was really on my way. This was better than a dream. I started to sing the words to Bob Segers' song, "Against The Wind," in my head as I rolled down the highway . . .

I had a loose plan of the route I would take. I wanted to pick up old Route 66 before I got out of California. My plan was to ride north and east, then catch it at Amboy just south of the I-40. Most of the road between here and Amboy was desolate. A good part of it went through the Mojave Desert with little or no people traveling it. This could be a dangerous stretch, but that's the route I wanted to take. I wasn't much for the beaten path with crowds of people.

I weaved my way through the state, alternately taking roads north, then east, then back north again. The scenery stayed pretty much the same, desert wasteland, periodically dotted with small towns. I rode the length of the Anza-Borrego desert, then at some point, I'm not really sure where, I entered the Mojave Desert . . . I think when I crossed the Chocolate Mountain range. It got its name from the color of the terrain. It had the distinct hue of a chocolate milk shake.

By the time I got to the middle of the state the people began to get scarce. The tiny towns became few and far between. It felt like

I had the whole state to myself so I kicked up my speed to seventy-five miles an hour, a good cruising rate for the open road.

It took about four hours when I started to get close to Amboy and came to a couple of dry lakes just south of the small town. It was eerie riding over a dry lake. I could tell that the earth here had once been under a large body of water and had now crusted up in big, flat pieces curled at the edges.

The temperature was somewhere between one hundred-ten and one-twenty. The sun was pounding down on the dry, dusty earth. It was easy to understand why these lakes didn't stand a chance out here.

The road dead-ended at Route 66 in Amboy. I could see the end of it ahead and what looked more like a gas stop than a town. I rolled up to the stop sign and looked both ways. "So this is 66," I said to myself.

I turned right, headed east, then pulled into Amboy and rolled past a sign at the edge of town that said, *Amboy, founded 1856, Population 20.* As I rode through, I could see the old buildings, and the equipment used to mine the chloride, behind locked fences.

My lips were dry and starting to crack. My throat was parched so I rode off to the side into a closed, boarded-up gas station to get a drink of water. I parked in the shade of the canopy and took out my water bottle. I sat on the small step that once led into the station office and looked around. The hot wind was blowing brisk and steady across the barren, dusty ground. It was hard to imagine living out here for any length of time. I still hadn't seen another human being in a while.

Just then, I caught something move out of the corner of my eye. It was about a foot away along the step I was sitting on. I held still and turned my head. It was a scorpion walking the length of the step trying to keep out of the sun. I slapped my hand on the wood and it scurried across the desert sand and disappeared out of sight behind some old tires.

I leaned back against the boarded-up door and closed my eyes. I'd been on the road a few hours now and I was getting used to it. I pictured Jo in my mind and how she felt in my arms. It brought a smile to my face. I was starting to miss her already.

I opened my eyes and listened to the whistling sound the wind made as it blew across the scorched land. I almost felt like I was in one of those science fiction movies where suddenly all the people on earth disappeared and I was the only one left. What a scary thought.

I tried to imagine how this town was before the interstate was laid. It must've been a thriving center of activity, being the only town for miles in either direction. Now it was reduced to a ghost town with the desert wind slowly wearing away what was left. It was probably hard for the people here to make the changes that progress brought along with the superhighway twenty miles to the north.

I better get back on the road, I thought as I picked up my water bottle and got up to leave. As I walked to my bike, I noticed a fine coat of road dust starting to cling to it. I laughed. "It's gonna get a lot dirtier by the time I'm through."

I stashed my water bottle away and sat on the seat. I was glad I was just passing through and not staying. The conditions here could best be described as brutal. It took a certain kind of person to live in this extreme and I wasn't that type. I liked my time alone, but I had to have people around me, too.

I fired up the engine and pulled back onto the pavement. For being a little-used road it was in good shape. I was about two hours outside of Needles, California. I could take the interstate and get there faster, but that would take the fun out of it and I wasn't in any hurry.

I took one last look around, hit the throttle and got up to highway speed. As I got closer to Needles, I started seeing more cars and people. After being out in the middle of nowhere for hours, it was a welcome sight.

About a half-hour out of Amboy I felt nature's call. I pulled over, left the engine running and ducked behind a rock. As I walked back to my bike, I noticed my headlight was out. I didn't know if the bulb was burned out or there was a problem with the wiring or switch. I had all my tools with me so it shouldn't be a problem. I hit the bright switch and the light came on. I flipped it back to the low beam and it went dead. I couldn't drive with the bright light on and blind oncoming traffic, and most of the states I would be going through had a headlight law, so I had to get it fixed. "Shit." It was probably a burned-out headlight but I'd better find a Harley shop just in case it was something more. It was Monday afternoon and I wasn't far from Needles so I should be able to get the parts I needed.

Once in town, I headed for the center of Needles and thought, *I hope this isn't an indicator of the way my trip's going to be. I'm not even out of California yet and I'm having problems.*

I cruised through town and got directions to an after-market Harley shop. It shouldn't be hard to find since old 66 cut through the middle of Needles. I had hoped to get a good distance into Arizona by the end of the day, but it didn't look like that now.

It took about five minutes to get to the shop. It was on the left side of the road in the middle of the block. I stopped and as I waited for the traffic to clear to make a left turn, I saw one bike on the gravel lot in front of the store. It was an older Harley. It looked like an antique, but was in perfect condition. I noticed a guy standing next to the bike looking hard at it.

The traffic cleared and I made the turn. I parked on the other side of the lot and shut my bike off. I didn't realize just how big the guy was till I got off my bike. He had to be at least six feet five inches tall, maybe more. He was wearing a leather vest with no shirt underneath. His body was covered with tattoos and his upper arms were bigger than my thighs. The blood vessels running along his forearms looked like huge soda straws under his skin.

His jeans were tattered and his boots looked like they were older than he was. Drops of sweat were dripping off his stringy beard and he didn't look like a very happy camper. He glanced at me from under his straggly, long blond hair and looked like he was about to chew someone's head off, so I headed straight for the door, avoiding his gaze, and minded my own business.

I walked through the door and saw a middle-aged biker dude sitting behind the counter. "How ya doing? Can I help ya with anything?" he asked with a crooked, but friendly, grin.

"I think I got a burned-out headlight. It's not really that old, but I figure I'll start with the easy stuff first."

He got up and disappeared into the back room. He came out holding a new headlamp, "This ought to do it," he said, as he handed it to me.

I took it from him and gave him the money. "I sure hope it does the trick," I said, and headed for the door.

"You need any tools?" he asked.

"No, thanks, I got everything I need." I stopped as I reached the door and asked, "That guy out there having trouble with his bike?"

"Yeah, he's been trying to get it started for the past twenty minutes. I'd leave him alone if I were you."

"No problem," I said as I stepped through the door and onto the lot where the big guy was trying to kick-start his bike. He was so big he didn't even have to put his full weight on the pedal, he just stepped down on it. I walked to the other end of the lot to my bike, watching him out of the corner of my eye. I didn't want to look straight at him 'cause he looked real agitated and I didn't want to irritate him any more.

I got busy changing my headlight and noticed he had stopped to rest between kicks. From the sound of his bike I could tell it wasn't going to start. I had no idea what the problem was, but it wasn't even sputtering when he kicked it. I finished with my bike and turned on the ignition switch, then flipped on the light. It came on bright and strong. "Got it," I said under my breath.

I carried the old lamp back into the shop. "That was the problem. I don't understand how an almost new headlight could burn out so soon, but it did. Do you have a place to throw this out?" I asked as I held out the light.

"Sure, I'll take care of it for you," he said as he took it from me and tossed it into a trash can behind the counter. He looked at the license plate on the back of my bike and asked, "What part of California you from?"

"Borrego Springs, a little town about ninety miles from the coast."

"Yeah, I heard of it. Where you headed?"

"New York."

"Damn, that's one hell of a long ride." I didn't want to go into detail about it but I didn't want to be rude either so I explained the plan to him. He listened without speaking, then said, "Hey man, I wish you all the luck and I hope it goes good for you."

"Me too," I said, as I headed for the door again, "but this is only the first day and I'm already fixing things."

When I got back outside I glanced at the big guy. He was bent over turning the screws on the carburetor. I noticed it was slowly dripping gas from the overflow hole.

So that's why it won't start, I thought to myself, *it's flooding. I wonder if I should help him? If the carb is flooding, turning the screws wasn't going to help solve the problem. It had to come apart to be fixed properly.*

I started to walk away and thought, *he doesn't look very friendly and probably doesn't need my help.* I stopped halfway to my bike for a moment, almost turning around, then said, "Naw, forget it," and kept walking.

I got on my bike and turned on the ignition switch. I grabbed the handlebars, held my thumb over the start button and hesitated. "Damn it. I just can't ride away without trying to help that guy."

I turned off the key and looked over at him. He was trying to kick-start it again and I knew that wasn't going to work. I put the kickstand down on my bike and walked over to where he was. I stood there waiting for him to stop trying to kick-start it.

When he finally did, I said, "I don't mean to butt in . . ."

Before I finished the sentence he snapped back in a deep, raspy voice, "Well then, if you don't mean to, don't!"

I held up my hands in self-defense, "Okay, okay, you don't have to bite my head off. I was just trying to help."

I turned to walk away when he yelled, "Hey!"

I froze dead in my tracks, the little tiny hairs on the back of my neck standing on end. *Oh shit,* I thought to myself, *now I'm in for it.* I wasn't sure if I should try to make a run for it, but if I did I'd probably never make it to my bike, so I turned around expecting the worst.

He hesitated for a moment, then asked, in a tame voice, "You know about carbs?"

"Yeah. I rebuild 'em for a living. I used to own and operate my own shop."

I saw his eyes widen ever so slightly, "You did, huh?"

I looked at his carb and pointed to it. "It's never going to start with that flooding the way it is."

"I've tried to rebuild it a bunch of times and it never works right," he mumbled.

"There's a lot to rebuilding carbs that people don't know about," I answered.

He stared at me with an unsure look on his face. "Do you think you know what's wrong with it?"

"It's one of two things, but it has to come apart to fix it."

He stood up, hovered over me, then looked at me for a couple of long, hard seconds. "I'm at the end of my rope and I'm about willing to try anything to get it fixed. Do you think you can fix it?"

I wasn't sure if it was a wise idea to get involved with a guy that could double as a brick wall, but I answered, "Yes, if this shop has the parts I'll need. You want me to try?"

He stared at the bike for the longest time, then looked at me. "Go ahead, if you think you can."

"All right. You take the carb off the bike and I'll go inside and get the parts."

"Just tell Mark to put it on my tab. He knows who I am," he said as he grabbed his tools and bent down to remove it.

I went back into the shop and Mark was sitting on the stool. I walked to the counter and said, "I'm gonna need some carb parts for that bike out there. I'm not sure about the year and the model, though."

He looked at me kind of funny. "No problem. I know all about that bike. He buys all his parts here." He went to the back and was gone a few minutes. He came out with the stuff. "Well, I got everything you need here," he said, as he looked at me strangely.

I wondered why I was getting the funny looks, but I didn't ask. He handed me the parts, then he finally asked, "Are you going to work on his bike?"

"Yeah. Why?"

"Just wondering. Do you know him personally?"

"No. Why do you ask?"

"Well, I've known that guy for years and he's never let anyone touch his bike. In fact, I don't think anyone's ever touched that bike 'cept him since he's owned it."

"Is that right? I guess there's a first time for everything, huh?"

He shrugged his shoulders, "Yeah, I guess."

I took the parts off the counter and stopped as I got to the door. I turned and asked, "By the way, what's his name?"

"He's called Maddog."

"Oh great," I said, "he's big, bad and mean and now I find out he's got rabies, too. Oh well, can't back out now," I muttered under my breath.

I walked outside and he almost had the carb off. I watched him work with his gigantic hands. I think he could use them as sledge hammers if he needed to.

He pulled the carb off and held it up to me. I reached out to take it and he instinctively pulled it back. I stood there with my hand out and he finally gave it to me.

I walked to a shaded area and began taking it apart. It took a few minutes, but I found one of the problems and showed it to him. He just nodded and didn't speak. He kept his eyes glued on me as I replaced the parts and adjusted the settings. I was a little nervous as he remained silent and just kept staring. I knew it wouldn't flood any more and was hoping that was the only problem. I remembered working on cars that had multiple things wrong with them and I hoped that wasn't the case here. I'd hate like hell to put this carb back on and have it still not start. That'd ruin my whole day.

I put the last screws in and said, "Well, this should work now," as I handed it back to him. He took it, walked to his bike and started to put it on. I stood in the background and kept quiet as he worked. I was getting more and more nervous as he got closer to finishing. I was starting to sweat.

I walked over to him as he connected the final line. "Let's see if you really know what you're doing," he said as he put his foot on the kick-starter.

I crossed my fingers as he stepped down on it. The engine didn't do anything. He stepped on it again and nothing. He looked at me like a lion looks at a lamb when he's about ready to have lunch.

"Oh, shit," I said under my breath. I was starting to sweat bullets now. I looked at my bike, figuring the best thing was to try and make a dash for it. Then it hit me. "Wait! The spark plugs are still wet from it flooding. We have to take 'em out and dry them off before it'll start," I said as I grabbed the wrench and reached for the plugs.

He caught my hand in mid-air and looked at me with suspicion. He grabbed the wrench out of my hand, " Gimme that. I'll do it."

I think whatever trust he had in me was quickly diminishing. I watched as he pulled out the plugs and dried them off, all the time looking at me out of the corner of his eye. He put them back in the bike, then said, "I hope for your sake you're right about the plugs."

"Me too," I mumbled.

He turned the ignition back on, cranked the throttle, lifted his leg onto the kick-starter and pushed down. I held my breath and the bike sputtered and died. I grinned 'cause I knew now it would probably start. He lifted his leg onto the kick-starter again and pushed down. This time it sputtered and roared to life. I smiled wide and let out a deep breath. He revved it a few times to clear it out and I said, "Let it warm up a bit and I'll adjust it for you."

He looked at me and I swear I saw a gleam in his eye. He didn't strike me as the type to crack a smile, but I think I saw the corner of his lip curl up just a little as he nodded and said, "Sure enough." When the bike warmed up I fine-tuned the carb and stood back. Maddog stood about a foot away staring at it. "Man, this thing ain't idled this smooth in years. I gotta hand it to you, you know what you're doing. You must have a lot of experience on these carbs."

"Not really. That's the first time I've rebuilt one like that."

His eyes got wide again, "Huh?"

Maybe I shouldn't have told him that and I stuttered, "Uh . . . it's cool, all carbs are basically the same. They operate on the same principals."

"Well, if you say so. It sure is running damn good." He watched it idle and revved it up a few times. "Wait here. I want to take it down the road apiece."

I nodded as he swung his leg over the seat and backed away from the front of the store. As he pulled away, I noticed how massive he looked on his bike. His body stuck straight up in the air and made the motorcycle look tiny. When he got a little ways down the road he hit the throttle hard and shifted through the gears, his long, sandy blond hair trailing in the wind. I could hear the engine rev loud and smooth without spitting or sputtering. I grinned, knowing he'd be happy with it.

I heard him fade off in the distance, then get louder as he headed back. He pulled up to where I was standing, but I couldn't tell by the look on his poker face whether he was pleased or not. He stopped in front of me, put the kickstand down and got off, leaving it run. He looked at me and said, "I don't know if this cycle has ever run so good, partner. I'm damn sure pleased I ran into you. There's one more thing I want to check," he said as he shut the engine off. "I want to see if it'll start again after sittin' a few minutes. You're not in any hurry, are you?"

"Nope. This is the first day of my vacation and I have lots of time on my hands."

We stood there waiting for his bike to cool down to see if it was going to start again. He looked at my bike. "That sure is a pretty machine you got there."

"Thanks. Your bike's in good shape, too."

He didn't seem to be much of a talker so we waited in silence for his bike to cool down. After five minutes he said, "Well, I guess I'll give it a shot now." He turned on the ignition key and put his foot on the kick-starter pedal, then pushed down. It fired up on the first kick and he stepped back, "This is almost too good to be true. It started on the first try. It's never done that before."

I didn't know what to say. All I did was rebuild the carb and check a few things that over the years I had learned to look for. "A carb can make or break a bike. I try to pay attention and usually things work because of it," I said.

He stuck out his hand to shake mine. I reached out my hand and he took it in his, "My name's Maddog, what's yours?"

"Ron, Roadside Ron."

"Well, Roadside, what do I owe you for taking care of my carb?"

"Nothing. I'm glad I was able to get it to work."

"I gotta give you something. It's not my way to be beholden to anyone."

"It's no problem, you don't owe me anything."

"I can't let you leave without doing something for you."

"If you try to force me to take anything, you're gonna cause a fight to start, then you're gonna feel bad for kicking my ass."

He almost smiled, then said, "I still don't like the idea of owing anyone."

"I'll tell you what, the next time you see someone on the road that needs a hand, just pass it on. Then we'll be even."

"All right. Can't I even buy you dinner, or a beer or something?"

I looked at the sky and it was getting to be late. I wanted to at least be in Arizona by nightfall. I was only about thirty miles from the state line and I wanted to get rolling. "I really have to get back on the road. Maybe some other time."

He looked at me, "Hey, if you're ever by this way again, you better look me up and we'll have a beer. I won't be hard to find. Everybody in town knows me." He stuck out his hand again, "You keep the shiny side up and the rubber side down now, ya hear."

His huge hand just about swallowed mine up. "Okay," I said, "you do the same."

I walked to my bike and sat on the seat. Maddog kicked his bike and it fired on the first shot again. He looked at me, nodded, stuck his thumb in the air, then swung his leg over the seat. I nodded back as he pulled away and roared down the road.

I packed up all my tools and stood by the side of the road for a minute. I sure felt good that I stopped to help him. I got on my bike, pointed it east on 66 and thought, *I should try and find a place to get a post card and mail it to Jo.*

I stopped and got one before I hit the edge of town and stuffed it in my shirt, thinking I'd write her when I stopped for the night.

I rode out of Needles and had to catch the interstate for a couple of miles to get back to 66 at the California-Arizona border.

The next part of 66 was a stretch of road that went between Topec and Kingman in Arizona. It was about seventy miles of desert and mountains that, from what I'd heard, was rugged and deserted.

When I got to the state line, I crossed over the Colorado River and got off the interstate. There was a small cafe and I figured I should stop and get something to eat. I didn't think there would be any place to stop between here and Kingman and it was getting late. I pulled onto the dirt lot in front of the place, got off the bike and dusted myself off. The sun was low in the sky so I'd probably pull over soon and get some sleep.

I walked through the door and looked for the bathroom so I could wash the gas and grease off my hands. There was only one customer in the cafe as I made my way to the john. When I finished, I came out and got a table by the window where I could keep an eye on my bike.

I grabbed a menu as the waitress came over. "Nice bike you got there."

"Thanks," I said without looking up. There wasn't much to choose from, so I ordered a steak and salad. She wrote it down and walked away.

I looked out the window and the sun was just about to set. I remembered the post card stuffed in my shirt and pulled it out. Now was a good time to write while I was waiting:

> *Hi, Jo,*
>
> *I'm just the other side of Needles. It's almost dark and I'm barely out of California. I stopped to help a guy in town and that's why I didn't get very far today. I don't know how far I'll get tomorrow, but it really doesn't matter. I'm not in any hurry and I want to see as much as I can. I wish you were here with me and I miss you. I'll write you again soon.*
>
> *Ron*

I drew a smiley face on it and stuffed it back in my shirt. The waitress brought my order and I asked, "Is there any place to mail a post card around here?"

"I can take it and give it to the mailman with our mail tomorrow if you like?"

I wasn't sure I wanted her to read it. "Well, I need to buy a stamp, too."

She walked away and came back with a stamp, "Here you go, hon. Are you sure you don't want me to mail it for you?"

I thought about it for a second, then dug it out of my shirt. What the hell, it's only a post card and anyone who handles it will be able to read it. "Okay, but make sure the mailman gets it. It's for a special lady."

"Your sweetheart?"

I looked out the window for a second, then smiled and replied, "Yeah, my sweetheart." As soon as I spoke those words, I felt a warm glow inside.

"Aw, that's so sweet," she said as I handed it to her. She took it, then walked away so I could finish my meal.

The sun had gone down behind the mountains by the time I finished eating. I had a cup of coffee and rested before I set back out on the road again. I didn't get very far the first day, only about three hundred miles. That was no problem, though. I didn't want to push myself. I calculated that I had about three thousand more miles to go. I figured that if I got to sleep early tonight and got up early tomorrow I could rack up some good miles.

I paid the bill and left a generous tip for the kind waitress. She thanked me and said, "Now don't you worry about that post card ya hear. I'll be sure it gets mailed."

I got up to leave, "Thanks, I'd really appreciate that."

She waved as I walked outside. It was a warm night and it should make for comfortable sleeping in the desert tonight. I checked all the stuff tied to my bike and headed up old 66. I rode about ten miles and it certainly was deserted. Not one car passed me the whole time since I left the cafe.

I slowed down to look for a good spot to camp. It was a cloudless night and the moonlight lit up the desert floor. I found a place and pulled off to the side of the road. It was kind of spooky not seeing any cars pass in either direction. Even in Borrego when we slept in the desert a car would come by every so often.

I unpacked my sleeping bag, laid it next to my bike then sat on it. I leaned up against my motorcycle as the desert air blew soft and warm across my face. The stars were bright and numerous as usual. I didn't think I could ever get so used to this that I didn't appreciate it any more. Every now and then the wind would blow a sagebrush across the sand in the eerie moonlight, which made it look like the ghost of some poor lost soul trying to find its way home.

I laid on my back and gazed up into the heavens and pictured Jo in my mind. I closed my eyes and could smell her perfume and feel her gentle touch. Different scenes of us together ran through my mind like a movie. I went over the things we had said by the little stream today. After an hour or so, I finally dozed off with a smile on my face.

Chapter Eleven

The sound of a car rushing past on the highway brought me back to consciousness. Before I even opened my eyes my first thought was, *I'm in the Arizona desert and I'm really on the road.* The sun wasn't over the horizon yet and it was still cool from the night. I knew it wouldn't take long for the air to heat up once the sun came into full view.

I got up, stretched and took a couple of deep breaths of the clear, fresh desert air. I gathered some twigs to make a small fire, then rolled up my sleeping bag and tied it onto my bike. I had a little metal stand and a steel coffee cup with a removable handle to heat water. It was perfect for morning coffee. One of the things I made sure I remembered to bring was my instant coffee from the garage for occasions just like this. I got the twigs to ignite and placed the stand over the fire. I took some of my drinking water, poured it into the cup and set it down on the stand. As I waited for the water to heat up, I looked around. I didn't get a chance to see the scenery last night 'cause it was too dark. I stared in both directions down the road and couldn't see anything man-made. It was pretty country, though. This road used to be the main route from east to west before they built Interstate 40. Now all the traffic was zipping around in a big loop to Kingman. If a person ever got lost out here, it would probably take weeks to find them, if they ever did.

The water was hot enough now so I put some instant coffee in it. I sat sideways on my bike seat and sipped from the cup as I thought about how Jo was doing and I wondered if John was busy or not.

I watched as the sun came into full view over the horizon and could feel its heat on my skin. I'd have to put my shirt and bandanna on soon to protect me from the intense rays. I was almost finished with my coffee and getting ready to leave when I heard a sound off in the distance coming from the direction of Topec. As it got closer, I recognized the low, deep rumble of Harleys. From the sound of them, there was a bunch and they were moving pretty fast.

I drank the last swallow of coffee and picked up my stand. The riders were almost upon me and I could just barely make them out. I stood up and waited for them to pass so I could check 'em out. As they got to where I was, they slowed down to look me over. There were about ten of them and they were grubby. I waved and they looked hard at me and rolled by. I thought about waving again but they didn't seem like a friendly bunch so I decided against it. As they cruised by, I could see they were wearing colors which meant they belonged to a motorcycle club or gang.

I stood still and waited till they passed before packing my camping stuff away. Those guys were headed in the same direction I was going and I didn't care to run into them again if I could avoid it.

I heard the sound of their pipes fade off into the distance and breathed a little easier. I gave them a few minutes to get down the road before I got on my way. I hadn't packed my pistol because there were states I was going through that had some pretty stiff gun laws and I didn't want to get busted. I wished I had taken it with me now.

I let about ten minutes go by before I got back on the road. The day was starting out nice and clear. I wasn't sure where I would stop to eat. I might have to wait till I got to Kingman. There was a little town on the map halfway between Topec and Kingman called Oatman and they might have a place to get a sandwich. I rolled out onto the highway, sat back in the seat, let the wind blow across my face, then kicked my feet up on the highway pegs, "It don't get no better that this," I said to myself.

I'd only gone about five miles when I spotted a group of people on the side of the road. It didn't take long to recognize it was the bunch that rode by me a few minutes earlier.

I looked straight on down the road as I passed them, making sure I didn't look at them. They were sitting on their bikes as I rolled by. I looked into my rearview mirror after passing them and sure enough, they pulled onto the road behind me. My thoughts started racing in my mind. I didn't like the idea of being out in no man's land without any protection and a bunch of gangsters on my ass. I thought to myself, *don't panic, just keep your head, Ron.*

I held a steady speed hoping they would pass, but they stayed a fixed distance behind me. I started to get nervous and figured, *maybe I should try to outrun them. No, I better not do anything stupid. Maybe they'll just follow me for a while and go around. Or, maybe there might be a town or a place with people up the road where I can pull over and let them pass.*

I held my handle bar grips tight and maintained a steady speed with the wild bunch right behind me. After a few minutes they pulled closer. It looked like they might pass and be on their way. One of them rode alongside me and gave me an "I want to kill you" look, as he drove in front of me. Then another one went around in front of me. A couple more rode alongside me and the ones behind me pulled right up on my ass. I was boxed in. A thought suddenly hit me like a knife blade in the gut. *These guys are out to get me. Any chance I had to outrun them was now gone.*

"Shit, why didn't I speed up when I had the chance?" I asked myself. They started to slow down and at the same time pull over to the side of the road, forcing me with them. There was no way I could get past them without running into one of them. *Maybe I should chance an accident. No, that's not going to work. I was hoping they just wanted to hassle me and let me be on my way.*

As we pulled off to the side of road, they completely surrounded me and forced me to a dead stop. I looked at the ones in front of me and asked, "What's up?"

One of them looked back at me, slowly getting off his bike. A couple of other ones got off their bikes, too. They looked like they'd been up partying all night, the smell of stale booze filled the air.

They had their bikes blocking any way out so I couldn't get by. *Ain't this the shits,* I thought. *When I woke up this morning I was the great road warrior. Now I was about to be reduced to lunch meat.* I kept my eyes on them as they slowly circled me. The grubbiest one stood in front of me, "Where ya headed, pal?"

"New York."

He looked at my plate on the bike, "You one of them California yuppies?"

"Nope."

"You fly colors?"

"Nope. I don't belong to any gangs. I ride solo."

He grinned a sinister grin and exposed some rotten teeth at that news, "Nice new cycle you got here. Your daddy let you take it out for a Sunday ride?"

I didn't say anything to that remark. One of the other ones came up on the other side of me and said, "Let's take him, Wolf."

I dug my feet into the dirt, got ready to rev up the engine and barrel my way out of here if I had to. I was willing and ready to run my bike right up this asshole's nose in front of me.

"Now, calm down, Peanuts," he said to the idiot standing next to me. "We ain't looking for any trouble, are we, boys?"

They all laughed and said, "Hell, no," in unison.

The grubby one in front of me, the one called Wolf, walked right up to me and put his face in mine, "We don't care much for strangers riding up and down our roads, 'specially no California, punk yuppies."

I had to hold my breath as he spoke to keep from smelling the stink of his stale, hung-over breath. He backed off a little and I said, "I'm on a cross-country ride and I ain't out to fuck with no one. I'm just minding my own business."

He walked back up to me and shoved my shoulder, "You getting smart with me, punk?"

His friend started to jump up and down, "Yeah! Get 'em, Wolf."

My gut reaction was to smack him in the jaw, but if I did I knew I'd have the rest of these animals all over me. I kept my cool, but it started to look like I wasn't going to get out of this alive.

He ran his fingers along my gas tank. "I sure wish I had one of these nice, new, shiny machines. Maybe you'd be feeling generous and trade yours for mine? Or, better yet, why don't you just give this to me, yuppie punk."

"Over my dead body."

Immediately right after I spoke I thought, *bad choice of words.*

"Maybe we can oblige you. If killing you is what it takes, I've got a couple of boys here that wouldn't mind. I don't know if you noticed, but there ain't nobody out here but you and us."

I looked around and all I could see was a bunch of toothless goons grinning at me. They started to close in so I gripped the throttle tight, *if I'm going down, I'm going down fighting.* I was just about to whack open my throttle, pop the clutch and run my front tire into Wolf's nuts when I heard a rumble down the road. They heard it too, and stopped in their tracks. *It's probably just another one of these scums,* I thought, as I aimed my tire right between his legs. The rumble got louder and I could tell for sure it was another Harley. As the rider came into sight, all the gangsters turned to see who it was. I figured this might be my only opportunity to escape, but I would have to kick a couple of bikes out of my way to get free. The trick was to stay upright in the process.

I started twisting my wrist on the throttle and was about to lift my feet off the ground when I looked over at the approaching rider. As he got a little closer, I recognized the huge frame of the man sticking straight up in the air. He slowed as he got to us and nonchalantly looked us over. I sat upright in my seat hoping he would see me. He rolled past us a little ways down the road, then stopped. *I think he saw me.* All eyes were on him now. He made a U-turn and came back. He rode up to the group and pushed his way through the crowd with his bike. They all moved out of his way as he stopped with his front tire coming to rest an inch from mine. He slowly reached down and shut his ignition off. No one spoke as he got off his bike and walked up to me, stuck his hand out and said, "How you doing, Roadside?"

At that moment he looked like the biggest angel I'd ever seen. I reached my hand out and replied, "Things could be better, Maddog."

Wolf looked surprised and spoke up. "Hey, Maddog, how ya be?"

He slowly turned to him, "Not bad. I see you met my partner, Roadside."

"Uh . . .he's your bud?"

"Yeah. You weren't giving him any shit, were you?"

He started to stutter, "No. We were just checking out his ride, right, boys?" They all nodded as he continued, "We didn't know he was your pal. Hell, any pal of yours is a pal of ours, right?"

They all nodded again. Maddog stared down at Wolf, "You ain't no friend of mine and don't you forget it. Now get the fuck out of here."

"Okay, Maddog, stay cool. We're outta here right now."

They got on their bikes, fumbled as they started them, kicking up a lot of dust and almost running into each other trying to get back on the road. After they left, Maddog looked at me, "They were fuckin' with you, weren't they?"

"Man, am I glad to see you," I said, as I let out my breath, "I'm not sure, but I think they were going to try and kill me. They thought I was some yuppie punk."

"I doubt that. There're just a small-time, two-bit gang. They might have ruffled you up, though. And to tell you the truth, when I first saw you yesterday, I thought you were a punk, too. Till you said you were a mechanic."

I looked at him, puzzled. "I don't get it. There are ten of them and they wouldn't mess with you. How come?"

"I got a pretty bad reputation. I used to belong to one of the biggest and meanest motorcycle clubs in the area, and they know it. I still have a lot of friends that belong and if those guys ever gave me, or any of my friends any trouble, all I have to do is make a phone call."

"That makes sense. I'm really glad you showed up when you did."

"Seems to me I remember you saying yesterday that if I saw someone in need of help, I should give 'em a hand. Then that would make us even."

I smiled, "Yep, I did say that, didn't I?"

"I figure me showing up when I did, and you just about to get your face rearranged, makes us even, huh?"

"I guess it does."

He turned on his key and was about to kick-start his bike when he looked up and asked, "Where are you headed?"

I explained my plan and he turned the key off and sat back down on his seat. "I rode this thing around for a couple of hours after you rebuilt the carb. It didn't act up once and started every time on the first kick. This cycle hasn't ran this good in years."

"Well, that makes me happy," I grinned.

"I've been wanting to see my ma in Indiana, but I couldn't trust this thing on a trip that far. I've been having trouble with the carb for a long time. And I guess I'm just too stubborn to buy a new one."

I looked down at my gas tank. "You're lucky. My mom passed away a few years ago. I wish I could visit her."

"Mine's getting up in years and I wanna get back there before it's too late. That's why I packed up early this morning and got on the road. I was thinking 'bout leaving tomorrow, lucky for you I didn't."

"You can say that again."

He sat and stared at me like he was trying to make a decision, then spoke, "I usually travel solo, but as long as you're heading east, we can ride together, if that's okay with you. I wouldn't mind taking my time riding old 66. Besides, if anything goes wrong with my bike, I'd have my own personal mechanic."

"Gee, thanks. Nothing like being tied to someone else's bike," I said. *Hell,* I thought, *it'd be like having my own bodyguard riding with this guy.* "Yeah, that's cool. We can ride together."

He almost smiled again and asked, "So, what's your plan?"

"I got this map of where Route 66 still exists. And I want to follow it as much as possible. I'm not sure how long it'll take, but it's a once-in-a-lifetime trip for me. I don't know if I'll get another chance to do this again."

"From what I remember, 66 ends in Chicago, doesn't it?"

I nodded, "Yes, it does."

"I guess I can ride with you as far as my hometown. It's just south of Chicago, almost on the Indiana-Illinois border," he said.

"Sounds good to me. I was going to stop and eat in Oatman. I'm hungry after that run-in I had with that bunch of outlaws, but I'm not sure what's out there."

"I've been through Oatman many times and there's a few places to eat."

"Sounds good to me. Lets get moving."

He started to reach down, then hesitated. "You ain't carrying anything illegal, are you? Like drugs?"

"No. Why?"

"When you look like we do, and when we get into other states, we might get hassled by the cops. So, it's better not to give 'em a reason to bust ya." It was easy to understand his concern. He looked like an outlaw biker. I wasn't sure I did, but when you're riding a Harley that makes you one in some people's eyes. "Let's get outta here," he said. "You ready to ride?"

I nodded and we fired up our bikes, rolled onto the road and headed for Oatman. From what I could tell by the map it was about thirty miles away. This part of the country was almost like Borrego except it got cold enough to snow during the winter. It's at a higher elevation and more mountainous than the desert around Borrego.

I glanced over at Maddog as we cruised down the road. He looked solid as a rock. His bike had high ape hanger handlebars and his shoulders were still higher than the bars. I'm not sure if ten of those guys could have taken him down. It felt good to have a fellow rider along and I think I was going to enjoy riding with him. I had a gut feeling that he wasn't as mean as he looked, even if he didn't smile.

We cruised along side by side and before I knew it we were riding into Oatman. It was an old mining town turned tourist attraction. It had one main street and that was 66 itself. As we rode in, there were wild burros roaming freely back and forth across the road with tourists feeding them carrots and taking their pictures.

There were a few small restaurants on either side and I motioned to Maddog to pull over. We stopped in front of one and shut our bikes down. It looked like we might make some pretty good time today if nothing else happened. We stood at the sidewalk, which was a wooden walkway like in the old western movies. And they even had horse rails where you could tie up horses.

Maddog looked up and down the road. "I spent a lot of years around here and this place is getting worse each time I come through."

"How do you mean?"

"It's a tourist trap. There was a time when you could come out here and be alone." He didn't say anything more. He looked around as though someone had taken something away from him.

I wasn't sure if I should speak, "I guess it's like everything in life. Nothing really stays the same, even though we want it to. Things get different no matter how hard we try to keep them from changing." I'm not sure if he heard me. He just kept looking down the street. I spotted a shop that looked like a deli. "I think I'm going to take a walk over and get a sandwich and a soda. How about you? Want something to eat?"

"Sure," he said as we walked in that direction.

We got our food and sat outside on a bench watching the tourists feed the donkeys and snap pictures. I looked at the license plates on the cars and trucks and most were from out of state. Maddog ate in silence, not too happy with all the people milling about. I could tell he wanted to get out of here quickly and I didn't care much for the crowds myself. One good thing about this was that most of the people came here from Bullhead City on a different route than old 66 and would probably go back the same way. So we wouldn't have to deal with them on the highway.

I pulled my map out of my shirt and checked the route. The next major city was Kingman, and from the map I guessed it to be about thirty miles away. It looked like the road went through a mountain stretch from the way the line curved on the map.

Maddog looked over at me, "You pretty much got that figured out yet?"

"Yeah," I said as I gulped down the last of my soda.

"You ready to get back in the wind?" he asked.

"Yep, ready whenever you are."

He nodded and we stood up and walked to our bikes. When we reached them, I stood alongside mine and waited for him to start his. He flipped on the ignition switch and stepped down on the pedal. It came to life on the first try. He looked over to me and said, over the rumble of his pipes, "Partner, you sure dialed this thing in just right."

I grinned, swung my leg over my seat and started my bike up. We drove onto the street and weaved our way between the tourists and donkeys on our way out of town. Once back on the open road, the wind began to kick up as we got further into the mountains. The road narrowed and the curves got sharp so Maddog fell in behind me, letting me take the lead. I felt kind of honored that he would follow me, since he didn't seem to be the type. I also noticed he had a lot of road discipline, which made him easy to ride with. I could tell he'd racked up a lot of miles on that bike.

I settled back in my seat and enjoyed the scenery. There were a few small towns, if you could call them that, along the way but not many people. This was still harsh desert and not for the meek or weak. Arizona was one of the last open range states and people carried loaded firearms out here. It was legal as long as it was in a holster and in plain view, not concealed.

It didn't take long before we came into Kingman and the traffic started to pick up. Just like Oatman, Route 66 went right through the center of town. We came to a stoplight and I looked at Maddog. "You want to stop or ride through?"

"Let's ride through, too many people here for me."

"I can go with that," I said as the light changed and we continued on.

It wasn't quite noon yet and we were moving right along. We got to the other side of Kingman and 66 continued eastward just north of the interstate. It then swung in a big loop going about thirty miles north through several small towns, then came back to the 40 at Ash Fork, according to the map. I followed the historic Route 66 signs and continued east. It was an uphill climb to Flagstaff and the scenery began to change.

As we rode through these towns, it became apparent how they had become cut off because of the interstate. Each town had the same boarded-up businesses and the weathered, deserted houses. I could tell they had been abandoned long ago. It struck me as sad the changes these people had to make because of progress. Every so often we passed someone walking along the road, and each time they smiled and waved.

We followed the old arch of the road with only the sound of the pipes in our ears and the wind in our faces. The terrain began to get greener the higher we climbed, but was still desert in nature. As we approached the other end of the loop, 66 would end for a while and we would have to get on the interstate at Ash Fork.

We finally merged back onto 40 and headed for Flagstaff. I wasn't too happy about riding the fast, trendy freeway and from what little I knew about Maddog, I'm sure he wasn't too crazy about it either.

We cruised along and it wasn't twenty minutes or so when I saw a sign for Williams, another town along the way. What really caught my eye was a sign that said, "Grand Canyon this exit." I motioned to Maddog that I wanted to get off and he signaled that he understood. I pulled off the freeway and he followed behind me. I stopped at the bottom of the ramp and he stopped alongside me, "Something wrong?" he asked.

"No," I said as I pulled out my map. "From what I can tell, 66 rides along I-40 for quite a distance. It's in bits and pieces for the next stretch and I thought we might take a side trip to see the Grand Canyon, if that's okay with you? Hell, it's a perfect day. The weather's warm and clear and it's still early. And besides, it's only a couple of hours away and it beats riding on the boring interstate."

"I got no problem with that. It's been a long time since I been on a real trip. So you got the map, lead the way."

I tucked the map back into my shirt and headed north on Route 64 to 180 in the direction of the south rim of the canyon with Maddog right alongside me. As we cruised toward the canyon, the scenery kept getting better and better. The traffic was on the light side considering it was a big tourist attraction and that made it easier to look around. Maddog was right beside me and I think he was really digging this, though he would never admit it.

It'd been almost an hour since we left the interstate when I saw a car parked on the side of the road up ahead. We both slowed down as we came to it and I noticed the rear tire was flat. We slowed down further and I could see two middle-aged ladies in the front seat with several children in the back. We looked at each other and intuitively knew to pull off to the side of the road in front of the stranded auto.

As we rolled to a stop I looked at Maddog, "Should we see if they need help?"

"Yeah, let's go."

We shut our bikes off and started to walk back to the car. As we did, I saw them look me over, then look over Maddog. They rolled up the windows as I got to the car and Maddog stopped short when he saw their reaction to us.

I stood alongside the rolled up window, "Are you ladies okay?" They looked at each other for a second, then nodded that they were. "Do you need any help?" They hesitated, then shook their heads "No", as they looked at Maddog. "Do you have help on the way?"

Again they hesitated and looked at each other, then turned to me and said through the window, "Yes, we have help on the way."

I thought she was lying and just scared. So I offered, "If you want, you can take your trunk key off the ring, give it to me and we can change the tire for you."

She paused, then said, "No, thanks. We'll just wait."

"I understand," I said as I turned to walk away.

I started to walk away when she rolled down the window about an inch and said, "Wait. Here's the key."

I walked back and she stuck the key through the narrow opening. "You can stay in the car if you feel safer," I said, as I took the key.

She nodded and I went to the back of the car. Maddog walked around the other side while the women watched him as he passed by. I opened the trunk and Maddog grabbed the spare while I got the bumper jack out. I jacked up the car and he took off the flat and put on the spare. I let the car down and we put everything away. I shut the trunk and we both walked to the window. I handed the key back to her through the opening. She took it and tried to hand us some rolled-up bills, "Here, take this," she said.

I put my hands up at the same time saying, "No. You don't owe us anything."

She looked puzzled. "I want to pay you for your help."

"Nope. We can't take any money."

That's when Maddog spoke up. "I'll tell you what. If you happen to see anyone who needs help on the road, stop and give 'em a hand. That way we'll be even."

Hey, I thought, *that's my line.* I looked at him and I could tell he was laughing inside.

She looked up at Maddog and I could see the fear begin to drain from her face as she rolled the window down and said, "If you won't take any money, please accept my thanks." She started up her car. "We really appreciate you boys stopping to help us."

We nodded as they both waved and drove away. I looked at Maddog. "I guess we spooked 'em."

"Not us. It was me they were scared of," he replied.

"Naw, we both look like banditos."

"You don't have to humor me, I'm used to it. It happens to me all the time. I guess it goes with the image."

I could tell it still hurt him no matter how hard he tried to hide it. I changed the subject. "The Grand Canyon is right down the road waiting. You ready to go check it out?"

"Yep. Let's get to it," he said as he turned to his bike.

I followed, and as we got on our bikes I said, "Sure does give you a good feeling to help someone, huh?"

He looked back and thought about it, then said, "Yeah, sure does."

He kicked down on his kick-starter, I fired mine up and we roared off in the direction of the Canyon.

It didn't take long before we were at the park entrance. We paid our fee to get in and rode along the rim of the canyon. I wanted to stop at one of the overlooks so I motioned to him and we pulled into the next one we came to.

I parked my cycle and Maddog did the same. As we walked to the edge, I asked, "You ever been here before?"

He looked awestruck, "No. I ain't never seen this in person. I heard a lot of people talk about it and now I know why."

"I was here once before and I'm still blown away at this sight." I looked down at the bottom and could see the narrow Colorado River snaking through the canyon, "It's amazing how that tiny river did all of this."

He looked down. "That river did all that?"

"That's what they claim." We walked to the edge and gazed at the cavern walls and the sheer immensity of the canyon. The colors were spectacular and the sunlight gave them brilliance.

Maddog stood there looking and seemed to be hypnotized by the view. I had the feeling he never got much of a chance to see the sights of the country. After a few minutes he said, "Man, that's really something. I'm glad we came here. I've been this way a few times but never took the time to stop and check this out."

We sat at the edge absorbing this gigantic, natural phenomenon for about half an hour. He started to fidget so I suggested we get back on the road and he replied, "Yeah, I feel better when I'm in motion."

We got back on our bikes and cruised through a couple more turnouts on our way out of the park. It was getting late in the afternoon and I thought we better be on our way if we were going to log more miles before we stopped for the night.

We took Route 64 out of the park and followed it to the end, which was Route 89 into Flagstaff. When I got to 89, I stopped to check my map and saw there were two ways we could go. I looked at Maddog. "We could head back to Flagstaff and catch the interstate. Route 66 pretty much is right on, or right next to the 40. Or we could head north for a bit and catch Route 264, a two-lane highway which goes through the Navajo Indian Reservation. It'll take us to Gallup, New Mexico, where we can pick up 66 again."

"Hey, partner, you been doing fine so far. Whatever you say is all right with me. You point us in the direction you want us to go and I'll be right behind you."

If I didn't know any better, I'd say he was having fun letting me make all the decisions so he could kick back. "I planned to sleep alongside the road tonight and I think it will be easier to find a place on a deserted stretch rather than along a busy interstate," I suggested.

"Suits me just fine. I planned to sleep outside on my bedroll anyway."

"It's settled then." I stashed the map in my shirt and headed north on 89 to 264, then turned east. I didn't think we would make it to Gallup tonight and there weren't many towns on this road. I hoped we could find one where we could stop and eat. I knew I'd be hungry in a little while and I was sure Maddog would be, too.

This road took us smack through the middle of flatlands and high plateaus. We rode through the Painted Desert and the Petrified Forest. The terrain was brightly colored in lines of red to sandy gray. It was as though nature came out here with a paintbrush and did some of her best work. This was truly God's country.

The scenery was beginning to mesmerize me. My thoughts started to drift as the pavement rolled away under my wheels, the highway sound ringing in my ears. I thought about the past two years of my life. *What did my future hold? What was down the road for me?* I pictured Jo in my mind, then her father's image appeared. *Would she ever be able to let him go and make her own way? What was Gloria like? Would I even be able to find her?* The thoughts started to race through my head and I was unable to stop them. That's when Maddog pulled slightly in front of me to get my attention. There was a small town ahead and he pointed to a restaurant sign. He wanted to pull over and I signaled back.

We rode onto the gravel lot in front of it and stopped. He looked at me. "Hell, partner, I'm almost outta gas. I didn't think you were ever gonna stop."

It was then that I realized we'd gone almost two hours since we turned onto this road. I shut my bike off and looked back, "Sorry, I guess I got carried away. My mind wandered and time just slipped away."

"Man, when you cruise, you cruise."

"Next time if you want to stop, let me know," I said apologetically.

"Hey, it don't bother me. This is the way I like to ride. It's just my speed. Take in a sight, then chew up a chunk of road. I can hang with that." He turned off his cycle and we walked to the restaurant. I looked around and realized we were right in the middle of the Navajo Indian Reservation.

There was an older, Native American gentleman sitting on the front porch of the restaurant in a rocking chair. As we passed him, he said, "How you fellas doing today?"

I answered, "Okay, and how 'bout you?"

"I'm doing just fine. Nice day for a ride on them motorcycles."

"Yeah, we've had great weather so far."

He smiled, "You fellas enjoy your meals now."

"Thanks, we will. And you have a nice day." He nodded and continued rocking in his chair. We went inside and sat down at one of the tables. I looked around and the walls were decorated with brightly colored tribal Indian artifacts. Some of them were very intricate and fascinating. Just then the waitress came over and I ordered a hamburger, fries and Coke.

"Gimme the same, only with a beer instead of a Coke," Maddog said.

"Be right up," she replied as she walked away.

I pulled the map out of my shirt and laid it on the table. He looked at me. "You been picking good roads to ride. You ever been out this way?"

"I've been cross-country, but never on the back roads like this. And not on a motorcycle."

"You ride like you know what you're doing," he said.

"Yeah, I've put some miles on. This is my first Harley, though. I just got it."

"Well, you handle it pretty good."

I nodded and could see the waitress coming with our food. We ate and when we were finished, Maddog called her back over again. "I'll have another order of the same."

Damn, I thought, *that was a big burger and a healthy order of fries. I was full and he's getting another? Well, he is a big boy.*

As he ate his second helping, I tried to figure out, by looking at the map, how far we should go tonight. It was almost dusk and I didn't want to ride on any unfamiliar roads in the dark. "We're almost to the New Mexico state line and we should probably find a place to sleep in an hour or so," I said half to myself while tracing a road line with my finger.

"Sounds good to me," he mumbled with a mouthful of French fries.

After checking out the map a little more, I stashed it back in my shirt and waited for him to finish eating. The more I looked at the works on the wall, the more intriguing they became. There seemed to be something spiritual about them. One thing for certain, they were pleasant to look at.

Maddog's voice broke my train of thought. "I'm done. You ready?"

"Yeah. We better gas up before we get out of town. From the looks of the map, there ain't nothing out there till Gallup."

We used the bathroom to wash up. We got gas, then set out on the road. The sun had just set and it was getting hard to see anything alongside the road. We cruised for a while, our headlights cutting a bright path through the darkness. The moon looked like it would be full in a couple of days and helped light our way.

I spotted a clearing off to the side and motioned to Maddog as we passed it up. We pulled over. "That looked like a good place to spend the night," I said, pointing back over my shoulder.

He looked back and said, "Yeah, that'll work."

We made a U-turn, rode back to it and shut our bikes down. It was right next to a several small trees. I figured if we sleep against them, we wouldn't get run over by any stray cars.

We stood next to our bikes and looked around, the moonlight lit up our surroundings. After a moment, Maddog spoke. "Man, it sure is quiet here."

"Uh-huh, we're in the middle of no-man's-land."

"I'll tell you, partner, this sure beats riding the interstate."

I took off my sleeping bag and he did the same. If we could get to bed early, we could get a nice start tomorrow. I cleared a spot next to my bike and laid my bag down on it. The sky was clear and we shouldn't have to worry about rain till we got further east.

I laid on my sleeping bag and Maddog laid on his. We both stayed silent for a few moments looking into the night sky. I finally broke the silence. "I'm glad I ran into you. My day could have turned out a lot different if I hadn't," I said.

"Hey, the same goes for me. If I hadn't seen you I would've took 66 to Kingman, then hit the interstate and took that all the way to Indiana. I don't get to do much sightseeing. The crowd I used to hang with wasn't into seeing the sights. A lot of other things, but not that."

"You mentioned you ride solo now."

"Maybe I'll explain it to you sometime." He was quiet for a moment. "I wouldn't even be riding with you, 'cept for one thing."

"What's that?" I asked.

"Remember that look the lady with the flat tire gave me the first time she saw me?"

"Yeah."

"Well, people react to me one of two ways. Either they're scared shitless of me or they want to pick a fight to try and prove something. That's happened all my life no matter where I go." He stopped again for a second, then continued, "When you came up to me the first time at the Harley shop, you wanted to help me. You weren't scared of me and you didn't want to prove anything. You treated me like a regular person and I appreciated that."

"Well, you are a regular person, aren't you?" I asked.

"Because of my size and my tattoos and the fact that I ride a Harley, a lot of people don't think so."

"Maybe you got to give them a chance to get past the first impression of you."

"It's not that easy. That's why I spend most of my time solo."

I didn't know what to say. I'd never had that problem so I couldn't relate. I guess I had to believe it was a problem for him if he said it was.

"Well, partner, I think we should get some sleep," he said, yawning.

"You're right. See you in the morning." I stared up at the stars and had a funny feeling more was going to be revealed to me before this trip was over. I crawled into my sleeping bag, pulled it over my head and was soon asleep.

Chapter Twelve

"Hey, partner, you gonna sleep all day?"

I was right in the middle of a dream as Maddog's voice shattered it. I peeled one eye open, trying to collect my senses. Looking around, I saw Maddog sitting sideways on the seat of his bike with one arm lazily hung over his handlebars, "Sun's almost up. We can't stay here all day."

"Yeah, I can see the sun's not quite over the horizon yet."

Just my luck, I thought, *I team up with a guy who only needs two hours of sleep a night. Naw, that ain't true. It'd been more like six or seven hours. I just wanted to finish the dream 'cause it had Jo in it.*

I opened the other eye, took in a deep breath of the fresh pre-dawn air and sat up. I noticed the air felt a bit more humid here and there was a light coat of dew on my sleeping bag. The further east we got, the more this would be the case. I climbed out of my bag and saw his was still on the ground, "How long you been awake?" I grumbled.

"A few minutes."

"You want a cup of coffee before we hit the road? I have to have my morning shot of caffeine."

"How are you gonna do that?" he asked.

I pulled the metal cup out of my bag, "If we make a small fire, I can heat the water in this and I have an extra cup."

"All right," he said, as he picked up some twigs and placed them in a small pile.

I rummaged around in my saddlebags for some matches and lit the wood. I filled the tin cup from my water bottle. He watched me, then said, "You got everything you need."

"Well, everything for a cup of coffee."

After the water got hot, I made him a cup of instant coffee and one for myself. I leaned against my bike seat, looking around as I sipped from my cup. It was neat to watch the pre-dawn gray turn to bright sunlight.

Maddog looked at me. "This ain't bad."

"What? The coffee?"

"The coffee, the scenery, this whole business."

I nodded in agreement. Only a few cars had passed by since we woke up, which made it feel like this was all ours. I took the map out and checked the route. It would take us through New Mexico, the panhandle of Texas, then into Oklahoma. I wasn't sure how far we'd get today, but it didn't matter. I looked at Maddog, who was gazing out across the landscape, "Maddog, how about we get a room tonight? It's been a few days since I had a shower and I could use a good night's rest on a real bed."

"Sounds good to me. I could use a shower, too."

I'd have to plan the route so it'd put us in a town at the end of the day. I think I could handle that. I had to wash my clothes too, so that would work out perfectly.

I put the map in my shirt and finished the rest of the coffee. Maddog finished his and handed me the cup. We packed up our gear, got ready to leave and he turned to me, "Let's find a bathroom and a place to eat breakfast."

"We're on our way," I said, as I started my bike.

He hit the throttle twice and stepped down on the kick-starter to prime it. Then he turned on the ignition and stepped down hard. It started, then sputtered and died. He went through the motions again and the second time it sprang to life. "Hmm," he said, "two times. That's not bad, not bad at all. It usually takes five to ten tries first time in the morning. I gotta hand it to you, partner, you sure got your shit together."

I didn't say anything, I just grinned a little. He got on and nodded he was ready for me to lead the way. I pulled onto the road and headed toward Gallup, with Maddog right alongside me. The day was starting out warm, beautiful and sunny. I adjusted myself in my seat and sat back to enjoy. The road we were on led right into Gallup so when we hit town, we stopped at a truck stop restaurant and had a good breakfast. I knew we'd be on the road most of the day and would probably rack up a lot of miles since it was still early. There was nothing like a good meal and an early start.

We left Gallup and crossed under I-40 on old 66. Most of the original road was still here and it wasn't long before we were riding over the Great Continental Divide, which put us right in the middle of the majestic Rocky Mountains. The crisp air and the scenery were different east of the divide. It didn't have that dry, desert feel that was characteristic west of the divide.

We cruised along the old route, riding through small towns that used to be populated before the interstate. The further away from the interstate exits we got, the more the towns were of the ghost variety. No matter how many of these I rode through, it still struck me as eerie and sad that they had to die. But I guess all man-made things come to an end sooner or later.

Maddog and I fell into a road trance as we drove along the two-lane highway. We weaved up and down and in and out of the great mountains' valleys and peaks. I gathered up as much scenery as I could so as to remember this journey. As we rode, I remembered something about this state that I'd heard once. It'd been said it was placed here by the gods and had a spiritual sense to it. Maybe because it was high in elevation, which made the air unusually crisp and clear and the sky was so deep blue it would grab even the most unaware person's attention. That's if you weren't in a hurry and looked around instead of straight ahead. Being on a motorcycle, exposed to all the elements instead of being cooped up in a car, even furthered that connection to nature.

I glanced at Maddog and knew he was having a good time. The soft, warm summer wind in our faces and the sights so clear here mesmerized the senses.

We reached the center of the state and crossed the Rio Grande River, which ran all the way from Colorado down to the Texas-Mexico border. The miles were flying by and I knew it would be sad to leave New Mexico, but we had to move on.

I motioned to Maddog to pull over to the side of the road. I wanted a drink of water and to check the map. We stopped, got off our bikes and I took out my water bottle. I took a long swig and handed it to him. He took two gulps and almost emptied it. I pulled my map out and said, "Forty goes straight east and 66 rides in a big loop to Santa Fe, then through Las Vegas, New Mexico, then goes back to 40. You want to go the loop?"

"Man, this is great. Let's stay on 66."

"Okay, 66 it is."

I didn't know there was a Las Vegas in New Mexico. Another casualty of the interstates, I thought, as I stuffed the map back in my shirt, put the water bottle back in my bag and rolled out onto the road with Maddog right alongside.

We continued on through the rest of the state and soon hit the interstate through Texas. A lot of Route 40 was laid right on the top of old 66 so we had no choice. We had about two hundred miles of Texas to ride and it was a large contrast from New Mexico. It was basically flat land made up of cattle ranches and farms. We rolled onward and I was still enjoying the landscape. I think the contrast made it interesting.

It was getting to be mid-afternoon and I tried to calculate in my mind where we would stop for the night, probably somewhere in Oklahoma. We had to stop and eat soon, but I didn't want to eat too early 'cause that would just tire me and I knew I wouldn't want to ride much further after that.

We rode for several more hours and finally came to the Oklahoma state line. We crossed over it and I was beginning to feel a little weary. Every chance we could, we rode old 66 and that made it even more tiring.

I got new energy, though, when the scenery began to change to green, rolling hills and valleys. Mother Nature was out here again playing with her paintbrush and her brilliant colors were everywhere.

From what I knew of this state, it was a Wild West place. A lot of famous outlaws hung out here. Also, the actual transition from west to midwest happens somewhere between the Oklahoma border and Oklahoma City.

The sun was getting low in the sky and the shadows began to get long. We were about seventy-five miles west of Oklahoma City when Maddog got my attention. He put his hand to his mouth as though he were eating. I nodded that I understood.

We pulled over at the first restaurant we came to and parked. We got off our bikes and stretched. My bones were starting to get sore and Maddog was riding a hard tail with a four-speed transmission, so he had to be hurting, too. But if he was, he wasn't showing it. He was probably the type who showed no pain, no matter what.

I looked the place over and saw it was a beat-up bar and grill, but at this point anything looked good. We walked toward the door together and as he turned to me he said, "I sure am hungry, partner, how about you?"

"Yeah, it's been a long day and we covered a lot of miles. After we pass Oklahoma City we'll start looking for a motel. It should be dark by then."

"Okay by me."

We went in and found a table by the window so we could keep an eye on the bikes. There was an older gentleman sitting with the waitress at the counter. She waited till we sat down, then came over, "What can I get you boys? Would you like to see a menu?"

"Naw," I said. "I'll just have a burger, fries and a Coke."

"Me, too," Maddog added, " except make mine a beer."

"Coming right up," she said, as she turned around on her heels.

I sat back in my seat and peered out the window, "Sure is an old, dusty town."

"It sure is," Maddog responded, " nice, though."

"I guess it's not really much different than Borrego, 'cept for the weather."

We both fell silent waiting for our food. When she came out and placed it on our table, I said, "Damn, those are some big burgers." They were huge, but Maddog didn't say anything. He just picked one up and started eating.

I had trouble finishing all the food, but I did. I sat in my seat not able to move. Maddog ordered another beer and when he finished said, "I gotta go to the john, be back in about ten minutes."

That was fine with me. I needed to relax a bit more before we headed back out. I settled in my chair and had a cup of coffee to stay alert. I pulled out the map and noticed that the interstate east of Oklahoma City was a toll road and that 66 rode right alongside it. I figured we wouldn't have much trouble finding a motel room 'cause it looked heavily traveled.

The sun was low in the sky now and I sat staring out the window reminiscing about the sights we'd seen today when an old beat-up pick-up truck with one of the front fenders hanging down pulled up onto the lot in front of the restaurant. Three guys were crammed in the front seat and a fourth was riding in the back. They sat there for a moment with the engine clanging, then the driver shut it off.

The guys in the front slowly got out and the one in the back fell out over the side. As his feet hit the ground he staggered against the truck. All of them were swaying slightly. They didn't look like a fun bunch as they headed toward the door. It appeared as though they'd been out on an all-night binge and were still chugging along on their last legs. As they passed our bikes, they stopped and pointed. They exchanged some words with each other, which I couldn't make out and figured they were Harley admirers.

They staggered through the door and looked around as they headed toward the counter. The place was empty now and I was the only one with a Harley shirt on, so it wasn't hard to figure out who the bikes belonged to. I waited for the usual nod and smile as they sized me up, but instead they just glared. As they sat down on the stools, one of the grubbier ones grabbed his crotch and intensely scratched his balls. They looked at me again and now I sensed trouble.

I tried to mind my own business, hoping Maddog would hurry up and get out here. We were definitely in the wrong neighborhood. I stared out the window and overheard one of them mumble something about, "Fuckin' biker trash."

I gulped and thought, *they must be related to Jerry the goon back home.* I sat quietly as they shot snide comments back and forth loudly to each other, making sure I could hear.

Finally, Maddog came out of the john and the four of them eyeballed him as he walked to the table. At first they looked a little shocked, but that didn't last long. As he sat down, the comments started again.

I leaned over and whispered, "I think we got trouble."

He nonchalantly gazed over at them, "Naw, they ain't nothing."

"Well, maybe not, but there's four of them and only two of us. If you do the math it means we're outnumbered two to one."

He looked out the window. "So?"

Okay, I thought, *if he's not worried about it, then neither am I.*

We sat there looking out the window listening to them mouth-off when Maddog said, "Well, partner, you 'bout ready to hit the road? It kinda stinks in here." That got their attention and I thought, *shit, we ain't getting out of here now without a fist fight.*

We slowly got up and so did they. As we walked toward the door, they moved in a position between the exit and us. Maddog walked right up to the one with the biggest mouth, who looked like the leader of this bunch, and stood nose to nose with him. Well, not really nose-to-nose since Maddog was at least six inches taller than he was.

He looked Maddog in the eye. "What'd ya mean by that remark?" he asked in a slurred voice.

"Just what I said, it stinks in here." I was a step behind him and a little to the right. I placed my hand on the back of a chair ready to pick it up and start swinging.

He stared at Maddog, then he asked. "You boys ride with any clubs?"

He responded, "I used to, but now I ride solo. What's it to you?"

"Look, boy, it's like this, we don't like outsiders coming 'round here." His three buddies nodded in agreement.

Maddog's jaw muscles tightened as he said, "Well, pal, I don't particularly give a fuck what you like." I knew the shit was about to hit the fan so I grabbed the chair tightly and got ready to start swinging.

There was a deafening silence between the two as they stared each other down, then the leader said, "My daddy always told me, the bigger they are, the harder they fall," as he took a swing at Maddog.

I lifted the chair into the air about to start smashing heads when Maddog caught the big mouth's fist in mid-air. He grabbed it tightly and the guy's eyes opened wide. Maddog then said, "Wanna bet? You better have another talk with your daddy."

The others froze as I raised the chair over my head. The room was deadly silent again as Maddog and the big mouth stood face-to-face with his fist lost in Maddog's massive grip. Then Maddog's knuckles started to turn white as he began to squeeze. Big mouth grimaced in pain as Maddog squeezed a little harder and the guy's face began to contort. Maddog kept squeezing and the guy let out a little groan, and mumbled, "Son of a bitch. Okay, okay."

Maddog clenched his teeth, squeezed down even harder and I heard one of the guy's fingers give a loud pop as the guy let out a high-pitched, blood-curdling scream. His knees started to buckle under him. I grimaced a little myself. Maddog didn't let up, he kept on squeezing. The guy dropped to his knees whimpering, his friends standing behind with shocked looks on their faces. I held the chair at the ready just in case.

Maddog gave one final squeeze and I heard another loud pop. The guy's face was so contorted by now that he was totally unrecognizable. He moaned loudly and crumpled to the floor in a heap of quivering jelly. Maddog let go and it was clear that a couple of his fingers were broken. Maddog faced the other three, "Well? How about you fellas?"

They all shook their heads and one said, "Nope, we got no problems."

"Good," he replied, as he shoved his way through the middle of 'em.

I put the chair down and followed closely on his heels. I didn't want to be the one to get stabbed or shot. As I passed the bunch, I couldn't resist jerking my arm back a little and watching them flinch.

We walked outside and as we headed to our bikes, Maddog picked up the pace and said, half under his breath, "Let's get the hell out of here. If they make it to their truck, they might come up shooting."

"Gotcha," I replied as I made a beeline for my cycle.

As Maddog reached his bike, he grabbed the handlebar and muttered under his breath, "Come on darlin', don't fail me now."

I jumped on my seat and fired mine up as he slowly primed his. I looked toward the front door and the wild bunch was stumbling out toward their truck. Maddog didn't even have his ignition switch on yet, *Damn, he's taking too long. Even if they don't have guns they can run us down if they get to their truck.* I kicked my bike into gear, at the same time releasing the clutch, which brought my front tire high off the ground. I pointed my bike between the crowd and their truck. I barely beat them to it, scattering them in all directions as I zipped by. I stopped, turned around and figured one more pass ought to buy us enough time for Maddog to get his bike going. I nailed the throttle again and popped the clutch, kicking up a cloud of gravel and dust, just missing them again as I made the second pass. I pulled up alongside Maddog as he was lifting his leg over his seat, "Let's get the fuck outta here," I yelled.

He was still being nonchalant about it when I looked in my rearview mirror and saw one of them reach through the open window of the truck and pull out a sawed off shot-gun. Maddog saw it, too, and that got his attention as he hollered back over his pipes, "Good idea." He slammed his bike into gear and we hit the pavement, our rear tires almost skidding out from under us. I kept one eye on my mirror as the guy with the shotgun tried to draw a bead on us. He was weaving back and forth as he squeezed off a round, which whizzed way over our heads into an open field.

Maddog and I both crouched down in our seats as they piled into the truck, hot on our heels. We shifted through our gears as quickly as we could and headed into the curves so fast that I scraped my highway pegs on the asphalt. I caught a glimpse of them on a short straightaway and I saw the muzzle flash of another round going off. I knew we were too far away by now for it to do any damage, but we poured the power on just in case.

We rode down the two-lane highway at top speed for at least ten minutes before we pulled over. After rolling to a stop I said, "I think we lost them. But just to be sure, we better get to I-40 as fast as we can."

Maddog nodded and said, "That was a real sweet move you made back there, partner," and he stuck out his hand to "high five" me.

I smiled, "What are friends for, anyway?" as I swung my hand out and connected with his.

We opened up our throttles wide and sped down the road. I doubt if that truck could go over forty-five miles an hour, but we weren't taking any chances. We hauled ass as fast as we could to the first road where we could turn south to get to the 40. Once on the freeway I began to breathe easy, but my heart was pounding madly as we cruised eastward. I glanced over at Maddog, who was cool as a cucumber, and thought, *this didn't even phase him. I bet he's been in this kind of situation before.*

We rode on the interstate for about an hour and a half till we reached Oklahoma City, then got back on Route 66 just before the Interstate became a toll road. It was getting late and I remembered when the sun set about an hour ago there were what looked like rain clouds in the sky behind us off in the distance, heading our way.

When we came to the first stoplight I leaned over to him, "Let's wait till we get out of the city before we get a room."

He nodded and we followed the 66 signs into the country. We rode till we came to what looked like a small town. I spotted a "mom and pop" motel with a restaurant and a laundromat just across the street from it. This would work out just right. We could do our clothes in the morning and eat breakfast while they were washing.

As we came to the driveway, I motioned to Maddog that I was pulling over and he fell in behind me. I stopped in front of the office and there was an older gentleman sitting behind the desk. It was a one-story place and it looked like we'd have no trouble getting the bikes into the room with us.

We went inside and the desk clerk got up. "Howdy, fellas, what can I do for you?"

I walked to the counter, "We need a room for the night," I said.

"One room coming up."

He took out a registration paper and I started filling it out.

"Will that be cash or charge?"

"Cash," I said as I pulled out the money.

Maddog walked up to the counter, "Here, let me pay half."

The guy looked up, "One bed or two?"

I was about to say we wanted two when Maddog spoke up,

"One bed will do."

The clerk quickly looked back down and started shuffling papers around. I stood there thinking, *oh, shit, what'd I get myself into?* There was an eerie silence for a second as the clerk kept shuffling the papers and I tried to figure out how to get the hell outta here.

Maddog spoke up again. "We'll only need one bed 'cause I sleep on the floor in my sleeping bag. I haven't slept in a bed in over fifteen years."

I breathed out a sigh of relief and said, "I knew that. Yeah, I knew that."

I looked at the clerk. "You knew that, too, didn't you?"

He mumbled nervously, "Uh, yeah, I knew that," keeping his eyes glued down to the counter. He finished the paperwork, handed me the key and said, "You're in Room 5," without ever looking up.

We turned towards the door and when we got to it, Maddog slapped me on the shoulder, "Had you worried there for a moment, didn't I, partner?"

"No, not me," I stuttered a little skittishly.

We rode our bikes to Room 5, which was way in the back. I think the old guy put us there on purpose so we'd be out of the way. That was all right with me, though. I liked the solitude.

I opened the door and checked to see if there was room for the bikes. Since there was only one small bed, they'd fit with no problem. I looked back outside at Maddog. "It'll work. The room's big enough."

I pushed mine in and he followed me with his. There was a clock on the wall, 9:30 p.m., the timing was just right. If we got to sleep now we could be up and out of here early. I wanted to call Jo and see if she was home. It was later there, but I didn't care. I wanted to talk to her. I looked at Maddog, "I'll be right back, I have to make a phone call."

I went outside to the phone booth and fished in my pocket for change. I put the money in the slot and dialed her number. It rang and the machine came on. *I hated that machine.* After it finished, I said after the beep, "Hi, Jo, it's Ron. I'm in Oklahoma and everything's going fine. I miss you and I hope everything's okay there. I'll see you when I get back." I hung up and was sad that I couldn't talk to her. I went back to the room and said, "I'm about ready to hit the sack. We put on a lot of miles today."

"Me, too," he replied. He undid his bedroll from the back of his bike and I pulled the covers down off the bed. We both used the bathroom and I turned out the light, got undressed to my birthday suit and got in bed.

I lay there for a minute, then asked, "What's your real name?"

He paused for a second, then answered, "Kipp."

"Kipp, you said you belonged to a motorcycle gang. What happened? Why'd you quit?"

He hesitated again and I wasn't sure he wanted to tell me, but he began to speak. "Back when I started high school, my height shot up to where I am now, but I was skinny as a rail. All the kids used to make fun of me and shove me around, so I got into a lot of fights because of it. I became a loner and when I was seventeen I started hanging with a biker club. I saved up and got my first Harley a few years after that. While I was in the club nobody fucked with me anymore. I really didn't like a lot things that they were doing, but they treated me right so I stuck around. In the meantime, I started to fill out and figured I could take care of myself if I had to. After being with them for a little over ten years, I woke up one day and couldn't continue on with the stuff they were doing, so I pulled away from the gang. I still have a lot of pals in it and that's why people don't mess with me, like that punk gang you ran into yesterday."

"Did your gang give you the name 'Maddog'?"

"Yeah. Sometimes when I get into a fight, I lose control and I have to be pulled off or I might kill the guy."

"Oh, I see."

I laid there for a moment, then explained my situation with Jo and how I met Gloria and was going to visit her. Then he asked, "So you met this babe on the Internet, huh? What kind of computer you got, a Mac or an IBM compatible?"

I was a little surprised he knew anything about computers and remarked, "You sound like you're familiar with that stuff."

"Yeah, a little. Just because I'm big doesn't mean I'm dumb."

We talked a bit more about it, then we both fell silent. I was ready to go to sleep and I think he was, too. Just then I saw a bright flash of lightning which lit up the dark motel room. It took a few seconds for the thunder and Maddog said, "Looks like we got here just in time."

I agreed and laid on my back, looking at the ceiling waiting for the next flash. It came seconds later and I waited on the thunder. It was only moments before it rumbled through. First in a low, deep sound, then it built to an earth-shaking pitch, then subsided. It'd been two years since I'd experienced a real good thunderstorm and I wanted to go outside and watch it, so I slid my pants on. "I'm going outside for a little while."

Maddog grunted as I walked towards the door. The rain began to fall as I opened it. I stood under the motel overhang and watched the large drops splash against the asphalt driveway. There was something life-giving and refreshing about a good, healthy rain.

As the storm passed over, the rain became intense and started coming down in heavy sheets. Each time the lightning struck, it momentarily lit up all the dark crevasses hidden by the night. It took a few minutes and the lightning got farther off in the distance as the storm moved on. The rain finally let up a little and became a mild, constant shower. That kind of rhythm put me into a trance-like state. I stood there for a while and it let up to a trickle. I hoped it would be gone by morning so we could move on. It was getting late so I went back inside and went to bed. Maddog was already asleep and the light patter of the rain put me into a deep sleep also.

The sharp, crisp rays of the early morning sun poked around the edges of the window blinds and I knew the storm had passed during the night. I looked over on the floor and Maddog was still sleeping. I slept well and wanted to get up and take a shower, but I didn't want to wake him. *Aw, what the hell, he woke me up yesterday morning.* I slid out of bed, took the last of my clean clothes out of my bags and went into the bathroom. I took a long, hot shower, then dressed. When I came out of the bathroom, he was awake and standing by the open front door. The clock on the wall said it was 6:45 a.m. He turned around, "Looks like the rain's done," he said.

"I hope so. We've been lucky with the weather so far." I walked to the door and looked out. It smelled fresh, like just cut grass. I looked at Maddog. "Did you say you wanted to take a shower, too?"

He nodded, "Yeah, I better get moving."

He went into the bathroom and I walked to the road and watched the cars drive by. I didn't get a chance to see this place in the dark last night. It wasn't even a town, just a little more than a roadside stop where two main roads crossed. I glanced across the street at the restaurant and wanted a cup of coffee real bad, but figured I'd wait for Maddog. I noticed two girls who appeared to be in their mid-twenties sitting in a booth at the front, eyeballing me as I looked back at them. They were cute and were probably wondering who I was being a stranger here.

I turned around and strolled back into the room. I couldn't hear the shower water anymore and heard Maddog moving around in the bathroom. He came out a few minutes later with his long, stringy blonde hair hanging down in wet clumps over his shoulders. He ran the towel through it a few times and asked, "So, what's the plan?"

"Let's put our clothes in the washer and have breakfast."

"Sounds good. But let's roll the bikes out front first so we can keep an eye on 'em."

I had the room key and was going to turn it in, but decided to hang on to it until we left. We had the room till twelve noon, but I was hoping we'd be long gone by then.

We pushed our bikes outside and rolled them to the front of the motel where we could see them from the restaurant. I looked across the road as we took our clothes out of our saddlebags and saw the girls eyeing us intently now. I motioned to Maddog to look and he peered at them. He then nonchalantly went back to what he was doing. I guess he was used to this sort of thing. We took our clothes and headed to the laundromat with the girls watching our every move. We tossed everything in the same washer, then headed to the restaurant.

We walked through the door and Maddog headed to a booth

two down from where they were sitting. As we sat down, they smiled at us and started chatting to each other. I looked over at them and one was doing most of the talking, while the other one just listened.

The quiet one was wearing shorts and a loose T-shirt. The talkative one was wearing shorts also, but they were high and tight and she had on a clinging, low-cut spandex top that looked like she was about to pop out of any minute. We ordered and while we waited one of them spoke up. "Those are nice Harleys."

Maddog was facing them and just nodded. I really wasn't interested in starting anything with anyone since I was involved with Jo and I had no intention of cheating on her.

As we ate, the one who made the remark about how nice the bikes were kept talking loudly, saying things like, "It would be so nice to go for a ride on one of those bikes."

The other one wasn't as forward and remained silent for the most part. We finished eating and had a cup of coffee. I looked at the clock and said, "I'll go put the clothes in the dryer. I'll be right back."

I went to change them and when I got back, the girls were sitting at our booth with Maddog. The shy one was sitting on my side of the booth and the outspoken one was sitting with Maddog. The shy one moved over and made room for me to sit down next to her. The one across from me stuck out her hand. "Hi, my name's Sarah and this is my friend, Tracy," she said, as I shook Tracy's hand.

I introduced myself and asked, "Do you live around here?"

Sarah replied, "Yep, we're from around here and it's boring. Where're you guys headed?"

I explained my plan and Maddog just said he was going to visit family. Sarah then sat up and looked at Maddog. "Come on, take us for a ride. We'd do just about anything for a ride on those Harleys."

Tracy sat up straight, "Sarah!"

"Oh, Tracy, loosen up. Let's have a little fun."

Tracy tilted her head down and glared at Sarah, but she just brushed it off and turned back toward Maddog again. "Well? What about it? You gonna take us for a ride?"

He looked at me, "What do ya think, partner?"

"I guess a ride wouldn't hurt any. A short one, that is. It'll take about half an hour for the clothes to be finished anyway."

I looked at Tracy. "Will they be safe if we leave them?" She nodded, then I said, "Let's go."

Maddog and I paid our bill and we all walked outside to the bikes. Sarah was almost jumping up and down, but Tracy was subdued. I don't think she was happy about the situation. I sat on my seat and waited for Maddog to start his bike, then I nodded to Tracy that it was okay to get on the back of mine. As she got on, I asked, "Any good roads to ride around here?"

She pointed and I followed her direction with Maddog right behind. We took the back roads past farms and ranches. It was pretty country with a lot of trees and thick, green shrubbery. I was having a good time, but this lady felt nothing like Jo. All I could think about was Jo, and how I was really beginning to miss her a lot. I glanced into my rearview mirror and could see Sarah was all over Maddog.

We rode for about half an hour and Tracy directed me back to the laundromat. We pulled up in front and shut off the bikes. Maddog came up to me and asked, "You still got the motel key?"

"Yeah," I said and handed it to him.

"We'll be back in a little while, partner," he said as he and Sarah walked across the road arm in arm.

Tracy watched as they disappeared into the room, then said, "Oohhh, that girl! She's gonna get in real trouble someday."

I didn't know what to say so I replied, "I think I better check the clothes, want to come along?"

"Sure, why not?"

I felt a little awkward as we went inside. I looked and the clothes were done, so I separated them and she helped me fold them. I then went outside and put mine in my bags and Maddog's in his. We stood there for a minute, then I said, "Would you like a cup of coffee?"

It took a second, then she smiled and said, "Yeah, why not?"

We went next door to the restaurant, got coffee and sat down. She meekly looked at me. "I'm not that kind of girl. Sarah is, so I don't want you to get the wrong impression about me."

I took a gulp of coffee. "I didn't think you were, and just so you know, I'm not that kind of guy."

"That's funny, I didn't think you were." We sat quiet for a minute, then she spoke again, "There's not much to do around here, so sometimes when we get a chance to do something different, we jump at it."

"I can understand that. Boredom would just about kill me. That's why I always find things to do."

She looked into my eyes. "You seem like a nice guy. Do you have a girlfriend back home?" I told her about Jo and my plan to go cross-country. After I finished, she said, "Gee, that sounds real exciting and your girl sure is lucky to have a guy like you."

"No, I think I'm the lucky one to have a girl like her. I just hope I didn't screw it up by taking this trip."

"Don't worry, if she really loves you, she'll be waiting when you get back."

I stared into my coffee cup. "I sure hope so."

She looked out the window for a moment, then said, "If you ever do decide to break up with her, come back and look me up."

I blushed a little, "But only if I break up with Jo."

"It's a date then," she said, as she smiled wide.

I saw Maddog and Sarah walking back across the road toward us and Tracy remarked, "I must have a long talk with that girl. I know it won't do any good, but I will anyway."

They walked through the door and Maddog set the key on the table. "Here, you guys wanna use the room now?"

We looked at each other. I smiled, then said, "No, not today. Maybe another time."

Sarah looked at her. "Aw, go on Tracy, give a little. Go have some fun."

"I'm having fun, right, Ron?"

"Yep, we're doing just fine."

"Boy, you're a real deadbeat."

She smiled at me and remained silent. She knew that I understood and no words needed to be spoken.

"How's the clothes?" Maddog asked.

"Done and packed away."

"Hey, thanks, partner," he said, as he sat next to Tracy with Sarah sitting next to me.

I noticed she smelled like sex but I kept quiet, turned away and minded my own business.

Sarah asked Tracy one more time. "Are you sure you don't want to use the motel room? I have to get you to loosen up somehow."

"No! And I'll be the one who decides when, and where I loosen up."

"Oh! Excuse me for trying."

"Sarah, drop it. I'm not that kind of girl and he's not that kind of guy. Besides, he's got a girlfriend and I respect that."

Sarah snorted as though she'd just been slighted and replied, "Have it your way, but don't blame me for your boring life."

"I haven't yet, and don't worry, I won't either," she replied sarcastically.

Maddog looked at me with that "It's time to get outta here" look and I think he was right. I tapped my fingers on the table. "I guess we better be heading out. We've got a lot of ground to cover today."

Maddog added, "Yeah, we better git."

Tracy stuck her hand out. "It was nice meeting you, Ron, and you too, Maddog."

Sarah grabbed a piece of paper and quickly scribbled something on it, then handed it to Maddog. "Here's my number. If you ever get by this way again, call me, ya hear."

He took the paper, shoved it in his pocket and nodded without saying anything. We stood up, said goodbye to them and walked out to the bikes with Sarah hot on Maddog's heels. I think if he'd stayed there for any length of time, he'd become a married man.

Tracy walked me to my bike and said as I got on, "Be careful and if you come through here again, maybe I'll see you. We're always here at the restaurant."

"If I'm this way, I'll be sure to stop by."

Maddog was trying to keep Sarah from pawing him. It was

funny to watch, but I wasn't going to let him catch me laughing at him.

He stopped her long enough to kick-start his bike and I fired mine up so we could get out of here. I knew he wasn't having fun anymore. I waved and we pulled out onto the road.

At the first stop sign we came to, Maddog looked at me. "Damn, I think that lady was getting too personal." I just smiled and didn't say anything. I had a lot of sarcastic comebacks for that remark, but figured it best to not say anything. "Well, what's the plan now, partner?" he asked.

"From the looks of the map, we'll follow 66 up along the toll road to Tulsa, then we'll stop and see how the road goes."

It was a little after 9:00 a.m. and I was hoping to make it to Chicago tonight and spend some time with my kids. Maddog was going about an hour south of Chicago and I wasn't sure if he wanted try to make it home tonight also. I guessed it to be about seven hundred fifty to eight hundred miles away. If we averaged sixty miles an hour, we could make it by ten or eleven, which wasn't all that late. It didn't make much sense to camp out on the road if we were that close to home. I'd wait till the afternoon to ask him, that way we'd have a better idea of where we stood.

We headed along I-44 in a northeast direction, which put the sun in a different position in the sky. I noticed that the further we drove, the more populated it seemed to become between towns. The long stretches of empty spaces were beginning to disappear. Route 66 between Oklahoma City and Tulsa was not like the previous part. There was much more traffic now, probably because the road of choice was the free road instead of the toll road. It was a nice change of pace.

I felt refreshed with a good night's sleep, my laundry done and a hearty breakfast. The day started out right, even though Maddog got a little nooky. That didn't make me jealous since I'd been making love on a regular basis with Jo. I think taking a break now was a good thing for both of us. Besides, with a guy like Maddog, it was probably a good thing for him to get laid as much as possible.

As we rode toward Tulsa, I was having a good time checking

out the scenery and the people. It was hard to describe. Since it was the transition from west to midwest, the people here could best be described as a combination of both, not really western, not really midwestern. The towns were pretty much spread apart and the entire route looked very much alive.

Every time I got on the road and drove through small towns, I would look at the people and wonder, *What did they do for a living? Where did they live? What did they do for fun? What were their lives like?* I would see folks coming and going and I always wondered just where they were coming from or going to, and there certainly were people along this route moving to and fro.

The road meandered slowly through the middle of each and every town. When we hit the open road between them, we made pretty good time. But as we cruised the towns we were held to stoplights and thirty-mile-an-hour speed limits. Suddenly it hit me that I was in that "hurry-up-and-get-there" frame of mind I would get into every so often. When something had to be done, I would slip into that "let's-get-to-the-end-of-it" kind of thinking. That wouldn't work here. I was supposed to be kicking back, taking it easy and enjoying everything about this trip.

I gave myself a mental slap, told myself I needed that and smiled. I then started to look around again instead of straightforward. I glanced over at Maddog and he seemed to be at one with the road. His stone face was expressionless as he rode along in the wind, nodding at the people who gave us the thumbs-up as we cruised through the towns. I knew now that there was a real human being stuck under that thick, hard exterior.

The time slipped by quickly as we rode through Tulsa and headed toward the Kansas border. I noticed a clock in a store window that said it was 2 p.m.

Not long after leaving Tulsa, Maddog signaled that he had to stop for gas. We were between towns and we stopped at the first station we could find that was still open. There were many boarded-up businesses along the old route and we were lucky to find one still open this far away from an interstate exit.

We rolled up to the pumps and I couldn't help but notice it was somewhat like John's station. It was a small, independent one with a service garage. The place was old and greasy with rusted spare parts strewn all over. I looked in the direction of the garage and saw an old hound dog lying half in and half out of the door. He opened his eyes when we drove up without moving his head. He stared at us for a second, then closed them again. I heard some wrenches clang in the garage, then an older gentleman appeared through the door. He walked up to us. "Need gas, fellas?"

I nodded as I took the pump nozzle and started to fill up my tank. When I finished, I handed it to Maddog and he filled up. The old guy spoke again. "Nice day for a ride. Where ya's headed?"

I said, "New York," and Maddog kept silent.

"Taking 66, are ya?"

I nodded again. "Yeah, we wanna see the country."

"Great way to do it, on a Harley," he added.

I agreed and we paid the bill. I looked at Maddog, "Want to get a soda?" He nodded and we pushed our bikes to the side and went to the soda machine. I stuck a dollar in the slot and got a can for me and one for Maddog, then we stood in the shade alongside the building.

I waited a moment, then spoke. "I thought we might get to where we're going tonight, but it's mid-afternoon and we ain't even out of Oklahoma yet. At this pace, we might get halfway through Missouri by nightfall."

"So, what's wrong with that?" he asked, "Do we have some sort of schedule we have to keep?"

"Nope. I get into a hurry-up mode sometimes."

"I'm having a good time and I ain't in no hurry. Hey, partner, relax, have fun. We'll get there when we get there."

He was right. I had to slow myself down. I looked around and said, "This is like the station I work in, 'cept ours is a lot cleaner."

"Looks like a place I wouldn't mind working in if I was a mechanic," he said.

"At our place, we're laid back and there's no pressure. John, the owner, is a real nice guy to work for."

"I work in a machine shop and I got it pretty good," Maddog said. "They let me take this time off to go see my ma and the guys I work with are all right."

The longer we were together, the more he opened up, and I could see that he really was a regular guy, which was a good thing for me 'cause he could have been a raving lunatic. We drank the rest of our sodas and he looked at me. Without speaking words, I nodded and we got on our bikes. I took the map out of my shirt and said, "We should be out of this state in a little while. It looks like 66 cuts through a tiny corner of Kansas before we get into Missouri."

Maddog responded, "Sounds good to me. Lead the way."

We fired up the bikes, waved to the old guy and rolled back onto the road. The sun was shining and the sky was dotted with big, white, fluffy clouds over us, probably left behind from the storm last night. It was picture-perfect.

We pulled into the town of Vinita and stopped alongside the road to check the map again. It appeared the road zigzagged back and forth between here and Joplin, Missouri. I had a pretty detailed map and it looked like it turned left and right about twenty times. This was going to be a real challenge to follow it through all these twists and turns. The interstate continued on in a relatively straight northeastern path right into Missouri, bypassing Kansas. There were what looked like at least six small towns we would pass through on our way, so if we got lost, I guess we could always stop and ask. That's if there were any people left to ask.

Maddog sat on his bike watching me before finally saying, "Is there some kinda problem?"

I hesitated. "No. I'm just trying to figure this out. You should see how this route goes," I said as I ran my finger over the map in an exaggerated manner.

"Hey, you been doing pretty good so far. I got faith in you. Whatever way you say is good enough for me."

"We have plenty of gas and if we get lost we can camp out along the road." I stuffed the map away, kicked my bike in gear and headed back onto the road with Maddog right alongside me. The road crossed the interstate, then doubled back before heading in a northerly direction toward Kansas. The map gave the old and new route numbers, which I followed. The first town we came to was a ghost town and the next two were alive and well.

It didn't take long before we hit the Kansas border and rolled into Baxter Springs. It was a place that looked like it was stuck back in the fifties and sixties. The road went a little further north, then turned directly east to the town of Galena, Kansas. The Missouri border was only a few miles away. We crossed the Missouri state line and rode into Joplin, a short distance down the road. The view began to change as we entered the Ozark Mountains. It was a real old mountain range and pretty much worn from years of weather and erosion. But it was awesome, nonetheless. The combination of sandstone earth and deep emerald green trees and brush made up for what it lacked in height. The state was pretty much a lot of gentle rolling hills flushed with greenery. A nice place to send post cards from. I wondered if Maddog was enjoying this as much as I was. He appeared to be.

We'd been in the seat for about nine hours now; it was getting late and we had to stop and get something to eat. I was right about the guess that we'd make it halfway through Missouri tonight. I was used to making estimates from traveling the interstates, but we hadn't been on one for a while. We were somewhere between Springfield and Waynesville when I spotted a small cafe alongside the road. I motioned to Maddog to pull over and stop.

I shut off my bike and so did Maddog. I straddled my bike for a few minutes, flexing my fingers. They'd gone numb some time ago. I stretched and said, "Damn, that was one hell of a long ride."

Maddog looked back at me as though this was par for him, and it probably was. He swung his arms back and forth a few times, then said, "Yeah, I guess you could say that. It sure builds up an appetite, though."

I got off my bike and looked the cafe over. It seemed to be a nice, quiet place and I was hoping we didn't have any trouble this time. I looked at Maddog and wasn't sure if I should say this, but I did, "You think we can maybe eat and leave peaceable this time?"

"Hey, partner," he said defensively, "I didn't start it, and I usually don't. But if they do, I'm going right through 'em."

I half-nodded and said, "This looks like a pretty mellow place and we should be able to get outta here with no problem."

"You gotta consider the way we look. Two dusty, bug-splattered biker dudes. People aren't going to take to us too quickly," he warned.

"Yeah, we do look scummy, huh?"

We went through the door, getting a lot of stares as we made our way to a back booth. It wasn't so much me, but more Maddog. He seemed used to it and brushed it off. It appeared to be a family place and the stares would probably be as bad as it got, I hoped.

We ordered and ate without incident. I had a cup of coffee and wanted to call Jo real bad. I looked at Maddog. "I'll be right back. I gotta make a phone call."

He nodded and I got up and walked to the public phone, dialed and held the receiver in my hand, hoping that she would pick it up. It rang twice before her father picked it up. *Damn,* I thought.

I spoke, "Hi, this is Ron. Is Jo around?"

He paused before answering, "No, she isn't. Can I take a message?"

I was really upset now and said, "No, thanks. Could you just tell her I called?"

He paused again, which was strange for him, then said, "I'll make sure she gets it," and hung up.

I walked back towards the booth and stopped at the counter. There was a post card rack and I rotated it, looking for that special one to send Jo. I found it and asked the lady behind the counter for a pen. She handed it to me and I moved to the side and wrote:

> *Hi, Jo, I'm in the middle of Missouri with Maddog. I just called and your father said you weren't home. I really was hoping I'd get to talk to you. I should see my kids in Chicago by tomorrow night. We're riding old 66 and it's taking longer than I expected, but I'm having fun. I miss you and wish you were here. I hope you're doing okay and I'll see you when I get back. Hugs and kisses, Ron.*

I stood by the cash register and wondered how I was going to mail this. The lady behind the counter watched me and asked, "Is there something I can help you with?"

"Yeah, there is. Do you know where I can get a stamp and where I can mail this?"

"Sure. I have a stamp here and there's a mailbox right outside the door."

"Good," I said, as I paid for the stamp and placed it on the card. Outside at the mailbox, I held the card for a moment. I wanted to say more, but there wasn't any room left, so I dropped it into the slot. I slowly walked back to the table and sat down. Maddog looked at me, "How'd it go partner?"

"Uh . . . the lady I was calling wasn't home so I mailed a post card." He nodded and took a swig of his beer. I took the map out, looked at it and said, "The next town is Waynesville and it's about halfway to Chicago from where we started today."

"Hey, man, that's no problem. The road's been great and I'm having a good time. So we'll get there tomorrow. That's pretty good timing."

"I gotta admit that this is a great ride so far. The sun's going down so we should probably stop for the night somewhere around Waynesville."

"First place you think is right, we'll stop" he said, between swigs of beer.

He finished his beer and we got ready to leave. The terrain was different here than the sandy desert. I figured it might be a good idea to find a boarded-up abandoned place to sleep. There were plenty of them on old 66, which was a benefit of sorts.

We paid the bill, used the bathroom and went outside. The weather was hot and muggy, not like the desert. It was almost as uncomfortable at night as it was during the day. We headed out again on 66 and rode through a few small towns. Right after we got to the other side of Waynesville, I started looking for a place to sleep. Not long after that, we came across several abandoned buildings and I motioned to Maddog to pull over. We stopped at the side of the road and I said, "We might as well sleep in one of these, otherwise we'll have to sleep in the damp grass."

"And if it rains, we'll at least have cover," he added.

I nodded and we picked one where we could roll our bikes into.

The door was missing and all the windows were gone. It had some broken pieces of furniture lying around and all the walls were busted out. The tiny pieces of walls that still existed had graffiti scribbled all over them. It was a shame to think that this was once someone's livelihood and now reduced to rubble. I believe, though, that where one thing disappeared, another thing popped up somewhere else and life evened out. It was still good enough to spend the night in.

We pushed the bikes through the doorway, took out our bedrolls and laid them down. I was really beat and knew I wouldn't have any trouble sleeping tonight. I figured Maddog was, too, but he'd never admit it. As I lay on my bag, I blurted out, "Man, I'm tired."

To my surprise he replied, "Yeah, me too."

Oh well, so much for my psychology assessing. He laid down too, and we didn't speak much. I just listened to the silence and the occasional chirp of a cricket. I climbed into my bedroll and was out like a light in no time.

I was rudely awakened by a bright light in my eyes. I could hear the static and occasional chatter of what sounded like a police radio. I squinted against the glare of the flashlight and raised my hand to block it, then heard a commanding voice say, "Keep your hands where I can see them, both of you."

The light swung over into Maddog's face. Now I could see the vague outline of a human being behind the light. I could tell he was a cop from the Smokey Bear hat he was wearing.

He then said, "Climb out of those sleeping bags real slow and keep your hands out where I can see 'em." We both did as he ordered and as he stood up, he held the light on Maddog's huge frame, then rested his hand on the butt of his holstered gun, "Now don't either of you fellas move. I want you both to walk over against that wall and have a seat." We did as he said, then he walked toward us. "You place your right hand out," he said to me, then looked at Maddog, "and you, place your right hand out."

He handcuffed us together in such a way that if we tried to run, we'd be facing in the opposite direction. The cuff almost didn't go around Maddog's wrist. "You're not under arrest. I'm just doing this for your protection and mine."

As we sat with our arms crisscrossed and handcuffed together, he patted us down for weapons. He took Maddog's folding knife out of the case on his belt and said, "I'll return this to you after I check you out." It was still dark outside and I guessed it to be around 3 a.m. The officer backed up a step, then said, "Let me see some I.D."

We both fumbled awkwardly to get our wallets out of our back pockets and Maddog got his out first. He slid it across the floor to the officer and I did the same.

He looked in Maddog's. "You're Kipp Anderson?"

He answered, "Yep."

The officer asked, "Are you carrying any contraband or weapons?"

He answered, "Nope."

"Which bike is yours?"

"The black one."

He then looked at my I.D. "You're Ron Healy?"

"Yes."

"And I assume the other bike's yours?"

"Yep."

"Are you carrying any contraband or weapons?"

"Nope."

"Do either of you fellas have any wants or warrants out on you?"

We both answered "no" simultaneously.

He then said, "You fellas just sit tight while I check to make sure these bikes aren't stolen and you're both clean. If that's the case, you can go about your business." He called in our names and our registration numbers on the bikes. While he waited for the information to come back on his radio, he searched our sleeping bags and our saddlebags. Maddog looked at me, "See, I told you, it's not wise to carry anything illegal on the road looking like we do. It's for sure we'll get stopped somewhere along the line."

After the officer finished searching everything, he said, "We have to keep an eye on these abandoned buildings. Every so often we get folks using 'em for illegal things like drug houses."

I responded, "We're heading cross-country and it got late, so we pulled over to get some sleep. We weren't doing anything wrong."

"Well, if the report comes back with no warrants, I'll let you go back to sleep, but be sure you're gone in the morning. Sometimes we get squatters here who try to move in."

"Don't worry, we'll be on our way at first light," I assured him.

Maddog just sat quietly. I think he'd had plenty of run-ins with the police and wasn't happy about our situation right now, and I hoped he didn't have any warrants 'cause I was gettin' used to riding with him.

We both stayed silent as the officer stood over us waiting for the information, his radio crackling every so often, breaking the stillness of the night. It took a while when I heard the voice speak my name, then say, "No outstanding warrants and the motorcycle is clean."

We waited for Maddog's information. He looked pretty calm, but I was tense and worried that he might be taken to jail tonight. After a few stressful minutes, the voice spoke his name, then followed with, "No outstanding warrants and the motorcycle is clean."

The officer moved toward us, reaching for the cuffs and said, "Looks like you fellas are all right." He unlocked the handcuffs and said, as he handed us our I.D.'s. "I'll leave you fellas be now, and remember, one night's no problem, but don't camp out, all right?"

I nodded as he stepped back. He still had Maddog's knife stuck in his belt and he turned to leave. When he got to the motorcycles he stopped and placed the knife on Maddog's seat. "Don't take this till I'm gone."

Maddog remained motionless. The officer took another step, stopped, and held his flashlight on the motorcycles. "Nice bikes. Ride easy and keep the shiny side up, rubber side down," he said as he walked out to his car.

I heard his door slam and a minute later he backed up and drove down the road. I looked at Maddog. "Well, he seemed to be

He didn't say anything. He got up and walked to his bike, then said as he picked up his knife and put it back in its pouch, "Cops are like people, there's good guys, then there's cops that take the job too seriously and it goes to their heads."

It occurred to me that this was a touchy subject, so I dropped it, laid back down again and he did the same. "I guess we got time for a few more hours of sleep," I said as I got comfortable.

I heard Maddog say a faint, "Yeah," and I finally dozed off again.

Daybreak came all too soon and we were up and ready in no time. "Think we should have a cup of coffee before we head out?" I asked.

"Sure, why not? It'll only take a few minutes, then we'll be outta here."

I got my coffee stuff out. "I'm not sure where the next restaurant is, so I'd rather have a cup in me to start the day right."

Maddog went outside and found some dried twigs. I followed and we made a small fire just outside the building. We packed our stuff up as we waited for the water to boil. "Looks like you're gonna make it home tonight, and I'm going to make it to Chicago. We only got half of Missouri and all of Illinois left," I said as I sipped the coffee.

He didn't say anything. He just stared at the small pile of burning embers.

"I mean we should make it if everything goes okay," I added.

He nodded, his eyes transfixed on the embers. We finished our coffee in silence and got ready to go, then he came to life, "So what's the plan for today, partner?"

"Hit the first restaurant we find and eat. I'm starved."

"Me too, so let's get on the road."

We gave our bikes a once-over to make sure everything was all right and fired them up. I rolled to the edge of the roadway with Maddog beside me and said, "To breakfast . . ." and hit my throttle.

We were less than five minutes on the road when I saw a car approaching from the opposite direction. As it got closer, I could see the emergency light rack on the roof and knew it was a police car. I wondered if it was the guy who checked us out last night.

As he came upon us, he waved and I recognized him and waved back. I noticed Maddog ever so slightly stick his hand out. Just barely noticeable and I thought, *Ha! He waved.* I settled back in my seat and whispered to myself, "It's gonna be a good day."

It took about thirty minutes before we came upon a small roadside cafe, which was open. I could smell breakfast cooking as we pulled up to the front. I shut my bike down and got off, "Man, I'm hungry."

Maddog was right behind me. We walked in and it looked like an old place right out of the sixties, linoleum floors and tables with cheesy tablecloths on them, and jukebox selection gizmos at every booth. The counter had old-style, swivel, red-topped vinyl stools.

We found a booth and sat down. I didn't have to look at the menu. I knew what I wanted . . . eggs, pancakes, sausage and the biggest orange juice they had. The waitress came over in the sixties hairdo and dress of that bygone era and took our order.

We pretty much ate in silence and I began to think about a few things. *Maddog and I would soon part company. I would get to see my kids after two years, and would be in New York meeting Gloria soon. Chicago was about two-thirds of the way to New York. It would probably take two days from Chicago to the East Coast and I wasn't sure of the roads I'd ride. Maybe some side roads and maybe some interstates. I'd make up my mind when I got there.*

We both finished our breakfast about the same time and had another cup of coffee. I looked around the café. "This is what old 66 must have been all about. The fifties and sixties were probably its hottest time. Then the interstates began to appear and slowly sapped the life out of it."

I looked out the window. The temperature was in the mid-nineties and the humidity hung thick in the air like a damp, stale washcloth. I noticed the people on this route were older, more stable looking, probably from the fact they grew up with 66. It seemed as though the people along this road moved slower, took their time, not running like the hectic pace of interstate riders. There were spots that were stuck back in time and almost made me wish I could go back there. But I knew that was impossible.

Maddog got my attention, "You ready to leave?"

I nodded and we both got up. We walked outside and the sun beat down unmercifully through the hot, humid air. The only relief to be had was to get in motion on our bikes. I sat on my seat and pulled out the map. It was getting moist from perspiration. The road between here and St. Louis snaked in and out around the interstate and was a curvy line on the map, which meant it was hilly. That would make for a pretty ride at least. I looked at Maddog, "Looks like a nice stretch of road to St. Louis."

He nodded and said, "Let's get in the wind, I'm dying just sitting here." It was hot, so I fired up my bike and he did, too. I stuffed the damp map back into my shirt and we rolled out onto the highway.

The road consisted of a lot of hills and valleys and there were a couple of spots where 66 dead-ended, so we had to make short trips back on the interstate. But for the most part, the old road was still intact with all its small towns and people. Another thing I noticed was that there were a lot more rivers here. It was odd, since living in the desert, to see so much water everywhere.

It took about four hours to get to St. Louis. The heat was even worse here. There was absolutely no breeze and the air was exceptionally humid, probably because of the Mississippi River. The terrain was made up of small bluffs, thick foliage and rolling hills along both sides of the river. I followed my map and we weaved through the city streets of St. Louis till we reached the river itself. It was also the state line between Missouri and Illinois.

I began to get butterflies in my stomach knowing that as soon as I crossed the river, I would be in the state of my birth. The map guided us to an old steel bridge that was the main river crossing before the interstate. We crossed the bridge and rolled into Illinois. Route 66 now followed Interstate 55 the rest of the way till it ended in Chicago. It also changed direction to almost straight north.

It felt good to be in my home state and the smells and sights brought back memories. In a way, I was happy to be visiting, but knew I'd be on my way again soon, and that made me sad.

As the miles rolled away under my wheels, my anticipation began to grow the closer I got to Chicago. I started to recognize the scenery from having lived and traveled all over this state. It felt good to see the familiar surroundings again.

Illinois, once you got away from the Mississippi River, was a flat prairie state, with Route 66 being fairly straight and no nonsense. The state had its own kind of personality. The towns began to get closer together and there were virtually no open, empty spaces between them. The farms were smaller and packed tighter together. I figured the rest of the country from here to New York would be as heavily populated, if not more so.

We were a few hours into Illinois when Maddog pointed to his gas tank signaling he needed gas, so we stopped at the first station we came to and we shut down our bikes. I was wet with perspiration and Maddog had a thin layer of sweat on him also.

We gassed up and rolled them over to the side to get a cold drink and take a break. As we sat on the curb in the shade, I remarked, "I'm all sticky and sweaty. I can feel layers of road grime on my face and hands." He nodded and wiped his neck with a handkerchief that he carried in his back pocket and I continued, "Sure is nice to live out west where the air blowing off the ocean hasn't had a chance to get polluted yet."

He took a big swig of his soda and said, "Yep, it sure is. This humidity will kill you. That's one reason I live in the Arizona desert." He paused for a second, then said, "I'm gonna peel off of 66 at Route 136 and head east to Route 41 in Indiana. My mom lives just south of there."

I looked at the perspiration-soaked map, then replied, "It looks like 66 is mostly on the interstate past 136. I'll tell you what, I'll ride with ya to 41, then head north to Chicago from there. On the way back, I can always ride that piece of 66."

He looked at me for a second. "Fine with me if you want to ride along."

"I'll probably spend two or three days with my kids before heading on to New York."

He didn't say anything. He just laid his head back against the building and gulped down the rest of his soda. We sat there for a while before he spoke. "We better head on out of here. It's getting unbearable to sit still." I agreed and we got back on the highway.

The wind felt good on my face, and I was still sticky and grimy, but loving every second of it.

Old 66 weaved through many small towns and took up a lot of time. At most we could do thirty-five miles an hour, but it was well worth it. We finally got to Mc Lean, halfway between Lincoln and Bloomington, then turned east on Route 136 and Maddog took the lead. I guessed Route 41 to be about an hour and a half away.

This part of Illinois was all farmland and the air was full of bugs. Most of the time they didn't bother me, but every once in a while I got smacked by a big one, and it was painful. But that's the price you pay for being a biker. I figured it would be like this all the way to New York and back, so I resigned myself to just accept it, and roll on.

It seemed like no time at all before we crossed the Indiana state line and were coming to the junction of Routes 136 and 41. I felt sad that I'd be going my way and he'd be going his. He motioned for me to pull over at the crossroads and we stopped together with our engines idling. He looked at me, then spoke, "Guess this is where we part company."

"Uh-huh," I nodded.

He was about to take off and head south when he asked, "You got a pen on you?"

I felt in my pocket, "Yeah, somewhere."

I found it and handed it to him. He took out a piece of paper and wrote on it, then handed it to me. "Here's my ma's phone number. When you head back, and if I'm still here, give me a call and I'll ride back with you."

I took the paper from his hand. "Will do. Let me give you my son's number so you can reach me if you need to."

We exchanged numbers and he extended his hand. "If we don't meet again, it's been a pleasure riding with you, partner, and keep safe, ya hear?"

"You too, and maybe we'll hook up for the ride back west." We shook hands, then he took off and made a right turn, south on 41. I sat watching him disappear in the distance before I turned left and headed north to Chicago. I already had a strange and empty feeling not having him alongside me.

Chapter Thirteen

I was well-rested as I gassed up at the corner station down the street from my son's house. I'd spent three days with my kids and we had a good time together, plus I had a chance to clean up and get my energy back. I was itching to get on the road and the weather was right, so I decided to head on to New York and get this trip done with.

I'd tried to call Jo several times and got the damn answering machine each time. I was getting nervous about not being able to talk to her since leaving Borrego Springs. It had been over a week now and I was really beginning to miss her voice, her touch and her fragrance. The thought occurred to me that I could always turn around and go back, but something was driving me on. Besides, I told everyone that I was going all the way across country, so now I had to.

I paid for the gas and took my map out to check my route one more time. I figured I'd stick with the interstate until I got far enough away from the congestion around Chicago, then ride on side roads whenever I got the chance. It was getting harder and harder to take my time the longer I went not talking to Jo. I should've been able to catch her at least once by now, but no luck.

I made my way to the freeway and headed east. It was a typical, hot midwest summer day. The air was hazy with humidity and the traffic was extremely heavy. It felt good to be on the road again, but some things were nagging at me, things that had to be answered for my own satisfaction. One good thing about this part of the trip was that it forced me to be alone with myself and my thoughts, and that's just what I needed.

I focused on the road and started thinking how the last couple of days my thoughts had been mostly centered on Jo. I felt this yearning deep down inside me, not just to make love, but to be near her. To be in her presence and feel her energy. It scared me in a way, but then again it felt good to have that feeling.

It wasn't long before I was crossing the Indiana state line and the traffic began to thin out. The houses started to get scarce and the scenery began to get green again. Whenever I drove in Chicago, I always had this sense of anxiety and that was beginning to leave me the further I got into the country. I couldn't handle much more than three days in the city anyway.

As I rode, my mind began to get into that familiar highway trance that was almost like a potent, intoxicating drug. The pleasant countryside of mid-America started to swallow me up. People again started to smile and wave as they passed me and I waved back.

I kept looking over my right shoulder, expecting to see Maddog. I'd really become accustomed to him riding with me. *Damn*, I thought, *it's real easy to get attached to people, which is good when they're with you, but painful when they're not.* My mind then turned to Jo and the feelings I had for her. They were real strong and I couldn't deny that any longer. They were strong to the point of losing myself totally in her, and that's what I think frightened me most, to get completely lost in another person again.

I focused my mind back on the road in front of me and rode the interstate for about a hundred miles when I decided to gas up, take a break and check my map. I exited and drove into the first station I saw. I got a soda and sat outside trying to decide if I should stay with the interstate or find a side road. According to the map, there was a parallel road not too far up the way and I made up my mind to ride it for a while. I finished my soda and hopped back onto the interstate to where I could meet up with the side road.

When I got to the exit, I pulled off and took the surface road. The Interstates were okay, but they were so impersonal and business like. Their purpose was to get you from point A to point B in a straightforward manner, and they did just that. The side roads had people and personalities, plus they distracted me enough so that I didn't drive myself crazy with my own thoughts. On the interstate all I could do was think, and too much of that wasn't healthy for me.

Before I knew it, I was crossing the Ohio state line. Time was sure going by fast. I'd been on the road so long now that I was getting used to just letting the pavement slip by under my wheels without even noticing it.

I jumped back on the freeway and rode past Toledo and stayed on the freeway for a while. I didn't want to ride through the big city streets 'cause I knew what they were all about. I'd rather spend time in the small towns if I could. The day was pretty much going along smoothly. The weather was hot and muggy, but sunny, so that gave it some redemption.

The mileage chart said it was eight hundred miles from Chicago to New York. At the pace I was moving, I should get about four hundred to five hundred miles in today. I'd try to make it closer to five hundred if possible, that way I'd only have to travel three hundred tomorrow and that would give me more time to find Gloria. *Man,* I thought, *one more day and I'd be in New York City meeting the girl from the computer, if I could find her, that is.* I was having trouble enjoying the ride from all the things going on in my head.

From what I remembered from the map, Interstate 80 parted from 90 just before Cleveland and went straight across Pennsylvania right into New York City proper. It was mid-afternoon and it looked like I'd be stopping in Pennsylvania for the night. I was beginning to get butterflies in my stomach knowing that I was so close to doing what I'd planned for so long. Just then I realized that I was getting narrow-sighted again and not paying attention to the things around me, so I tried to focus on the journey and not destination. I settled into my seat, lightened my grip on the handlebars and took in the sights of the Ohio countryside.

By the time I got to the Pennsylvania state line, I was beginning to tire and was getting hungry, but there was still a couple of hours of daylight left so I decided to push on a little further into the state before I stopped for the night. My thoughts were beginning to run wild again in my mind, and the further away I got from California, the more intensely I thought of Jo and the times we had together. Damn it! I kept slipping back into this crazy, scattered thinking no matter how much I tried to enjoy my surroundings. It's funny, when I planned this trip, I never figured on the other stuff to be going on at the same time. I thought it would be kicking back with the sun and wind in my face without a care in the world. Ha! Was I way off.

I checked my odometer and it was getting close to five hundred miles since I left Chicago, so I started looking for a place to stay for the night. I didn't feel like camping out on the road, and the further east I got, the harder it was to find an isolated spot.

The sun was getting low in the sky when I spotted an exit that had a small cluster of motels and restaurants. I got off the freeway, then found the side street with motels on it and picked a not-so-fancy one so I could roll my bike inside. The clerk was taking a nap when I walked through the office door, which jolted him back to life. I paid for the room and asked where I could get a decent meal. He pointed and said, "Just down the road. It's walking distance."

I took the key and rolled my bike into the room. I sat on the bed staring out into the gray dusk of the early twilight of night, my mind heavy with thought. *If I don't figure out what's going on with me soon, I'm gonna explode,* I thought as I got up and walked to the diner.

I ate dinner in silence, totally consumed in thought. *Would I be able to locate Gloria? All I had was a few street names and several landmarks she had mentioned every so often. I would give it my best shot, and if I couldn't find her, that was okay by me. At least I tried.*

I finished dinner and had a last cup of coffee, then slowly walked back to my room. I wanted to go to bed early and get on the road by 7:30 if I could. I undressed and laid down staring at the ceiling, my eyes wide open. I lay there a few minutes with my mind racing. "Shit!" I said as I sat up and swung my legs over the edge of the bed, "I can't sleep."

I dressed and walked outside into the cool night air. I looked up and down the road, to the left was the interstate with all the businesses and to the right looked like an isolated country road. I turned to the right thinking a long walk might tire me enough so I could get to sleep.

As I walked, I looked around at the trees, hills and valleys that were visible in the moonlight. The fireflies were busy darting back and forth doing firefly things, and the crickets were chirping loudly to each other. Every time I got close to one, it would fall silent waiting for me to pass, afraid I might locate it.

I walked quite a distance when I started thinking about Jo and how I felt about her. *Why do I keep telling myself I need more time? What exactly is it I need time for? I've been out of my marriage long enough. Just what was my problem?*

I suddenly stopped dead in my tracks and it hit me. I was falling in love with Jo. All this time I was subconsciously trying to keep that from happening. All at once it was crystal clear. I was in love with her and I couldn't deny it any longer.

Right then, a deep sense of calm and peace settled over my whole body and being. The fight was over. I was no longer in a raging battle with myself. It blew me away to find how simple the answer was. *I was in love with Jo,* I repeated in my mind.

"I'm in love with Jo," I whispered to myself. Then I let out a big holler, "I'm in love with Jo!" so the whole world would know. I spun around, faced the small town and hollered again, "I'm in love with Jo!" so they knew too.

I turned and looked at the moon floating effortlessly in the heavens and thought, *I wonder if she can see the same moon right now? Is she looking at the sky thinking of me at this very moment?* I wanted to let her know right now, so I turned back toward the motel and hurried to the room. I unlocked the door, sat on the bed and held the phone in my hand thinking, *it's late there and I'll probably get the answering machine. I can't leave this on the machine.* I hung up, and thought, *I can't tell her this over the phone or in a post card. I have to tell her this to her face. I wasn't sure if I could wait till I got back, but I'd have to try.* I got undressed again and had no trouble drifting off to sleep this time.

I could tell by the hazy shade of light that it wasn't quite daybreak yet. My first waking thoughts were of Jo and my realization last night. I threw aside the covers and leaped out of bed into the shower. I dressed and went to eat breakfast. For some reason, everything looked slightly different. The colors around me were a little brighter and the people seemed to be in a better mood. Maybe it's because my whole insides were singing and my thoughts were all about Jo.

I ate and was having coffee when the waitress came over with the check. "Will that be all for you today?"

I smiled wide, "Yep, I'm fine." She started to turn, then stopped and looked at me. I looked back, "Is there something wrong?"

"Oh, nothing. You look like you're glowing. Your whole face is smiling," she replied.

I thought a moment, then shyly said, "I'm in love."

"Ahhh," she said, then turned and walked away.

After finishing breakfast, I went outside and noticed how bright and clear the day was. Man, did I feel good.

I walked back to the motel room and checked the map one more time. I wanted to get to New York, find Gloria, say hello and get back to California. I was about three hundred miles away and it was early, so it should be a little after mid-day when I got there.

I rolled out of town, hit the freeway ramp, twisted the throttle and shifted smoothly through the gears till I reached highway speed. The bike sounded and felt just right under me. This new day and the scenery seemed especially brilliant. The whole countryside was radiating around me. Everything was perfect, the bike, the surroundings and the feeling in my soul. For lack of a better word, everything seemed so alive.

I was looking cool and feeling good cruising along the Pennsylvania interstate with my feet kicked up on the highway pegs, leaning back as far as I could. I started humming some old tunes to myself as I closed in on the New Jersey state line.

As I rode along, I felt so light and free that it was almost scary. I think for the first time on this trip I really enjoyed the things around me. I noticed everything . . . the trees, the road and the sky. It reminded me of how I felt when I was with Jo and how, for some reason, my senses were always so acute when I was with her. I had only one major concern now, getting safely back to California and being by her side. I smiled all the way to the New Jersey line.

The traffic started to get heavy again and people started to drive real rude, but that didn't bother me. I really didn't care 'cause I wouldn't be here long anyway. Besides, nothing could get to me right now, except someone stealing my bike. Now that would really piss me off.

New Jersey was a small state and I should be out of it and into New York in less than two hours. I would have to stop somewhere in New York and get a detailed map so I could pinpoint where Gloria lived. This wasn't going to be easy, but I had faith in myself and the fact that she gave me enough information to find her.

After going through all the long states I'd already traveled, I was at the end of New Jersey in no time. I followed the signs to New York City and stopped at a gas station mini-mart as soon as I crossed the Hudson River. I gassed up and bought a map from the station clerk, then went outside and sat down to look at it. Gloria had said she lived in Scarsdale and I located it just north of the city. I had no idea what it was like 'cause I'd never been on the East Coast before. I planned my route, memorized it and stashed the map in my shirt. I decided to have a soda and rest a few minutes before heading out.

I walked to the soda machine, stuck my coins in the slot and retrieved the can from the opening at the bottom. I sat back down and looked around. People seemed to be moving at a hectic pace. It looked like they all had to be somewhere right this very moment. Just watching them move started giving me that sense of anxiety I always had in Chicago. It was starting to drive me nuts, so I finished the soda, tossed the can in the trash and got back on the road.

I headed north in the direction of Scarsdale and guessed it to be about forty-five minutes, or so. The people were driving so close together and in and out of lanes that all I wanted to do was get the hell out of there. I threaded my way to the Bronx River Parkway through a maze of freeway interchanges, almost getting nailed a couple of times by irate drivers. While cruising, I noticed all the houses were packed tight on either side of the road, really crammed together. It reminded me of Chicago, or any other big city for that matter, where space was at a premium. Some people felt safe snugly tucked away amongst others, but not me. I'd take the wide-open spaces any day.

Following the highway signs as I got closer to Scarsdale, I began to get curious about the kind of area it was. When I got to the outskirts, I started looking for Grand Avenue. I remember Gloria saying she lived not far from that street. I spotted the exit and got off. I pulled over to the side and figured I'd try west first. She talked about a certain church being on the corner of Grand and her street, so I headed west looking for it.

I hadn't gone very far when I saw what resembled a building like the one she spoke of on the left side of the road, so I pulled over. I wasn't sure if I should turn left or right, so I took a right turn and slowly rolled down the street looking for a small park she said she frequented. As I cruised down the street I looked at the houses and they were all very expensive mansions, real upper-class stuff. Maybe the reason she wouldn't tell me anything about herself was that she was afraid. Maybe she was a nanny or a housekeeper and was embarrassed. It didn't matter what she was 'cause I didn't judge people by the work they do. Or maybe her father was very wealthy and she felt because I was just a mechanic, she didn't want to embarrass me. I was really getting curious now. Every house I passed had to be worth millions.

The street dead-ended and I didn't see any small park, so I rode back to Grand and tried the other way. Again, I slowly rolled down the street and it was lined with expensive mansions on both sides. I rode a couple of blocks when I came to a small park that looked like it could be the one she went to. If it was, then I had it narrowed down to these two blocks, that is if the church was right and the park was right. I sat alongside the park and thought, *now what am I going do? Should I knock on every door and ask? I was sure I'd get thrown in jail in this neighborhood.* I slowly rolled back in the direction I came from, looking at the mansions, trying to guess which one she might live in. I'd gone about a block when I saw a maid standing at the front door of one on them. I decided to pull onto the driveway and ask if she might know Gloria. I rode past the neatly trimmed lawn and stopped in front of her. She looked a little frightened at the sight of this road-worn Harley rider. I tried to be as nice as possible so as not to scare her since she was looking at me like I was a common criminal.

"Hi there," I said in my most pleasant voice. "I'm trying to find a friend of mine and I'm not sure where she lives. Her name is

Gloria," and I went on to describe her.

She looked at me for a second with suspicion, then said, "That sounds like Gloria who lives right across the street."

My eyes widened. "Really?" I said, in disbelief.

This is unbelievable, that I was able to find her so quickly, that's if it was the right Gloria.

I stared at the mansion across the street and my eyes drifted over to the Rolls-Royce parked next to the house. *This was outta my league,* I thought, *maybe I should just start heading back and forget it. If she was hired help, I didn't want to make her feel uncomfortable. And if she owned that mansion, I didn't want to make myself feel uncomfortable or embarrass her.*

I was about to turn around and ride away when a Mercedes pulled into the driveway and the maid said, "Why, there's Gloria now."

I recognized her from the picture she sent. I turned to the maid, "Thank you very much for your help." I kicked my bike into gear and rolled to the edge of the street and stopped. Aw, what the hell, screw the feelings. I might as well go over and say hi as long as I came all this way.

I hesitated at the end of the drive to give her a chance to park. She got out, walked to the passenger side, opened the door and stuck her head inside to get something. I slowly rolled across the street and pulled onto the driveway behind her. She was bent over getting what looked like a bag of groceries from the front seat and as she lifted it out, I revved my engine. She stood straight up, startled, then dropped the groceries to the ground, spun around and looked at me as her mouth dropped open. Her eyes got real wide and she gasped, "Ron?"

"Hi, Gloria, I didn't mean to scare you. I just wanted to surprise you."

She stood motionless, transfixed for a second, then quickly said, "You can't be here. You have to leave, now." She bent down to pick up the groceries strewn on the ground. I hopped off my bike to help her. She looked at me with frightened eyes, "You can't stay here, you must go now. Please!"

"Gloria? What's wrong?"

"I can't explain right now. Just go."

The fear in her voice was bordering on panic. I helped her put the stuff back into the bag and we stood up. I looked into her eyes, "Gloria, I'm not leaving till you tell me what's wrong."

I could see the pleading on her face as she said again, "Ron, you don't understand. I can't explain it to you right now. If you don't leave, you'll get me in trouble."

"Why would you be in trouble?"

She started to answer when the front door swung open and she nearly jumped out of her shoes. A well dressed, middle-aged man appeared. "What's going on out here? Who the hell is this?" he asked, eyeballing me. I didn't know what was going on, but I sure didn't like it. He walked toward her at the same time saying, "Is this one of your secret boyfriends? Huh?"

He grabbed her arm and started shaking her. He shook so hard the bag fell out of her arms again. He raised his hand as though he was going to slap her so I jumped in between them and took hold of his arm, "Hey, pal! I don't know what the fuck's going on here, but you ain't smacking no one."

He shot back, "Let go of me. This has nothing to do with you."

I took a step forward, which put us nose to nose and growled, "Wanna bet? Now let go of her or you're going to be making a dental appointment today."

He stood firm so I yanked his arm and he lost his balance. He then let go of her and whirled around. "You have no idea who you're messing with, you piece of trash," he yelled.

I squared away, raised my fists and said, "Come on, fuck, I really don't care who you are. As far as I'm concerned, you're about to become dog meat."

"You better not touch me."

I looked at Gloria, "Who the hell is this guy?"

She was shaking uncontrollably. "He's my husband," she muttered.

"You're married to this jackass?"

She gulped, "Yes."

The jerk looked at Gloria. "I think you better get in the house." He looked at me. "I think you better get out of here before I call the police."

I looked at her, "You're not going in there with him, are you?"

She lowered her eyes in shame, then said, "Maybe you should go, Ron. I'll be all right."

"You better do as she says or I'll have the police escort you out," he snorted.

"It don't take no rocket scientist to figure out what's going on here and I'm sorry, I ain't leaving." I stood there with no idea what I was going to do next, but I knew I couldn't leave her here like this. I thought for a second, then looked at her. "Does he physically abuse you?"

Her husband took a step forward. "Hey, buddy, that's none of your damn business."

I turned toward him, cocked my fist back and he retreated several steps, then I said, "You're pushing it, pal. I'm about ready to rearrange your nose."

"That's it, I'm calling the police," he shot back.

I thought for a bit, then replied, "Yeah, go ahead. Why don't you? I think that's a good idea. That way, maybe we can straighten out what's going on between you and her. I'm sure the cops will be interested in that."

Gloria lifted her head. "That won't do any good. He's a very powerful person in this state. I've called them before and they haven't done anything."

"She's right, they won't do anything to me. Now why don't you be a good fellow and get on your motor bike and leave?"

I was getting real pissed off. "So, he has abused you!" I knew now that she was in a bad situation and it would only get worse if she stayed. I couldn't make her leave and I didn't know what else to do. I looked at her and her lower lip was quivering. "Gloria, I don't know if I should say this, but you can't go in there with him. If he's hurting you, you owe it to yourself to leave right now."

"Where am I going to go? My life is here. I can't just leave. How will I survive?"

"You can do it. People do it every day, even though they think they can't. They just do it. If you really think leaving is such a bad decision, think of the alternative. What do you really have to look forward to if you stay with him?"

He stood there tapping his foot. "Well, make up your mind. Are you going to listen to this fool or are you going to come to your senses and tell him to go? You know you'll never make it on your own."

I looked back into her eyes. "If you really want me to go, I will. But you have to tell me to. Before you do, though, I want you to think about it first. You can set yourself free if you want to. But I can't make that decision for you. You have to make it yourself."

She looked down at the groceries strewn all over the ground, then bent down to pick them up. I helped her put them back in the bag. Her husband grinned and said, "I'm glad to see you've come to your senses. I think it's time you left, mister."

I stood up, wanting to nail him right in the jaw. She walked up to him, then shoved the bag into his gut, catching him off guard and knocking the wind out of him. "Here's your food. Make your own dinner." She turned to me, "Can you wait here while I change clothes and then can you give me a ride?"

I gulped. "Sure, I'll wait right here."

"You can't do that, Gloria. Where will you go? What will you do? You'll never make it out there. You're nothing without me," he pleaded.

She looked at him eye-to-eye. "Suddenly the thought occurred to me that I'm nothing with you."

She turned to me. "Maybe it was a good thing you showed up after all. The talking we did with each other, and seeing you in person just gave me the courage to finally make a decision I should have made a long time ago. I'll be right out."

"No problem. I'll wait here. And don't worry, he won't touch you."

"It's funny, I'm not worried," she said as she went in the house to change.

He was enraged as she walked past him, then he looked at me. "You'll never get away with this."

"Get away with what? Telling her she has a choice and she doesn't have to take any more shit from you?"

"She'll be back and I'm not sure if I'll take her back."

"You're one sick Bozo, aren't you? I don't think she will and I'm gonna do my best to talk her out of that idea."

"And look at you," he smirked, "just what do you have to offer her?"

"I don't know what you think is going on between us in your warped mind, but for your information this is the first time we've met in person. And this ain't about who has the most toys."

"Ha! I don't believe that. She knows your name. She's about to leave with you, and you expect me to believe you just met her? Ha!"

"Hey, pal. Listen, I don't expect you to believe anything. You don't have a clue, do you?" I flicked my hand at him in disgust and turned away. I didn't want to carry on a dialogue any further with this jerk. I walked over to her car and leaned against it. The thought suddenly came to mind, *how am I going to explain this to Jo. Oh well, I think under the circumstances she'll understand, I hoped.* He turned to go into the house. I jumped up and ran to the door before he could shut it and said, "Oh, no you don't. When Gloria's out of there, then you can shut it."

She came down the stairs dressed in faded jeans, boots and a black leather coat. He let go of the door and started to plead with her, "Gloria, don't go. I want you to stay. You can't walk out on me like this."

"It won't work this time. First the begging, then the beatings. I know now that it's never going to stop," she said as she walked past him. He reached out to grab her arm and she jerked it away. "You're not going to touch me anymore," and she continued out the door. She brushed by me and said, "Come on, let's get out of here."

I got on the bike and she hopped on behind me. I fired up the engine and her husband came to the door, "You can't do this to me! I'll make you pay for this, you hear me!"

"Please, let's go," she said as she turned her head away from him.

I rolled down the driveway past the rows of manicured trees on either side. I had no idea where I was going or what I was going to do. I figured maybe we should stop for a beer or coffee and get a plan.

When we stopped at a stoplight, I made that suggestion and she opted for coffee. But first she wanted to ride for a while to get away and clear her head.

We rode for about forty-five minutes when I saw a fast-food restaurant and pulled over. We went inside, each got a cup of coffee and sat in a booth at the far end away from all the people. I looked into her face and she was even more beautiful than her photo. Her eyes were moist so I kept silent until she felt like speaking.

After a few minutes she said, "Thanks for being there. I'm sorry we had to meet like this. I'm so scared right now. I have to stop and think a minute."

"That's okay, just take it easy. We'll figure out something. There's nothing that can hurt you right now. Drink your coffee and try to relax."

She cupped it with both hands, brought it to her lips and sipped slowly. She gazed out the window. "I feel like a heavy weight's been lifted off my shoulders. For the first time in a long time I feel free. Scared, but free."

I didn't want to say anything, but I was a little scared myself. Here I was a long way from home with a very beautiful, vulnerable lady sitting across from me. I knew deep down in my heart nothing would happen between us, though. All I could think about was seeing Jo again. I hoped this trip didn't blow it between her and me. It would break my heart.

I looked at Gloria. "He was real bad, huh?" She just looked at me and I could see the deep hurt in her eyes. I sat quietly and waited until she was ready to talk.

She drank a few times from her cup, then said, "I don't know what was wrong with me. I had just moved here from Minnesota and was working as a fund-raiser for a senator's re-election campaign when we met. My husband was the major contributor to the campaign. I was young and naive and he had wealth and power. He made millions in stocks and various private business ventures and is a financial genius. He was so kind and showered me with gifts and attention. I grew up on a farm and we always squeaked by. I was really impressed by all of that."

I sat drinking my coffee, listening. I didn't want to interrupt her.

"We started dating and I fell in love with him. He bought me this engagement ring," she held out her hand, "and it cost a fortune."

I looked at the diamonds and I was no expert, but there was a big rock in the center with a bunch of smaller ones around it. I knew it had to cost a bundle.

"We got married almost three years ago and when we did, I really thought I knew who he was. Right after that he started to change from a kind, loving, giving, person to a mean, selfish, hateful person. At first I thought I'd done something to change him."

I couldn't help interjecting, "I don't think so."

"Well, at first I did. And because I thought that, I set out to try and fix it. But he only got worse."

Her eyes began to fill with tears. I reached over and took her trembling hand, "Listen, you don't have to say anything more."

"Yes, I do. I've had this dammed up in me for three years and I have to let it out. Please don't stop me."

I gently squeezed her hand. "That's okay, talk as much as you like and I'll listen, and stop when you feel like it."

"Thanks. It means a lot to me."

I sat back and got comfortable. She fingered her coffee cup, trying to collect her thoughts. She stared into her cup, "After we'd been married about six months, he started screaming and yelling about little petty things. It wasn't long after that he began to hit me." She paused for a moment, "That's about the time I got on the Internet. It became a release for me. Of course I didn't tell anyone about my situation. I guess I was too embarrassed, or scared. I really don't know which. It was about a year after that you got a computer and we started exchanging e-mail. I remembered you because you were kind and didn't pry into my life. You were one of the few people who talked about real things and not a bunch of sexual innuendoes."

I nodded and sipped my coffee. She looked up at me. "I'm

sorry. I didn't even think about you. Here I am laying all my woes on you and not even giving you a chance to say anything."

"Gloria, I think it's good for you to get this out. I have no problem just listening."

"You're sure it's all right?"

"Yes. Go on, tell me more."

She looked away for a moment, then looked back at me. "You were open with yourself. You told me a lot about yourself and I admired that. I think I was secretly jealous that you could do that and I couldn't. There were times I wanted to tell you, but I was afraid that if I did, you would stop writing, and you were my only link to reality."

"If you would have told me how it was, I certainly wouldn't have stopped. Matter of fact, just the opposite," I assured her.

"Well, I couldn't take that chance. For the past few months, I've been trying to get the courage to leave, but I just couldn't find it. Then you showed up out of nowhere. When my husband came to the door and I saw that look on his face, I knew I would get beaten for being seen with you." She paused and gulped hard, then continued, "I knew that when you left I would pay for something I didn't do. Then when you said that there was nothing there for me, for some reason it clicked that you were right. I looked at you standing there and to me you meant freedom. The way you talked about your life while we were communicating on the Internet was inspiring. All I needed was one final push. Another thing is that you were the first person I ever saw stand up to my husband. Not even the police would challenge him."

"I guess maybe that's 'cause I'm stupid and I have nothing to lose."

"You're not stupid. I've talked to you far too long to believe that."

I noticed her cup was empty and asked, "Would you like more coffee?" reaching out to take her cup.

"Yes, but you sit here. Let me get it."

"That's okay, I'll get it."

"No, please let me. You've done a lot for me already," she insisted.

She took the cup out of my hand, got up and walked to the counter. I couldn't help but watch her as she did. *How could anyone hurt her like he did?* I thought. *Oh, well, I knew better than to try and figure people out. I was usually wrong when I did.*

She came back with the coffee and handed me a cup. "Here. It's the least I can do. I want you to know that all the time we've been communicating has really helped me a lot."

"I'm glad. I just wish I would've known your situation."

She sat down and took a drink of her coffee. She looked a bit more relaxed. I knew that talking about it would help. "Do you have any friends here?" I asked.

"Just one. And that's where I usually go when things get rough. She's been a real sweetheart but I don't want to go there this time. He knows I'll be there and always shows up begging and pleading with me to come back and I always do. I really want to break it off this time so I want to stay away from there. I want to make sure I do everything I can to get away from him for good."

"That's a good idea. If you don't want the same things to happen over and over again, don't repeat the same behavior."

"It's easy to know the right thing to do, just hard to do it. I have to figure out what I'm going to do next. I don't have any cash with me and I'd like to go back to Minnesota for a while. I need time to be with my family and get my head together. What are your plans?"

"Well, like you already know, I wanted to ride my Harley cross-country. I got it a month earlier, so I wanted to meet you and surprise you. So, here I am."

She smiled for the first time. "Oh boy, did you ever."

"Then I planned on heading back to Borrego Springs."

"How are things with you and Billy Jo?"

"I realized that I'm in love with her. I haven't talked to her since I left almost two weeks ago. I'm beginning to worry. I've sent her post cards and called a couple of times, but all I get is the answering machine or her father. I sure miss her. She's all I think about."

She looked away, and appeared saddened. Probably because she wanted her marriage to work and it looked like it was over for

her. She looked at her watch. "The bank will be closing in a little
while. I've got to make a withdrawal so I have some money. Then
I guess I should get a ticket to my hometown. Do you think you
can give me a ride to the bank?"

"Sure. You want to get something to eat first?"

"Maybe after we go to the bank. I'm not really hungry right
now, and I want to make sure I get there before it closes."

"I'm ready when you are."

She nodded and we got up to leave. "I want you to know I
really appreciate all that you're doing."

"It's no problem. I'm glad to be of help."

We got on the bike and rode through the streets of New York
City in the direction of her bank. It'd been quite a while since I'd
been in the heart of a large metropolis. I couldn't help but admire
the old, but sturdy architecture. We navigated through narrow
streets with tall buildings on either side reaching up to the sky,
blocking out the sun.

When we got to the bank, she motioned for me to pull over and
park. I did and she asked, "Would you like to come in?"

"Okay," I said as we got off and walked toward the door.

We entered the lobby and it was huge with a three-story
ceiling. I guessed it to be nineteen twenties or thirties in design. It
was impressive. She walked up to one of the representatives sitting
at a desk. He looked up at her and said, "Hello, Mrs. Johnson. How
are you today?"

"I'm fine, Mr. Rauls."

She sat down in a seat across from his desk, "I'd like to make a
withdrawal."

"How much would you like to withdraw?"

She thought a minute, and said, "Ten thousand dollars."

He shuffled in his seat, "I'll have to have the manager clear
that amount," he said as he got up.

He walked over to another desk where an elderly gentleman
was sitting. They exchanged some words, then looked in her
direction. He got up and they both walked back to where Gloria
was sitting. Then the other gentleman spoke, "I'm sorry, Mrs.
Johnson, your husband has put a freeze on your joint accounts. I'm

afraid I can't let you make a withdrawal without his permission."
She turned white. "That's something he would do."
He spoke again, "I'm really sorry, Mrs. Johnson," he repeated.
"It's not your fault. Don't worry about it." She got up and we
walked to the door. "I guess I came into this relationship with
nothing and it looks like I'm leaving with nothing," she blurted
out.

We walked to my bike and I said, "If you need some money, I
have a little. At least I can get you home on a bus, if worse comes
to worst."

She stopped and looked down at the rings on her finger, "Wait!
Maybe I'm not leaving penniless after all. I've got an idea. Can
you give me another ride?"

"You bet. Just point the way."

We rode for several blocks and she motioned to an upscale,
fashionable jewelry store, "Pull over here. This is where my
husband bought my wedding rings." They didn't look to be open.
She got off and walked to the door, "Damn! There're closed
already," she said as she pushed on the locked door.

She was on the verge of tears and about to come unglued. I
hopped off my bike and quickly went over to her. "Don't worry,
we can come back tomorrow when there're open. It's no problem."
I could see this was really starting to get to her. I put my arm
around her shoulder and we slowly walked back to my motorcycle.
"Why don't we find a place to get something to eat and sit for a
while?" I suggested. She nodded and we got back on the bike. I
didn't know where I was going so I rode for a little bit straight
west. I saw a small cafe and stopped in front. "Is this okay?"

"Yes. It's fine. I feel like a real burden to you, Ron."

"No, you're not. You're going through a difficult time and a lot
of things are beyond your control. But we'll get everything
straightened out, somehow." I had no idea how that would happen,
but I knew that if we sat down and had dinner, something would
come to mind.

We found a table and she ordered soup and I got a sandwich.
We sat quiet for several moments, then she said, "Maybe I could
stay at my friend's house tonight. I really don't want to because I

know he'll be there."

I sat thinking for a minute, then replied, "We could get a motel room for the night and then tomorrow you could do whatever you were going to do at the jewelry store."

She looked at her rings, then into my eyes. "I'm going to sell these back to them. They're of no use to me anymore. I'm not sure how much I'll get, but it should be enough to get me back home. Then I can take care of resolving my marriage. I'll pay you back after I sell them."

"That won't be necessary, you don't owe me anything. I made sure that I had enough money when I left Borrego. And I have plenty to get back."

She reached over and touched my arm. "You're so kind and understanding."

I felt myself get flushed, then I looked down at my food. "We better finish eating."

I ate my sandwich and looked out the window. It was beginning to get dark. I didn't know my way around and thought it best that we get a room soon and get to bed early so we could take care of her business first thing in the morning. Then the thought struck me that maybe she would be more comfortable in her own room. I'd better ask her. "I can get two rooms, one for each of us, if you like. That way if you need to be alone . . ."

"Oh, no, I don't. And I trust you. One room will do just fine. I'm okay with that. I don't think I want to spend the night by myself anyway."

I felt a little funny. Paul's words ran through my mind about meeting Gloria. And now we were about to spend the night together in a motel room. Not something Jo would be happy about. I'd get a room with twin beds. All we were going to do was try and get some sleep. I really had no desire to sleep with anyone but Jo and I'm sure Gloria was in no mental condition to want anything more than sleep. Why then was I getting nervous about this? Oh well, not to worry. I reassured myself nothing's going to happen. We'd get back to the jewelry store and, hopefully, she'd be able to sell her rings and be on her way home.

She ran her spoon around the edge of her empty soup bowl and

I thought we'd better get going, "Maybe we should start looking for a room?" I suggested.

"Yes. I could use some rest. This hasn't been a good day for me," she replied in a strained voice.

"Do you know where we might be able to find one? I have no idea where to look." She mentioned a few places and I knew they were high-rise motels where I wouldn't be able to keep an eye on my bike.

"I think we should look for one of those economy motels where I could park my bike in front, right outside the door. I'd feel better if I could watch it. I'd sure hate to wake up in the morning and find it gone."

"I didn't think about that. Wherever you feel you want to stay is all right with me."

Actually, I wanted to bring it into the room with me, but I didn't think that would be a good idea, so I didn't bring it up.

We were about to leave when I looked into her eyes. I remembered how I felt when I made the final break with my ex-wife, that ultimate feeling of being lost and so alone. If she was anything like me, this was the beginning of a journey for her which would be full of mixed emotions. I wished there was some way I could spare her, but I knew better. She would have to walk through this and get to the other end herself. There were no short cuts. I realized just then that it must have been the breakup of her marriage that I was intuitively relating to all the time we were talking on the Internet. All her comments were now beginning to make sense.

"Are you ready?" she asked.

"Yeah. How far is the airport from here?"

"A few miles. Why?"

"We stand a better chance of finding the kind of motel I'm looking for near the airport. At least there'd be a bigger selection. I just want to make sure I leave here the same way I arrived, on my motorcycle."

"I understand. I'll show you how to get there."

I paid the check, then we went outside and got on the bike. She leaned against my body as she reached around me and pointed up the street. "Go that way."

I started the bike and she slid her arms around my waist. It made me a little uncomfortable, but I shrugged it off. She held me tightly as we roared off to the airport.

I couldn't help but notice the scenery around me. The lifeless, cold asphalt and concrete was a far cry from the spacious country I'd become accustomed to. It occurred to me that people weren't meant to be stacked up on top of one another like they were in big cities. For some reason, it didn't seem natural.

Gloria tapped me on the side and motioned for me to turn at the next light. I did and the street was lined with motels. I picked a two-story one with the doors facing the street, hoping I could get one on the ground floor, then park my bike right outside the door.

I stopped in front of the office, shut the bike down and got off. "I guess this'll do."

Gloria got off also. "It's fine with me," she said.

We went inside and I looked at the clerk. "I'd like a room for two with double beds."

The clerk offered the usual paperwork, then asked, "Cash or charge?"

Reaching into my pocket, I said, "Cash."

Gloria quickly responded. "Let me pay the for the room, Ron."

"You don't have any money."

She slapped a charge card down on the counter. "I'll charge it. And I hope my husband gets the receipt." The clerk cleared his throat and nervously fingered the papers in his hand.

"No, I can take care of it," I said.

"Please, Ron, I insist. You've done more than enough," she said as she handed the card to the clerk.

"Okay, if you want to, and if it'll make you feel better, go ahead." The clerk tried to take the card and remain inconspicuous. I didn't think he wanted any part of this. I stepped back and walked over to the door. *Was I doing the right thing?* I thought to myself. *She needed help and, by the luck of the draw, I was there. Why was it bothering me so much? I knew why. I felt like I was cheating on Jo. I knew I wasn't, but the feeling was there nonetheless.*

She walked up alongside me. "We got a first-floor room right around the corner."

"Good. I'm parking my bike right in front of the door."

She walked to the room and I rode my bike over to it. She opened the door and looked inside. "This room's big enough. Why don't you bring your motorcycle in?"

"I was going to suggest that, but I didn't know how you'd feel about it."

"Shoot, that won't bother me any." She stood there startled for a moment. "I'm talking like I'm back home already and I haven't even left New York yet. I think that's a good sign," she said with a puzzled look on her face.

I just smiled and turned off the bike. I looked around to make sure no one was watching, then said, "Could you hold the door open while I push it in?" She did and I guided it through. I put it alongside the wall and set it on the kickstand. "Perfect," I said smiling.

"Now you won't have anything to worry about," she said, smiling back.

I suddenly got nervous and flipped on the TV. "Maybe I can catch the weather report. I'll be heading back tomorrow afternoon and I'd like to know if it's going to be nice outside."

"Good idea," she said, sitting on one of the beds.

I sat on the other bed and tried to focus my attention on the television, feeling very awkward. I had no idea what to say or do, so I asked, "Would you like something from the vending machines in the lobby?"

"No, thanks. But go on and get something for yourself if you'd like."

"I think I'll have a soft drink," I said, as I got up.

"I'll have one, too. If you don't mind," she said quickly as I walked towards the door.

"No problem. I'll be right back."

I went into the lobby and stood by the machines, staring blankly at them. I thought I'd better suggest we go right to sleep when I got back to the room. All I had to do was keep my cool till tomorrow morning. Besides, I knew she had too much on her mind for anything otherwise.

I got two sodas and a candy bar and headed back to the room. As I opened the door, I noticed she was already under the covers and her jeans and coat were folded up in a neat pile next to her bed. She still had her blouse on so I breathed easy. I walked alongside her bed and handed her a soda. "Would you like a piece of candy bar?"

"All right. A small one, though."

I broke some off and handed it to her. She took it, then said, "I shudder to think where I'd be right now if I'd have stayed. I know I'm doing the right thing. The more I think about it, the more I know I should be with my family."

"I agree. Breaking up is a hard thing to do. Even when it's a bad marriage, it's still hard."

"I remember when you told me about how you'd been married for a long time and then your marriage fell apart. It gave me hope to see you start over again."

"I did what I needed to do. I basically put one foot in front of the other. Some days were harder than others. I know that time heals all wounds. It just depends on how deep they are."

She gazed blankly off into space. "My mind is so mixed up right now. One minute I want to laugh and the next minute I want to cry. Then I'm happy, then sad."

"That's part of it. I sure remember the feelings. At first you go through major extremes. Then as time goes by, the ups and downs level off."

She stared at the TV and I knew she was going through a lot of pain. I wanted to go to her and hold her, but under the circumstances I knew that wouldn't be a good idea for either of us. I stood up. "Maybe we should try to get some sleep. It's going to be a busy day for both of us tomorrow," I said, turning off the television.

"Yeah, that's a good idea."

I shut off the light and got into bed. I hated to sleep with my clothes on, but I thought it better to do so. I got under the covers and noticed how quiet it was. At least outside under the stars there was wind and nature noises. I turned over with my back to Gloria and started thinking about Jo. I missed her smell and her touch. I thought about how we met, and the first time we made love. The first time we rode a horse together in the mountainous forest. After a while, I dozed off. Sometime during the night I dreamed I felt Jo snuggle up behind me. I slowly woke up and realized Gloria had crawled into bed with me and snuggled up with me. I froze and held my breath. This wasn't right, not for me anyway. I gently touched her arm, "Gloria. We can't sleep in the same bed together. I hope you understand, but I just can't."

She buried her face in my back. "She really means a lot to you, doesn't she?"

"Yes, and I'm not sure if I already screwed it up by taking this cross-country trip. But it doesn't matter. Right now I can only sleep with one lady and that's Billy Jo."

She slid away from me and sat up on the bed. "You're right. I can't expect you to sleep with me, even though we wouldn't do anything. It's still not right."

She got up and sat back down on her bed. I felt bad. "You're a very beautiful, and desirable lady. If I didn't already have someone in my life, I would have no problem with it. But I do."

"It was wrong for me to do that," she said.

"No, it's okay, Gloria. You need comfort. I'm just the wrong person right now. And you didn't do anything wrong. It's natural to want compassion, especially in a time of need."

I went over, sat down next to her and put my arm around her shoulder. "If you want, we can talk. I'll stay up with you."

"God, you're so understanding. I wish I could meet someone like you."

"You will. It might take some time and you might have to wait to get over this one, but you will."

She put her head on my shoulder and we sat quietly for a few minutes. She lifted her head. "I'm okay now. We better try and get some sleep. We're going to need it." I nodded and went back to bed. It took a while, but I finally drifted off to sleep again.

The morning light seeping around the curtain edges brought me back to consciousness. I looked over and Gloria was still sleeping. I'm not sure when she finally did go to sleep, so I thought I'd lie here and maybe try to catch a few more winks to give her a chance to get as much rest as she could.

I must've dozed off because the next thing I remember is hearing the shower water running in the bathroom. I sat up and after a few minutes she came out. "Wake up, sleepyhead."

"I'm awake. I woke up at dawn, but went back to sleep so you could get as much rest as possible."

She was a lot more cheerful as she walked up to me, cupped my face in her hands and kissed me on the forehead. "I appreciate that. I did need the rest and I feel a lot better now."

I sat on the edge of the bed collecting my senses. "It takes a few minutes for me to wake up," I said, rubbing my eyes.

She walked toward the door. "You want some coffee and a sweet roll? I'll get it from the office."

"Sure, I could use some coffee, and I'll take it black."

"You got it," she said as she swung the door open.

I was glad to see she was in a better mood, but I knew it would be up and down swings. I thought that after she got home she'd be in a better mental frame of mind.

I tried to shake the sleep out of my head and decided to take a quick shower. I took some clean clothes out of my saddlebag and went to the bathroom. I quickly showered and could hear Gloria milling around in the other room when I got out.

"I got your coffee and roll," she hollered through the door.

"I'll be right out," I answered as I got dressed. I went into the other room and picked up the coffee from the dresser. "Thanks, I really needed this."

The door was slightly ajar and it looked to be sunny and warm out. I picked up the sweet roll, walked to the door and looked outside. Gloria stood alongside me, "Things sure do look different from one day to the next."

I thought a moment, then said, "I think it's a combination of what happens to us and how we take it that affects us."

"Hmm, could be. I just know I feel like everything's gonna be all right," she said.

"It will. Just give it some time." I looked at her and realized she didn't have any clean clothes. All she took were the clothes on her back. I had an extra flannel shirt, "Would you like a clean shirt? I have a spare one."

"No, thanks. If I can sell my rings I'll stop at an inexpensive department store and pick up some things for the trip home."

"Are you sure?"

"I'm sure, thanks anyway."

I walked outside and looked around. It was hard to find any grass or dirt. There were a few trees, but they looked out of place, like they didn't belong in this maze of brick buildings and concrete pavements.

Gloria stood in the doorway. "Are you almost ready?"

"Yeah," I said and gulped the last of my coffee and ate the last bite of my sweet roll. I went inside and backed my cycle out the door into the parking lot. "You'll have to direct me back to the jewelry store. I have no idea where I am."

"Okay," she said as we got on the bike. She slid her arms around and scooted up close. I could feel her firm body against mine and, being a human, it started to arouse me. I fired up the engine, kicked it into gear and focused my attention on the road. The traffic was so thick that it didn't take long for me to lose that feeling.

She guided me through the streets of New York City. We went through neighborhoods where there were tall apartment buildings standing side by side. Little kids were playing in the streets for lack of any open areas. Then we cruised down streets with neat, small single-family homes. These weren't as crowded, probably because the people were in their backyards.

I considered myself lucky to be able to see that narrow band of America that I'd seen so far. The country appeared to be divided into three sections as far as I could tell: the relative open newness of the west, the transition past Oklahoma to the midwest, and then past the Great Lakes to the crowded, older eastern seaboard. Each had its own distinctive personality. The people had a lot in common as people, but temperaments and habits were a little different, not to mention dialect. I thought that at the time this country started to develop, no one could have predicted the path it would take.

Gloria tapped me on the side and I realized we were downtown again, with the tall skyscrapers blotting out the life-giving rays of the sun. She motioned for me to turn right at the next light. I did and we were right in front of the jewelry store. I parked between two cars.

"Come in with me," she said as she lifted her leg over the seat.

I nodded, turned off the bike and we went inside. This was no small-scale jewelry store. The clerk greeted Gloria by name.

"Can I speak with the manager or owner, please?"

"Yes, Mrs. Johnson. One moment, please." He went into the back and reappeared with another gentleman.

She leaned over to me and whispered, "Good, that's the owner."

He walked up to her smiling, "And what can I do for you today, Mrs. Johnson?" he said with a foreign accent.

"I'd like to talk with you in private if I can."

"Why, certainly. Come this way." We followed him to his plush office. He sat behind his desk and we sat in the chairs in front of it.

She paused for a moment, then said, "I'm in a monetary bind at the moment and I'd like to know if you would be willing to buy these rings back from me?" she asked as she held her hand out.

He looked surprised. "Those are your wedding rings, Mrs. Johnson."

"I know," she hesitated as she looked at her finger, "but my marriage is over."

His surprise turned to suspicion as he leaned forward on his desk, raised his eyebrows and looked at me. "Are you all right? You're not in any danger, are you?" he asked her while keeping his eyes trained on me.

She looked at him staring at me. "Oh, no. Ron is a friend of mine. He's been a real help to me these past few days."

"Are you sure?"

"Yes. Please don't worry about him. It's my husband that's the problem."

He sat back in his chair but still eyed me with caution. He turned back to Gloria and said with his accent, "This is highly irregular. We are in the business of selling jewelry, not buying it."

"I'm aware of that and I'll take whatever you feel they're worth."

He ran his fingers over his thick, black mustache thinking, then said, "Could you remove them from your finger, please?"

She did as he asked. He took them, got up and walked to the door. "I'll have to let Vito look at these and appraise them. I'll return shortly."

She nodded and sat staring at the wall, not speaking. I waited a few minutes, then said, "I hope he gives you what they're worth. They look expensive."

"They are. I'm not sure how much he paid for them, but I know it was over a hundred thousand dollars."

I took a deep breath and thought, *wow, that's a lot of money.* I sat quiet since I didn't think she wanted to talk right at this moment. I knew this was hard for her and I wished there was something I could do to help ease her pain.

The owner came back and sat in his chair facing her, "This is not customary for us, but I can make you an offer. I do not wish to insult you, but I can only offer you a fraction of what they're worth. I can buy them back for twenty-five percent of their retail value."

She sat thinking, "And how much would that be?"

"Thirty-thousand dollars."

Damn, I thought, *that means he paid one hundred twenty thousand dollars for those rings. And this jerk is only going to give her thirty thousand bucks back. What a deal for him.*

She sat staring at the rings in his hand, then cleared her throat and said, "Okay, I'll take it."

"I'll make out a cashier's check," he said as he got up again and walked to the door. "I'll return with it."

I didn't know if I should speak, but I couldn't help it. "Those rings are worth a lot more retail. Are you positive you want to sell them back to him? Maybe if we shopped around, you could get more?"

"No, I just want to get this over with and get home. I really don't care how much I get as long as I can leave and have some money to last me a while."

I understood how she felt. I did the same thing when I left. The things and stuff weren't important anymore. Well, thirty thousand isn't a trifling amount either. She wasn't talkative and the silence was deafening. It seemed an eternity before the owner came back with the check.

He handed it to her. "I'm sorry your marriage isn't working out. I wish you the best of luck and if I can be of any help to you in the future, please don't hesitate to call."

She took the check and stood up, "This will help me out tremendously. I'm sorry things worked out the way they did myself."

I got up and we walked toward the door. The owner stayed behind his desk and waved goodbye as we left. She hurried to the front, rushed out the door and stood on the sidewalk with tears beginning to form in her eyes. I walked in front of her, then put my arms around her. "That's okay, go ahead and cry. Let it out." She buried her head in my chest and sobbed for a while. People passing by stopped and stared. I wanted to scream, mind your own business, but thought that's not such a good idea at the moment.

She regained her composure and lifted her head. "Could you take me back to the bank so I can cash this check?"

"I sure can. Come on, we're on our way."

She wiped away the tears from her eyes and got on the bike after me. I waited a moment, then asked, "Are you ready?"

"Yes. Go that way," and she pointed to the right.

I pulled into traffic and followed her guidance through the overcrowded maze of streets. I was beginning to get claustrophobic here and I knew I would have to get out of this city soon for my own sanity.

It didn't take very long before we were in front of the bank. I pulled up to the curb, shut the bike off and sat on the seat. She swung her leg over and asked, "Aren't you coming with me?"

"If you want me to."

"I want you to."

I got off and we went inside. She walked to the manager's desk where we were before and the man looked up again, surprised.

"Why, hello again, Mrs. Johnson. How can I help you?"

She sat in the chair in front of his desk and held out the check. "I'd like to cash this."

He looked at it, then said, "I'll have to clear this with my manager. I'll be right back."

He walked to the same desk he had gone to before. Gloria fidgeted nervously in her chair. This had to be very uncomfortable for her, to say the least. I put my hand on her shoulder, "There shouldn't be any problem cashing that check."

"I hope not. I don't think I can handle another setback right now."

The clerk came back alone this time. "Could you endorse the back of this please?" he asked as he handed it to her. She took it, signed it, then handed it back to him. "How would you like the bills?"

"Hundreds will be fine." He nodded and went to the gate behind the teller's cages.

"See, I told you, no problem."

She forced a smile. He came back with thirty bundles of hundreds banded together. He set them on his desk in front of her, "Is there anything else I can help you with?"

"No thanks. This will do for now." She stood, shook his hand, picked up the money, then turned to me and said, "I'm ready to go now." She put the money in her purse and we walked to the door. As we reached it she pulled out a bundle of hundreds and tried to hand them to me. "Here, I want you to have this."

I threw up my hands and backed away. "No way, I can't take any money. You keep it, you'll need it more than me."

"Please take this. It's the least I can do for you. After I get home, I'm going to file for divorce and I know I'll probably get a large settlement, so take this."

"Nope," I said, as I kept my hands up, "I can't accept any money."

She put her arms down to her sides, "Ron, I want to do something for you, now take this."

I walked through the door at the same time saying, "Nope."

I hurried to my bike and sat on the seat. She followed me and stuck the bills back in her purse, "Can I ask you for another favor?"

"As long as you don't try to pay me."

"I won't. I want to pick up a few things before I leave. Could you take me to a department store?"

"I'd be more than happy to, just show me the way."

I followed her directions through more crowded streets and an endless array of traffic lights. I was amazed that anyone ever got to his or her destination in this town. I guess I'd been in the wide-open spaces too long. I was beginning to miss my home and I felt an emptiness not being able to see Jo. After Gloria was safely on her way, I was going to stop and give her a call. I hoped she'd pick up the phone and not her father or that stupid machine.

She tapped my shoulder and broke my concentration. She was pointing to a shopping mall. I turned into it and she directed me towards a department store. I didn't care much for shopping, but I'd go in with her. It probably wasn't a good idea to leave her alone for any length of time.

We parked and went inside. She immediately went to the women's section. I reluctantly followed. She bought a couple of undergarments and an extra pair of jeans and a couple of blouses. She also picked up a small knapsack to put the things in. We went through the checkout counter and she paid for them with her credit card.

We went outside and stood by the bike, then she faced me. "I guess I should decide how I'm going to travel."

"Uh-huh, that would be a good idea."

"I don't suppose there's any way I could talk you into driving me to Minnesota?" she asked coyly.

"No, I couldn't do that in good conscience. If I wasn't involved with Jo, I wouldn't hesitate."

"I didn't think you would, but it didn't hurt to ask."

She had a sadness in her eyes but I had to be true to myself and I felt I owed it to Jo. I didn't mind going out of my way to help her, but I couldn't drive her all that distance. Besides I was anxious to get home. I'd been on the road long enough and going to Minnesota would put an extra thousand miles on my ride back.

She looked at me as though she were in deep thought. "Should I go by train, plane or bus? If I go by train or bus, it'll take days." She thought a minute more. "I guess I'll take a plane. I just want to get home."

"Yeah, you might want to be with your family as soon as possible," I added.

"You're right. Could you take me to the airport?"

"I'd be happy to. Just point the way."

We drove to La Guardia and I stopped at the parking gate. "Do you want me to come in and wait with you? It might take a while for the next flight out to where you're going."

"What about your bike?"

"I'll park it right here next to this attendant's booth and ask him to keep an eye on it."

She looked at him. "Yeah, it should be safe here."

I pulled alongside the booth and asked, "Is it okay if I park my cycle here by you so you could keep an eye on it?" as I handed him a five-dollar bill.

He smiled, took the money and replied, "You got it, chief. Ain't nobody going to bother that motorcycle."

"Thanks."

Then Gloria said, "You make real sure nobody touches this bike."

He nodded and flashed the peace sign as we got off and started walking towards the terminal. Gloria paused as we got to the door and touched my arm, "Are you absolutely sure there's no way I could change your mind about giving me a ride? I'd take care of all the bills and it wouldn't cost you anything. I'd really love to ride on your bike."

"That would take me at least a thousand miles out of my way and I want to get back. I'm beginning to miss my home."

"And Jo?"

"Yes. And Jo."

"I must tell you, she's one lucky lady to have you in her life." She started through the door, then paused again. "I don't want to lose you as a friend. I want to keep in touch," she said.

I agreed and said, "Let me give you my phone number and

address."

I wrote it down on a piece of paper and handed it to her. She took it. "I'd give you mine, but I'm not really sure where I'll be. So when I get settled, I'll send it to you."

"Make sure you do," I insisted.

We went inside to the counter and she inquired about a ticket to St. Paul and the agent replied, "There's a flight to Chicago in an hour. Then you can transfer to a connecting flight from there to St. Paul."

"I'll take it." She used the credit card again. "When he gets the bills, he'll know I really left. And I hope it hurts him."

I didn't say anything. I knew she wanted revenge and I hoped she would get over it in time. "I'll wait with you till your plane leaves," I said as we walked to the boarding gate, "My bike should be all right where it is."

When we got there, we sat looking out the window. It took a while before she spoke. "I've really enjoyed talking with you on the Internet and I hope when I get another computer we can continue to talk. I mean as friends, just so Jo will understand."

"I'm sure she will. Just send me your e-mail address when you get back online."

"I will," she said as she stared out the window again watching the planes landing and taking off.

We sat quietly till they announced her plane was boarding. We both got up and walked to the gate. She turned to me and put her arms around my waist, then put her head against my chest and hugged me tightly. "Thank you for all you've done for me. I don't think I can ever repay you and I'll never forget you."

We hugged for a minute, and then she lifted her lips to mine and gave me a short, friendly kiss. She squeezed me one more time and quickly turned around and hurried through the gate. I watched her disappear into the plane, then I walked back to the window and waited to watch her plane take off. There was a sadness deep inside me. I knew it was going to be hard for her, but I had faith she'd get through it. I hoped she'd keep in touch.

Her plane lifted off and I slowly walked back to my bike. I waved at the parking attendant and he remarked, "No one ever came near it."

"Thanks, I appreciate that."

"No problem, bro."

I was about to swing my leg over the seat when I noticed that the flap on my saddlebag was pushed in. I thought, *someone was fuckin' with my bags.* I was just about to jump all over the parking lot attendant when I saw something was stuck up under the flap. I unlatched the strap and lifted it. And there, stuffed in the bag, were two bundles of hundred dollar bills. I picked them up and looked into the sky to the west in the direction of her plane. "Ooooohhhh, that was sneaky, Gloria."

Smiling to myself, I stuffed them to the bottom of the bag and latched it back up, then rode around to the attendant's booth and handed him the ticket. He looked at it. "That'll be ten dollars and fifty cents please," he said.

I handed him two twenties, "Keep the change. You earned it."

His face lit up like a Christmas tree, "Hey, man, thanks. You have a nice day now."

"You too," I replied, then hit the throttle and roared toward the interstate that would take me out of town.

"Whoa! What's wrong with me," I said. I can't leave New York City without stopping at a local Harley dealer and picking up a few T-shirts. I have extra money now, why not? I'd feel like a jerk not bringing anything back for Jo.

I pulled into the next gas station and looked up the addresses of a couple of dealers and wrote them down. I went inside, asked the clerk for directions to the closest one and headed toward it. It didn't take long to get there and I went on a mini-shopping spree. I got something for Paul, Diane, John and Jo. I got some shirts and a real nice jean jacket Jo would look real hot in. I also got one for myself. I had to buy an extra bag to attach to my sissy bar to carry everything.

I packed everything away and headed for the interstate out of town. I crossed over the Hudson River into New Jersey, grinning from ear to ear now that I was on my way back cross-country. I heaved a big sigh of relief.

I wanted to stop and call Jo just to hear her voice. It was

getting to be late afternoon but I didn't want to stop till I got all the way out of town into the country. It was three hours earlier in California so I had plenty of time to call. I had a pleasant, peaceful feeling deep down inside my gut now that I was headed west. I settled back in my seat and let the road hum under my wheels. I'd become a regular country boy since leaving Chicago.

The farther I got from New York City, the faster the traffic was able to move. God, it felt too good to be rolling along at sixty-five miles an hour again. Two days in a big, fast, crowded city was more than I could handle. As the miles rolled away under my wheels, the deeper and easier I began to breathe.

I headed west on Interstate 80 through New Jersey. The sun was sitting low in the sky and shining in my eyes. It was as though it was a beacon pointing the way, beckoning me to follow. As I got closer to the west end of New Jersey, the country opened up. I began to feel that sense of freedom I'd lost in New York.

I crossed the New Jersey-Pennsylvania state line and had to make a decision when and where I was going to stop for the night. The sun was ducking down under the horizon and the temperature would probably drop. The next major town was Milton, Pennsylvania, about a hundred and twenty miles away. I'd stop and get a room there with a phone so I could call Jo. I wanted to meet up with Maddog again if he hadn't left yet. I'd give him a call just to let him know I was on my way back.

It was close to 10 p.m. when I pulled into Milton. I cruised around looking for a motel where I could bring my bike in with me. I found one and while paying for the room realized I hadn't eaten yet. The only thing I had was the coffee and roll this morning. "Is there any place to get something to eat around here?" I asked.

"There's an all-night diner right down the road a bit."

He gave me directions and I got the room number and key, then went to eat. I figured it would be about eleven when I finished and got back to the room to call, which would be eight in California. That wouldn't be too late. I didn't want to irritate Jo's father any more than I had to.

I finished dinner and hurried back to the motel. After making sure that no one was looking, I rolled my bike into the room. I sat on the bed and stared at the phone on the nightstand. After reading the instructions, I picked up the receiver and punched in Jo's number. I didn't expect anyone to pick up on the other end. I thought the machine would come on as usual. I really wanted to hear Jo's voice bad.

It rang once, then twice. Finally, someone picked up. It was her dad's voice. "Hello, Thompson Ranch. Can I help you?"

I didn't know whether to speak or hang up. He probably never gave her my messages anyway.

After I didn't say anything, he said, "Hello? Is anyone there?"

I finally responded, "Hello, Mr. Thompson. It's me, Ron. Is Billy Jo there?"

"Uh, no she isn't, but I can take a message and make sure she gets it."

That was strange, he's never said that before. I hesitated, then asked, "Do you know when she'll be in? I'd really like to talk to her."

He paused for a second. "She's out of town and won't be back for about a week."

Out of town? Why would she be out of town and where would she go? "Could you give her a message?"

"Yes. What is it?" He was being awful cooperative and I was beginning to worry.

"Could you tell her I'm on my way back and should be there in about a week?"

"I'll see that she gets it. That's if she gets back before you do."

There was a silence on the other end like he wanted to say more. He would usually just hang up right away. This was out of character for him and it was beginning to scare me. After a few seconds he said, "Goodbye." He waited till I said goodbye to him before he hung up and that was unusual, too.

I slowly set the receiver back on the phone and sat there looking at it. *Where would Jo go? And for a week or more?* I was getting nervous. I'd never spoken that many words to her dad since I'd known him.

I sat back on the bed and leaned against the wall. I looked at my bike parked at the foot of the bed. It was dusty and dirty. *Was this worth it? Did I mess it up with Jo?* I had the urge to jump on the bike and start riding back to California right now, but that wouldn't do any good. She wasn't there. Maybe I'd call John in the morning. Maybe he knows what's going on. I could try to catch Paul also before he goes to work.

I could have sworn her father wanted to say more to me. Should I pick up the phone and call him back? No. I'd wait till tomorrow and call Paul and John.

I flipped on the television, but couldn't concentrate on the program. My mind kept wandering back to Borrego and Jo. I knew I shouldn't second-guess myself about this trip 'cause everything has a reason and a purpose, even if it wasn't clear to me right now.

I couldn't wait. I picked up the phone and dialed Paul's number. If he was home he should still be awake. It rang several times and I started to get antsy. "Come on, Paul, answer the phone."

He fi, Paul, what's up?"

"Ron, how you doing?"

"Pretty good. I'm in the middle of Pennsylvania and I'm headed back."

"Cool. So, did you meet Gloria?"

"Yeah, I'll tell you all about it when I get back."

"Oh, man, you gonna make me wait, huh?"

"When I get back. The reason I called is 'cause I just talked to Jo's father and he says she's out of town. Do you know what's up?"

"No. All she told me was that she had some business to take care of and she'd be gone for a while."

"That's all she said? What about Diane? She must've told her."

"If she did, Diane's keeping the secret real good. She says Jo told her the same thing she told me."

"Something's up and I want to know what it is."

"I really can't help you there. If I knew, I'd tell you," he assured me.

"I know you would. But she's okay otherwise?"

"Far as I know she is. She just went off somewhere."

"Damn, I bet Diane knows. Jo tells her everything."

"Well, if she does, I'll try to pry it out of her and I'll let you know."

"Thanks, do that will you?"

"Okay. So, how you doing?"

"So far no problems. I met this guy in Arizona and we rode together for a while. He stopped in Indiana to see his mother and I'm going to try and hook up with him if I can. I gotta tell you about him when I get back."

"Sounds like you're having a lot of excitement."

"Yep. Now I'm ready to head home."

"And you sound a little tired, too."

"I am and now I'm worried about Jo."

"Don't worry about it. I'm sure it's nothing major."

"I'll try not to. I'll let you go and if I don't call you, I'll see you in about a week. Oh, yeah, I almost forgot to ask. How is Jerry the jerk behaving?"

"He's minding his own business and not bothering anyone. He came into Jay's a few times and stayed to himself."

"That's good to hear. It's a load off my shoulders. I'll see you soon."

"Take care and ride safe," he said, then hung up.

I hung up and was a little relieved. But I still wanted to know what was going on. I looked at the clock and it was getting late. I'd better try and get some sleep. I'll call John and Maddog in the morning and head for Indiana if he's ready to leave. I lay on the bed and stared at the ceiling. The street light filtered through the curtains and gave the room an eerie glow. I lay still for a while before finally drifting off.

Chapter Fourteen

The sound of cars starting up outside in the parking lot woke me. I looked at the clock, 8:30. *Damn, I slept late. Oh, well, by the time I showered and shaved John should be at the station when I call.*

I got up and moped to the bathroom. I took care of business, cleaned up and shaved. It was close to 10:00 a.m. when I finished, which would make it 7:00 in California. I walked to the phone and dialed the station.

He picked up the receiver and said, in his familiar western drawl, "Morning. John's Service Station. John speaking."

"Hi, John. Ron here."

"Well, howdy, Ron. Good to hear from you. How's everything going?"

"Just fine. And you?"

"Just the usual, not too fast and not too slow. A few people have been asking about you. Told 'em you were taking a well-needed vacation. Oh, yeah, I got your post cards. Where are you?"

"I'm in Pennsylvania on my way back. By the way, have you seen Jo?"

"Not for a few days now."

"So you wouldn't know where she went?"

"No. Did she go somewhere?"

"Yeah. She went out of town for a while and no one knows why."

"Is she all right?"

"I think so. It's just bothering me that I don't know what's going on."

"Well, seems to me there's nothing you can do about it. So you might as well have a good time and you'll find out when you get back."

That's true, I thought. *I have no choice and I'm powerless to do anything till I get back.* "I'll try. I have to make one more phone call. I'll see you in about a week."

"Take care and if you need anything, give me a call, ya hear?"

"I will. Bye."

I hung up and searched my wallet for Maddog's mother's number. I found it and dialed. A soft-spoken, lady's voice answered, "Hello."

"Hi, is Mad . . ." I stopped and corrected myself. "Uh, is Kipp there?"

She took the phone away from her mouth and hollered, "Kipp. It's for you."

"Good, he's still there," I whispered.

His deep, burly voice resonated through the phone, "Hello?"

"Hi, Maddog. It's me, Ron."

"Hey, there, partner. Where are you?"

"I'm in the middle of Pennsylvania."

"Are you on your way to New York? Or are you on your way back?"

"I'm on my way back. Are you ready to head out?" I asked.

"When do you think you'll be here?"

I had the map in my lap. "It looks like I'm about four hundred miles from you. It's almost 10:30 here. I'm gonna stop for a quick bite to eat and I figure I should be there between 6:00 and 7:00, depending on traffic."

"That's a bunch of hard driving. You going to want to leave right away when you get here?"

"If I get there as planned, we'll still have a couple of hours of driving time left. If that's all right with you."

"Sounds good to me. Give me a call when you're about a hundred miles away and I'll meet you on Route 41, the same spot where we parted."

"Yeah, I remember where that was. I'll give you a call in a few hours," I said.

"I'll be waiting. Keep the shiny side up, the rubber side down."

"You got it. See ya." I hung up and backed my bike out the door. I looked up at the sky to the west and it was cloudless. So far the weather was cooperating.

I rode a little way down the highway and stopped at a convenience store, got two muffins and a cup of coffee. I went outside and sat on the curb alongside my bike. As I drank my coffee, I watched people go in and out of the store. I thought back to the hectic pace in New York. It seemed that the people in the big cities were moving extremely fast, but not covering much ground. And out here in the country, people were moving a lot slower, but they were going great distances. Somehow it appeared a paradox, but it was true.

I watched a pretty, young lady pull up in an old Mustang muscle car. She eyed me, then my bike. She got out of her car, headed toward the door and as she passed me, she smiled and said, "Nice bike."

I smiled back and replied, "Thanks."

She lingered for a moment, then went inside. I finished my coffee and muffins and got up to leave. The girl came back out and glanced over her shoulder at me. She looked at my license plate on my bike, "Long way from home, huh?"

"Yeah, I'm on my way back."

She smiled and slowly got in her car, started it up and waved as she backed away out of the parking spot. *That girl was trying to hit on me,* I thought. *Yep, the country had the city beat hands down.*

I swung my leg over the bike and sat on the seat. I had a lot of miles to ride and figured I better get started. I fired up my engine and got back on the interstate. I rolled westward over the gentle, grassy plains of Pennsylvania. It was late summer and everything was still deep green and blooming. As I rode, I checked out the farms and ranches that were the backbone of this country. I tried to enjoy the landscape, but the fact that Jo had gone away was gnawing at me. I could call her father again and just ask him. The worst that could happen was he would not tell me and hang up. Yeah, I'm going to call him again, but I'll wait till I need gas before I do.

The countryside rolled by and I was making pretty good time. I wondered if I should stop in Chicago again and see my family before heading west with Maddog. I'd wait until I got just south of Chicago before I made that decision.

I was getting close to the Ohio state line and I noticed I needed to pull over and get gas. I rode into a service station and stopped alongside a pump. I gassed up, got a handful of change for the phone and pushed my bike over to the side. I was nervous as I dialed, partly because I wasn't comfortable about questioning her dad and I wasn't sure if I'd be happy to know where she was.

It rang twice and he picked up. "Hello, Thompson Ranch. Can I help you?"

"Hi, this is Ron again. I hate to bother you, but I'm worried about Jo. Could you tell me where she is?"

There was a long pause, then he said, "I think I'd rather let her explain that to you when she gets back."

I hesitated a moment, then said, "I understand. Sorry to bother you."

He paused again, "I don't think it's my place to say, so I'd rather let her explain." At least he was being nice about it.

"All right," I said, "I should be back in about five days or so."

"She should be back by then also."

"Okay, I don't want to keep you any longer."

He said goodbye and we both hung up.

I stood by the phone and thought, *he's been more open with me the last two times we've talked than all the time I've known him.* I walked to my bike and got on. I sat staring across an open wheat field wondering where she could possibly be. I didn't have a clue. I fired up the engine and said to myself, "I won't get home sitting here." I hit the throttle and headed toward the Ohio state line.

I was making real good time going through Ohio. The traffic was averaging about seventy miles an hour and I decided to stay on the interstate all the way through to Indiana. I stopped outside of South Bend and checked the map. I was about a hundred miles from where I left Maddog. I found a roadside phone and stood by it, trying to decide if I should make a side trip to Chicago again, or just pick up Maddog and keep heading west. To hell with it, I gotta get back to California. I'm sure my family will understand. Besides, I just saw them on the way here.

I picked up the receiver with a twinge of guilt and dialed Maddog's number. I waited for someone to pick up. I heard Maddog's voice. "Hello?"

"Hey, it's me, Ron."

"Hey Roadside, where are you?"

"I'm just outside of South Bend."

"Damn, man! You're cooking. What's your hurry?"

"I'll explain it to you when I see you. You gonna be ready to go?"

"Yeah. It should take about an hour and a half for you to get here. Or maybe less the way you're riding. I'll meet you where we parted."

"Sounds good. If you're not there, I'll wait."

"I'll be there. See you then."

I hung up and thought as I walked to my bike, *I am really moving. I should stop in Chicago, but I have to keep moving. I think I was becoming obsessed with getting back.*

I tried to keep my speed down and was beginning to feel every bump in the road. I thought that after I met up with him we could ride an hour or two, then stop to get something to eat. This was the longest, hardest day on the road for me so far this trip.

When I got to U.S. 41, I turned south and headed toward the spot I had dropped him off. It took about thirty minutes when I spotted him sitting on the other side of the road facing me. He was leaning back on his sissy bar, his foot propped up on his handlebars, smoking a big, fat cigar. I rode past him, made a U-turn and pulled alongside him. He stared at me without speaking. I guess I looked a little road-weary. I was dirty and full of bugs. I don't think I looked like a happy camper by the way he stared.

He finally spoke, "So, how'd things go in New York?"

"I'll tell you about it later. Are you ready to roll?"

He stared at me again, not speaking, then said, "You look like you been riding hard. Did you stop and see your kids?"

"I did on the way to New York, but not on the way back here." I was getting irritated and finally said sarcastically, "Are we gonna sit here and shoot the shit all day, or are we gonna ride?"

He looked at me and remained expressionless, then raised his left eyebrow ever so slightly. He bent over, slowly crushed out his cigar on the pavement and lowered his leg to the ground. He looked at me again and said, "I forgot something at my mom's. Let's take a ride over to the house. It'll only take a couple of minutes."

"So lead the way," I replied, agitated.

He kick started his cycle and pulled out onto the road and I fell in behind him. *Damn,* I thought, *why was he pussyfootin' around? I wanted to get some more miles behind me tonight.*

We went south for about five minutes, then turned down a dirt road onto a large farm. We went a little further and rolled up to a neat, well-kept farmhouse. We shut off our bikes and got off. I could barely straighten up. An elderly lady appeared from behind the screen door and stood on the porch alongside a swing swaying in the light breeze. She was very petite and couldn't have been an inch over five feet tall. Her gray hair was pulled back tightly in a bun on top of her head. Her ankle-length plaid summer dress gently swayed in the breeze under a checkered apron. She vaguely reminded me of someone. Connie, that's who she resembled. As big as Maddog was, she was just the opposite. It was hard to believe this was his mother.

"Mom, this is Ron. The fella I told you about."

She peered at me through her horn-rimmed glasses. "Well, hello, Ron. Kipp has spoken highly of you. He said you helped him fix his motorcycle."

"Oh, ma, come on," he said, embarrassed.

I looked at Kipp and whispered, "What's her name?"

"Oh, it's Elsie. Sorry about that. Everyone just calls her mom."

"Hi, Elsie. Nice to meet you."

She looked into my eyes, "Have you had supper yet?"

"Uh, no. Not yet."

"Well, you come on in here and let me fix you something."

I looked at Maddog, wanting to get back on the road. He looked back at me. "If you didn't eat yet, my mom will take care of ya. You can't turn her down and hurt her feelings now, can you?"

I did want to stop and eat. Might as well do it now. "A quick bite," I said, "Then we'll head out." Maddog nodded and headed towards the porch.

She turned and went back through the screen door. I followed him up the wooden steps and across the porch. He stepped inside the house with me right on his tail. I looked around and everything was as neat as a pin. There were knickknacks strategically placed throughout the living room. There were doilies on every piece of furniture. Over in the corner, a grandfather clock loudly ticked away the seconds as though it, and it alone, had complete control of time.

Maddog pointed to a sofa and said, "Have a seat and she'll call us when it's ready."

I sat down and he sat in a rocking chair across from me. "When's the last time you had a home-cooked meal?" he asked.

I laughed, "I can't remember that far back."

"My mom's the best cook around. I know you'll like it."

I sat on the sofa nervously tapping my fingers and shuffling my feet. I glanced over at Maddog and he had his legs crossed with one ankle propped up on his knee. He had his head tilted back with his eyes closed. How could he be so relaxed at a time like this? Well, I haven't told him anything yet, that could be why.

The only sound in the room was an occasional noise coming from the kitchen, and the clock ticking. After a few moments the slow, rhythmic ticking got louder and more annoying. My mind was moving a hundred miles a minute and that damn clock was ticking so slow. Suddenly, I realized that this anticipation was going to kill me. And if I didn't slow down, I might do something stupid on the road and never get back. The more I listened to the clock, the more I started to relax. I put my head back and closed my eyes. The ticking began to soothe me and I let the rhythm carry me away.

I almost dozed off when Elsie yelled from the kitchen, "Supper's ready."

My eyes snapped open and we both got up and walked through the kitchen door. The aroma was overwhelming. This smelled much better than Connie's cooking did, although I didn't think anything could.

I pulled a chair away from the table and sat down. Maddog did the same. She set a large plate of roast beef in the center of the table, then followed that with some freshly mixed vegetables and a bowl full of steamy mashed potatoes. She set the gravy down and said, "Help yourself."

Maddog replied, "Yeah, go on, dig in."

He grabbed his fork and speared a couple of healthy slices of roast beef. I followed suit with two heaping tablespoons full of vegetables on my plate, then handed them to him. I spooned the mashed potatoes and watched the steam rise as I piled them on my plate. I smothered them in gravy and poured some on my beef. If I didn't shove something in my mouth in the next few seconds, I was going to start drooling uncontrollably. His mother sat down and watched me shovel my food in my mouth. I thought I was in heaven. Maddog wasn't moving too slowly either.

I had second helpings of everything and started to slow down. I hadn't tasted food like this in years. I was tempted to camp out here for a few days. I scooped up the last bit of food from my plate with my fork and shoved it into my mouth. His mother looked at me. "Did you have enough?"

My eyes were bulging. "I can't eat another mouthful."

"Oh, my, but you must have some pie ala mode."

I looked at Maddog with pleading eyes. I was about to explode. He looked back at me and shrugged his shoulders. "Maybe if you wait a half an hour, you'll have room."

I still wanted to get on the road but I couldn't move if my life depended on it. I looked out the window. "It's getting late and I think we should get going."

He tapped his fingers on the table, "Even if we leave right now, the most we can ride is a couple of hours and you've been on the road all day. I'll tell you what, why don't you spend the night here and we'll get up at the crack of dawn and just ride a little longer tomorrow? And didn't you say Route 66 starts in downtown Chicago?"

"Yes, it does."

"And you want to ride the route's distance, right?"

"That was my plan."

"Why don't we get up early and ride to Chicago. It's only about an hour and a half from here, and while you're there you can stop and visit your kids."

"I really wanted to try and make it back to California in five days or less, if I can."

"No problem. Even if we take our time, we can still get back in less than five days. We can ride five hundred miles a day. That would only be at most ten hours on the road each day."

I thought about it and he was right. There really was no sense in leaving tonight. His mother added, "Yes, and you can sleep in one of the spare bedrooms. We have plenty of room."

Maddog persisted. "Spend the night. You can wash your bike if you stay. It's really dirty and it sure looks pretty when it's all cleaned up."

I couldn't argue with that. I should visit my kids before heading back to Borrego Springs. It was only right. I was too full to move anyway and it was late. My bike was filthy and could use a good washing. There was no way I could argue. I looked at Maddog, "Okay, I'll stay. I'll wash my cycle and by the time I'm done, I'll have room for that pie."

He stood up. "Come on, I'll get the hose out."

I stood up with him and followed him to the door. We went outside and I noticed there was still about an hour of daylight left. I took my saddlebags off and untied my leather coat from the handlebars.

He laid out the hose and got a bucket with soap in it. I filled the bucket with water and hosed down my cycle. He sat on the stairs with his massive arms folded across his chest, watching me wash my motorcycle. As I soaped up the bike, I explained what happened in New York. I also told him about Jo going out of town. He didn't say anything, he just listened.

I finished soaping up the bike and picked up the hose to rinse it off. I hesitated before turning it on. "I'm worried about Jo. She didn't mention any plans about going anywhere before I left. I think I might have screwed it up between her and me."

Maddog calmly looked at me, then said, "So that's why the big rush. If you get there before she does, what can you accomplish?"

I didn't respond.

"If you get there after she does, what can you accomplish?"

I straightened up and rung out the rag. "Nothing, I guess."

"And you can't do nothing till you get back, so I suggest you take care of the stuff in front of you, like rinsing off that bike before the soap dries on it." I did as he suggested and he remained silent as I dried off the bike. He then stood up as I finished, "You ready for that pie?"

I set the towels aside. "Yep, I got room now."

We went back inside and sat at the kitchen table again. His mother pulled out two huge, steaming hot slices of homemade apple pie from the oven. She set one in front of me and the other one in front of Maddog. She took the vanilla ice cream out of the freezer and set it on the table, "Take as much as you like."

I scooped the ice cream onto the hot pie and it immediately began to melt down the sides. I devoured it in record time, then sat back in the chair. I wasn't sure if I would ever recover from this. I was fully fed and had a clean motorcycle . . . what more could a man possibly ask for? I thought of Jo and instantly felt empty inside.

"Would you like another piece?" Elsie asked.

"No, thanks. I think I'd hurt myself if I had one more bite. I haven't had a meal this good in years. Thank you very much for inviting me to this great dinner."

"It was my pleasure. I'm glad you fixed Kipp's bike so he could come and visit me."

She got up, took a few plates and walked to the sink. I stood up. "Do you need any help with the dishes?"

"Oh, no. You boys go out and relax. I can take care of these."

"Are you sure? I wouldn't mind helping at all."

"No, you relax. You boys are going to do a lot of riding tomorrow, so you rest up."

"Come on, let's go outside," Maddog said. "Mom don't let no one touch the dishes."

We walked out onto the porch. "My mom's old-fashioned. She has complete control of the kitchen and the only thing she'll let anybody do in there is eat, nothing more."

"I sort of figured that."

I looked to the west and the sun had just set below the horizon. The sky was scarlet-red with a few bands of thin clouds streaking across it. I muttered, "Red sky at night, sailor's delight."

Maddog said, "Huh?"

"Oh, nothing. Looks like we might have good weather tomorrow."

He walked down the stairs and took in a deep breath of fresh country air, "Let's go down the road a bit. I'll show you where I grew up."

We walked down a dirt road between two cornfields lined with tall shade trees. We must have gone about a half a mile before he spoke. "My dad farmed this land up until the day he died."

"How long ago was that?"

"About fifteen years now."

We came to a spot of high ground where we could see the fields stretch out for great distances in the moonlight. He put his back to the wooden log fence, lifted himself up and sat on it, then looked over the land. "My dad wanted me to be a farmer, but it wasn't in my blood. I think it broke his heart. I got two brothers and a sister, and I'm the youngest. One of my brothers went off and joined the Navy. He's a lifer. My other brother became an Indiana State Trooper. My sister married a guy, had two kids and moved to Indianapolis. That left me to carry on with the farm. Three sons, and I was his last hope to carry on the farming tradition. I think the pressure my dad put on me just drove me further away. The harder he tried to make a farmer out of me, the harder I resisted."

He stopped talking and looked out over the fields again. After a few minutes he continued, "I left home at seventeen to try and find my way. I became the black sheep of the family because of the people I hung with, the outlaw biker gang. My dad died of a heart attack one day while plowing the fields and I never got a chance to talk with him to settle our differences. I'm sorry I never got to do that." He fell silent and I knew he was hurting.

"So, does your ma do the farming?"

He coughed, then replied, "No. After my dad died she leased out the land and other people farm it. That's how she gets by. There are times I feel guilty and think I should move back here and work the farm, but I don't know how. If I tried, I know I would screw it up."

"Well, your mom's doing good, isn't she?"

"Yeah. And I know she wouldn't want me doing something I really don't want to do."

"There you go, sounds to me like it's working out the way it's supposed to."

"I guess it is, just sometimes it's hard to accept."

We stayed there a few minutes, then he hopped off the fence. "We better get back. Mom's probably wondering where we are." We walked down the dirt road back to the farmhouse. Just before we went in, I eyed him with suspicion. He looked back, "What?"

"When I met up with you on the road earlier today, you said you had to come back here 'cause you forgot something. You really didn't, did you?"

He stared at me for a moment, then replied, "Maybe I did. Maybe I didn't. Does it matter anyway?"

"No, it doesn't." We walked a couple of more steps, then I said, "Thanks." He nodded without speaking.

We went into the house and his mother was sitting in the rocking chair with the clock ticking in the background. "Did you boys have a nice walk?" she asked.

"Yes," I replied.

"Where did ya go?"

"We went up towards the main field, near the back forty." Maddog answered.

"Oh, that's nice."

I stood in the middle of the living room feeling awkward when Elsie said, "Why don't you show Ron his room, Kipp?"

"Okay, follow me."

We walked through a long hallway with rooms on either side and we stopped at the last one. He opened the door and said, "We gave you this one in the back so you'd have privacy. You got your own bathroom, too."

"Thanks," I said as I stepped inside through the doorway. The furniture looked to be old, dark brown oak and finely polished. The room was in the corner of the house and had two windows at right angles to each other. The bed was queen-sized with a massive headboard with an intricate design carved on it. The dresser matched the bed and was supporting a large mirror.

Maddog stood in the doorway. "If you need anything just holler. I'll be right down the hall."

"All right, I will. Thanks."

"You want the door closed?"

"Yeah, could you?" He shut the door and I heard him walk down the hall. I figured I'd stay in the room and give him time with his mother before we left. I was tired anyway 'cause I didn't get a whole lot of sleep the night before.

There was a soft, warm breeze coming through the windows blowing the curtains back and forth. I walked over to one of them and sat down. *California seemed so far away at this moment,* I thought. I stared into the night sky and all I could hear was the crickets chirping to each other looking for a mate. Seems people and creatures are always doing that. We aren't complete unless we're with a mate. I thought about Jo as I gazed out the window and watched the fireflies blink their bright lights to each other to show their way. The moon lit up the tall wheat blowing in the wind. It looked so soft and appealing, like a giant feather duster being swept back and forth by nature's hand. A body could get real comfortable here.

I sat there just staring out over the fields for the longest time. I was tired, but this was almost more soothing than sleep. It was getting late, though, so I decided to go to bed. I pulled down the covers and the sheets had a clean, fresh scent about them. I stripped to my birthday suit and laid on the firm, comfortable mattress. I closed my eyes and the last thing I remember was hearing the crickets chirping in the night.

The heat from the rays of the sun shining through the window onto my face woke me up. I took in a deep breath and the aroma of fresh farm sausage frying in a skillet filled the air.

I got up and looked out the window. It was a warm, sunny, breezy day. *God,* I thought, *I slept like a rock. The best I'd slept in a long time. I'm glad I listened to Maddog and stayed the night. This was just what I needed.*

I went into the bathroom and took a quick shower. When I got out, Maddog was at the bedroom door. "Breakfast is almost ready.

Hope you're hungry."

"I am. I'll be dressed in a minute." He nodded and went back to the living room.

I walked down the long hallway and Maddog was sitting in the rocking chair looking out the screen door. He glanced at me as I entered the room. "How'd you sleep last night?"

"Good, real good. Matter of fact, like a baby."

"I like that room myself. It was my oldest brother's before he left."

His mother came in from the kitchen. "Breakfast is almost ready. Would you like to do your laundry while you're waiting?"

I thought about it and figured I'd have to do it anyway, so I might as well do it now and get it over with. "Yes, I do have some dirty clothes."

I took them out of my saddlebags and Maddog led me to the washer. I put my clothes in and then went to the kitchen for breakfast. His mother had already set the food out. There were fried eggs, homemade sausage patties and pancakes. Even though I stuffed myself last night, I was starving.

I sat at the table and Elsie said, "Take as much as you like. Don't be shy."

I wasn't. I piled the eggs, sausage and pancakes on my plate. So did Maddog. We ate in silence for the most part. I liked being here, but I really wanted to head back to California. I missed my home and Jo.

We ate like people who hadn't eaten in days. The food was so good and the aroma was so appealing, it was hard to eat like a gentleman. I finished a glass of freshly squeezed orange juice and sat back in my chair. I was glad it was going to take a few minutes for my clothes to be ready. I needed that time to digest the food so I could move.

Maddog stood up. "I'm going outside to check my bike before we leave."

I got up with him. "Good idea. I should look mine over, too. I've put quite a few miles on it and haven't really checked it."

We walked outside and it was starting to get hot. There was a stiff breeze blowing, which made the humid temperature bearable.

Maddog checked his tires and chain. He looked over the engine and trans and checked the bolts. I did the same and secured my saddlebags back under my seat, then tied my leather coat onto the handlebars. I made sure the two thousand dollars was still in the bottom of the bag.

It's a good thing I stopped here instead of riding straight through, I thought, I would have kept going until I dropped. Then done the same the next day. I'm not sure I would have made it back home that way. I was going to make it a point to try and kick back and enjoy the rest of this ride. I'll get back to Borrego Springs when I get back. I knew it would be gnawing at me in the back of my head, but I'd just have to keep it in check.

Elsie came out with my clothes all folded up and handed them to me. "Thanks," I said, as I took them and put them in my saddlebag, "You didn't have to do that."

"Oh, it was no trouble."

Maddog looked at her. "We'll be leaving in a few minutes."

She appeared a little sad. I turned to her and said, "Thanks for your hospitality. I really ate and slept well."

"You're welcome. And if you ever get by this way again, stop by and say hello."

"You bet I will."

Maddog looked in my direction. "You almost ready, partner?"

"Yep," I said, as I climbed on my bike.

He walked over to his mom and hugged and kissed her. She reached up and held his face in her hands. "You be careful now, you hear."

"I will, mom," he relied, sheepishly.

"You better." She looked at me. "It was nice meeting you, Ron."

"It was nice meeting you, too, Elsie."

Maddog got on his bike and we started our engines. His mom stood at the edge of the road and waved as we started to roll away and we waved back. She folded her arms across her waist with her long dress blowing in the wind, watching us as we hit the road.

We kicked up some dust, got on Route 41 and headed toward Chicago. I didn't plan on staying long and I had already called my kids to tell them I was on my way. The closer we got to the city the more closely packed the houses became. The traffic began to get dense and people started to dart in and out, trying to make up a couple of seconds here and there. They were probably in a hurry to get home so they could sit and watch TV.

We crossed the city limits and the traffic became congested. Our cruising speed slowed from a constant sixty to forty, then thirty as we got closer to the downtown area. It was a hot day and the humid air clung to our skin. I guess I'd become acclimatized to the desert.

We traveled through the downtown area to the north side where I motioned to Maddog to get off at a particular exit. We stopped at the first light after getting off. Maddog leaned over to me and said, "When we get where we're going, point me to the nearest bar and I'll wait for you there."

"You sure you don't want to come along? You're welcome."

"Naw, this is something you gotta do alone partner. I'm just excess baggage."

"Suit yourself. But you're welcome to come if you like." He shook his head and we moved on when the light turned green.

We cruised through the narrow city streets of the neighborhoods where I grew up. People turned their heads as we passed. They were probably checking out Maddog, who stuck up over the roofs of the parked cars as he sat straight up in his seat, stoned-faced.

Even though I didn't live here anymore, this would always be a part of me. All these places were etched in my memory. They all helped shape who and what I was.

We rode through a section of town with closed-down factories and warehouses, where now-deserted railroad tracks used to bring freight trains on their journey to pick up their cargo for other parts of the country. This was one of the blue collar, working class neighborhoods I used to live in. I remember playing on the tracks and having to keep an eye out for the big, powerful train engines that slowly rumbled by every now and then.

As I rode through the streets, the scenes triggered memories of my childhood, then through my teenage years up to, and through, my young adult life. Each part had its own chapter full of feelings and emotions locked away in special places in my mind. The corner grocery store across the street from my old elementary school where I used to stop and buy penny candy. The spot in the schoolyard where the class bully picked a fight with me and we punched it out to a draw, which didn't bother me any since he was a lot bigger than me. The place where I used to stand alongside the school building and watch the first girl I had a crush on from a distance because I was too shy to approach her. All the very neat single-family homes tucked between the three-story apartment buildings I would pass every day on my way to school. My best friend's house that was long ago vacated by his family and taken up by another one. The place my ex-wife grew up before we took up residence together as man and wife. The apartments we rented until we finally moved into a place we could call our own.

All the emotions welled up inside me like a giant tidal wave about to sweep over me. I got hold of myself as I stopped in front of a corner bar and turned to Maddog, trying to keep my emotions in check. "My kids are right down the street. You sure you don't want to meet them?"

"You go on. I'll wait here. Take your time. I'll have a few beers and shoot some pool."

"All right," I said, as I turned my bike down the narrow side street while Maddog parked in front of the bar.

I cruised down the street and my kids came out to greet me when they heard my Harley. My daughter had become a beautiful young lady and my son was now a handsome, strong, young man. I don't know what I did right, but somehow they turned out okay. It must have been the big guy in the sky more than my doing. I never got my hands on the rule book of life so I had to figure my way as I went along and play it by ear. It's kinda like on-the-job training, I guess.

I stayed with them for about three hours and felt guilty about leaving to go back to California, but my life wasn't here anymore. My home was in Borrego Springs, and they were young adults going on with their own lives. When I left a couple of years ago, it was to deal with a lot of the pain and grief of a divorce. Since then,

I'd built a new life in the desert and I could never move back here and be happy.

We said a few lingering good-byes and I rode away with a tear in my eye, back to the bar where Maddog was waiting. I regained my composure as I walked through the door. "Sorry I took so long," I said, as he shot a ball into a pocket.

He looked up. "No problem. You coulda taken as long as you wanted. I'm in no hurry."

I sat on a stool and waited for him to finish his game. When he did, he looked at me. "You ready to head back?"

"Yep," I said, as we both got up and walked toward the door. When we got outside I turned to him, "Hey, Kipp, thanks again."

"For what?" he asked as innocent as he could.

I smiled and answered, "Just thanks."

He nodded and swung his leg over his bike. I got on mine and he asked, "So, what's the plan, partner?"

"From the looks of the map, we have to head downtown where 66 starts, then ride out on interstate 55 for a while."

"Sounds good to me. Lead the way so's we can get home."

We fired up the bikes and rode south to the middle of the city, then turned onto the interstate. As we rode past the suburban homes toward St. Louis, my thoughts and feelings were running wild again. A wave of different emotions ran through my mind. I was overjoyed to be heading home. I was worried that I hadn't heard from Jo all this time and the fact that she left town. I was so pleased that I was in love with her and I wanted to share that with her so bad. And seeing Chicago after two years brought back a lot of memories.

I was consumed in thought when Maddog got my attention, which snapped me out of my trance. Some time must have passed as we were out in the country now and I hadn't even realized it. He was trying to signal that he needed gas. *Damn, it must have been at least an hour since my last conscious thought of my surroundings.*

We pulled into the first station and gassed up. Maddog looked at me. "Let's get a drink and take a break."

I nodded in agreement and we sat along the shady side of the building. He was silent for a minute, then asked, "Are you okay, partner?"

I paused, then answered, "Got a lot of stuff on my mind."

"Try not to let it get to you 'cause there's really nothing you can do about it right now. The only thing you can accomplish at the moment is getting home, then you might be able to take care of things."

I looked at him with one eyebrow lowered and thought, *this big lug's got a lot of wisdom under that rough exterior, and he hides it well.* I answered, "Yep, nothing I can do about it until I get there. I guess I'll try to enjoy the trip."

I gazed at my soda and thought, *it's gonna be hard, though.* Maddog took two long swigs of soda to try and get some relief from the hot, muggy midday heat, then turned to me. "We've been ridin' the interstate for a while now, thought the point was to ride old 66. Is it anywhere around here?"

"I completely forgot," I said as I pulled the worn, tattered map from my shirt. I studied it for a minute, "Yeah, there's a large chunk of 66 running along the freeway here. We almost passed it up."

"Well, point the way and let's get to it."

We finished the sodas and tossed the cans in the trash. We rolled out of the station and got back on the road and I led the way to old 66 again. It sure felt good to be back ridin' with Maddog. I tried to imagine making this trip without him and I'm sure it would have been real boring. He didn't say, or do, much, but his presence could really be felt.

We hooked up with the old route again and rode through the flat farmlands of Illinois. It took a few hours for my emotions to finally settle down. Riding through the small towns in the middle of summer helped take away the intensity of the things I was feeling. They weren't gone, just eased a little.

We crossed the Mississippi River into St. Louis and the country changed from flat to rolling, lush green hills. The heat and humidity became unbearable again and we kept moving fast to keep the wind on us. We stopped for gas a few times and Maddog checked on my well-being.

It was getting late and I saw some threatening clouds in the sky on the horizon. We were halfway through Missouri and I wasn't sure how far we'd get today, but we were making real good time. It's a good thing we both had a chance to rest up at his mom's house before we started back on the road.

We were close to the Oklahoma border when I figured we should stop, eat and look for a place to stay for the night. I stopped to check the map. We were between towns so we had a way to go yet.

As we rode, I could smell the moisture in the air. We hadn't got caught in the rain yet, but I think our luck was about to run out. I could see the lightning flashes off in the distance and hear the thunder, and we were riding head-on into it. I motioned to Maddog to pull over and when he did, I asked, "Want to try and make the next town?"

"Sure. If it starts raining, we'll just pull over and wait it out."

"Okay," I replied and we got back on the road.

The storm must have been moving fast because it was no time at all before the sky got dark and the clouds were right overhead. The rain started, lightly at first, then quickly became a blinding downpour. We rode the shoulder of the road until we found an abandoned building, then hurried and pushed the bikes into it.

I sat against one wall with rainwater dripping down my face and into my eyes. Maddog sat against the opposite wall directly across from me, soaked to the bone, too.

He stared at me for a bit, then cracked a tiny smile. He grinned widely for a minute, then broke out in a big, hearty laugh at the water dripping off my hair into my eyes. I watched him, then asked, "What's so funny?"

He pointed to me. "You are."

"What'd you mean?"

"You look pathetic, partner," he blurted out between laughs.

I looked at him a little miffed. "You don't look so hot yourself, big guy."

I realized that I'd never seen him crack a smile, let alone laugh. Then our situation struck me funny and I began to laugh myself. We laughed hysterically for about five minutes before I realized we'd better get into some dry clothes so we didn't get hypothermia.

We changed and I said, "Man, I'm hungry. I hope this rain doesn't last long."

"Me, too, but it's almost dark and most places along here probably close up early," he warned.

"Well, if it keeps up we might have to spend the night here and skip dinner."

I pulled out some candy bars I had stashed in my bags in case of times like this and handed two to Maddog. "We might as well eat these while we're waiting. I got more if you want 'em."

He nodded, "Thanks, partner," and ate them in no time.

So I handed him two more and he did the same with them. I ate mine and it didn't look like the rain was going to let up soon, so I remarked, "From the looks of things, we'll be staying here tonight."

"Yep, sure looks that way."

We waited about thirty minutes more before we got our bedrolls out and settled in for the night. At least we were dry and our bikes were out of the rain. He drifted off to sleep and I lay there quietly, listening to the soft patter of the rain falling onto the roof and onto the ground outside. I thought about all the things that happened so far on this trip and smiled. It was happening exactly the way it was supposed to. Everything had its meaning and purpose, even if some of the things did make me sad or worry. They all had their place and knowing that, I was able to roll over and let the rhythm of the rain lull me to sleep.

The sound of someone moving around jarred me awake. It was dawn and the sun was just coming up. Maddog was rolling up his sleeping bag and said, "Hey, partner, I don't mean to rush you, but I have to get some grub real soon. My stomach's been raising up a storm."

I looked at him groggily. "Uh . . . I'm up."

I crawled out of my bag and stretched. I slept like a rock last night all the way through and was glad I did. I figured it wouldn't be a good idea to suggest having a cup of coffee before we left. It was clear he needed to get food quick. I tied my stuff to my bike and we got ready to leave. I looked outside and it appeared to be clear. The sun was out and it looked to be a nice day.

We rolled our bikes outside and I waited for Maddog to start his. He kicked it over and it gave a loud backfire and died. He looked down at it, slightly perplexed. He kicked it again and it started, but sputtered and backfired a few more times as he worked the throttle to keep it running. He glanced at me with a look of surprise. My first thought was, *Oh, shit, I knew it was too good to be true, to make it all this way without trouble.*

I looked back at him, "Could be from getting wet last night. Let it run a few minutes and give it a chance to dry out."

He nodded and we sat there for a while, letting his bike warm up. It smoothed out and he shrugged his shoulders, "Maybe it was a little wet and needed to dry out. One thing for sure, if not, I'll find out. But right now, let's get some food before I keel over. I'll worry about the bike later."

We got back on the road and stopped at the first open restaurant we came to. His bike popped a couple of times on the way, but it ran. I had a funny feeling we were going to be fixing it somewhere along the line. Call it mechanic's intuition.

We pulled into the lot in front of the restaurant and Maddog was off his bike and on his way through the door before I could get mine shut off. I followed him to a booth and when the waitress came to give us water, he blurted out, "I already know what I want, steak medium and eggs over easy, as soon as possible."

She looked at him, surprised, then looked at me. "Do you want a menu or are you ready to order, too?"

I didn't want to hold up the waitress for one second so I replied, "I guess I'll have the same." She walked away and Maddog sat fidgeting in his seat. He was usually pretty calm, but not this morning. I wanted to talk to him about his bike, but I thought I'd better wait until after he ate. If I asked now, he wouldn't hear a word I said.

It didn't take long for the food to arrive and Maddog gulped his down and ordered another. I was real hungry so I ordered a side of pancakes myself. Ridin' all day yesterday, then going to sleep without dinner was not the way to go. I sure wouldn't want that to happen again, and I knew Maddog wouldn't either.

I waited till he finished his second order to where he calmed down enough to ask, "You think your bike's gonna be all right?"

He thought for a moment. "I'm not sure. It feels a little funny. I don't think it's the carb, though."

I was glad to hear that. I'd hate like hell to have something I fixed screw up, especially on his bike. "So, you want to try and ride it and see how it goes?" I asked.

"Yeah. If it gets worse, I'll just have to stop and fix it."

I checked the map. He was going to Needles right on the Arizona-California border that looked to be about a thousand miles from here. I told him that and he just nodded. He peered out the window. "I'll make it home somehow. I always do, one way or another."

He sure didn't seem to be worried about it. It looked like it was gonna take two days to get to Needles, with or without problems. I guess I'd better plan on it taking three days before I'd see Borrego Springs. I drank the last of my coffee. "Well, you wanna give it a shot?"

"Yeah, let's git," he answered as we got up and walked outside. He stopped as he got to his bike. "Hey, partner, I'd rather take as many of the back roads as we can. I hate getting stuck on the interstate."

"That's good enough for me. We'll see how your bike runs." It took a couple of kicks before it started and I knew the problem was getting worse, but maybe we could baby it home before it got too bad to ride. We headed out again and it wasn't long before we crossed into Oklahoma. If we could get four of five hundred miles behind us today, that would put us somewhere near the New Mexico state line.

His bike popped every so often but we just kept heading west. We stayed on the free road, which ran along the Oklahoma turnpike. It was well-traveled and there were a lot of places to get help if we got stuck here. I glanced over at Maddog every once in a while and he nodded that he wanted to keep going. It was awful hard to enjoy the ride knowing that any minute his bike might quit.

We made it past Oklahoma City and his bike seemed to be

running about the same. I kept us on 66 as much as possible in case we had to pull over. Only problem now was that people, places and things were starting to get scarce. I carried enough tools with me and Maddog had his share, but if we needed a specific part, we were screwed.

It was getting to be late afternoon and we were about a hundred miles from the Texas state line when his bike started to pop and backfire like crazy. He motioned to me that he was pulling over and I fell back behind him and followed him to the shoulder. I pulled alongside him and he looked at me. "I think this is as far as I'm gonna get, partner, until I fix this thing."

I shut my bike off and he shut his down. We got off and I asked, "Any idea what it might be?"

"I'm not sure, but it feels like it might be an ignition problem."

I stood there staring at his bike, then asked, "When's the last time you tuned it up?"

"A while ago."

"How old are the points?"

"Pretty old."

"Well, let's start there. If the points are burnt, then the timing's off, so let's check it."

"How can we? We don't have a timing lamp."

I looked up and down the highway. We were on a dusty, isolated stretch of asphalt and the closest town was miles away. *It figures. It would break down in the middle of nowhere.* I stood there thinking for a minute, then said, "I got an idea." I rummaged around in my bags and found a spare light bulb, and I always carried a couple of wires. I walked back to his bike. "We can make a timing lamp with this."

He looked at me slightly amazed. "You're right. That'll work."

We got busy taking the points out and filed off the burnt tips. We put them back and timed it with the makeshift lamp. Then we put it back together and he got ready to kick-start it. "Man, I sure hope that was the problem," he said, stepping down on his kick-starter. The bike sprang to life. He revved it up, then let it idle. It was real smooth again and didn't pop or backfire once. He looked at me with a smirk. "Damn, partner, you're good."

I was kind of embarrassed. "Naw, just a lot of years of experience is all."

He hit the throttle a few times and it sounded loud and strong. I looked up at the sky. "It's gonna get dark soon. We better find a place to eat and then look for a place to sleep. We're not far from Texas."

He revved the engine a few more times. It sounded healthy so that had to be the problem. I got on my bike and said, "That'll get you home, but you should put new points in when you get back."

He nodded as we got back on the road and I could swear he was smiling. I guess I would be, too, if it was my bike and I just got a reprieve from the barren Oklahoma plains.

The knot in my stomach eased a little knowing that his bike was running smooth, now. What I really wanted to do was to hear Jo's voice and feel her in my arms. I wanted to know where she went and what she was doing, but I figured it wouldn't be wise to pressure her dad.

We found a place to eat right before the Texas state line and I wanted to call to see if she was back yet. So, after I finished eating, I found a phone and dialed her number. I held my breath as it rang, then someone picked up, "Hello, Thompson Ranch," her father said.

I wasn't sure if I could take much more of this as I said, "Hi, Mr. Thompson. Is Jo back yet?"

He paused as usual, then answered, "No, Ron, not yet. I expect her back in a few days." Wow! That was the first time he ever said my name. I didn't even think he knew it.

"Uh . . . okay. If she gets back before I do, could you please tell her I called?"

"I'll make sure she gets the message," he assured me.

Man, this was getting weirder by the minute. If I didn't know better, I'd have sworn he was almost being friendly with me.

I walked back to the booth totally perplexed now. I didn't know what to think. I sat down and Maddog asked, "Is she back yet?"

"No, not yet. Not for a few more days, I guess."

"See, and you were in a big hurry. Now you can relax and take your time."

I nodded and stared out the window. My mind was already back to Borrego Springs but my body was at the Texas state line. If only I could get the two of them together for the rest of the trip.

"Hey, partner, think we should get lookin' for a spot to bed down?"

"Uh, yeah," I answered in a daze.

We paid the bill and walked out to the bikes. Maddog flipped on his ignition switch and got ready to kick-start it. "Well, let's see how many kicks it's gonna take to fire this muth'a up." He stepped down and it started right up on the first kick. He grinned out of one corner of his mouth. "Man, is that ever sweet."

I was surprised he even knew such words, let alone use them. He was gettin' more amazing by the minute.

I got on mine and fired it up. I was impressed with these new Evo engines. My bike was as strong and smooth as ever.

We got on the road and went the short distance into Texas before we found an abandoned building and stopped for the night. We went right to sleep and got up early the next morning.

We had quite a ways to go to Needles today and most of the trip would be on hot, dry desert land. I was glad to get away from the hot, muggy weather of the midwest. The heat coupled with the humidity was too much for me. I made some coffee for us before we left, just in case it took a while before we found a place to eat. Even though we were going in the opposite direction from when we began this journey, everything still looked fantastic. The towns and the landscape had their own particular traits, which made them unique. We stopped and had breakfast, then got right back on the road. Even though Maddog was telling me to lay back and enjoy, I sensed he had an equal desire to get home, too.

As we rode through Texas and into New Mexico, our bikes purred together real smooth and I thought, *I could get used to this, just cruising all over the country with a fellow rider.* As we headed into the interior of New Mexico, I got that spiritual sense again that this state was so famous for. I watched the scenery go by and it put my mind at ease somewhat. I knew things would turn out all right if I just had a little faith, and right now I really needed something to calm my racing thoughts. The closer I got to the California state line, the faster my heart began to pump.

I tried my best to appreciate the things around me and got into my rode trance. The ride through New Mexico was just as spectacular as it was coming through from the other direction. Before I knew it, we were crossing the Arizona state line. It was late afternoon and I figured we'd probably reach Needles just before dark.

I motioned to Maddog that we better stop, get gas and take a break. We pulled into a station and after filling up, we took up our usual spot on the shady side of the building with our sodas.

Maddog looked at me. "Hey, partner, by the time we get to Needles and eat, it's gonna be dark. You don't plan on riding all the way back to Borrego tonight, do you?"

"I'm not sure yet. I'll make up my mind when I get there."

"Well, if you want, you can stay the night in my apartment and head out tomorrow. To ride all the way back today is a lot."

"Let me think about it."

"My place isn't much, but it beats the street and you're welcome to stay."

"Thanks," I said, as I stared out over the open plain.

We stayed silent and finished our sodas, then got back on the road. As we neared the California border, the sun got low in the sky and was right in our path. It was as if we were chasing it to the horizon. We got to the mountains just before the Colorado River and the sun would duck behind a hill and when we would get to the top of it, the sun would pop back out again. It appeared to be teasing us by setting, then reappearing every time we got to the top of a hill.

It felt so good heading west and getting so close to home. I'd been on the road long enough now. I had to make up my mind soon whether to spend the night at Maddog's, or try and ride the rest of the way tonight. I was getting tired and my hands, ass and feet were getting numb, so the idea of staying was looking better and better.

We crossed the Colorado River and it took about fifteen minutes before we were riding down the main street of Needles.

We pulled to a stop sign and Maddog leaned over. "Follow me and I'll take ya to a place where we can get some good grub."

I nodded, "Okay, lead the way."

We rode to the center of town and pulled up to a small diner. The sun had set and every bone in my body was sore. I couldn't feel my hands and feet anymore and my ass hurt like hell. I knew that once I got off this motorcycle, sat down and ate, I wasn't going to want to go anywhere tonight.

I followed him through the door and a customer and the guy behind the counter both said "hi" to him as we found a booth. I sat down and thought, *that's it, I'm staying in Needles tonight. Ain't no way in hell I'm riding the last few hundred miles.*

We ordered and Maddog looked at me. "Hey, partner, that was one hell of a ride. I think I saw more of this country in the past few weeks than I have in all my years of riding."

"Me, too. I had a great time."

We ate dinner and when we finished, he asked, "So, have you made up your mind yet about staying?"

"Yeah, I'm too sore and tired to go on tonight. I'll stay and head out in the morning."

"Wise decision. It's late, and that's too much to ride in one day."

I painfully nodded in agreement. The check came and he grabbed it. "I'll take care of this."

"No, man, I'll pay mine."

He was very persistent. "Nope, I got it."

He took care of the bill and we walked outside into the warm, dry night desert air. I stood next to my bike, "How far do you live from here?"

"Just down the road. Follow me." He kick-started his bike and I fired mine up. We rode a few blocks and stopped in front of a storefront. He pointed toward the back. "I live in a room behind the store. We can park right next to the back door." I followed him to the back and we rode through a hinged gate into a fenced yard. He shut the gate behind us and said, "No one will bother the bikes. Anyone around here knows if they fuck with my bike, they're dead meat." *That was good to know, but what about mine,* I thought. *Aw, hell, I'm sure it'd be okay here.*

As he untied his bedroll, he said, "You better bring in your sleeping stuff 'cause you're gonna need it to sleep on." *Oh, yeah,* I thought, *he must not have a bed in there.* I took my stuff off my bike and we walked through the door. It was dark so he fished around for the light switch and flipped it on. I stood there amazed as the room filled with light. The walls were covered with charcoal sketches. They were tacked up everywhere. I walked up to one wall and started looking at them. "Who did these?" I asked completely awestruck.

He didn't say anything as he fidgeted with his bedroll. One by one I checked them out, and as I did, I couldn't help but feel a sense of real appreciation for the beauty of these sketches. I blurted out, "Man, these are really good. Well, good's not a very accurate description. Great would be better." I looked at him again. "So, who drew these?"

He looked at me, then looked away and mumbled, "I did."

"Wow. You really got talent. You know how to draw."

I continued looking at them and slowly made my way around the room, making sure I checked each one out. There were drawings of the desert, some of cowboys on the range and some mountain scenes. Each one was of superior quality and artsmanship. I was completely speechless as I went from one to the next. Maddog stayed silent as I carefully looked each one over. When I got to the last one, I asked, "Do you ever sell these?"

"I've sold a few, but I feel funny taking money for them. I was given the talent free, so how can I charge for 'em?"

I thought a minute, then replied, "You're not charging for the talent, you'd be charging for the time you put into them."

His eyes widened for a second. "Huh, I never thought of it that way. Just the same, it would still be hard to take money."

I went back to one sketch that I really liked a lot. It was of a cowboy sitting alone with his horse at a campfire out on the desert plain.

Maddog walked up to it. "You like that one? It's my favorite."

"Yeah. This one really has feeling."

He reached up and took it off the wall, "It's yours, partner."

"Oh, no!" I exclaimed as I stepped back, "I couldn't take that."

"Hey, you fixed my bike twice and I'd probably still be back at the Texas border. So, I want to do something for you. Now take it."

I was a little choked up and reluctant as I reached out and took it from him. I looked at it again and it really stirred something deep inside me. He walked to the other side of the room and picked up a hard, cardboard tube, "Let me put it in here to keep it safe till you get it home."

I nodded as I handed it to him and he carefully rolled it up and put it in the tube. He taped a cap on the end of it and handed it back to me. "If you see any others you like, let me know and they're yours."

"No, this one's more than enough."

"Okay, but if you do, just speak up."

As we got ready to go to sleep I looked around again. It was a big, one-room studio type apartment with a small kitchen area, a living room and a bathroom. "Not a bad place you got here," I said as I sat on my sleeping bag. Then I noticed a phone in the corner.

He saw me looking at it. "You want to make a phone call? Go right ahead."

"It's long distance," I cautioned.

"That's no problem. It's late and I'll get night rates so it won't cost hardly anything. Go on, use it."

I got up and dialed Jo's number and her father picked it up again. After he spoke his opening line I said, "Hi, this is Ron. I hate to keep bothering you like this, but is Jo back yet?"

"Not yet. I expect her any day now."

"Thanks. I should be back in town late tomorrow afternoon myself." I wanted to tell him to let her know that I loved her, but that wouldn't do. I had to tell her that myself, so I said goodbye and hung up.

Maddog didn't say anything for a moment, then asked, "You ready to get some sleep, partner?"

"Yeah. I'm beat and I could use the rest."

"Me, too," he said as he turned out the light. I tossed and turned trying to find a spot on my body that wasn't sore so I could lie on it. I finally did and drifted off to sleep.

Chapter Fifteen

Maddog's voice woke me. He was already up and about. "Hey, partner, you want breakfast?"

"Yeah, sounds good to me," I answered, yawning.

"If you're gonna take a shower, get to it. I'll walk across the street and get some fresh eggs and orange juice."

"All right," I said as I jumped up and got in the shower.

He was back from the store by the time I got out. "I'll make the eggs," he said, "you make the toast."

"You got it." I took two slices of bread and put them in the toaster, then started packing my stuff.

"How do you want your eggs?"

"Any way is fine with me," I said as I put two more slices of bread in the toaster and buttered the ones I just took out. I finished packing by the time breakfast was done and we sat down at his small kitchen table to eat. We didn't speak much as we ate and I kept looking at the drawings all over the walls. He could make some real money if he ever decided to sell them. But that was not for me to push. I'm sure he already knew that. I thought about how good it felt to finally be back in California and back in the desert. I hadn't realized how attached I'd become to this place, till I left it.

Just as we finished eating, Maddog looked at me and lowered one eyebrow, "Hey, partner, if I ever hear you came by this way and didn't stop to see me, there's gonna be hell to pay."

I smirked a little. "No way I'd ever do that." He nodded and ate his last bit of toast. I lingered a little more, then said, "I better be gettin' on my way. I want to get home to see if Jo's back yet."

I got up, picked up my gear and walked to the door. Maddog got up, too. "Hey, I'll ride to the edge of town with you, partner."

I nodded as we walked out to the bikes and I tied my stuff on. I watched as he primed his bike, then kick-started it. It sputtered and died as usual for the first cold start of the morning. He hit it a second time and it came to life. He looked at me and hollered over the noise of his pipes, "You got the touch, partner."

"Naw, you're the one with the talent," I said as I fired mine up and rode through the gate onto the street. I headed for the main drag, which was also Route 66, and turned west with Maddog right alongside me.

When we got to the edge of town, we both pulled over to the side of the road. He looked at me, then stuck his hand out, "You're one hell of a guy, partner, and I'm glad to know you."

I replied, "So are you. I'm glad to know you, too."

We both sat silent for a moment, then he waved and said, "Keep the shiny side up, rubber side down. I'll catch ya in the wind, partner."

A lump started to grow in my throat so I couldn't respond. I just nodded, hit my throttle and got back onto the road. I watched him make a U-turn in my rearview mirror with a tear in my eye. I stayed choked up for a while as I headed off into the barren desert.

The further I got away from Needles and more into California, the more I recognized the terrain since it was the same road I took on the way to New York. I thought I might stop at John's station to see if he was still there before I headed to Jo's ranch. I wasn't sure if I'd get back in time before he closed up for the night. It didn't matter. If I missed him, I'd see him tomorrow morning.

It didn't take long before I was at Amboy again so I pulled into the abandoned gas station that I stopped in coming from the other direction. I shut the bike off and sat on the wooden step in the same spot as before. I looked around and this time it was familiar to me . . . which made it look, and seem different than the first time I saw it. The old trash was still in the same position as it was the last time I was here. Seems the only thing that was different was my mind and the memories in it. I looked at my bike and it was caked with road grime. I smiled and thought, *it's only dirt, and it'll come off with a little soap and water. It's funny how I got here on my first day out and had so many unanswered questions, and now I sit here on the last day of this trip, knowing the answers to a lot of them.* "Life is strange," I said to myself as I stood up and got back on my bike.

I turned off of 66 at the same spot I first picked it up, headed south over the dry lake bed and rolled the power on. After riding through no man's land for about an hour and a half, I came to a gas station right outside of Joshua Tree National Monument. I avoided the park on my way to New York and didn't really check it out. I have enough gas and thought to myself, *this time I'm gonna slow down, ride through it and really enjoy it.*

I rode easy through the park and let my mind wander. I found a shady spot, parked and took my water bottle from my saddlebag. I sat under a shade tree, leaning against it and letting my thoughts drift to Jo and where she could possibly be. *She'd been gone almost as long as I had. I was beginning to make myself sick with worry. I was sure her dad would tell me if there was anything wrong. Just then a chilling thought sent a shiver down my spine. What if she dumped me because I took this trip and met Gloria? Now the knot was real tight in my stomach. If I didn't stop this thinking, I was going to drive myself crazy.*

I don't know how long I sat there, but some time had passed, so I stashed my water bottle and got back on the road. It was getting late and I'd probably miss John today. The way my mind was running wild, I could sure use a good talk with him right about now. I had to calm myself down or else I wasn't going to make it back in one piece. The road began to get more familiar the further I rode into California and that eased my thinking some.

As I got closer to home, old, familiar sights came into view. This was the first time I'd been away from this scenery for any length of time and everything looked slightly different. I knew it really wasn't; it was probably just 'cause I'd been away from it and I appreciated seeing it again. It had the clarity that taking things for granted usually dulled. I was just happy to be back.

I'd been on the road almost three weeks now and I could feel every foot of the pavement under my wheels. My hands and feet were numb and my arms and legs felt like pieces of lead. My rear end was so sore I couldn't feel it anymore. I'd picked up a few bugs on my body this last day of my journey and it was hard to keep my head up. It was all I could do to keep my hands on the handlebars and guide the bike to stay on the right side of the road. Every bone in my body ached, but in spite of all this, I wouldn't have traded any moment of the trip. Each mile I got closer to home seemed to give me renewed strength to keep going.

It wasn't long before I saw the town limit sign of Borrego Springs. It looked so good I wanted to stop and kiss it. I didn't, though, and kept on to John's station. I rode up to the driveway and it was locked up as I expected. I looked around and everything seemed to be as it was when I left.

I turned my bike out of the driveway, pointed it toward the mountains and headed to Jo's ranch. It was a half an hour down the road and I knew I could make it the rest of the way. I was getting my second wind. It was about 7:00 p.m. and there was still a little daylight left.

I traveled down the roads I'd traveled many times before on my way to see Jo. Borrego Springs was relatively new to me, yet I guess I'd lived here long enough that it held its memories. I thought about the times I'd driven Jo home and the times that Paul and I rode back and forth on this road. It was as though I knew every twist and turn, which I probably did by now. I watched as the scenery changed from sandy desert to lush mountain green. The temperature soon dropped about twenty degrees as it always did.

I rode for about thirty minutes, checking out the valleys and plateaus around me when I saw her driveway entrance. My stomach tightened up as I turned onto it. I didn't know what to expect and I naturally expected the worst. As I approached the house, I looked for Jo's Jeep and it was nowhere in sight. *Damn,* I thought, *she's probably not back yet.* I saw her dad's truck parked in front of the porch and wondered if I should even bother knocking.

I stopped in front of the house, letting my bike idle, trying to decide whether to leave when her father appeared in the doorway. He swung open the screen door, looked at me a moment, then said, "Hello, Ron. Could you come in for a second? I'd like to speak with you."

I sat there on my bike, which had two thousand five hundred miles worth of road grim on it and me being all dusty, thinking, *oh shit, something's up. I wasn't sure I wanted to go in with him. What if it was a plan to do away with me and he was going to shoot me once he got me inside the house.*

He stood there holding the screen door open. I had to make a decision quick. Oh, well, might as well go in and find out what's going on. I shut off my bike and slowly walked up the stairs. He pushed the door further open and stood aside to make room for me to walk by. I entered the living room and he followed. He stood next to a chair and motioned to me. "Have a seat. I've got something to tell you and it's not going to be easy for me to say this, so bear with me."

I nodded as I replied, "Okay."

We both sat down, him across from me in a large, cushioned chair. He looked at me, cleared his throat, then spoke. "I owe you an apology."

I looked back at him, startled, "For what?"

"Well," he paused, "when I first met you, I didn't like you. The more you came around here, the more my hate for you grew and I couldn't figure out why." He shuffled his tall, thin frame nervously in his seat. "I thought you were just biker trash and were probably going to stay awhile, then move on. At least that's what I was hoping."

He took his large, tanned, leathered hand and rubbed it across his lean, sun-beaten face. I could tell he was having a hard time talking so I said, "Mr. Thompson, you don't have to explain it to me, I understand." I didn't, but I guess I didn't need to know.

"Yes, I do," he responded. "I must get this out."

"If you say so."

He adjusted himself in his chair. "There were two reasons I didn't like you and I didn't know what they were until right after you left. Then they hit me like a ton of bricks." I wanted to ask where Jo was real bad, but I figured I'd better let him finish first. "When my wife died, I literally shut down. I built a wall around myself and wouldn't let anyone in. I watched you and I picked up bits and pieces from Jo about you. I guess I was jealous that you came out of a long-term marriage and didn't just sit and stagnate. You made some moves, you took some chances and that angered me. That you could and I couldn't."

"Well, my situation was a lot different than yours. You tragically lost your wife and it was totally unexpected," I said.

"Maybe, but you moved on nonetheless and tried to start a new life. That's one reason I didn't like you. The other one was that I was afraid you were going to take Jo away from me."

He paused to collect his thoughts, then continued, "I didn't realize when Jo's mother died that she took her place and tried to take care of me. Maybe I did realize it, but was unwilling to do anything about it. I kept Jo prisoner by not allowing her to get on with her own life. I should've pushed her onward, but I kept silent. Then you showed up and became a threat to me. I was afraid I was going to lose her."

Now I shuffled uneasily in my seat as he continued. "She didn't tell me much about you, but I knew what was going on. I watched her change and I knew she was falling in love with you. I still thought you were biker trash," he cleared his throat again. "You took a chance and moved out here. Then you took another chance and rode to New York. I know about the girl in New York, too. Jo doesn't know that I know. I might not say much, but I listen real well."

He knew everything and he was spilling his guts to me. *Why?* I thought.

"You had courage and you followed your dreams, even though you might have lost what you had."

"I wouldn't call it courage," I replied.

"Yes, it was, and you did. I finally took a long, hard look at myself and realized it's about time I made some changes myself. Some inner changes and some outer changes." He stood up, "Would you like a beer or a soda?"

"I think I could use a beer right about now," I gulped.

"I'll be right back," he said as he disappeared into the kitchen.

I sat there wondering why he was telling me all this. *Maybe he was still going to do me in and he just wanted to gain my confidence. He really went into the kitchen to get a loaded gun. I looked around at all the trophy heads on the wall and wondered where he would mount mine after scattering the rest of my body throughout the desert for the coyotes.*

He returned and to my surprise he had two bottles of beer in his hands. He gave one to me and I said, "Thank you." *I'm wrong again. I'm bad at trying to figure people out.*

He sat back down and looked at me. "So that's why I'd like to apologize and at the same time, thank you."

"That's not really necessary," I said, still a little nervous.

"Yes, it is, for me. I'd like to apologize for treating you the way I did and I'd like to thank you for opening my eyes."

"All I was doing was trying to get through life myself, the best I could. I didn't think I was doing anything special."

"Maybe you didn't think so, but you were."

I figured now's a good time to ask. "Uh, if you don't mind my asking, where did Jo go?"

He fumbled with his bottle of beer. "I should probably let her tell you, but what the hell. All the time she was going out with you she secretly wanted to finish college. You had your degree and she always felt less than you. She mentioned it a few times and, of course, I just brushed it off. She didn't say anything to you because she wasn't sure, so she kept quiet about it. She only needs one more semester to graduate."

"I think she should. It would be a real benefit to her if she finished."

"Yes, and I agree with you, now. Right after you left, she made up her mind to go to L.A. and get living quarters so she could register for the fall semester. That's when it really hit me that I should have encouraged her to go back a long time ago."

I smiled widely. "So that's where she is, going to college." I was happy. Now I could put to rest all those morbid things running wild in my head.

"I'm not pleased with myself for holding up her life and I'm glad you came along and upset the apple cart."

"I had to set things to rest in my mind also. That's one reason I took the trip," I said.

He stared for a moment. "Yes, I guess no matter who we are, or where we are, we all have things to confront in our lives."

There was silence for a couple of minutes as we drank our beer. He then spoke again. "Jo's been trying to get me hooked up with a lady for a while now and she doesn't know this, but I've been doing business with a lady rancher in Temecula for a few months. We went on our first date right after Jo left for L.A. and we're interested in each other. I've been waiting to surprise Jo with it and I'll let her know when she gets back."

"When will that be?"

"Oh, I forgot to tell you. I expect her back tomorrow morning. She's only about two hours from here."

I paused for a moment. "I really want to see her. I missed her so badly while I was on the road."

"I don't know if I should tell you this either, but she really loves you."

"I know. And I want to tell her something that I came to realize on the road." He didn't respond. I think he knew.

I looked at the clock and figured it was time for me to get going. "It's getting late and I should get home and clean up."

We both stood up and he stuck his hand out to me. I shook it and he said, "Thanks for listening. I hope there's no ill feelings."

"Not on my part. I bear no grudge."

"Good. Maybe we can start this off on the right foot from here on out."

"Sounds good to me."

I walked to the door and he said, "Jo should be here around nine or ten tomorrow morning. Do you want me to tell her you're back?"

"No. I'd like to surprise her."

"No problem, mum's the word."

I stepped past the screen door onto the porch and Mr. Thompson followed, "You're going to stop by tomorrow?"

"Bright and early," I smiled.

"I'm leaving after Jo gets back and I'll be gone most of the day. I hope I see you before I leave."

"Okay," I said as I swung my leg over the seat of my bike.

I fired up the engine, waved and made a U-turn back toward the highway. As I rode back to John's station, I noticed the sun had set behind the mountains. The light was in that strange transition between day and night, an eerie shade of gray. It would be dark by the time I got back and I wanted to call Paul.

As I cruised, a real peace settled over me and I thought about what had just happened between Jo's father and me. I never would have guessed it would work out the way it did, not in my wildest dreams. It's really odd how life unfolds.

I rode through Borrego Springs with a good feeling in my gut. I pulled onto the driveway of the station and shut my bike off. I unlocked the door, stepped inside, looked around and everything was just as I left it. John's toolbox was alongside the wall, neat as a pin. Mine was across from his, untouched, the way it was when I left. My bench was also in order.

It felt so good to be home. I opened the overhead garage door and rolled my bike in. I walked by my computer, stopped in front of it and stared. After looking at it for a few minutes, I flipped it on. Out of habit, I went into the mail section and to my amazement, there was mail waiting. There were two letters, both from Gloria. She must have written them while I was on the way to New York. I read them and it was the usual stuff, only now it all made sense to me. I deleted them and shut the computer off. I stared at the dark screen thinking, *this thing will never be the same for me now.*

I looked at the clock. It was a little after nine. I picked up the phone and dialed Paul's' number. It rang a couple of times and he picked up, "Hello?"

"Hey, Paul, what's up?"

"Ron, where are you?"

"I'm at the station."

"John's station?"

"Yep. I'm back."

"All right! How'd everything go?"

"Pretty good. I got a lot of stuff to tell you."

"Hey, man, hang on there. I'll be right over."

"I'll be waiting." I said as I hung up, sat on the stool and leaned backwards on my bench looking at my bike. It was caked with dirt and road dust. It sure looked good, though. I started to reminisce about the trip, about Maddog, about Gloria, all the scenery I was able to see.

I sat on the stool relaxing when I heard Paul pull up outside. I got up and opened the door. He shut off his bike, walked over to where I was standing and stuck out his hand. "Hey, man, how you doing? Long time no see."

I shook his hand. "I'm good. How about you?"

"Great. You gotta tell me how it went."

We went into the garage and he walked over to my bike. "Damn, this thing is dirty. But I bet you had a lot of fun," he said as he grinned at me.

"Yep, I sure did."

I walked to my saddlebags and fished around the bottom and found the two thousand bucks. I pulled it out as his eyes widened and his mouth fell open, "Where'd you get that? You didn't rob a bank while you were on the road, did you?" I didn't answer him right away. I slowly walked back to my stool, waving the money in the air. "Come on, tell me where you got it."

I looked at him for a few seconds, toying with him, then said, "Gloria stashed it in my saddlebag."

"No way! She gave it to you?"

"Yep." I told him what happened and he sat there wide-eyed the whole time.

After I finished, he said, "Wow, that's unreal. She gave you two grand, huh?"

"I want to send it back to her, but I have no idea where she is."

"Why? You should keep it. She said she's probably going to get a large chunk of money when she gets divorced, so why not keep it? Two grand will mean nothing to her."

"Well, I just don't feel right keeping it. I didn't earn it."

"Yes, you did. And besides, she really wanted you to have it. Otherwise she wouldn't have given it to you."

"Maybe you're right. I guess I could use it."

"There you go, and don't feel guilty about it."

I nodded and told him about Maddog and all the things that happened to me, and to us. He sat across from me awestruck as I unraveled my tale.

He gazed at me, then said, "Man, I really wish I could have gone along with you now. It sounds like the ride of a lifetime."

"It was. And maybe I'll do it again, next time to Florida. Maybe we can plan it so that I can take Jo along and you and

Diane can come, too."

He smiled ear to ear. "Yeah, we gotta get together and do that. Maybe next summer, and I'll try to trade my bike for a newer Evo. Oh, yeah, did you ever find out where Jo is?"

"She went to L.A. to register for college to finish her degree. I had a long talk with her father a little while ago. And we straightened out some things between us." I didn't want to go into the particulars since that was personal.

"Cool. I know he had some bad feelings for you."

"We got that all cleared up now." I stood up and put the money back in the saddlebags and turned to Paul, "Well, the plan sounds good to me and I'm ready. We just have to get the rest of you homebodies in gear," I said, ribbing him.

"Hey! Believe me, I'm gonna try."

"It's settled then. Next summer, the big trip."

"You got it," he snapped back.

He looked at the time, "Whoa! It's late and I better get home to bed. I have to work tomorrow."

"I'll see you," I said as I walked him to the door. He nodded and got on his bike. He kicked it once and it sputtered. He kicked it again and it fired up.

I hollered over the noise of his pipes, "We gotta look at that carb this weekend."

"All right, we will," he said as he rolled the power on and rode away.

I walked back into the garage and realized I hadn't eaten yet. I was dirty and needed a shower desperately. I didn't feel like going out so I rummaged around and found a can of tuna fish. I made a tuna salad, which I ate like there was no tomorrow. I got undressed and stepped into the shower. I turned the water on as hot as I could stand it and stood under it for what seemed like a half an hour. It felt so soothing on my aching muscles that I wanted to stay forever, but I knew the hot water would run out soon. So I washed, rinsed off and got out. I wrapped the towel around me and walked past my bike and stopped. It needed to be washed real bad, but it would have to wait till tomorrow. I continued on to the doorway and locked the door behind me as I headed to my van. I knew I would sleep like a baby tonight.

I slid open the side door of my van and everything was just as I left it. My bedroll looked so inviting. I gazed up into the heavens and considered myself fortunate. I didn't have a lot of things and stuff, but what I had was enough for me. And because of that, I didn't have to worry about how I was going to keep the stuff I didn't have. I crawled into my sleeping bag, leaving the door open so I could look out into the desert and watch the stars in the sky. I had a very secure feeling laying here. Kind of like a small child in the safe and warm arms of his mother. God, it felt so good to be back. I thought about seeing Jo tomorrow and I wondered how she would react. I hadn't spoken to her for almost three weeks. I was a little worried, but that didn't matter. All I wanted to do was see her. I also wanted to see how John was doing. I hoped he was all right.

I was lying on my back looking up when I saw a shooting star streak across the sky. I guess I was supposed to make a wish. I thought a moment, then said, "I wish happiness and good health for all." I knew that was a large order, but it never hurt to ask. I continued to look up in the sky and said, "I did it. I really did it. I rode all the way across the country." It was still hard to believe. I lay there a while thinking I would close the door before I went to sleep, but I never got the chance. I was off into dreamland before I knew it.

Chapter Sixteen

I heard John's voice and I thought I was still dreaming until I opened my eyes and saw him standing outside my van. The sun was already up and he said, "You made it back safe and sound."

I sat up a little groggy, "Yeah, I got back last night. What time is it?"

"Seven a.m. You want some coffee?"

"Sounds good to me. Let me get dressed and I'll be right in."

I rummaged around for some clean clothes and put them on. I slid out of the van and walked to the station. The sun was shining strong as usual. I could tell it was going to be another hot and dry one today and it really felt good.

John was sitting in his squeaky chair in his usual position. "Coffee's almost ready," he said as I walked through the door. I nodded and sat on the uneven three-legged stool. It was unbalanced so I tried to readjust it. I almost got it level and settled for that.

He tilted his head down, peered at me over his glasses and asked, "How'd your trip go?"

"Boy, have I got a lot to tell you."

"Did you have fun?"

"It was the experience of a lifetime and I had a great time. I'd do it again in a heartbeat."

"I'm glad you enjoyed it and made it back in one piece."

I glanced at the coffee and could see it was ready. I turned to John as I got up. "It's done. You want a cup?"

"Yeah, black, please."

I poured two cups, walked to where he was and handed him one. I took my position again on the stool from hell. I proceeded to tell him about my trip and all the details. I told him about Maddog, Gloria, the two thousand dollars and Maddog's mother. He sat and listened with his fingers interlaced together resting on his stomach, his eyes closed in his usual form.

I finished and he sat expressionless, not moving. Then he finally opened his eyes and said, "Yep, sounds like you had a real adventure. Have you seen or heard from Jo yet?"

I told him about her going to school and he looked pleased. "She should be back sometime this morning, and I want to surprise her."

"Well, you go and see her if you want. Everything's fine here."

"I think I'll get breakfast first, then come back and call to see if she's home." He nodded and rocked slowly in his chair, squeaking in time with his motion.

I went to the back, got washed up and rolled my bike outside. I headed for the town diner and ate a huge breakfast of eggs, pancakes and sausage. I was one hungry man. I then went back to John's and looked at the clock, 9:50 a.m. Her dad said she'd be back between 9:00 and 10:00 so I picked up the phone, my stomach tied in knots of anticipation, and dialed.

It rang several times, then her father answered. "Hello, Thompson Ranch. Mr. Thompson speaking."

"Hello, it's me, Ron. Is Jo there yet?"

"Hello, Ron. She got back about twenty minutes ago. She's upstairs unpacking. You want me to tell her you're on the phone?"

"No. I want to surprise her. She doesn't know I'm here yet, does she?"

"I haven't said a word, and I won't if you don't want me to."

"Don't. I'll be there in about half an hour. She's not going anywhere, is she?"

"Not that I know of."

"Good, I'm on my way." I hung up, hurried toward the door, passing John on the way out. "She's home. I'm going to see her. I'll be back later," I said as I rushed past him.

"Drive careful now. Take your time. It won't do you any good if you don't get there."

"I will," I blurted out as I jumped on my bike, fired it up and rode off the driveway and out onto the street in one fast, smooth motion.

I rode out of town trying to keep to the speed limit. It wasn't easy since I hadn't seen or talked to Jo for so long. My emotions were getting the better of me and I thought I should slow down or I might not make it there, like John said.

I got hold of myself and headed the bike toward the mountains and Jo's ranch. I rode past the scenery I'd driven by so many times. I tried to concentrate on it, but my mind was consumed with my destination. I forced myself to take it easy the rest of the way there.

I finally reached the ranch driveway, almost losing traction on the gravel as I turned onto it. I rolled up to the house and could see her Jeep parked out front. For some reason, it looked real good. I stopped under her bedroom window and revved my engine. She stuck her head out the window and said, "Ron, you're back!"

I hollered up to her, "I've got something to tell you," but before I could say it, she smiled and ducked back into her room.

I set my bike on the kickstand and shut it off. She appeared at the screen door as I got off the bike. I faced her as she stepped out onto the porch. I stood next to my dirty bike while she stood on the porch eyeing me with a smug look. I gazed into her sparkling, light blue eyes. Her long blonde hair, tied in a ponytail under her white Stetson, was gently blowing in the warm breeze. She slowly stepped down the porch stairs, her boots sounding sharp against the wooden planks. I wanted to rush to her and take her in my arms, but I could tell she was holding back, restraining herself so I held back, too. She got to the last step and cocked her body a little sideways toward me. She placed her hand on the tight, faded jeans, hugging her hips, and said, "So, how was New York?"

"It was no big deal as far as New York goes."

"And how's Gloria?"

"No big deal either, as far as she goes."

I watched her soft, lush lips move as she talked and it was driving me crazy. I wanted to kiss them so bad, but I knew I'd better wait.

"Did you do anything with her?"

"No. I said I wasn't going to, and I didn't."

I saw a sigh of relief on her face. She took another step towards me, stopped and tilted her head again slightly. I looked deeper into her eyes. "I called and called and your dad said you weren't here. I was worried about you."

She looked surprised, "You were?"

"Yes. I care a lot about you."

"Well, I care a lot about you, too." She stepped right in front of me and it took all my self-control not to reach out and touch her. "My dad said you called and I got all your post cards. Thanks."

"I wanted to talk to you and hear your voice."

"You did?"

"Yes."

She looked longingly into my eyes, "I was worried about you the whole time you were gone. That's a long way to ride a motorcycle."

I couldn't restrain myself any more. Her presence in front of me was too much for me to bear. I reached out, slid my arms around her waist and pulled her close to me. I softly touched my lips to hers and felt her melt against my body. She parted her lips, her tongue searching for mine. She pressed her entire body against me and almost drove me out of my mind. Then she laid her chin on my shoulder, putting her lips next to my ear and whispered, "I missed you so much."

"I missed you, too," I whispered back. She drew her head back and I looked into her moist eyes. She looked back at me and I said, as our eyes locked together, "I love you, Jo, and I'm deeply in love with you."

Tears began to form in the corners of her eyes, then rolled down her checks as she smiled from ear to ear and said, "Oh, Ron, I love you so much."

She gently pressed her lips to mine and I could taste her tears of joy. Then she dug her head into my chest and clutched me tightly, at the same time trembling. We stood in that position locked together for a few moments when a convertible with the top down pulled in front of the house. A sporty blonde lady who looked to be in her fifties stood up in the seat and asked, "Is Tom around?"

Jo looked surprised and tried to compose herself as she wiped her eyes. "You mean Mr. Thompson, my father?"

The lady looked back, "Uh . . . yeah, Mr. Thompson. Is he here?"

I guess Jo figured it must be business and turned to go into the house when her father appeared on the porch. "Well, hello, Martha," he said.

"Hi, Tom, is this your daughter?" the lady asked. "We've never met."

Jo stood between me and her father, completely taken aback by the whole series of events unfolding in front of her.

Her father spoke. "Martha, I'd like you to meet my daughter, Billy Jo. And this is her boyfriend, Ron." We both said hi in unison. He then said, "Ron, Jo, this is Martha, my date."

Jo's eyes opened wide, "Date? Did you say date?" She stood paralyzed for a moment, then ran up to him on the porch, tears streaming down her cheeks uncontrollably again, "Oh, daddy," she said, throwing her arms around his neck and hugging him tightly. She stood there sobbing for a few seconds as we watched. I was beginning to get choked up myself and had to turn away and clear my throat. Jo then turned to Martha, "I'm sorry. Please excuse me. This has been a very emotional day for me so far."

"That's okay, honey, I have days like that myself," Martha replied.

Jo wiped the tears from her eyes as she walked back in my direction. Her father spoke again, "I'm going out and I'll probably be gone most of the day." Jo nodded, too emotional to speak. He said as he walked to the waiting car, "You two have a good time now, ya hear."

He stood at the door of the car, turned, smiled at me and winked, then got in the car. Jo caught that and gazed at me in amazement, her mouth wide open. She stood speechless, looking back and forth between her father and me as he drove off. She stared at me, then said, "I don't get it. Did I miss something along the way? What's going on between you and my dad?"

"We had a long talk last night and we straightened some things out between us."

"He knew you were back and didn't tell me?" she asked, miffed.

"I asked him not to. I wanted to surprise you."

Her face softened and she looked at me with a girlish pout, then meekly said, "Oh."

I walked around to my saddlebags and undid the straps. "I've got something for you."

Her eyes got real wide. "You brought me a gift?"

"Yes," I said as I handed her the T-shirts.

She took them and held them out. "Oh, Ron, they're so nice," she said as she held them up to her body.

"I got one more thing for you," and I pulled out the jean jacket.

Her mouth dropped open and she gasped as I handed it to her, "It's gorgeous," she said as she put it on. "Oh, I love it." Then she threw her arms around my neck and kissed me hard and long.

"I got one for myself so we have matching jackets."

"Ohhhh, let me see. Put it on," she said, almost jumping up and down.

I took it out and pulled it over my arms and she cooed, "My, my, don't you look hot." She swayed gently back and forth with her head tilted to one side. "Want to come upstairs and help me unpack?"

"Okay," I said, as my pulse quickened.

I pulled the jacket off and threw it over the seat of my bike. She turned and walked toward the house. I followed her up the porch stairs and through the door. I looked around as we walked past the living room and the things didn't appear as sinister as they once had. The guns no longer looked threatening and the stuffed heads on the wall weren't mocking me anymore.

Jo started up the stairs to her bedroom with me close behind her. I watched her hips swivel in front of me at eye level as she stepped up each stair. I reached out and, ever so gently, ran my fingertips along the outline of her hips. She stopped, put her head back and sighed. I stepped up to the next stair below her and kissed the back of her neck while reaching my hands around to her stomach, the blood pounding madly in my temples.

She moved away from me slightly. "Uh, you have to go help me unpack," she gulped.

We continued the rest of the way up the stairs with me as close as I could get behind her. We walked through her bedroom door and the light fragrance of her room filled the air. There were a few things folded on the bed and she picked them up. She walked to an open dresser drawer and placed them inside. I walked over to where she was standing and stood beside her. "When do you start school?"

"Next week. I've rented a room with another girl and I'll be staying the weekdays there."

"That means I won't be able to see you during the week?"

"It's only two hours away, Ron. If you're not busy, drive up."

"Yeah, I could do that. You'll be here on the weekends?"

"Yes. Except if I have tests, then I might stay there. But you could still come and visit me. It'll only be for four months, then I should graduate."

"Good. I'm happy you're doing this."

"Me, too. I've waited long enough."

I stood next to her and felt her magnetism pull me to her as she fumbled with the clothes in the drawer and kept rearranging them. I reached out and took her hands in mine and she turned toward me. I put my face right up to hers and ran my tongue lightly around the edge of her silky soft lips, then fully put my mouth on her soft, tender, sweet lips. She shivered and put her arms around my neck, moving her body forward against mine. I was fully erect by now and she pushed her groin against me while rotating it. I placed my lips to hers, again feeling her hot, quick breath on my face.

I let my hands fall to her buttocks and pressed her even harder against me and she responded by rotating her hips faster. I slid my arm around her shoulders and the other one under the back of her thighs, at the same time lifting her up and carrying her to the bed while keeping our lips locked together.

I gently lowered her onto the bed, then knelt alongside her. I pulled the jacket over her shoulders and clumsily fumbled with the buttons on her shirt as she looked at me with lips slightly parted and her eyes half closed. She stroked my chest as I pulled her shirt out from under her and unhooked her bra. Her firm breasts stood pointing up at me, begging to be massaged. I took them in my hands and gently, but firmly, rubbed the mounds of flesh while manipulating her nipples. She let out a soft moan and squirmed beneath my hands, then she reached out and caressed my bulging hardness, about to rip through the fabric of my jeans, and sent an uncontrollable shiver through my body.

I let my hands trail down her stomach to the button on her jeans, then unbuttoned them and slowly undid the zipper, letting my fingers drag on her firm, lower stomach. I knew she was reaching a feverish pitch as she raised her hips in the air to let me pull her pants off. I tugged them down over her hips to below her knees, exposing her moist vagina. I scooted down to her feet and pulled off her boots so I could remove her jeans completely. I stood alongside the bed gazing down at her near-perfect body lying before me.

She reached up and pulled at my jeans. "Come on now, you have to take off your clothes." I yanked my shirttail out of my trousers and unbuttoned the top three buttons. I didn't want to bother with the rest of them, so I pulled the shirt over my head. I undid my pants and started to pull them down along with my underwear. As I did, my rock-hard penis popped out and Jo reached over and stroked the length of it, making me clench my teeth and tightening every muscle in my body.

She looked at it. "My, my, if you get any bigger, you're going to burst right through your skin."

She was absolutely right, I thought as she ran her fingertips up and down the length of my penis, which caused my hips to jerk with sheer pleasure. I finished taking off my pants and boots, standing completely nude in front of her.

"Come here," she said softly as she held her arms outstretched to me. I was strained to the limit, but I wanted to take my time and go slow, to make it last.

The soft, warm breeze blew through the window, tossing the curtains back and forth, and the birds in the tree next to the window chirped a mellow tune as I climbed onto the bed next to Jo. I rolled on top of her, resting my weight on my elbows, then closed my eyes and slowly rubbed my hardness up and down on her. She spread her legs as far as she could and moved her hips in rhythm to mine.

Her sweet scent drifted into the air as our bodies began to sweat in the warm summer breeze. I laid my head next to hers and she whispered, "I missed you so much and I love you so much."

I put my lips close to her ear, "All the time I was on the road, all I could think about was you. Somewhere along the way I realized I was in love with you, too."

I could feel her start to get emotional again, so I placed my lips on hers and she moved her hips against me faster. Her breathing quickened as she grabbed my hips, pushing and pulling me up and down on her. I slid down a couple of inches and held myself right up against her, feeling her wetness. I slowly entered her and she moaned loudly, then lifted her hips in the air and strained to take in all of me.

"Oh, God, I think you're going to drive me crazy," she panted in my ear.

"I think I'm already there," I whispered back.

I propped myself up on the palms of my hands, my arms outstretched, and slowly started to pump. Jo reached up and grabbed my chest muscles, "That feels so good . . ." she cooed, "your whole body feels good."

I lowered my lips onto one of her nipples and started to suck, at the same time pumping a little faster. She grabbed the back of my head and pulled it deep into her breast.

My senses were heightened to a point of almost being metaphysical. She caressed the back of my head. "Don't stop," she said, sounding almost as though she were drunk.

I kept a slow rhythm for a minute or two, acutely aware of each place our bodies made contact. I not only felt her hot, smooth flesh, I felt the energy emanating from her very soul. I couldn't hold this slow pace much longer, being driven by the uncontrollable natural urge to complete this union between us.

She wrapped her legs around my lower body and pushed me a little harder and faster. Our bodies were moist with a light coat of sweat helping to further intensify the mounting fever. Any reasoning I had was taken over by the overwhelming sensations of Jo beneath me. I could hold back no longer. I started to stroke faster and Jo responded by moving her hips with me. I placed my lips on her and felt her quiver with passion.

I was on the verge of cuming and I raised my upper body into the air, propping myself up on the palms of my hands again. I pumped as hard as I could and convulsed in spasms of ejaculation. She dug her heels into my buttocks and clenched at my back, shoving me into her as deep as I could go, vibrating and pulsing in orgasm herself. She threw her head back and screamed out, "Oh, God!"

My lower stomach muscles jerked uncontrollably a few more times and I felt her inner muscles throbbing madly around me. She grabbed my shoulders and pulled me down onto her heaving breasts, clutching me tightly.

We lay there feeling each other's heavy breath and pounding hearts as I drifted into a semi-conscious daze. I felt the breeze from the window blow across my body, cooling me off, the birds still chirping in the summer sun. For the first time in a long time, I felt complete with another human being and totally at one with Jo.

I came back to awareness as she ran her fingertips up and down my back. She licked my ear lobe and said, "I'm so glad you're back."

"Me, too. All I could think about while on the road was this moment. I had trouble keeping to the speed limit."

"I want you to tell me all about your trip."

"I will, but not right now. I just want to lie here and feel you next to me."

I put my head alongside hers and felt the wetness of a tear. I raised myself up and looked into her eyes. They were moist with tears. "What's wrong?"

"Nothing," she replied.

"Are you sure?"

"Yes. I'm just happy," she said as she smiled and hugged me tightly.

I gently kissed her forehead, then placed my lips softly on her closed eyes, first one, then the other. I then kissed the tip of her nose and the tip of her chin. She giggled and squirmed a little as I slowly and gently put my lips on hers. She took a deep, long breath as I moved my lips on hers. After a few moments, she pushed me up and away, and said, "Take me into the desert. I want to go for a ride on your Harley."

"What about the ranch?"

"That's what we pay Dave for. I want to ride with you so bad. I really missed it."

"Sounds good to me," I said.

I sat up and she bounced to a sitting position on the bed, then slid to the edge playfully pushing me. "Come on, let's get dressed and go," she said as she picked up her jacket.

I yearned to ride our old, familiar roads with her. I picked up our clothes and handed hers to her. We watched each other get dressed, touching one another as we did.

After getting dressed, we went downstairs and through the living room. I stepped onto the porch and Jo stood beside me. The midday sun was bright and crisp. I slid my arm around her waist and she did the same to me. As we walked down the porch stairs to my bike, I felt like a little kid. That feeling of Christmas morning with all the presents under the tree. The sensation when you feel the love of your first love. The newness of things happening to you for the first time as you're growing up. It was a fresh, clean, new day and everything in it was fresh, clean and new.

As we got to the bike, I said, "Sorry it's so dirty. I haven't had a chance to wash it yet."

She walked to it and placed her hand on the tank. "It's beautiful, Ron, no amount of dirt could take away from your bike."

"Yeah, it's only dirt. It'll come off," I replied, not so embarrassed anymore.

She took my jacket off the seat and held it out. "Here, put this on." I did, then got on the bike and lifted up the kickstand. I put the passenger pegs down for Jo and she swung her leg over the seat and said, "Let's find a nice, quiet place out in the middle of nowhere so you can tell me all about your vacation."

"A place in the middle of nowhere, coming right up," I said as I pushed the start button and the engine came to life.

She slid her arms around my waist and held me tight, pressing her body up against mine while laying her head on my back. I made a U-turn and headed toward the main road, then pointed the bike toward the desert and rolled the power on. The pipes rumbled their loud, smooth, unmistakable Harley sound as we rode the mountain roads lined with trees and green brush. We got to a place where the road ran right down the side of the mountain onto the desert floor. From this point we could see thirty miles or so. The Salton Sea was visible, too. I paused at a scenic view halfway down and Jo murmured, "It's so beautiful here," then laid her head against my back again.

"It sure is," I said as I pulled back onto the road and hit the throttle, settling into my seat and getting lost in the scenery around me. Bob Seger's song, "Roll Me Away," playing loud and clear in my head as we got lost, following those endless white lines . . .